Shadow of the Raven

Millie Thom

SONS OF KINGS:
BOOK ONE

Contents

Dedication

Shadow of the Raven is for my husband, Nick, who has tolerated my obsession with both Alfred and the Danes, and trailed around numerous museums and historical sites with me in my insatiable desire for a better knowledge and understanding of the times.

About the Book

Shadow of the Raven is an historical novel that follows the early years of Alfred of Wessex and Eadwulf of Mercia (whose character is fictional, though his father is not). Their stories unfold during the tumultuous events of the mid-ninth century, when Danish raids render Western Europe in a state of panic and dread.

The Viking Danes were fierce, pagan warriors, whose moral codes and barbaric rites defied the laws of their Christian neighbours. Driven by what they deemed the demands of their gods they plundered more affluent lands than their own, showing no mercy to those who stood in their way, as well as those who did not. And yet, their home life and customs reveal a different picture.

Documentary evidence from the time maintains that the earliest raids on the Anglo-Saxon kingdoms began with that on Lindisfarne, over fifty years prior to the start of this tale. Continuing sporadically, primarily along the coasts and rivers of Eastern Britain during the next fifty odd years, by the 850's attacks had become frequent enough to be a real cause for concern.

This situation called for cooperation between the formerly rival kingdoms, who found difficulty in seeing each other as anything other than bitter enemies. One of the first steps towards unity was made between King Beorhtwulf of Mercia and King Aethelwulf of Wessex (father of Alfred, who later gained the title 'The Great'). The transference of a small section of Mercia to neighbouring Wessex around 848 is seen as the first mark of unity and friendship between them. The area transferred became the new Wessex shire of Berkshire, where Alfred was born at Wantage in 849.

This novel is about the sons of those two kings and their different stories as they grow. Although their lives take different routes and are set in different lands, they are inextricably linked through their families: links that will, one day, draw them together. It follows chronological events of the time, although, when it comes to Norse mythology, well, mythology it is! Many of the names, family relationships, dates and events come from a variety of conflicting sources. So I dipped into what seemed to fit best with my tale.

Other research relied initially upon *The Anglo-Saxon Chronicle* and *Asser's Life of Alfred,* filled out with detail from a variety of notable works of non-fiction, including: *Alfred the Great* by Justin Pollard; *Alfred the Great* by Richard Abels: *The Life and Times of Alfred the Great* by Douglas Woodruff; *In Search of the Dark Ages* by Michael Wood; *The Vikings* by Magnus Magnusson; *The White Horse King* by Benjamin Merkle; *Cultural Atlas of the Viking World* – contributors: Colleen Batey, Helen Clarke, R.I.Page and Neil S. Price and *Follow the Vikings* –a publication by the Council of Europe Cultural Route (purchased at Lindholme Höje in Denmark).

List of Characters

In Wessex:

Aethelwulf: King of Wessex (son of the great Bretwalda Egbert)

Osburh: his wife

Alfred: fifth son of Aethelwulf

Aethelstan, Acthelbald, Aethelberht and Aethelred: older sons of Aethelwulf

Aethelswith: Aethelwulf's only daughter

Cynric: Aethelwulf's nephew

Osric: Osburh's brother and Cynric's father

Osberht: Aethelwulf's ageing groom

Edith: Osburh's ageing nurse

In Francia:

Charles the Bald: King of the West Franks

Judith: Charles's daughter

In Mercia:

Beorhtwulf: King of Mercia

Morwenna: his wife

Eadwulf: son of Beorhtwulf and Morwenna

Burgred: Beorhtwulf's brother

Sigehelm: Eadwulf's tutor

Thrydwulf: Mercian ealdorman

Aethelnoth: son of Thrydwulf and friend of Eadwulf

Beornred: young thegn at Beorhtwulf's court

In the Danish Lands:

Rorik: Jarl from Aalborg

Egil: his right hand man

Ragnar Lothbrok: Jarl from Aros

Aslanga: his wife

Bjorn: Ragnar's eldest son

Ivar, Halfdan and Ubbi: sons of Ragnar and Aslanga

Freydis: Ragnar's only daughter

Thora: serving woman at Aros

Cendred and Burghild: Saxon slaves bought by Ragnar at Hedeby

Toke: Aslanga's old Norwegian slave

Hastein: Bjorn's cousin (on his mother's side)

Leif: Bjorn's helmsman

Jorund and Yrsa: Morwenna's son and daughter

Alfarin: king of Bornholm Island

Kata: Alfarin's daughter

Olaf: an ageing Norwegian seaman

Anglo Saxon kingdoms at the time of Alfred's birth, 849

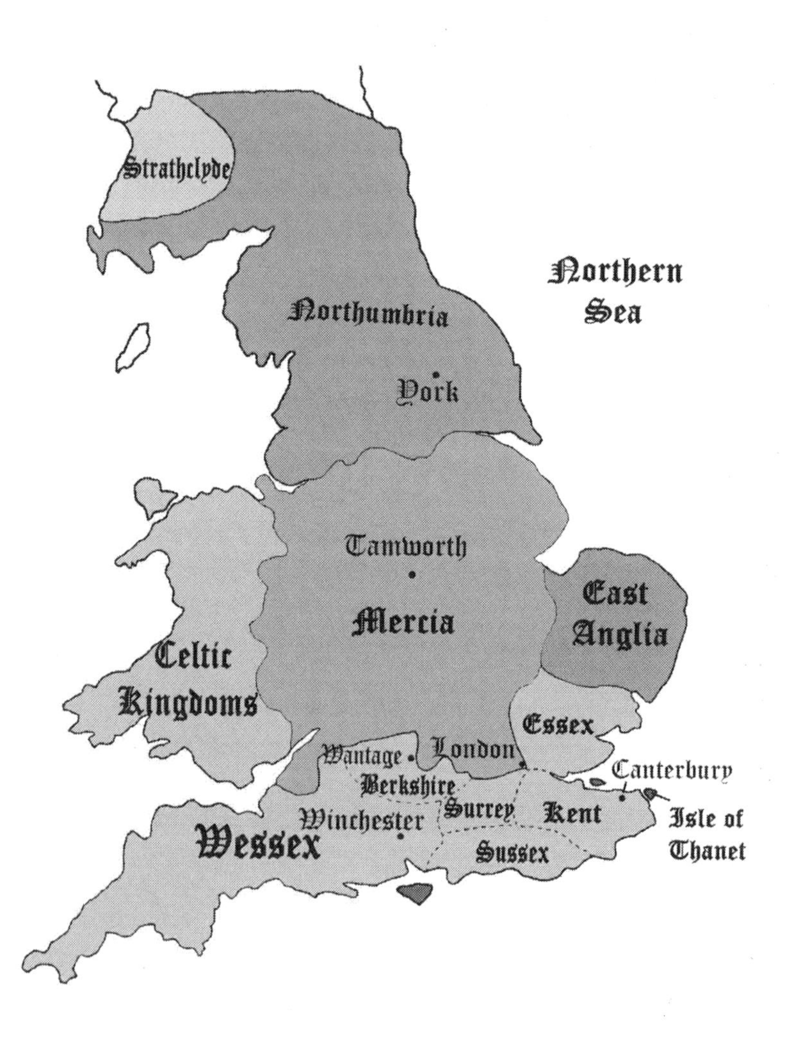

Norse lands in the ninth century

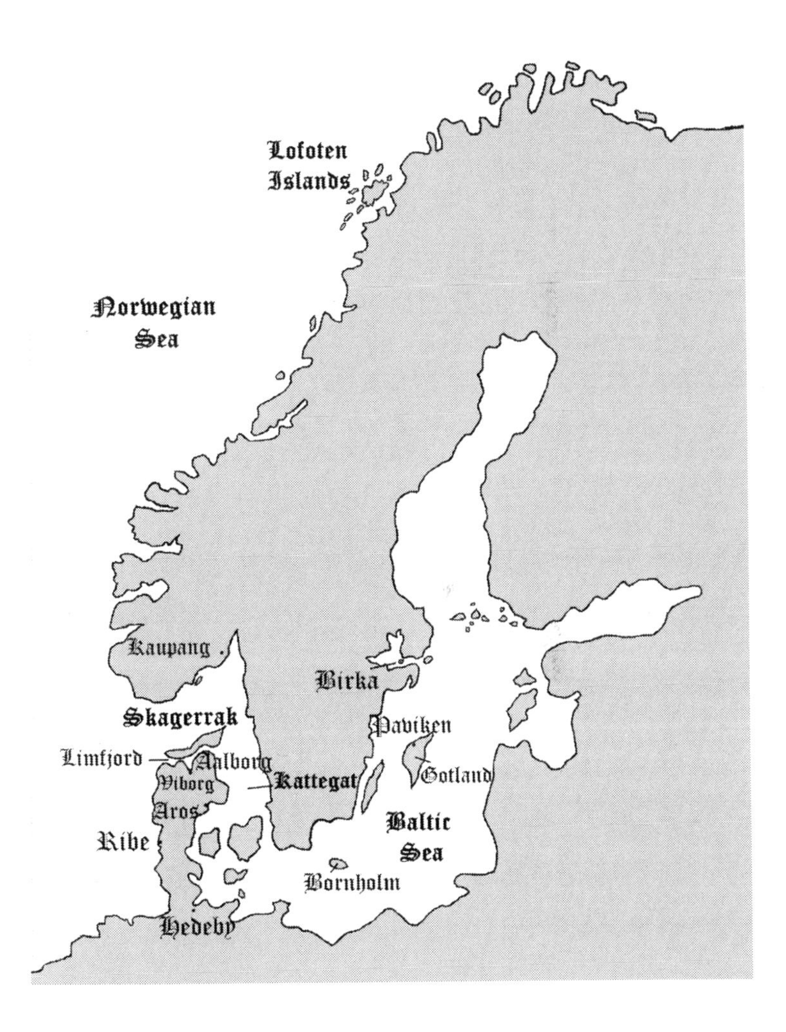

One

London, Mercia: late March 851

The snowball caught him completely unawares; a solidly packed pellet that smacked into the side of his head with considerable force, sending him reeling. His pulse raced, his temper boiled but, despite his outrage, Eadwulf grudgingly admitted that the thrower had commendable aim. And now the perpetrator was standing over him, watching him rub his burning cheek, grinning like a cat who had just devoured the tastiest mouse.

'That doesn't count!' he yelled at Aethelnoth. 'The match hadn't even started, so that's *cheating*!' He glanced at the two lads on his team, who were both nodding agreement. Aethelnoth's grin widened still further and Eadwulf half expected him to lick his lips.

'I suppose you're expecting me to apologise,' Aethelnoth said, struggling to suppress an outright guffaw. 'But since I don't call scoring the first strike "cheating", you could be waiting a long time...'

Eadwulf launched himself at the bigger boy, knocking him off his feet and straddling him on the dirt-churned snow – then dissolved into fits of laughter at the goggling surprise on his friend's face. The other lads gathered to witness the ensuing wrestling match that had, by now, become a familiar occurrence.

* * *

Being the son of a king could be so boring at times, Eadwulf decided, cursing the need to spend so much time at his studies, when his friends were outside, having fun in the snow. Reading was one thing; he was good at that. And he loved the stories his tutor told him. But writing ...! His fingers ached from gripping his quill and his mind would not stay focused. To make matters worse, the snows were now thawing, icicles along the eaves beginning to drip. Soon the Mercian Court would leave for Buckingham. Yet here he was, in this dreary hall, staring at mind-numbing letters, willing the morning meal to be ready soon. *Then* he'd get even with Aethelnoth for yesterday.

His father, King Beorhtwulf, had only intended to spend the Christmastide at his London vill, but the heavy snows of early January had rendered moving on impossible. All roads had become blocked. So they'd simply been stuck here. Not that Eadwulf disliked it here, as a rule. In fine weather there was plenty to do, like visiting the market in London, a few miles south on the wide River Thames. And once his lessons were over, he had Aethelnoth to keep him company. At eleven, just a year older than himself, the reeve's son had become Eadwulf's firm friend over the years, despite his outlandish sense of fun.

Yet during the winter months the hall was dim and stuffy. Little light penetrated the shuttered windows and though a ruddy glow emanated from the fire in the central hearth, so did thick, dark smoke, which snaked up to the hole in the thatch, wafting about whenever servants scurried past. Oil lamps gave only localised light, the corners of the large room remaining in gloomy darkness.

He scowled at his quill, willing his hand to put the implement to use. But it was hopeless. He wiggled his fingers and glanced about, his thoughts wandering in multiple directions. At the far end of the room his mother, Morwenna, worked at one of the looms with her women, adeptly creating the much needed cloth. Eadwulf tugged at the neck of his itchy, woollen tunic, wondering whether weaving was as boring as writing ...

If only he'd been allowed to ride out with his father on the morning hunt.

He peeked at his stern-faced tutor at the end of the table, who was still engrossed in his reading, his brown hair hanging lank about his face. Though not an old man, perhaps a little younger than Beorhtwulf in his fortieth year, Sigehelm behaved like one at times. He'd once trained for the priesthood but, for some reason, had left and become a tutor. A good decision in Eadwulf's opinion: the Church was for fat old men who could do naught but beg God for things. Sigehelm was always talking about God, which was annoying at times, since Eadwulf hadn't yet decided whether God was actually real.

With a resigned sigh he looked down at his morning's work ...and inwardly groaned. A dark, wet trail meandered its way from the horn ink pot, right across the detested parchment. Sigehelm would be sure to insist he write it all out again. Eyes focused on his tutor, he folded up the sheet, intending to dispose of it before it could be checked after the meal. Then he'd simply claim ignorance of its whereabouts.

'If I'm not mistaken, Eadwulf, you have something to say to me.'

Sigehelm's brown gaze was solemn. Had he spotted the

messy parchment, or was he merely querying why Eadwulf had folded it up early?

'I was just thinking it must be the end of the lesson, Sigehelm. I've worked hard since early morning and would like to stretch my legs before the meal.'

Not a complete lie; just not the entire truth. If that answer would suffice he could look forward to spending time with Aethelnoth. If not, it would be an afternoon inside this stuffy hall, copying out the dreaded letters again.

* * *

With his huntsmen and attendant thegns, King Beorhtwulf rode back from the forest, his two great wolfhounds loping along beside him. It had been a good hunt, confirmed by the quarry slung over the backs of the pack horses. Cooks flapped in appreciation as the huge deer and smaller game were laid outside the wattle-walled building that served as kitchen and bakehouse.

Beorhtwulf surveyed the carcass of the felled deer, an old stag with massive, branching antlers. The slow old beast had made easy prey. 'It hardly seems fair, does it, brother?'

'What doesn't seem fair?' Burgred squinted at Beorhtwulf as unaccustomed sunshine brightened the sky. The air had lost its penetrating bite and he fingered the brooch fastening his black cloak.

'To end a long life like this...' Beorhtwulf shrugged his broad shoulders, touching the toe of his boot to the lifeless form. 'He looks a noble creature; probably sired many calves in his time. To end up spitted over our hearth seems to deprive him of all dignity in death.'

'Your sentimentality is misguided brother. The beast would surely be pleased to know he gave many people much pleasure and kept our bellies full. And he was old ...would soon have fallen to the forest floor where his carcass would have slowly rotted away, or been eaten by woodland scavengers. Does *that* sound very dignified to you? Besides, what use would scavengers have for those antlers, when our craftsmen can turn them into such useful things? You know how Morwenna loves her antler combs and bits of jewellery. I'm partial to antler knife handles myself, and the men would be lost without their gaming dice.'

Beorhtwulf grinned at his younger brother, half a head shorter than himself, his red-brown hair less fiery than his own bright red. 'Point taken, Burgred. The meat will be more useful to us than foxes and the like. Let's hope today marks the onset of a warm spring,' he murmured, a note of optimism in his voice. 'Our people grow restless to sow the corn and move the stock out to pasture.'

But Beorhtwulf was a worried man. The onset of spring would bring a far greater threat to Mercia than the snows, and at tomorrow's meeting of the Witan there were urgent matters to discuss. With a heavy sigh he whistled for his hounds and strode towards the reed-thatched hall to share the morning meal with his wife and son.

* * *

Inside the hall, all domestic activity was suspended for the duration of the Witenagemot. Called in haste once travel had become possible, it was an unusually small gathering, several of the kingdom's leaders dwelling too distant to reach London in time. Food preparation was relegated to the kitchens and Morwenna and her women had retired to their bower with their embroideries, leaving the looms redundant for the morning.

Beorhtwulf sat on his high-backed chair at the centre of the high table, against which two long trestles had been positioned at right angles. He surveyed the waiting assembly, feeling quite grand in his dark green tunic trimmed with gold braid, specially made for him by Morwenna. 'The green will match your splendid eyes,' she had said, 'and the trim will complement your elegant crown.' To his right, Burgred and Thrydwulf chatted amiably as they waited for him to make a start; to his left, Bishops Wulfhere and Egfrith waited in silence, their position at the high table testament to their integral roles in the government of Mercia. As marks of holy office, each bishop wore a large ring inlaid with amethyst and carried a tall staff. Attendant nobles sat expectantly along the remaining tables.

'The time has come, my friends,' Beorhtwulf began, the hall falling silent as he rose to his feet, 'the time when we may have to fight for all we hold dear. You all know of the threat to Mercia of which I speak. The Danes have become bolder over the years. Their successes along coastal areas of Wessex and Northumbria have made them greedy for more. We have been spared from many of these raids by virtue of our limited coastline. *So far.* But now the situation has changed. The heathens have overwintered on the island of Thanet. With the spring they'll be on the move, sailing up the Thames and conducting their raids using their ships as base. London stands on the Thames! This manor – *your* home, Thrydwulf – is very close to the Thames. They'll load their ships with pillaged goods and sail back to Thanet before returning to their homeland, likely to repeat the process next year.'

Beorhtwulf waved away any untimely questions. 'The name of their leader is Rorik, a man feared throughout the Low Countries, particularly in Friesland. He raids under the sponsorship of a man claiming to be King Harald the Second of the Danes. Rorik is Harald's brother. These two have become rich at the expense of many in mainland Europe and now their greedy hands reach out to our lands.'

He regarded the faces before him: his kinsmen and ealdormen; holy bishops, and young men at the beginning of what should be a long and fruitful life. How many would still be here next year?

'Rorik is a shrewd leader,' he stressed, 'who means to maximise the plunder he can elicit from our people. We urgently need to devise strategies to stop him.'

Resuming his seat, Beorhtwulf allowed his councillors to share views amongst themselves. Most had believed that only the Welsh posed a threat to Mercia. Some of his most trusted ealdormen looked pale and shaken. The two bishops were stiff with outrage, while several younger men were putting on a show of outright bravado.

Thrydwulf raised a finger, requesting to speak. A big, sturdy man in his late thirties, the London reeve was experienced in both Council matters and combat, having led many armies against the Welsh, and had served Mercia loyally during Beorhtwulf's twelve years of kingship. Today, Thrydwulf's dark eyes matched his choice of tunic and cloak, contrasting with his thick, straw-coloured hair and beard. Beorhtwulf motioned for silence and Thrydwulf stood to face him, bushy eyebrows raised.

'We've all heard of this camp on Thanet, my lord, but know naught of its leader, or his intentions. What, or who, is your source of such information?'

'I'll leave my brother to explain that to you all, Thrydwulf.'

Beorhtwulf waited with a degree of anxiety, knowing that many viewed Burgred as an aloof character, too proud to mingle with the other men, though constantly surrounded by his own retainers. Some believed that Beorhtwulf relied too heavily on Burgred's judgement. Perhaps he did. But his brother had an astute mind, and had often proposed policies that had proved to be most beneficial to Mercia. It had been Burgred, after all, who had suggested the alliance with Wessex: give King Aethelwulf the area of land that Wessex had coveted for so long and propose unity between their two kingdoms.

'Thank you, my lord,' Burgred said, flashing Beorhtwulf a smile as he rose, elegant in his tunic of fine blue wool. 'As all of you, I'd heard talk of this Danish camp and, whilst residing at my Hertford manor in November of last year, I could not help wondering just what these pagans were scheming. So, a few days after Christ's Mass, before the onset of the snows, I set out for Thanet with seven of my retainers.'

The responses were mixed: outright disbelief that Burgred could undertake such a daring enterprise; scepticism; surprise.

But no disinterest, Beorhtwulf noted.

'We posed as vendors of a produce no red-blooded warrior could resist. Ale: fifty barrels of it from my own manors, loaded onto four horse-drawn carts. You may deem such a quantity excessive,' Burgred considered, his emerald gaze sweeping the faces. 'But my spies had been given estimates by Kentish villagers of a camp of over three hundred and fifty men – too large a force to be placated by a mere few barrels...

'So we journeyed south, fording the Thames at Kingston, then east through Wessex territory into Kent. Our coastal route avoided the ridges and forests inland but we had vast areas of marshes, lagoons and reed beds to negotiate and skirting these added miles to our journey. We had disguised ourselves as simple cottars, our threadbare tunics and cloaks not the warmest attire for late December. A bitter wind blew in from the Northern Sea and we prayed we'd complete our task before the snows made further travel impossible. Villagers were grateful to earn a coin or two for the use of a barn or hayloft and providing us with meagre provisions each night, and after two weeks of painfully slow travel we forded the River Wantsum to Thanet.

'The six hundred or so families on the isle have not been unduly troubled by the Danish presence, but few could ignore their potential to raid and kill. We simply took directions and set off to the camp.'

Bishop Wulfhere raised a finger and Beorhtwulf invited him to speak. A wiry man of late-middle years, encased in a thick, purple cape over his long white alb, Wulfhere's watery eyes blinked incessantly. 'Why weren't you all killed as you approached? The Danes are not renowned for negligence in such matters. Nor do they possess tolerance, compassion or–'

'Compassion the Danes do *not* possess, nor tolerance, my lord,' Burgred snapped. 'But their cunning and curiosity are boundless. Rorik would wonder why a group of rag-tag Saxons should be stupid enough to near a large enemy camp. Were we acting as bait, while an armed force made ready to strike?' He shrugged, spreading his hands to give emphasis to the question. 'So, we were herded back to their camp and rigorously questioned until they decided that we were what we claimed to be: simple merchants, pooling resources from several homesteads, risking our lives in the hope of sizeable profit.'

'You are surely not implying that this Rorik was willing to pay for the ale?' Raised fingers ignored, Bishop Egfrith's double chins wobbled as he voiced the question on everyone's lips. 'Is it not the Danish custom to simply *take* what they want and slay anyone who stands in their way? Their gods praise bloodlust and thieving in their warriors, so what made them treat you any differently?'

Burgred glared at the dumpy little bishop. 'It is true,' he agreed. 'The Danes aren't here to pay for anything. The only payment we received was to be able to leave their camp alive.'

'But why? Why didn't they simply take the ale and kill you all?'

'My Lord Bishop, isn't that obvious? Our ale had made them extremely happy...'

Amusement rippled round the hall and Burgred disregarded the indignant Egfrith. 'So, my lords, we were imprisoned in one of their tents while the Danes caroused late into the night, our fate to be decided when Rorik was sober. My intention was to gain information while our guards' tongues were, perhaps, a little loose. So we sang one of our own battle songs; loudly. Predictably, they hurtled in and ordered our silence: six of them, clad in tunics of stinking hides. They squatted across the tent's entrance, glowering. But I was determined to learn of their plans. Just how safe was Mercia?'

Burgred grinned at the sceptical faces. 'I applauded Rorik's awesome reputation. More sober men than our guards may have questioned the source of this praiseworthy reputation, since this was Rorik's first venture into our lands. Fortunately, a hardened warrior with a mane of unkempt, blond hair and a thrice-plaited beard readily extended my accolades. His name was Egil: Rorik's second in command.

'Rorik is a powerful jarl, he told us; blood kin to a king and rich from countless raids into the Low Countries. He has heard that our cities have great temples full of gold and silver, and that our God deplores wealth, demanding that his followers should live in poverty. So, Rorik decided to do our God a favour by taking the unwanted treasures to where they *would* be appreciated.

'In the spring another three hundred and fifty *shiploads* of Danes will arrive to join the four hundred men waiting on Thanet,' Burgred stressed. Outraged intakes of breath preceded stunned silence. 'They intend to take Canterbury in April and London before the end of May. My lords, we must act now if we are to survive!'

Before Burgred could seat himself, a dark-headed young warrior named Beornred asked, 'Did Rorik simply let you walk free from his camp, my lord?'

'In a word, yes,' Burgred replied tugging at his tunic, sweating in the fierce glow of the hearthfire. 'The next morning we were unceremoniously ousted, with thanks for our generous "gift". We were obliged to leave on foot, freezing in the biting cold. Luckily, the Danes were unaware of the coins concealed in our boots, and once well away from Thanet we purchased food and mounts for our journey home. By evening we reached a large homestead and were offered shelter in a sizable byre. But during that night, the snow fell thick and fast, and by morning, drifts blocked all roads, rendering further travel unthinkable. For the next few weeks, the reeking byre became our home. Then, a week ago, the snowfalls eased, so we set out. Some roads were still blocked in sections, entailing a few detours, but we avoided mishap other than one lamed horse, which stumbled down a pothole hidden beneath the snow.

'I deliver this tale with a heavy heart,' he declared, hand across his chest. 'I don't doubt Egil's words and believe we must prepare for May.'

An animated buzz filled the hall as Burgred sank to his seat. Defensive tactics were aired, punctuated by declarations of outrage from the two clerics. Beorhtwulf knew this was understandable; a raid on the scale described could mean the loss of many lives. Without doubt, Danish war-bands must be faced by war-bands of their own. The main obstacle to that was of sheer numbers – another three hundred and fifty ships, each carrying thirty or forty warriors. There was only one option Beorhtwulf could take.

'Trusted advisors and fellow Mercians,' he began, raising

his hand for silence as he stood. 'Burgred has earned our deep respect by risking his life in the service of Mercia; his brave venture puts us in a position to prepare for this onslaught. We have until the end of April. Not long enough, I hear you say. But *I* say, we are given no choice in the matter!'

Dismayed comments ensued and Beorhtwulf struck the table hard with his fist. 'When have Mercians ever conceded defeat *before* the onset of battle? I tell you: *never*! Mercia once ruled supreme amongst these kingdoms. The mighty Bretwalda Offa would surely turn in his grave if he thought his people baulked at the defence of their lands. And although Mercia has since been overshadowed by the escalating might of Wessex, we are still a formidable force. And Wessex is now our strongest ally.'

Having sown the seeds of his intentions, Beorhtwulf pushed on. 'These past days have shown that winter is at last drawing to a close. Most years we'd be celebrating, making ready our seed corn and ploughs. But not this year, for soon the Danes will be setting sail. And the major problem that plagues my mind is that of the vast number of enemy warriors compared to the far fewer number of trained Mercians. It is many years since the Mercian fyrd was mustered; our ceorls will take time to prepare for battle.

'My lords, I see only one solution to this problem.'

He stared, unsmiling, at the questioning faces. 'I intend to ride to Winchester, where the Wessex king has journeyed for the Eastertide. I believe Aethelwulf will aid us in this.'

It was said. The reaction was loud. But Beorhtwulf was not concerned with their protestations, though he knew many found it hard to view Wessex as an ally. He held up his hand for silence. 'I have agonised over this news since Burgred's return a week ago, and believe that Aethelwulf is our only hope. Wessex has been beset by Norse raiders for some years, and the Saxons have developed skilled tactics against them.'

Beorhtwulf's closing words were placatory. 'Come, my lords, are not Mercians and Saxons of the same peoples? Who is our greater enemy – Aethelwulf of Wessex, our ally, or the marauding Dane, Rorik?

'You know I do not need your answer.'

Two

London: late-April 851

From the doorway of the hall Morwenna gazed across the low-lying lands of the Thames Valley. The view was one of serenity and peace. It was the third week of April, the week following Eastertide, and the land had greened, fresh and fragrant beneath a cornflower-blue sky. Spring colours splashed meadow and woodland, breathtaking after weeks of monotone, silvery-whites. Scents of the freed earth were heady and she drank them in greedily before they drifted out of reach.

Inside the hall, Thrydwulf and Burgred were reviewing the training of the fyrd with the thegns who had not accompanied Beorhtwulf to Winchester. They'd spent days in the villages, preparing men who knew little of warfare for combat, readying them to advance as an orderly unit, and form a shield wall on a given command. Unable to afford weapons, most ceorls were armed with wood-cutting axes or wooden staffs, and hastily made shields; a few owned bows or spears.

Wishing to discuss her son's progress, Morwenna had summoned Eadwulf and his tutor to accompany her outside after the morning meal, away from the bustle of servants carrying surplus food back to the kitchens and stacking away the trestle tables. In the middle of the open area, a short distance from the lofty hall, with the spring meadows stretching out before them, Morwenna addressed her concerns to the learned scribe.

Sigehelm assured her that he had little to complain about.

Since the incident with the ruined parchment, Eadwulf had been a most diligent pupil. An afternoon repeating his letters had given him tremendous incentive to avoid careless mistakes in future.

And now Morwenna had her son to herself. She was so proud of him, and so was his father. Eadwulf was their cherished only child, although the 'only' status would soon be changed.

For some moments, they stood together, content to enjoy the bright spring morning, and she squeezed Eadwulf' shoulder, his linen tunic warmed by the sunlight. The soft buzzing of a bee carried to her ears and the April breeze played with the wisps of hair that escaped her head veil, making her feel so alive. All should have been well with the world; but it was not. Mercia was threatened and must be defended. She dared not think of the future beyond May, knowing that the babe in her womb may never have chance to be born. An involuntary shudder took her, and Eadwulf glanced up at her troubled face.

'Try not to worry, Mother. Father should be home soon, and I am here to look after you.'

'That is true, Eadwulf,' she said, smiling down at him, struck, as always, by his likeness to Beorhtwulf. 'You've been a great comfort to me these past two weeks.'

'He has a large bodyguard: thirty warriors. And he was certain the Wessex king would help us. King Aethelwulf has lots of sons too; five, I think, although one of them is still a baby! He was born at our old vill at Wantage – did you know that?' Morwenna nodded but said nothing, reluctant to interrupt his flow. 'And the eldest son, Aethelstan, the one who rules Kent, put up a good fight against the Danes in Canterbury last week, so Uncle Burgred told me. But there were just too many of them against Aethelstan's army, so he retreated. There's little left of Canterbury now. The Danes looted it and burnt it down.'

Morwenna felt a sickening dread in the pit of her stomach. Just too many Danes. The Danes had sacked Canterbury in April, as Burgred had said they would, and would sail up the Thames in May. But when in May? It could be barely two weeks away or as many as five...

'Well, isn't this a cheerful little party.'

Engrossed in her black thoughts Morwenna hadn't heard Burgred approaching and, startled, she spun round. 'Can anyone join in, or is it a private affair?' he asked, grinning. 'You're looking lovelier than ever today, Morwenna. That green gown suits your fair colouring well and reminds me of the freshness of spring. Yet your mood seems more in keeping with the bleakness of winter.'

'It's hard to feel cheerful, my lord, knowing what we must soon face.'

'Father won't let the Danes destroy London, Mother!'

Burgred guffawed at his nephew's exasperated assertion. 'May our king deliver us from all evil!'

'You make too light of the situation, my lord.'

'I appreciate the gravity of the situation only too well, Morwenna,' Burgred snapped, his expression blackening. 'We're not training those farmers to fight for the fun of it.'

'I know how hard you work for our kingdom,' Morwenna said quickly, wishing she could eat her words. 'If not for you we could not prepare for this dreadful threat.'

'We must all do our best for Mercia,' Burgred acknowledged with an indifferent shrug, and I'm sorry I offended you. The strain of these weeks is getting to us all.'

'You are right, brother.'

Burgred flinched, a reaction Morwenna had noticed before when she addressed him thus. She often wondered whether he resented her marriage to Beorhtwulf; believed, perhaps, that she'd married above her station, despite her father being a powerful Anglian ealdorman. 'We were just speaking with Sigehelm,' she said, eager to change the subject.

'Oh, not another decorated parchment! You really shouldn't adorn your work, Eadwulf. Sigehelm simply isn't the artistic type.'

'It's nothing of the kind,' Morwenna declared, before Burgred could ridicule further. 'Sigehelm is pleased with my son's progress.'

'Eadwulf,' a boyish voice called, 'I've something really interesting to show you. Can you come now?'

Glad of the distraction, Morwenna watched Aethelnoth bounding toward them from the stables, waving his arms wildly. The sturdy eleven-year-old was almost a head taller than Eadwulf, and his bear-shaped build, wild blond hair and laughing brown eyes were so like Thrydwulf's, his father. It was impossible not to like the lad.

'I beg your pardon, my lady. I should have asked your permission first,' Aethelnoth said in his most courteous tone. 'But could Eadwulf join me for a while before training starts with our sword master? Ocea says we'll begin later today.'

'Of course,' Morwenna replied, knowing how much Eadwulf enjoyed Aethelnoth's company. 'But don't dare be late back, or I'll have Ocea giving me earache.'

* * *

'Well, I'm afraid I can't stand around chatting all day.' Burgred flashed Morwenna a dazzling smile, perfect white teeth accentuating his good looks. 'I've an errand to run, so is there anything you need before I leave?'

'I don't think so,' she replied, choosing not to query the nature of this errand. 'We'll see you at the evening meal then?'

'Probably, although I could be a little late.'

'When do you think Beorhtwulf will be back?' she asked, wondering whether her husband was aware of Burgred's odd mood changes. 'Do you think his journey to Winchester will prove successful?'

Burgred's lips pulled taut. 'You ask questions to which I have no answers, Morwenna. I am not my brother's keeper! When Beorhtwulf has finished his discussions with Aethelwulf, he'll return and inform us of their plans. Unless they both become bored with such trivial issues as saving people's lives and decide to formulate laws stopping hunting in the forests instead.'

Shocked by such unbrotherly sentiments, Morwenna gasped. But she could not – would not – let such remarks go unchecked. 'The people are Beortwulf's prime concern, as you well know!'

Burgred turned away, his eyes downcast. Did he regret his outburst, or was he simply scornful of her trust in Beorhtwulf and the Wessex king?

'My brother is blessed to have you for a wife,' he murmured, facing her again. His eyes, moments ago so full of contempt, now seemed to hold profound sadness. 'I often wonder which of his qualities cause you to hold him in such high esteem.'

'I love Beorhtwulf the man,' Morwenna said quietly. 'As our king, he has kept Mercia strong in the face of adversity from the Welsh, and prevented further strife with Wessex by allying himself with Aethelwulf...' At Burgred's sneer, she faltered, but did not remark. 'But as a mere man, Beorhtwulf has qualities of kindness and thoughtfulness I could have searched a lifetime to find.'

'Again, I apologise, Morwenna. My temper is easily fired today.'

'Yet you treat me with such disrespect – and I have always treated you with sisterly affection.'

Burgred turned again to stare at the woods, almost a mile to the west. Sunlight played on his hair, picking out the reds and golds. 'That's just the point,' he replied, without turning. 'I don't want to be merely your brother. I want so much more from you than that.'

In stunned silence, Morwenna watched her husband's brother striding away in pursuit of his errand, tasting the salty tears that rolled down her cheeks.

* * *

The two boys ran fast and free, exulting in the warmth on their backs and the vast blue sky above. They ran until their legs could carry them no further, collapsing, breathless, on a grassy slope a short distance from the forest's edge.

Eadwulf rolled to face his friend. 'What was it you wanted to show me so urgently?'

'Oh, that was just something to say to convince your mother I *really* wanted you to come with me,' the tousle-haired boy replied, grinning. 'And it seemed to work, didn't it?'

'Well, don't try it a second time. Mother has a very good memory.'

Aethelnoth hooted at Eadwulf's grimace. 'As a matter of fact, I did see something in the forest when everyone was snoring last night.'

'Why, exactly, were you outside at that time of night?'

'Going for a piss, of course. It was so dark I couldn't see where I was treading; stubbed my big toe on a stone or something. Want to see a black toenail? It's hanging off...'

Eadwulf wrinkled his nose in disgust.

'No? Well, because it was so dark, the lights stood out.'

'What lights?'

'How should *I* know? They were over by the woods, about six of them moving about, so they could have been torches, carried by people. What do you think? You're so clever you should be able to work it out.'

Eadwulf stared at his friend. 'There's nothing to work out, stupid! It's most likely as you said. Torches carried by people.'

'Which people?'

'How should *I* know?' Eadwulf mimicked. 'I was in bed, where I was supposed to be.'

'Well, I reckoned we'd go and have a look round. You know, search for clues.'

'Sounds good to me,' Eadwulf agreed. 'But we'd better get back in time for Ocea's instruction, or we'll get more than earache.'

* * *

Burgred cursed. He'd waited for the two brats to leave their resting place, expecting them to turn back to the hall. But now they were heading straight for the forest. He hoped Egil and his men had the sense to stay hidden. The woods were expansive and the undergrowth should offer ample concealment, despite the sparse spring foliage.

His meeting with Egil was arranged for a place some distance into the forest, where a huge, gnarled oak, struck by lightning some years ago, sprawled across the forest floor. Its trunk and branches were charred lifeless and black, like a great, contorted sculpture. Burgred recalled Egil's sneering words as he'd stroked the blackened wood:

This is what your London will look like when Rorik is through with it.

From a distance he watched the boys for a while. Thankfully, they seemed to be keeping to the edge of the trees, searching through the litter of the forest floor. What strange game was this? Perhaps they were collecting insects, or looking for something they'd lost on a previous visit. Whatever it was, he hadn't the time to find out. Moving in a wide arc, he entered the woods some distance from where the boys were grovelling. His mood was thunderous following his encounter with Morwenna; he'd not intended to reveal the full extent of his feelings and wondered how he'd face her again.

But right now he must finalise details with Egil.

* * *

'What exactly did you think we might find? There's nothing here that couldn't be found in the rest of the forest.'

'Can't you see it's been recently trampled?' Aethelnoth retorted, trying to hide his disappointment. 'There are lots of broken twigs and – yes! Just look at this.'

Eadwulf scrambled over to his friend. 'A firebrand of some sort,' he deduced, pointing to the charred end. 'So this proves you did see torches, but not who was holding them.'

'Keep looking.'

The novelty of the activity was rapidly wearing off and Eadwulf rummaged half-heartedly. He inched his way along a narrow passageway between the undergrowth, his mother's warning about wild boars ringing in his ears. Something hard jabbed his knee and he winced. Recovering the object from the rotting leaves, he stared at it.

'I've found something,' he yelled.

Aethelnoth scurried towards him. 'Well, what is it?'

'A brooch,' Eadwulf said, passing it to his friend. 'One used to fasten cloaks. And, I may be wrong, but I think I've seen it before.'

'Really?' Aethelnoth studied the brooch. 'It's gold, and I think these red stones are rubies. Not a poor man's trinket then.'

'No,' Eadwulf agreed, trying hard to place where he'd seen the object before.

Aethelnoth rubbed bits of soil and vegetation from the brooch. 'Could've fallen from some nobleman's cloak whilst out hunting, I suppose.'

'Well, *I* think it's something to do with the torches you saw. Perhaps someone hid here, waiting for someone.'

'But it was dark,' Aethelnoth reminded him, 'and miles away from anywhere. Why would he need to hide? He couldn't be seen in the woods.'

'Maybe he needed to be sure the people arriving with the torches were the ones he was expecting.'

'Who, at that time of night?'

'I suppose poachers after our livestock could be about at night,' Eadwulf surmised, nodding his head. 'But I doubt that a nobleman would be meeting such people.'

'And poachers wouldn't carry torches. They couldn't risk being seen.'

'Who'd be there to see them in the middle of the night?'

'People going for a piss, like me.'

'People staggering around in the pitch black aren't generally looking at the woods, Aethelnoth. They're usually watching where they're going so they don't tread in pig shit, or bump their big toes on hard rocks.'

'This isn't getting us anywhere.'

'True; and anyway, I've a better solution.'

Aethelnoth scowled at Eadwulf's smug expression. 'Go on then, enlighten me.'

'It appears to me,' Eadwulf began, with an air of pomposity just to irk his friend, 'that these people with torches must have been strangers, come to meet someone.'

'But we still don't know the identity of either.'

'Eadwulf stared at the brooch in his friend's hand. 'You've forgotten one little detail. We have a useful piece of evidence here. I just need to remember where I've seen it before.'

* * *

Warm rays of the setting sun slanted across the valley, casting long shadows of the horsemen and scattered patches of woodland. Beorhtwulf sighed. Not far now.

They'd left Winchester the previous morning, escorted by a dozen of Aethelwulf's men as far as Chertsey, where they were housed overnight in the hall of a Wessex thegn. Riding again since mid-morning, they'd forded the Thames into Mercia at Kingston and followed the river downstream towards the London manor. The talks with Aethelwulf had confirmed the value of having Wessex as an ally. With the onset of May, West Saxon armies would swarm across the Thames Valley. A united front: Mercia and Wessex.

Beorhtwulf smiled at the thickset thegn riding at his side with a faraway look in his eyes. 'We've been away too long, Creoda. Thinking of home?'

'I was, lord. Werburh's due to give birth in a few weeks and she expected me home long before now.'

'None of us anticipated being in London this long, Creoda; first the snows and now this Danish threat.'

'Werburh will understand about the snows, my lord, but I've not sent word of the raids. How can I, so close to the birthing? A first child's a great worry to a woman.'

Beorhtwulf nodded, appropriate words evading him, and delved into silent contemplation. Beside them the Thames flowed full after the snowmelt, rays of the setting sun bouncing on its turbulent surface. Closer to London the land along the banks became marshy, its only use being in the thick growth of reeds for roofing thatch, but immediately ahead of them a stretch of dense woodland reached down to the banks. Veering to skirt the trees, the hairs on Beorhtwulf's neck suddenly prickled. It was too quiet; too still...

Too late he yelled, 'To me!'

Extended in a drawn-out cavalcade, the Mercians didn't stand a chance. The attackers came in waves from the concealment of the woods, their screeches obliterating the silence as they hurled themselves at his men. Vastly outnumbered, the Mercians were dragged from their mounts and brutally hacked down. As the inevitable end neared, only Creoda and young Beornred stood with Beorhtwulf for the final strike.

Creoda suddenly dropped like a winged bird, blood gurgling through his lips. The axe had come so fast that Beorhtwulf hadn't seen it coming. Then Beornred was dragged away and Beorhtwulf stood alone. Fur-clad shapes swooped on the dead to gather the spoils; like vultures stripping the very meat from their bodies. Fleeting images assailed his mind: of Morwenna and Eadwulf, and his brother, Burgred. He would never see them again.

'Kill me now, you filthy savages,' he screamed. 'What in God's name are you waiting for?'

The blow to his head sent him reeling. He retched with the pain and rolled onto his side, dizzy and disorientated. But he heard the voice.

'God? Which god would that be? Do you think the Christian god has been looking after you well today? No? Perhaps you should try Odin, the Danish god of kings. Thor is better suited to warriors, I'm told. But you resemble neither king nor warrior today, grovelling down there in the dirt.'

Beorhtwulf gaped, speechless, as Burgred loomed over him, hatred bright in his eyes.

'You can take that look off your face, Beorhtwulf. It truly is me, here to witness your long-awaited demise. And that young upstart, Beornred, can convey the sad news to Morwenna. No need to worry on my account,' he said, his voice thick with mock concern. 'Beornred will say naught of my presence at this unfortunate skirmish. He was moved well out of the way before I put in my appearance ...

'Oh yes, I've hated you as long as I can remember, dear brother, and at last I can be honest about it. You were the first born, and Father always loved you best. By the time I was born he wanted nothing to do with another snivelling brat. He actually told me that, did you know? Don't look at me as though I were mad; every word I say is true. And Mother was so old when I was born she was more like a grandmother, with a face like a wizened apple!'

Beorhtwulf dragged himself up on his elbows, striving to make sense of what he was hearing. 'But *I* have always loved you, Burgred. When you were a child, I sought to develop your mind, train you in skills for later life. Haven't I given you lands and manors in return for what I believed to be your loyalty to Mercia, and to me?'

'No doubt such skills will be useful,' Burgred admitted, examining his fingernails, 'and the lands will serve me very well. I've built up a large number of faithful followers in the kingdom. But I always saw you as a weak-minded man, not the stuff kings are made of.'

'And you think you can do it better, is that it?'

'Something like that.'

'By making yourself useful to our kingdom's enemies. But what use are you to them, brother? What have you promised them ...free rein to ravage Mercia?'

A dangerous light flashed in Burgred's eyes. 'You seek to anger me again. But you're not in a position to fare well if you do, are you?'

'You'll burn in the fires of hell for all eternity!'

Burgred threw himself at Beorhtwulf in an uncontrollable rage. Threats of hell-fire and damnation had always caused him nightmares.

'Enough!' A shaggy-haired Dane with a thrice-plaited beard hauled Burgred to his feet. 'Finish what you want to say to this cur and we'll be on our way.' His heavy features twisted midway between snarl and smirk. 'We've a certain royal manor to raze tomorrow.'

Beorhtwulf could no more prevent his anguished howl than he could his tears of frustration and rage. 'Dear God, Burgred, think what you're doing! Are they all to be slaughtered, like these men who so recently gave you their trust?'

'Chilling thoughts, eh?' Burgred brushed down his tunic, an ugly smile on his lips. 'But don't worry about Morwenna. She'll be fine, once she's my wife.'

'Surely all this carnage is not solely for the purpose of rendering Morwenna a widow so she'll turn to you? Do you truly believe she could accept you after such betrayal?'

'By all the pompous saints, Beorhtwulf, you must think me quite simple. Morwenna will never know of that. I shall return to the manor once Rorik has finished with it, to find Morwenna distraught in her bower, with Egil guarding her door. I'll be heard to dispatch Egil and she'll turn to me for support – as will the rest of Mercia, who'll see me as a fitting king.'

'You're mad, Burgred! You've forgotten how to be a compassionate human being, a Christian.'

'Remember, Beorhtwulf, not long ago I told that pathetic bishop that the Danes knew naught of compassion. As for being a Christian...' Burgred rolled his eyes heavenwards. 'As a king, Odin will look upon me in a very favourable light.'

'So you see yourself as one of them, do you? But do they see you the same way?'

'They will, when their tribute comes in regularly. Silver's a persuasive commodity.'

'You'll be no more than their puppet, a simpering mindless doll, taking orders from savages. Do you really believe you'll have any power in ruling Mercia?'

'I shall be king, and have much authority. I have Rorik's word!'

Ambition and jealousy had destroyed the brother Beorhtwulf thought he knew; greed blinded him to the lies and the drastic consequences of his actions. He searched Burgred's eyes for some glimmer of humanity but recoiled at the hatred he found. 'What about my son? What do you intend for him?'

'The brat will be dead by noon tomorrow.'

The second blow to Beorhtwulf's head rendered him unconscious as he launched himself at his brother to choke the last breath from his treacherous body.

* * *

The screams inside Beorhtwulf's head seemed to rise and fall ...rise and fall. Searing pains shot through his skull; acidic bile dribbled from his parched lips onto cold, wet earth and he realised he was lying on his belly, shivering convulsively, his hands tied behind his back. He was soaked to the skin and so very cold. He forced his eyes to open, striving to make sense of the wretchedness of his situation. Greyness enveloped him; late evening then, or daybreak perhaps. And it was raining: a steady, cold drizzle. Tortured screams resounded again inside his head – or *were* they in his head?

He dragged his battered body onto his side, pulling up his knees to kneel before straightening out his trembling legs to stand. He looked around him, battling his stagnant memory. Signs of recent encampment were evident; the site deserted now, camp fires long since burned down. But laughter sounded from somewhere close.

Sunset. The last thing he remembered was a glorious red sunset, and the ambush, sickening and bloody. Then threats about razing Thrydwulf's manor ...

And Burgred; treacherous, insane, Burgred.

'Where in God's name are you now, Burgred?' he yelled, his voice rasping in his throat.

'No point looking for your loving brother, Mercian. He left before dark last night.'

Beorhtwulf swung to face the Dane with the thrice-plaited beard and searched the hardened eyes of winter-blue. 'Can you not find it in yourself to show mercy ...Egil? It serves no purpose to slaughter innocents.'

The Dane nodded, acknowledging his name, and shrugged. 'Rorik must keep his subjects in fear and subservience or they'll deem him weak. Many of his people must die to carry this message to the rest.'

'But these are not *his* people!'

'Not yet, perhaps, but your brother is more pliable than soft clay, has little care for the people you show such fondness for. He'll be most useful to us.'

The piercing scream chilled Beorhtwulf to the core. 'In the name of all that's holy, what is happening?'

'So squeamish, King of the Mercians. How can your people follow a weakling?'

'I am no weakling, but mindless killing should give no man pleasure. My people have moved on from wanton slaughter, whereas your people have not.'

The kick to Beorhtwulf's stomach was hard and fast and he doubled over, gasping.

'You know nothing Mercian! Once we only raided lands close to our own, but now we are here in your kingdom. I say we've moved a good way on.' Egil's throaty chuckle at his own jest was broken by another agonised scream. 'He is not a brave man either. Hauk has enjoyed hearing him scream like a woman. You Mercians have no balls.'

'What in Christ's name have you done to him?' Beorhtwulf yelled as realisation struck. 'Beornred is but a boy!' His outburst elicited another vicious kick, this time in the groin. Agony exploded and he dropped like a stone, retching.

'As I was saying,' Egil sneered. 'You Mercians have no balls. Yours, lord *king*, won't be much use for some time. That young whelp won't have any at all by now. Last time I looked he did have his balls, though he squinted oddly through his one eye, causing our men some amusement. The other was smeared quite creatively across his face.

'Hauk likes to make the operation interesting: for the benefit of the audience, if you see what I mean.'

Three

Eadwulf shoved the untouched Latin script away in disgust, keen to be outside now that the sun was shining after the light rain shower of early morning. Sigehelm had instructed him to make a start before he'd disappeared on some errand or other, but in his absence, Eadwulf had allowed his thoughts to wander.

It had taken him little time to remember where he'd seen the rubied brooch before. Burgred had been wearing it on the day of the hunt, the day before the Witenagemot. As Eadwulf had begged to be allowed to ride out with his father, his attention had been momentarily drawn to the shiny red and gold brooch fastening Burgred's cloak. But he'd soon forgotten about it. His uncle had so many pieces of fine jewellery.

For the past two days Eadwulf had pondered over possible reasons for the brooch's appearance in the woods, in the very area where Aethelnoth had seen the torches. Of course the brooch could simply have been lost during the hunt and impossible to find beneath the forest debris. Yet if that were the case, Burgred would have returned to the hall that morning not wearing his cloak. Eadwulf could clearly remember his father walking in with his cloak across his arm, and Burgred entering moments later...

But was his uncle wearing his cloak?

However hard he tried, further details remained a mystery. He could hardly accuse Burgred of any crime, nor yet link the brooch to the rendezvous in the forest. Besides, a meeting of any kind – with or without Burgred – may have been quite innocent. Then why meet in the middle of the night, out of sight?

'So, nephew, learning your Latin like a good, future king?'

Eadwulf's head jerked back from the smirking features so close to his face, certain his thoughts had drawn his uncle to him. 'Delighted to see me, as always?' Burgred chortled, pulling himself up. 'Is that expression merely surprise, or do I detect a sprinkling of fear? Surely you don't fear me, do you, Eadwulf? For the life of me, I can't think why you should.'

'Of course I don't fear you; you just startled me. What did you want to say to me?'

'Nothing in particular; there just never seems to be time for little chats these days.'

'I can't say I've seen much of you lately, Uncle. Mother says you spend much of your time hunting in the forest.'

'Ah, hunting,' Burgred said, sitting on the bench beside Eadwulf and adjusting the leather belt around his brown tunic. 'Now there's a pastime to be extolled. To hunt down one's enemy, bringing him to ground from his lofty position in his own domain, gives a man faith in his own abilities.'

Eadwulf blinked, taken aback by the odd response. He realised the hunt gave men a sense of achievement, a pride in their skills of stalking, and indeed killing. The hunt could also become a battle of wits between hunter and prey. But he'd been taught to view the hunted creature with respect, the primary aim of the hunt to provide food. The animal should be viewed as a saver of lives.

'Do you see animals as your enemies, Uncle?'

'Animals are like people. The more important they are the further they have to fall and the greater the pleasure I experience in causing that demise.'

A shiver ran down Eadwulf's spine. Burgred was not talking about animals at all; he had greater prey on his mind.

'But no, nephew, I haven't been in the forest since the hunt with your father soon after my arrival here, though I do intend to hunt again, very soon.' Burgred stood to leave, an unctuous smile on his lips. 'Now I'll leave you to your Latin texts; you mustn't disappoint that humourless monk, I suppose. Will you be in here all morning?'

'I believe so. Why do you ask?'

'Just remembering when I was your age. A morning of study seemed an eternity to me, too. I'm sure your mother will soon be here to work with her minions over there.' Burgred flicked a hand towards the women preparing the meal. 'I must see her first ; we have one or two matters to discuss.'

'Unfortunately, Morwenna is quite unwell today,' a quiet voice uttered from the doorway. Sigehelm pushed the door shut and came to stand next to them. 'Your mother sends her apologies, Eadwulf; she won't be joining you this morning. She was coming to work at her embroidery when I met her just now. I must say, she looked so pale and tired I persuaded her to retire to her bower to rest.'

'Quite right, too,' Burgred stated. 'Morwenna has been overdoing things lately. Her bower's the best place for her this morning.'

The door closed behind Burgred and Sigehelm took his usual seat at the end of the table, his eyes full of concern. 'Not one of your better days, is it, Eadwulf? You can discuss your problems with me, you know. You can trust me. Something is troubling you and your mother would worry if she knew. No, I have not burdened her with more problems. She really isn't well and will probably not feel herself until your father returns.'

'Thank you, Sigehelm; I never doubted I could trust you.'

Eadwulf knew he could trust Sigehelm, yet to voice suspicions of treachery involving his uncle would appear as wild imaginings. His tutor had never witnessed Burgred's innuendos and explicitly hurtful comments, or seen the glimmer of hatred in his eyes. Eadwulf had felt increasingly more uncomfortable in Burgred's presence as the months had passed, yet he struggled to trust his own feelings. Perhaps he just *wanted* to find something incriminating in Burgred's behaviour.

'Eadwulf! Did you hear what I just said? Apparently not, if I read that startled expression correctly.' Sigehelm smiled tolerantly: not the usual reaction from his strict tutor. 'I said perhaps we should share a story or poem. You'll make little headway with your studies whilst your mind is elsewhere. What about one of the old Greek tales – of Heracles, perhaps? Or shall we examine events at the Siege of Troy? Do you know anything about Achilles?' Eadwulf shook his head. 'He was a mighty warrior who had only one vulnerable spot on his entire body. And that one weak place resulted in his downfall. Yes, we shall read his story; it will give you something else to think about, at least for a while.'

* * *

Perched on cushions of straw in a corner of the stables, Eadwulf and Aethelnoth listened enthralled to the story of Achilles. It had been Sigehelm's suggestion that Aethelnoth should join them, a suggestion that made Eadwulf smile. His tutor's motives were as transparent as water. But he was grateful, nonetheless. His friend's presence had helped to lift his spirits.

Eadwulf had known exactly where to find Aethelnoth, since the boy spent so much time with the horses he loved so much. Aethelnoth had witnessed his first foaling at the age of six, and helped his own mount into the world two years ago. But Aethelnoth was much less keen on his studies and frequently shirked his morning lessons. His face had lit up when Eadwulf entered the stables, only to darken rapidly when Sigehelm trailed in.

Yet Aethelnoth shared Eadwulf's captivation at Sigehelm's tale of the battle of Troy, the idea of the wooden horse leaving him dumbfounded. '*My* father wouldn't have fallen for such a cheap trick,' he scoffed. 'King Priam was obviously not a very wise man. Thrydwulf says that to out-think the enemy, we must keep one step ahead, get inside their heads or something.'

The snorting and stomping of the horses was the first indication that anything was amiss, then the panicked shouts; the reek of smoke assailing their nostrils only moments later. They hurtled to the stable door, aware that it could take barely minutes for wood and thatch to burn to a crisp, and reeled in horror. Searing waves of heat smacked into them. The hall was ablaze, its heavy thatch ready to collapse; angry red flames lashed at the wood-planked walls. People collided with each other, precious water slopping from their pails as they raced to quell the towering flames. Yapping, terrified dogs added to the pandemonium.

Sigehelm crossed himself, uttering a prayer for anyone trapped inside the blazing hall. 'Eadwulf; Aethelnoth; stay close to me,' he ordered, grabbing Aethelnoth's arm as the boy turned to lead the horses to safety. 'The stables are far enough away to be safe for now. If need be, I'll loose the horses when you're both safe with Morwenna. But may the Lord help these other buildings. The kitchens will probably soon be ablaze. We must hurry. I need to help to fetch water.'

It was then that the Danes struck.

Yowling men stampeded through the palisade's main gate, their entrance unchallenged as people fought to control the blaze. Yet they had needed neither to burn down nor scale the palisade wall. The gates must have already been open, contrary to Thrydwulf's insistence that they be kept locked and guarded.

Frenzied screams escalated. Sigehelm yanked Eadwulf and Aethelnoth behind the kitchens and, stooping low, they headed for the women's bower. Suddenly Eadwulf froze. Burgred stood outside the bower's door – and something about that was so very wrong ...

'Eadwulf, in God's name, child, we cannot stand and stare. We must reach your mother and try to flee from the manor.'

'Burgred's a traitor, Sigehelm!' Eadwulf spat. 'He was meeting them in the woods! And he must have started the fire: the hall was ablaze before the Danes came through the gate. He must have opened that for them too.'

Sigehelm gasped. 'He's betrayed us to these savages? But why would he?'

'I don't know exactly, yet. But I won't let him get to my mother!'

Eadwulf struggled to break free of Sigehelm's grip, just as two Danes joined Burgred: one tall, with flaxen hair and plaited beard, the other bull-shaped with straggling brown hair and beard. Sigehelm shoved the boys behind a wattle fence.

'Look, Burgred didn't run from them,' Eadwulf spat. 'He's talking to them!'

But Burgred slunk away, just as the bull-shaped man reached for the door. The other stood resolute, grinning at Burgred's glowering retreat.

'No!' Eadwulf yelled, bursting forward again. 'Leave my mother alone!'

Burgred's reaction was swift. He turned in his tracks, his face contorted with rage, and charged at his nephew.

* * *

Fitful and nauseous, Morwenna curled in a wicker chair, a blanket pulled up to her chin. The air in the bower's hall was chill after the night's rain, despite the glowing brazier. She had insisted her women leave her to rest and she relished the peace and quiet. If only she could sleep. Perhaps when she woke the debilitating nausea would have eased; perhaps Eadwulf would tell her what was disturbing him; perhaps Beorhtwulf would have returned ...

She realised how feeble she sounded, but this wretched sickness rendered her so physically drained, at a time when it was crucial to stay strong. But it would likely be several weeks before the sickness left her.

The high-pitched screams struck terror into Morwenna's breast. She hurtled to the window and wrenched back the shutters, recoiling at the chaos before her eyes. Orange flames and thick, black smoke billowed from the hall and people scattered from fur-clad savages hacking freely at moving targets.

Eadwulf ...! Eadwulf was inside the burning hall!

She flung back the door but a huge, terrifying shape loomed before her, barring her way: a giant of a man, with matted brown hair and a barrel of a chest.

'Not you, my lovely,' he leered through repulsive black teeth. 'It's not safe for a lady out there.'

'Let me get to my son!' she screamed, scrambling to dodge round the massive bulk. But for one so big he was nimble on his feet, and he caught her wrists to restrain her.

'Now that isn't part of the plan. You're to be kept safe from the fun outside. We're going to make our own fun in here, just you and me.'

The callused hand clamped across her mouth, cutting short her horrified scream. She kicked out wildly, but he jeered at her feeble antics. 'Now this can be nice and easy, or rough and wild, and you could end up covered in bruises. Either way I *shall* have you ...

For a few, terrifying moments Morwenna prayed she'd waken from the ghoulish nightmare. Then the brute shoved her against the wall, unfastening his belt and dropping his breeches before throwing up her skirts. 'By Odin you've a beautiful arse,' he drooled, his huge hands kneading her flesh. 'A man could stay abed forever next to that arse.'

Morwenna's panic rose almost to hysteria as he thrust into her. But she could barely move.

'The name's Jarl Rorik, by the way,' he slavered into her neck, once his lust was sated, 'leader of this foray into Mercian domain. I shall enjoy taking these lands if all its women are soft and fair like you.' His dark eyes narrowed. 'But just remember, if you're not extra friendly the next time I have you, I may decide to share your considerable charms with my men.'

'Beorhtwulf won't let you do this,' she croaked as he pulled back, turning to leave.

Rorik snorted. 'I can tell you, my lovely, King Beorhtwulf is no more.'

Morwenna choked back a horror-struck sob. 'You can't have killed him! He's not yet returned from–'

'From the court of that old fart, Aethelwulf, you mean? We know all about that little scheme to garner aid. But like I said, your husband is no more.'

'What about my son?' she hurled at his back as he reached the door. 'Is he dead, too? And Burgred? Are they all dead?'

Rorik turned and fixed her with a cold stare. 'Of your son, I can't be certain. Some of your people *may* have been spared; thralls are always needed on our homesteads. But I still have need of the king's loving brother. I shall enjoy playing with him.'

Morwenna fell to the floor, feeling utterly defiled. The Dane's foul stench filled her nostrils and she could feel his rough hands pawing her, taking away every shred of dignity. Yet her plight seemed little compared to that of others. She pictured the earth scarlet, strewn with lifeless bodies, including that of her beloved husband.

* * *

Eadwulf bolted, knowing that Burgred would kill him if he caught him. He dodged frenzied people and pillaging Danes, feeling no panic, no hysteria, only cold determination that his uncle would not bring down his intended prey this time. He sped towards the palisade, seeking the place where the dogs had tunnelled through to the outside, just big enough for him to wriggle through.

There, next to the pig-pens. He was almost there. Slower than Eadwulf, Burgred had fallen behind, so all he needed to do was get through quickly and head for the forest; hide until his father's return. But in his blinkered state he didn't see the four Danes nearing from the sides and suddenly he crashed to the earth, his knees and elbows taking the brunt of the fall.

'Well, here's a real lively one!' The young Dane who'd put out his foot to trip him, yanked Eadwulf up. 'Fancied your chances with the pigs, did you?'

'He's *mine*!' Burgred hissed, panting to a halt. 'That was the agreement with Egil. The brat was running from *me*.'

A tall, rangy Dane stepped forward, arms folded across his chest. 'As far as we know, Mercian,' he spat through his drooping moustache, 'you've kept your side of the bargain. And so have we! We've dealt with this royal manor as you requested. But I've no recollection of any agreements about who we take as prisoners.' His upturned hands and raised eyebrows prompted smirking head-shakes from his companions.

Burgred glared at Eadwulf with such loathing that the young Dane who'd caused his fall seemed impelled to speak.

'Such hatred, Mercian ...He is but a child, a relative I'd say from the look of you both. Save your hatred for your real enemies.'

'He *is* my most real enemy! He has to die – he and his father, my dear brother. They stand in the way of everything I want.'

'Then you needn't worry,' the tall Dane said. 'The boy will bother you no more because he's coming with us. Be content that one object of your hatred is dead.'

The words smacked into Eadwulf. 'No!' he screamed, frantically struggling against his captor's tight hold.

The young warrior's fingers dug into Eadwulf's arm. 'Be still boy, or we'll be forced to truss you up like a chicken. Your father is dead. But I'll tell you this: he was a brave man, a man deserving of respect.' He glared contemptuously at Burgred. 'He fought against our men valiantly and died like a king. That may not be consolation to you now, but perhaps later.'

'Don't get soft with the boy, Godfried,' the tall Dane urged. 'He'll need toughening up if he's to be much use on one of our homesteads.'

'Don't presume to teach me how to treat anyone! I sought only to quiet the lad.'

The tall man grunted. 'Your father will be pleased on our return,' he soothed. 'Plunder always puts a smile on King Harald's face. But your uncle won't leave until he's drained this land of its wealth. Rorik's not a man to do only half a job.'

Eadwulf's eyes met the smouldering green of his uncle's as Godfried dragged him to the palisade gate. Burgred could barely control his fury. He'll go to their leaders now, his *allies*, Eadwulf thought. God make them kill him for what he's done! If ever a man deserved to die, it was the man he'd once called Uncle.

* * *

The frenzied screams had ceased and a deathly silence prevailed. Morwenna huddled on the rushes in a corner of her bower, her knees pulled up to her chin, arms clasped around them. She rocked herself to and fro, her mind screaming grievance for her lost husband and son. Voices sounded now, drawing closer, and panic rose. Would Rorik give her to his men as he'd threatened? She'd rather die than suffer the pain and degradation of repeated, savage rape.

Rorik squeezed through the doorway, his scornful gaze finding her hunched in the corner. 'Come out and be good, my pretty, and I might be nice to you.'

For a fleeting moment she thought to laugh in his face, taunt him with his sexual inadequacies. Say anything that would make him kill her on the spot. But courage deserted her and she remained dumb and petrified.

'You won't play by my rules? Well, no matter, this time. There's someone here to make you take notice.' Rorik turned to a tall, blond-headed man. 'Bring him in, Egil.'

Morwenna's hopes surged. Beorhtwulf was alive, or Eadwulf!

The wreck of a man was dragged in by two of Rorik's men, his feet scraping through the rushes, his agonised groans heart-rending. Dried blood matted his hair and his left arm hung limp at his side. Further injuries were likely concealed by his stained clothing.

Egil grabbed the man's hair, yanking back his head. Morwenna stared at the empty eye socket: a deep hollow, black with congealed blood; then the swollen, split lips. The hideous mutilations momentarily obscured his identity; then realisation struck.

'You are animals!' she screeched, rising and stumbling forward. 'Beornred is only a boy!'

Rorik laughed, as though someone had just revealed the answer to some hilarious riddle. 'I was beginning to think I'd got you pegged all wrong But I see you *have* got that feistiness I love in my women.'

'I'll never be your woman. I'll kill myself first!'

'I'll take pleasure in discussing that with you later, but right now, you'll hear what this "boy" has to say. Boy he may be, but he fought like a man against my warriors. We've done no more than any warriors would to an enemy taken captive.' Rorik raised a fist, halting her intended outburst and turned to the mutilated figure. 'Now, you were brought here for a purpose, so get on with it,'

Between ragged breaths Beornred told of the fateful ambush and its predictable end. Tears coursed down Morwenna's cheeks. This wretched young man could think only of ensuring that her pride in her husband lived on. Of his own, indescribable agonies, he said nothing. She accepted the truth of his words. Deep inside she'd known Rorik hadn't lied. But now, even hope was gone. Nothing remained but the unbearable misery of her loss.

'Take him out,' Rorik snapped at his men. 'I've no further use for him.'

They would kill him now. Morwenna knew it was for the best. Beornred's mind and spirit were dead already; his butchered body would have soon followed.

Then Burgred stepped through the open door.

'I thought they'd kill you, too,' she choked, throwing herself into his arms. 'They tortured Beornred so wickedl. And they've killed Beorhtwulf, and may have captured Eadwulf. Pray God my son still lives.'

'He lives, lady,' Egil growled. 'Ask *him*, he's just seen him.'

Morwenna pulled back, searching Burgred's eyes in hope of explanation. But he held his silence.

'Speak, Mercian!'

'Eadwulf lives,' Burged admitted, his eyes flicking to the menacing jarl. 'He'll be taken to their lands and sold as a slave. You, Morwenna, will remain with Jarl Rorik as ...as his concubine.'

'Tell me the rest, *brother.* Tell me!' she yelled as Burgred's unforgivable treachery became clear. 'Let me hear from your own lips why you've betrayed your own brother, your own people.'

'Beorhtwulf had to die,' Burgred stated, his voice devoid of all warmth, all humanity. 'I'll make a better king than he ever could. He was weak, hadn't the head for ruling or the skills for policy making. Even the idea of unity with Wessex came from me. And I wanted you, Morwenna. Things have changed since you so favourably impressed the jarl, but I shall rule Mercia, our agreement on that still stands.'

Rorik grunted. 'How do we know we can trust a traitor to his own people?'

Burgred opened his mouth to protest but seemed to think better of it and made to leave. 'Goodbye, Morwenna.'

'Wait! Tell me where you saw Eadwulf!'

'If things had gone to plan the brat would now be dead, like his father. But I suppose a slave poses me no threat, and the few people still alive believe he died in the hall, along with his god-fearing tutor. And Thrydwulf is well and truly dead. I saw his body myself.'

Morwenna spat in Burgred's face. 'I hope they dangle you up high, puppet, then cut the cords and laugh as your body lies scattered across the Mercian lands you so grievously harmed. Be gone from my sight: you are worse than they.'

* * *

Thrydwulf's manor was no more. Of the proud, wood-planked hall, the small chapel, stables, kitchens and bowers, nothing remained but smouldering ash; the palisade a charred circle scarring the earth. By noon the pungency of lingering smoke mingled with the stench of roasted flesh; those who'd sought escape indoors had been given but a moment to emerge before their dwellings had become their funeral pyres. Of those who had hoped for mercy, most had been brutally hacked down. Mutilated bodies, almost unrecognisable as people, stripped of weapons, jewellery and usable clothing, lay where they'd fallen, carrion for the scavengers.

The handful of able-bodied spared had been herded out beyond the palisade: there were fewer than a dozen. They huddled together in one of the manor's carts, their terror-filled eyes darting. Those who wept too loud or too long gained a lashing. Eadwulf had known these people for most of his life.

His tutor, Sigehelm, and skinny Alric, one of the cooks, were the only male adults taken; the rest were women and girls, servants at the manor, or attendants of his mother. And his friend, Aethelnoth.

Of Morwenna's fate, Eadwulf was ignorant. All conquering warriors took slaves, he knew that; some for ransom, others as prizes of war. A king's wife would be seen as an exceptional prize. Grief engulfed him and he squeezed his eyes shut.

But he wouldn't cry; he would never let the Danes see him cry.

As the wagon moved out, he caught a flash of green, and flaxen hair, and he was certain that the man shoving someone into a wagon was one of those he'd seen outside his mother's bower. He strained his eyes until the smoking blackness that was once a fine Mercian manor disappeared from view, promising himself that one day Burged would pay dearly for his treachery.

Four

Winchester: April 851

'Our stomachs have been doubly assaulted, lord. To be confronted by the butchered body of my dear brother so soon after the sickening remnants and stench of Thrydwulf's manor...'

Burgred hung his head, hand across his breast, hoping his grief-stricken stance and haggard appearance looked convincing. God, he was tired, at least that was genuine. Joining his men in the forest after he'd left Morwenna's bower, he'd made his decision. Rorik had no intention of honouring him as king; what a fool he'd been to believe he would. His only hope now was Aethelwulf: convince the old goat he'd returned from his own manor to find the atrocities already committed.

Despite riding like the Furies, it had taken two days to reach Winchester. He baulked at the possibility that his plans might fail, but by taking the news of Beorhtwulf's death to Winchester himself, he hoped not only to gain Aethelwulf's sympathy, but his support.

'My men tried to shield me from the sight of Beorhtwulf's mutilated body,' he continued. 'But I saw what those animals had done, and the scavengers had already begun their work. We buried Beorhtwulf by the river, my lord, but had no time for the rest.'

Aethelwulf sat motionless on his high-backed chair, his direct blue gaze fixed on Burgred, cold and judgemental. Sweating beneath this raking appraisal, Burgred tried to focus on the court's attendants. To the king's right sat a young man so like Aethelwulf in build and facial features it could only be one of his sons, though the deep chestnut hair and eyes likely resembled his mother's, as well as those of the tall, elegant man of late middle years at Aethelwulf's opposite side.

The uncomfortable silence was broken by a sudden commotion outside. Horses skidded to a halt, shouted words were exchanged and within moments a small group of warriors entered the hall and fell to their knees before the king, helms clutched under their arms.

'Let's hear it then, Egric,' Aethelwulf demanded, gesturing to the men to rise. 'What news is so urgent it can't wait to be told?'

'The Danes, my lord. They're in Surrey!'

Aethelwulf shot to his feet with a rapidity that belied his years, his face thunderous.

'Our patrol witnessed their attack on London,' Egric panted. 'They burnt it to the ground, after they'd looted it and slaughtered everything that breathed! There were hundreds of them. Most of their ships set sail down the Thames, but others ferried men and horses across the river and moored on the Wessex bank. A dozen ships there were.' He glanced up warily at Aethelwulf, gauging his response. 'Then, leaving maybe half their number to guard their ships, the rest headed south into Surrey. Close on two hundred riders, we guessed.

'We were lucky not to have been spotted, lord,' Egric added as the king's chest heaved. 'The woodland is sparse along those banks, but the Danes were busy with their ships. We kept our heads low and our horses well back – couldn't risk them giving us away.'

Burgred watched with interest; this timely interruption could serve his purpose well.

Aethelwulf sank to his seat, striving for calm. 'You've done well to bring us this news, Egric, unwelcome though it is. Tomorrow your patrol will head for Osmund's hall at Guildford. My army will follow within the week.' His glacial eyes turned to Burgred. 'It seems the Danes had greater designs on Wessex than we'd realised, and Surrey can't be left to fend them off alone. It comes under Aethelstan's jurisdiction of course,' he explained for Burgred's benefit, 'but my son's depleted forces won't stand further battering. And ultimately, responsibility for the entirety of Wessex is mine.' His piercing stare sharpened. As the next Mercian king, Lord Burgred, I trust you will honour our newfound unity. I fear that darker times are yet to come.'

Aethelwulf's meaty fists clenched tight and he sprang again to his feet, almost toppling his chair. 'I swear I'll not rest until I put an end to their rampaging in my kingdom!'

'Father, won't you sit and take refreshment?'

The young woman had entered unnoticed and, as she approached the king, Burgred noted she was scarcely more than a girl, a comely one at that. So, this was Aethelwulf's only daughter, Aethelswith; fair haired and complexioned, like her father. Her blue tunic followed the curves of a body that had the slimness of youth.

'I just thought you didn't seem quite yourself when I peeped in,' she said tentatively, her cheeks flushed with embarrassment. 'I beg your pardon for interrupting, but I wondered whether a little wine might help you to ...to think.'

Aethelwulf's taut muscles loosened and he smiled. 'It's good to know you've a care for your old father, daughter. But I am well; it's just the task ahead that fills my thoughts. And yes, I do forgive your interruption, though only you or your mother would be forgiven such a sin.'

The young man at Aethelwulf's side winked at the girl and Burgred noted the many smirking faces. The king's soft spot for his family was evidently well known. Aethelwulf seemed to be a many-faceted character.

'Shall I fetch you that drink then, Father?' Aethelswith's cheeks glowed still brighter at the laughter her question caused.

'What you can do,' Aethelwulf said, placing a fatherly arm round her shoulders, 'is go to the kitchens and inform the servants that ale for all of us wouldn't go amiss.' He bent down, allowing his daughter to kiss his cheek. 'Then, I think you should see if your mother would like some company. She isn't in the best of health, and old Edith isn't as sprightly as she was. And young Alfred's quite a handful.'

'Say no more, Father,' Aethelswith replied, laying a hand on his arm. 'I know what my little brother can get up to. Edith would appreciate some help.'

'Then be off with you. That drink is well needed and we have plans to make.'

Aethelswith scurried off in pursuit of her errand, nodding politely as she detected a stranger at Court. The flash of her blue eyes caused a stab of guilt-laden misery in Burgred's chest. Only two days since he'd longed to look into the blue eyes of another. But he must move on. Aethelswith was a very pretty girl indeed, one he'd remember – once he ruled Mercia, with

Aethelwulf as his staunch ally.

Hadn't that been his advice to Beorhtwulf all along: keep on the right side of Wessex?

* * *

Already mustered at Winchester in preparation for moving into Mercia at the beginning of May, Aethelwulf's army was ready to move out within a day of Burgred's unexpected arrival. Aethelwulf surveyed the scene beyond the palisade, pleased with the impressive numbers. Over three hundred fighting men, comprising the ealdormen of Hampshire, Dorset, Wiltshire and Berkshire, with over a hundred thegns and two hundred men of the Hampshire fyrd.

'The ceorls will be pleased to see action earlier than expected,' Osric remarked, coming to stand next to him. 'They're desperate to get back to their homes. Spring sowing's been left to the women and the men fret they'll be greatly overtaxed. Our system of raising an army from the villages, and only when the need arises, is far from satisfactory. Though most ceorls are fit from working the land, they lack military skills and need training each time: not always possible in an emergency.'

They watched the men sparring for a while, many wielding shields as they'd been taught. 'Our present system *is* inadequate,' Aethelwulf eventually agreed with his brother-by-marriage. 'But to maintain a permanent army has never been our custom. We couldn't force free men to join an army.'

'I'm not sure they'd all need to be forced, Aethelwulf. There must be hundreds of able-bodied ceorls who'd be proud to serve their king, for a regular income, of course.'

'The idea certainly has its possibilities, and is one to be considered at some future stage. But for the present we continue as always, trusting our ealdormen to do their best. Now, I know we needn't go over our plans again, Osric, and your men know what's expected. If all goes well you could cover the sixty-odd miles to London in a little over two days, with several hours for rest before you strike.'

Leaving Osric to supervise the men, Aethelwulf headed for the paddock, needing to be alone with his thoughts. His feisty black stallion, Satan, trotted up to the fence and he caressed the smooth neck, mulling over his carefully laid plans:

He'd divided his forces into two: Osric, with the other three ealdormen, would lead twenty thegns and almost two hundred of the fyrd, the latter mostly on foot. Among them would be Osric's son, Cynric, a broad-backed young man whose battle skills matched those of the most hardened Wessex warriors. They would leave at dawn tomorrow and head to the Thames, where the waiting Danes guarded their ships. The attack was planned for the shadowy light of pre-dawn, when all but the enemy lookouts would be sleeping. Their orders were simple: spare no lives and fire the cursed ships.

Aethelwulf himself would lead the pursuit into Surrey, from where further reports confirmed that minor raids on homesteads were all that had occurred, so far. His army would be swelled by whatever numbers Osmund, the Surrey ealdorman, could muster, plus the twenty men of Egric's patrol, and consist only of mounted warriors: men on foot could not pursue mounted, fast-moving Danes. His second-eldest son would accompany him, the only one of his brood with the dark hair and eyes of his beloved wife, Osburh, and her brother, Osric. Like Cynric, eighteen-year-old Aethelbald had seen nothing of battle yet, but his leadership skills were evident. Aethelbald addressed the men with an easy style and his robust appearance and skilful handling of the fyrd ensured respect. Aethelbald would make an excellent king, provided he controlled the temper and impetuosity that so often resulted in inopportune or inappropriate action.

Aethelwulf closed his eyes, contemplating the days ahead. 'I'm all right, boy,' he murmured as Satan nuzzled his shoulder. 'Preparing for battle always rouses troubled thoughts. Pray God we all survive.'

* * *

The evening meal was a sombre affair, the absence of the king and most of his warriors leaving the Winchester hall in whispered silence. The men left to guard the manor were morose but resigned to follow their orders. Aethelwulf had entrusted them with the safety of those still in residence, and as true Wessex noblemen, they knew their duty. The events at London would not be repeated here.

April daylight had faded early. Ominous black clouds had scudded across the afternoon sky, bringing a steady downpour which now seemed set for the night. The warm glow from the firepit and flickering lamps did little to alleviate the anxious mood; even most of the shields from around the walls had gone: yet another reminder of events about to unfold.

Aethelswith gave up trying to eat and pushed her bowl away. By tomorrow her father could be dead; a thought too terrible to contemplate. And Cynric too; dear, wonderful Cynric, who could make her laugh and fill her with such joy. A feeling of warmth engulfed her whenever she thought of him. She'd heard people speak of 'love' and could only guess that it was love she felt for Cynric.

Catching Edith's eye she attempted a smile. The ageing nurse's expression reflected Aethelswith's own anxiety, and beside her, Aethelwulf's loyal old groom, Osberht, stared into his pottage as though something slimy had fallen into it. Two of the loveliest people Aethelswith had ever known, who'd long since lost their respective spouses; they had made a wonderful couple since their marriage eighteen months ago.

'I noticed you taking Mother's meal to her room again, Edith,' she said, moving to sit opposite them. 'Worrying about Father will be so hard for her to bear.' She choked back the tears, held so well in check all afternoon.

Osberht reached across the table and patted her hand. 'It's all right to be upset, my lady. We all feel the same. Just remember, your father's an experienced leader. He *will* succeed, and will soon be back with you.'

Aethelswith nodded, meeting the grey eyes that inspired such trust. 'I've never doubted Father's leadership, Osberht, or his bravery, but battles are battles and men can be lost. And having three of her family out there to worry about will do Mother's health little good. I've offered to take Alfred for a while but she insists he's happy where he is.'

'Your mother never rests while Alfred's awake,' the rotund

nurse confirmed with a fond smile. And believe me, he sleeps little. By rights a child of two should be fast asleep by now, but I'll wager he'll be extremely active for some time yet, and wake before the songbirds in the morning. Lady Osburh's been weak since giving birth to young Alfred, if I'm honest, though at times she seems full of energy. Some things fill her with such pleasure, like Alfred cutting a new tooth, or Aethelred's progress with his Latin. Now it is you, my dear, who fills her mind, and the way you're blossoming into womanhood. No, don't you go blushing now, 'tis naught but the truth – as any of the young men of the Court would tell you, if they'd be so bold. Your mother's keen to see a good marriage arranged for you.'

'I don't suppose she hinted at *who* she thought I should marry?'

'Edith flicked a stone-grey plait over her shoulder, smiling impishly. 'Maybe we did catch the odd name.'

'Please Edith, don't keep me in suspense. Tell me, *please*.' But, assailed by a sudden thought, Aethelswith stopped herself. She could be married off to some nobleman she'd never met, or even someone from another kingdom. Then she'd have to leave her beloved Cynric and Wessex for ever. 'On second thoughts, perhaps you'd better not.'

Osberht grinned. 'Oh, we think you'd approve of your parents' choice for you, Lady Aethelswith.'

'You know him?'

The groom's old eyes twinkled. 'Of course we do. And I think the whole court knows how you feel about the young man. The trouble is, the young man doesn't know how you feel, though why he doesn't is beyond me. But I'm sure he absolutely worships his cousin.'

Aethelswith's heart lurched. 'Cynric's my only cousin of marriageable age!'

Osberht grinned. 'You know, Edith, I think Lady Aethelswith's got the message. Your parents will be speaking to you after–'

'Thank you so much for telling me,' Aethelswith said, jerked back to the present and glancing at her seven-year-old brother who was staring glumly into the hearthfire. 'But now I must speak with Aethelred. He's as much in need of comfort as the rest of us.'

* * *

Halting at the doorway Edith threw a worried look over her shoulder. Grief hung over her mistress's chamber like a shroud. 'Are you sure I can't take Alfred for a while, my lady?'

'No, it's all right, Edith,' Osburh replied with a wan smile. 'Alfred's happy just now and may prove some distraction to his sister.'

Edith nodded, unconvinced. 'I'll not be far away should you need me.'

The door closed and Osburh moved to embrace her daughter, who had barely stopped weeping since hearing the awful news two days since. 'God works in ways we may find hard to understand, Aethelswith, but we must believe He truly cares for all his children. Time will heal your pain. You will find another.'

'Never!' Aethelswith sobbed, prising Alfred's grubby little hands from her skirt with uncharacteristic intolerance and throwing herself onto Osburh's bed. 'Cynric was my only hope of happiness.'

Osburh perched at Aethelswith's side and brushed the tears from her cheeks. 'Take comfort in knowing that Cynric died a noble death. It was bravery indeed to move into the path of a falling mast on a burning ship to save another. Had he not done so, it would have been his dear friend, Deormod, we bury tomorrow.'

Aethelswith was utterly distraught and had eaten nothing since the return of Osric's party bearing Cynric's crushed body. Osric had helped to carry his son to the church to await burial and not emerged from his own quarters since. Deormod kept constant vigil in the chapel.

'My brother is much in need of our support now,' Osburh said gently. 'We need to be strong for his sake. To lose an only son...' She faltered, struggling to control her own emotions; Cynric had been like a son to her. How could she comfort a young girl's romantic ideas? And yet, she trusted Aethelswith's feelings to be sincere.

'There will always be losses during combat, daughter, and loved ones waiting behind must be prepared to face the worst. We must thank God for your father's safe return. I prayed for him constantly during those awful days and my prayers have been answered.'

Osburh lifted Alfred up beside his sister and encircled them both in her arms. 'We will never forget Cynric, Aethelswith, but time does heal. Keep his memory locked in your heart.'

Five

Thanet to Hedeby: May 851

Half a dozen knarrs, the sturdy sailing vessels used by the Norsemen for carrying cargo, cast off from Thanet on a fine morning during the first week of May. The host of dragonships carrying throngs of warriors set sail with them, but their sails quickly picked up the strong south-westerly and soon became no more than tiny specks on the distant horizon.

In the hold of the knarr, *Njord's Bounty,* Sigehelm retched, though his stomach had long since ejected its meagre contents. He tried to focus on his silent prayers, his mind baulking at the reality of the situation into which he'd been thrust, and refused to look at the billowing water. Sigehelm had never been a brave man. Only once, eleven years ago, had he crossed the Northern Sea, and on that occasion, he had not been held captive. Yet even then he'd hated the sea. And the Northern Sea was notorious for being perilous and unpredictable. Storms could sweep in without warning to release their fury in ear-splitting thunderclaps and luminous, jagged streaks of lightning. Driving winds and rain could whip the sea into a frenzy, capsizing ships and sending their booty to the ocean bottom.

But for Eadwulf's sake, he *must* stay strong. The boy had no one else to turn to.

Huddled beside him, Eadwulf stared vacantly across the vast waters as though his mind had withdrawn to some distant place, a place that Sigehelm could not reach. He seemed unaware of the stinging tongues of icy water that lashed the decks and soaked them to the skin as the ship ploughed through the crested foam, and was unaffected by the unbearable nausea. Perhaps it was his way of dealing with the truth too awful to accept: that he'd never see his parents or homeland again. But two young women whom Sigehelm did not recognise constantly groaned in their misery. Bound at the wrist and linked to each other, the four were surrounded by sacks of looted goods and could barely move.

The first night at sea was a petrifying experience. Sea and sky merged into each other, the moonless expanse an all-consuming blanket of darkness, the silence broken only by the water's incessant slapping against the hull. The Danes slept in turns, sufficient crew remaining alert to man the ship. To Sigehelm, sleep became a distant hope and he almost envied Eadwulf his state of oblivion.

For four days and nights the weather held clear and the sea calm, a favourable breeze conveying the knarrs at a steady pace as the crew sang songs of their homeland. Sigehelm cursed the pagans to everlasting damnation, the small replicas of Thor's hammer, Mjöllnir, around their necks a constant reminder of their misplaced faith.

In the afternoon of the fifth day the lookout's cry of 'Landfall!' sent an excited buzz through the crew. Sick with foreboding, Sigehelm watched the Danish coast draw near: a narrow strip of sandy beach backed by low, grass-speckled dunes. Whatever happened now, their lives would not be easy in this pagan land.

The wind kept good faith with the ships, and they sailed

upstream for almost two miles. Coastal dunes gave way to large tracts of wetlands where abundant wildfowl hovered: coots and moorhens, mallard, marsh tits and red-necked grebes caught Sigehelm's eye, as well as the occasional whooper swan. He'd seen such species in his homeland, but recoiled from the possibility that this hostile world could be anything like Mercia. Smoke rising from the hearths in nearby homesteads purveyed an air of tranquillity that Sigehelm could not feel.

Then the port of Ribe came into view, lying on the northern bank of the River Ribea on a sandy, wooded peninsula, raised above the surrounding marshes. Several vessels were moored along the wharves, some being loaded ready for sailing, others seeming to have recently berthed. The striped sails of the knarrs were lowered and the Danes heaved at their oars, grunting with the effort of driving the ship steadily towards the jetties.

* * *

They spent their first night on Danish soil in a large, wood-planked warehouse along Ribe's quayside. Besides Eadwulf, few of the fifteen captives were familiar to Sigehelm. Young Aethelnoth was one of them. Like Eadwulf, the boy was sunk in despair, his head bowed as though to avert attention with which he couldn't cope. Another was Alric, one of Thrydwulf's cooks, who stared numbly at the wall, gaunt and exhausted. The third was a serving girl whose striking looks had attracted many a young man's attention in the London hall. But now she squatted, whimpering, scraping dried vomit from the front of her tunic.

Sigehelm's pity for these people welled. The terror of not knowing their fate was etched into their haggard faces as they huddled together on the straw.

Soon after dawn the next day, guarded by four of Rorik's rough-looking crewmen, they left Ribe on what proved to be a slow and uncomfortable journey. Bounced and jostled as the two ox-drawn carts trundled over the rough track, it would have been difficult to speak, even had they been permitted. The road was crammed with traffic moving in both directions, and livestock being herded to market at Ribe constantly forced them onto the verges. Bright May sunshine offered little comfort. Sigehelm ran his fingers through his hair, meeting a tangled thatch encrusted with sea water.

Next to him, Eadwulf stared ahead, unseeing and unfeeling.

In the early afternoon they turned south onto a road of substantial width and improved surface. Dense forests covered the slightly elevated land whilst vast expanses of water meadows and marshland flanked innumerable streams. Sigehelm shuddered. This was, indeed, a God-forsaken land, one in which the pagan gods played with the souls of the misguided.

They stopped each night at small homesteads where they were shunted into some kind of barn and fed a meagre meal before being locked in for the night. Then, as daylight faded on the sixth day, they approached a settlement that Sigehelm instinctively knew was their destination. It was larger than the homesteads of previous nights and near to the sea. The odour of salty air filled his nostrils and the harsh keening of seabirds added to the steady rumble of the carts' wooden wheels.

Daylight had almost faded as they trundled through the

town's narrow streets toward the waterfront, the buzz of voices and clamour of activity bearing evidence of a thriving community. Lamplight flooded through open shutters, glinting on the dark water as it lapped the wharves. In happier circumstances the melodic murmurings would have created a lulling sense of peace. But fear seized Sigehelm's chest so tightly he could scarcely breathe.

Rough hands grabbed his tunic and dragged him from the cart, hustling him inside one of the large warehouses that lined the quay. The low-roofed building was similar in design to that at Ribe – a wood-planked, thatched structure with a straw-strewn floor, empty but for the pitiful souls thrust inside. The raucous laughter and inebriated singing of night-time revellers carried through the walls long after they'd been fed the usual quota of dried rye bread and water; the racket gradually evolving into vicious arguments and brawls, and the screams and sobs of women.

Sigehelm knuckled his stinging eyes and massaged his throbbing head; he was so exhausted that merely standing was further punishment. He longed for respite from the reality of past weeks but, as dawn approached, he'd spent yet another night almost devoid of sleep. The other poor wretches had eventually succumbed to restless slumbers, some sobbing themselves into a state of total exhaustion. In the pre-dawn light he could just make out Eadwulf and Aethelnoth, curled side by side, their young bodies, for the moment, blessedly unaware.

What would the new day bring? Sigehelm prayed that he wouldn't be separated from Eadwulf, whose grief had remained buried throughout the tortuous journey. But once the harrowing memories eventually surfaced, the boy would have great need of guidance and comfort.

* * *

As the first glimmers of light squeezed through gaps in the wood-planked walls, Eadwulf roused from his sleep and rolled stiffly over. He blinked several times and glanced around before pulling himself up and tweaking stalks of straw from his salt-stiffened hair.

'Take heart, child; I am here,' Sigehelm said gently. 'You've been far away these past days, unaware of our sea crossing or our journey here.'

'I did see those things, Sigehelm, but somehow they just seemed like dreams.' Eadwulf's face contorted as cruel reality returned and his agonised groan tore at Sigehelm's heart. 'Sigehelm, my father and mother! The Dane who captured me said my father is dead, that he died like a true warrior. But I can't bear to think about it!'

'Months, perhaps years, will offer consolation and acceptance of your loss, Eadwulf. But for now you must focus on your survival. Conduct yourself with dignity and never give up hope of returning home one day. Such hope may keep you alive.'

'But I must know what the Danes have done to Mother! *She* isn't dead, I know she isn't. I saw her! I know it was her. I recognised her hair, and the green gown she wore so often. That ugly Dane was pushing her into a wagon just as we were leaving.'

Sigehelm's mind reeled. Pray God that Eadwulf was right,

though even if he were, finding Morwenna would surely be impossible.

'What will they do with us, Sigehelm?'

'If I'm correct,' he replied, holding Eadwulf's intense gaze, 'this place is Hedeby, an important trading town. Goods from as far as the Orient, Samarkand, Byzantium and even deepest Africa can be purchased here.'

'Have you been here before?'

'I have not, but I have been to other towns like it – Kaupang and Birka, for instance, both in the lands far to the north of here. All markets have many similarities but Hedeby is renowned for one particular commodity, for which purchasers will travel many miles.'

Eadwulf stared in silent expectation.

'That commodity is slaves, Eadwulf. I believe we'll be taken to the market place and sold to whoever offers a good price for us.'

'I already knew the reason for our capture,' Eadwulf huffed. 'But if I'm to become a slave, I shall escape!'

Sigehelm grunted. Now was not the time for lectures, but escape was as plausible as the sun falling from the sky. And without doubt, Eadwulf's life depended on his obedience to his new master, no matter how harsh his commands might be.

* * *

Eadwulf lay down beside the still sleeping Aethelnoth, the conversation with his tutor playing on his mind, his nostrils filled with the reek of putrid straw. He was weak from days without proper food, though the gurgling sickness in his stomach would not acknowledge hunger. He drifted in and out of a sleep where vivid images swamped his mind: of bloody slaughter and the sickening stench of burning flesh. Once fully awake he kept his heavy eyelids closed, unwilling to accept the wretchedness around him. A moan and a soft sob told him that others were beginning to stir; the rhythmic breathing at his side revealed that Aethelnoth still slept.

Beyond the warehouse the first carts were rumbling along the waterfront, just the odd one at first ...then another ...and another. Occasional shouts from what sounded like men loading and unloading cargoes mingled with the interminable screeching of the gulls. From inside the warehouse the sounds seemed far away and indistinct.

But Eadwulf knew they were not.

Six

Soon after daybreak the four guards entered the warehouse, gesturing to the captives to eat the thin gruel they'd brought. Eadwulf forced down what he could, under threat of a whipping if he refused. Their wrists were bound and the long cords used to link them together before the guards again departed. The hum of the town's business intensified as the morning wore on and Eadwulf envisaged the crowds of bargain hunters goggling at the human merchandise.

The gruel sat heavy in his stomach and he swallowed hard to keep it down.

On their return, the guards shunted them out into the sunlight, worsening the dread pounding in Eadwulf's chest. He sucked in calming breaths of briny air and watched the seabirds swooping to snatch scraps from the jade-blue water. The jetties were packed with barrels, crates and bundles being moved to and from the moored vessels. Fishing boats and trading ships sailed in and out of the inlet – which Sigehelm had told him was Haddeby Noor – to the Schlei Fjord, which connected with the open waters of the Baltic Sea.

They were goaded along wood-planked walkways towards the town's centre. The stall-lined streets swarmed with people of skins and clothing of diverse hues, all seeming intent on spending the silver in their purses, and the hapless captives were knocked and shoved as they struggled through, trying not to entangle anyone in their bindings. Along broader thoroughfares, ox-drawn carts competed with shoppers on foot and a few wealthier people on horseback. Between the streets, smoke seeped through the thatched roofs of domestic buildings to blend with the stink of putrid waste from the shallow ditches alongside the fences. In many yards, craftsmen were hard at work; in some, women threw scraps to honking geese, or drew water from their wells.

The peaceful normality of the town's everyday life was too much for Eadwulf to bear. He choked back an anguished sob; for him, nothing would ever be normal again.

In the heaving market place the aromas of cooked food failed to mask the gut-churning reek of raw fish and Eadwulf's stomach heaved anew. They were steered between merchants' tents and stalls surrounded by eager customers vying for a vast selection of wares – from exotic trinkets, fine silver, jewellery, glass, spices, amber, silks and furs – to more mundane household goods like soapstone bowls, beeswax candles, tools, knives, handsomely carved wooden chests, and leather shoes and belts. Eadwulf registered them all in trembling dread. His own ragged little group would soon be on display, like cattle, or fattened geese.

They were dragged to a vacant space and strung out like beads on a string. The guards called out, gesturing to their offerings, but for some time they were hardly given a second glance. Animated bargaining competed with the bleating of sheep and goats, the honking of geese and the shrill calls of traders enticing folk to buy. Loose dogs yapped and squealing children chased between the stalls, whilst overhead, the dirges of seabirds reflected Eadwulf's feelings of utter despair.

Gradually, customers began to wander over. A ragged boy

watched glumly as the churlish man he followed prodded Eadwulf in the ribs. An ugly purple bruise stained the boy's left cheek and Eadwulf knew there would be no kindness in his future life should this brute become his master. But the man turned away, the boy trailing miserably after. A ginger-haired young man wandered past, his fine blue tunic and darker blue cloak indicative of some high ranking family. He was so engrossed in eating a steaming delicacy he almost tripped over a yapping mongrel hurtling past. Yelling curses after the dog he sauntered off.

By mid-afternoon all the young women had been taken, so had Alric and Aethelnoth. His friend's new master seemed to be a wealthy lord, accompanied by the young man dressed in blue that Eadwulf had spotted earlier. Whether that meant that Aethelnoth's life would be any easier, Eadwulf couldn't begin to guess. Besides himself and Sigehelm only two of the little group remained: a matronly woman who barely raised her eyes to anyone, and a dark-headed man who scowled at any who neared, for which he'd been repeatedly lashed.

The crowds had now thinned and traders were packing away unsold goods. Eadwulf ached with exhaustion and his bound hands had long since gone numb. His legs suddenly buckled and he collapsed in a heap. One of the guards yanked him roughly to his feet, just as a fierce-looking man in a cloak of thick, dark fur appeared before them. His long, flaxen hair and plaited beard resembled those of many of the Danes that Eadwulf had seen during the day, but he emanated an air of power, like a chieftain. He spoke briefly to two armed men on his flanks, gesturing angrily at the stall.

Behind this trio, accompanied by four more armed men, were two boys, one of them astride a sturdy pony. Eadwulf guessed that both were a little older than him. Both were finely attired, but physically they were very different. The dark-haired youth slouched in his saddle, his misshapen back hunched, his feet in stirrups adjusted to suit his short legs. The other boy had a robust, muscular build, and was as fair as his companion was dark. Both stared at Eadwulf with arrogant disdain.

The scowling chieftain snapped at the two boys, then moved to tower over Eadwulf, his meaty knuckles pressed to his hips. Few men could compete with him in girth, though his height was not as impressive as Thrydwulf's, or even Beorhtwulf's. Eadwulf reeled as thick fingers yanked up his chin and piercingly blue eyes bored into his. Then the man stepped back, examining every inch of him, before subjecting Sigehelm and the two others to the same grousing scrutiny, continuously muttering and snapping at the two boys.

Attentions suddenly focused on Sigehelm, who had boldly addressed the chieftain. Eadwulf felt certain his tutor would be struck down for his audacity. But the chieftain's expression was one of interest and, after a short conversation, words were exchanged with the guards, silver was handed over and the four captives led away.

* * *

At Hedeby's waterfront the dragonship *Sleipnir* loomed, the maw of her monstrous, horse-like head snarling dislike of her master's most recent purchases. At the top of her mast, a flag depicting an eight-legged horse rippled in the breeze.

Eadwulf squatted on the wharf beside the other three, rubbing his wrists, chafed raw where the tight bindings had been. Household goods and wine barrels were loaded onto the ship and, eventually, crewmen took their positions at the oars and the new slaves hustled aboard to huddle with the cargo at the stern. The mooring ropes were released, the ship was pushed out and the *Sleipnir* glided into Haddeby Noor. The sail was hoisted and the helmsman steered the vessel towards the Schlei Fjord.

As the sun sank low in the western sky the *Sleipnir* veered from the mouth of the fjord and followed the Danish coast north. They sailed on through the night and as the sun hailed the new day, Eadwulf turned to speak to Sigehelm. But his tutor's head was bowed in prayer.

'Never held much with faith myself,' the dark-headed man said, shuffling uncomfortably beside them in the limited space between the wine casks. He grinned to reveal a wide gap where three front teeth must formerly have lodged. 'Knew someone just like him once,' he continued, jerking a thumb at Sigehelm. 'Killed he was, in Canterbury, when the Danes set about burnin' and killin' before King Aethelstan could do aught about chasin' the buggers off. No, faith didn't do Uffa much good. The name's Cendred, by the way. And I don't bow down to no heathens.'

'Then you'll not survive for very long!' Sigehelm snapped, making them both jump. 'If you value your life, think most carefully before you act, or speak.'

Cendred bridled but held his peace.

'I believe we'll reach our destination before noon, Eadwulf,' Sigehelm said with a weary sigh. 'I urge you to remain calm and do exactly as you're told. Your life will be very hard if you don't. We must hope our master treats his thralls well.'

Too terrified to think of what lay ahead Eadwulf nodded, shoving his clenched fists into the folds of his tunic to hide his trembling. 'What did you say that so interested the chieftain in Hedeby?'

'You'll remember at the market the chieftain was scrutinising us from head to foot?' Sigehelm whispered, his eyes fixed on Cendred. 'Well, it seems his wife wanted several young women for working around the hall, but their party arrived late at the stalls because they'd met up with some of their kinsfolk, so by the time they began looking for slaves, all the suitable women had been sold. But after looking us over he decided to take you and me and leave these two behind. The traders were not happy to be left with unsold goods,' he continued, his voice now barely audible, 'but resigned to keep them until the Midsumarblot – the midsummer festival – when they could string them up as offerings to their god.

'You are right to look aghast, Eadwulf. These people think no more of offering a human being to their gods than we do of slaughtering livestock to keep us fed. Their gods demand blood to keep them satisfied. Gods like Odin and Thor.' Sigehelm gestured to the flag atop the mast. 'That's Sleipnir up there: Odin's eight-legged horse. Odin is said to ride across the skies on the beast. So you see, child, it was in desperation that I explained how useful these two could be in his village. A woman of Burghild's age would be skilled in domestic chores and

Cendred's muscles could prove invaluable for manual labour. I could think only of the consequences should the chieftain *not* purchase them. Admittedly, I spoke before I had time to think. Pray God Cendred doesn't bring doom upon us all.'

'I thought the chieftain would strike you down when you spoke.'

'That thought crossed my mind too, Eadwulf, but I soon realised he was more interested in what else I could do. When I told him I was a tutor and learned in many things, he said he knew the very role for me in his hall.'

By late afternoon the *Sleipnir* swung into a narrow estuary and a few miles upstream the ship was moored along the bank, in sight of a large settlement. Eadwulf promised himself he'd do their work and pander to their whims, whilst over the months and probably years, he'd plan his return to Mercia.

Seven

In mid-May the remnants of Rorik's raiding party limped into their camp on the Isle of Thanet, licking their grievous wounds, a far cry from what Rorik had planned: a glorious summer of looting throughout the Saxon kingdoms before returning home to praise and admiration from his appreciative brother, whose eyes would sparkle like the mounds of booty presented to him. Rorik racked his brains to find excuses with which to placate the ill-tempered king, but could think of none.

That godly old man, Aethelwulf, must have calculated his moves so very well. His army had taken them unawares – asleep, if he were honest – having laid such a tight trap around that cursed plain at Aclea that Rorik himself had only escaped by the skin of his teeth. Leaving his men to face their fate, he'd fled with a mere half dozen men back to London, to be further assailed by the loss of the waiting ships. He'd had no option but to ride back to Thanet, trying not to contemplate Harald's temper when he learnt that the ships he'd financed were amongst those burnt to a crisp.

On Thanet only two of the longships landed in April remained: Rorik's own vessels, guarded by thirty men awaiting the return of their jarl with the dozen ships from London. The rest had cast off two weeks since with their booty. Did Rorik imagine it, or could he see scorn in the men's eyes as Egil informed them of the rout, and the destroyed ships?

He said nothing and headed for his tent. A night with the

Mercian woman would lift his spirits. Yanking back the skins of the tent flap, he was already unbuckling his leather belt.

* * *

Aros, Denmark: summer 851

At the beginning, Eadwulf's new life seemed unreal, like a nightmare that refused to end. Days became nights in regular succession but he'd withdrawn so much inside himself he barely noticed. As on the knarr, events seemed to occur around him rather than involving him. He detested the coarse woollen tunic and breeks he was given to wear, and carried out his tasks slowly and inefficiently, as though his body awaited orders from a mind that had ceased to function but was awash with horrifying and unnatural images. Scoldings and punishments were frequent, though he was too rapt in his own misery to care. But little by little his mind broke free of the nightmarish images and he was able to take stock of the village to which he now belonged.

Aros was a sizeable farming community, so named after the little river on whose waters its people depended, and ruled over by Jarl Ragnar Lothbrok, the fur-clad chieftain who'd plucked them from the slave stall. Little over two miles downstream the river widened and deepened to form the estuary that embraced the blue-grey waters of the Kattegat Strait. Cattle grazed on the water meadows aligning the banks, behind which the cluster of buildings nestled at the foot of a low rise and the undulating country beyond. On the drier slopes was the cultivated land, where Eadwulf now knelt, weeding between rows of cabbages.

He counted five farms within the jarl's community, stretching out along the river. One of these was Ragnar's own and on which Eadwulf's work was focused. Each farm consisted of half a dozen or so buildings of various size and purpose, along with vegetable gardens and animal pens, all enclosed within a fenced compound. The largest building on each farm was the longhouse, each one a hall in its own right, where the family and thralls lived, and in some cases, also the cattle during the winter. The jarl's huge hall stood at the centre of this community, dominating the view and presiding over his domain. An open, communal area reached out in front of the hall, where people could meet and festivities were held.

'Jarl Ragnar not only controls the farms in this village,' Sigehelm told him at the end of another long day as they made ready their beds against the hall's long walls, 'but a very sizeable portion of the surrounding area. Ragnar has far more power than most of the jarls in Danish lands. He's hailed as a king by his people and treated with the utmost respect. The people owe him allegiance and Ragnar owes them his service as both administrator of the Law, presiding over their Assembly, which they call the *Thing*, and as priest to the gods.'

'He's the strangest priest I've ever seen,' Eadwulf huffed. 'No Mercian priest dresses in wolfskins and eats like a ravenous bear.'

Sigehelm agreed with a shudder. 'Their pagan ways leave us quite bewildered.'

Jarl Ragnar's hall was a magnificent affair, well fit for a king, Eadwulf decided, climbing into his bed. It was over a hundred feet in length and towered far higher than any of the neighbouring longhouses. He recalled the first time he'd stood outside, thinking how Thrydwulf's hall would have paled into insignificance beside it. This huge building also had smaller rooms and compartments adjoining it, including sleeping rooms for the jarl's own family, and the fireroom, which housed the mealfire, where most of the bread, pastries and other delicacies were cooked.

The sturdy oak-planked walls were broken by a few small windows, their shutters flung open during the summer days. The jambs of the doorway were carved with swirling patterns and figures that reminded Eadwulf of the stories of ancient heroes that Sigehelm had so often told him. A thick reed thatch sat atop the walls to present a solid and compact-looking roof, with a hole at its centre to allow smoke from the central firepit below to find its way outside.

The idea that Ragnar's wealth and power depended on the proceeds of raids like that on Thrydwulf's manor filled Eadwulf with revulsion. A picture of Aethelnoth's laughing face flashed through his mind and he choked back a sob, wondering whether he'd ever see his friend again.

* * *

After the first few weeks Eadwulf came to understand what the Danes demanded of their thralls and his life took on a fairly regular routine. He learnt that to speak or act out of turn earned him a thrashing, and if he didn't complete his work satisfactorily he'd forego his evening meal. He soon realised that no one cared about his aching stomach and that punishments would be dispensed without lenience. But he also found that if he did exactly as he was told, he was well fed and provided with a warm bed for the night inside the jarl's hall.

And, very soon, he learnt that his mistress hated him.

Ragnar's small, dark-haired wife, Aslanga, was strict and unforgiving and insisted Eadwulf was punished if he refused to lower his eyes when she spoke to him or didn't complete a task to her satisfaction. He was denied food for a day simply for meeting her dark and scornful gaze, which was so like that of her strange son, Ivar.

'Stupid, ignorant boy!' Aslanga spat at him so frequently. She shrieked and ranted at her husband who infuriated her even further by grinning in response.

'Our mistress is livid that the jarl bought us instead of the female thralls she asked for,' Sigehelm told him one evening in early July as they stacked away the trestles after the meal. All was peaceful in the hall at that time of day with most of the young men away. The women sat repairing clothes or sewing tapestries in the light from the fire and oil lamps, while a few of Ragnar's men rolled their dice on a table in the corner. Rarely did anyone sit up late: most needed their sleep ready for the next day's work. The jarl's family would retire to their private quarters whilst the rest prepared their beds for the night.

Eadwulf's eyes watered and he stifled a huge yawn. The days were so long and started well before dawn: he'd never known life could be so hard. He'd spent the morning working in the fields and the afternoon helping with the dyeing of huge skeins of wool, which would be woven into clothes and blankets for the winter.

'I urge you to be very careful, Eadwulf,' Sigehelm whispered, glancing to make sure he wasn't overheard. 'Aslanga seems to have taken an unreasonable dislike to you. I'm unsure what the problem is, but during more than one of her tirades she's made rather sarcastic remarks regarding your red hair.'

'My hair? Well, I can't do anything about that. Surely she's not so simple as to overlook that fact.'

'No, but you could, perhaps, tie it back...'

'I know what you mean, Sigehelm, you don't have to demonstrate!' Eadwulf yelped, pushing the fumbling hands away from his flowing locks.

* * *

Eadwulf's first summer in the Danish lands passed quickly. He tried hard to do as he was told in order to avoid the constant lash of Aslanga's tongue and soon her derisive comments had lessened. But still, at times, he felt the heat of her scornful stare. All he could do was keep out of her way as much as possible. To make matters worse, Eadwulf had long since realised he must also avoid Ivar and Halfdan. Ragnar's two sons were hostile and vindictive, constantly finding ways of tormenting him and getting him into trouble with Aslanga.

The elder, dark-haired boy, Ivar, had some sort of disability and couldn't walk unaided. His short legs were extremely bowed; his back twisted and stooped like that of a hunchback, though his arms were thick and muscular. Ivar's whole body looked out of proportion and his facial features were decidedly ugly, and much too old for the face of a boy. He was accompanied everywhere by two aides, on whom he leaned heavily, and a fearsome dog that resembled some snarling wolf with a menacingly feral glint in its yellow eyes. Whenever Eadwulf neared, a deep growl emanated from its throat. Ivar himself constantly accused Eadwulf of time wasting, and threatened severe punishment if Aslanga found out.

Ivar's behaviour puzzled Eadwulf, since he'd never consciously done anything to annoy the boy. His only crimes seemed to be that he was Mercian, and a thrall. He came to see Ivar as a pitiful person, with whom life had dealt most unkindly. His twisted body would never know the joys of running, climbing trees or swimming in fresh, cool streams.

Halfdan, just a year older than Eadwulf, also found it a great game to belittle and poke fun at the new thrall. But unlike his brother, Halfdan was healthy and agile, spending much of his time practising battle skills. And rarely did any of the other lads best him at wrestling – an activity prized more for its sporting and entertainment value than its use in combat.

Images of the times he and Aethelnoth had rolled around in the sunshine always hovered close. The bright flames of his memories burned through every fibre of his being, dominating his thoughts as he worked, possessing his dreams as he slept.

And along with Eadwulf's memories was the ever-present desire for revenge.

Eight

The warriors' return in the autumn was eagerly awaited by their loved ones: wives, mothers, children and grandparents, and others, whose eyes sparkled in anticipation of the plunder they would bring and the great feasts planned to welcome them home. And with the onset of September, expectation of their homecoming heightened.

'Once the young men return,' Thora explained as they weeded between the clumps of scented herbs in the vegetable gardens, 'the women will be freed to pursue tasks needful before the frosts and snows set in. There are so many jobs that get neglected in the men's absence; we have so little time, and after supper we're all ready for our beds.' The Danish woman glanced at Eadwulf, her brown eyes twinkling. 'We need to pay heed to the weaving, so we have woollen cloaks and blankets, and complete the embroidery on new wall hangings to stop cold winds whistling through cracks in the wood planking of our longhouses. Many folk will require new winter tunics too, or repairs to their old ones. We must soon begin the preparation of winter foodstuffs as well.'

Eadwulf enjoyed working with Thora because she chattered away and explained about the Danish way of life. She was not a young woman, possibly around her fortieth year, he estimated, and garbed in the usual attire of a thrall: a dress of thin, grey wool with a sleeveless, white tunic over. Her grey-streaked fair hair was mostly hidden beneath a white kerchief, and her round face and ready smile ensured she was well-liked by the other thralls. Even Aslanga treated Thora well, if not exactly kindly.

'The autumn months will be just as busy as the summer,' she said as they continued their weeding. 'Many foods need careful preparation so they last through the winter. We make preserves from forest fruits and berries, and pickle vegetables from the gardens: nothing is wasted if we can help it. We brew mead from the honey from our hives and beer from harvested barley and hops. There's cheese and butter to be made, hazelnuts and logs to be brought from the woods, and peat to be cut to supplement the logs as fuel. Oh yes, Eadwulf, you'll be kept *very* busy,' she said, smiling as she put down her garden fork, 'especially with Aslanga watching over you. As you probably know, our mistress runs the hall with an iron fist. She'd not insult Ragnar by having him go short of anything. Between you and me,' she added with a conspiratorial wink, 'I think she still feels the need to compete with Gudrun.'

Eadwulf had no idea who this Gudrun was, but felt no inclination to ask.

'I imagine you'll be given the job of collecting fruit, or cutting peat, though you may well end up making cheese with me, Eadwulf. I should like that, you're better company than some I could name.'

'And I would quite like to see how cheese is made. I've often wondered how milk suddenly becomes solid.'

Thora laughed and ruffled his hair before becoming serious again. 'During Blotmonath we slaughter all but our best breeding stock, so we'll be busy preserving the meats: some will be salted in vats of brine and some smoked in the big barns, like that one over there,' she said, pointing to a large barn at the other side of the byre. 'Some of it we simply hang to dry.'

Eadwulf nodded. On his father's manors the November practice had been similar, although he'd never actually been involved with Blotmonath before.

'Well, I can't see a single weed hiding in there, can you, Eadwulf?' Thora stood and brushed down her skirt. 'Ouch,' she winced. 'If I stayed in that position much longer I swear my knees would lock solid and I'd never rise again.' Her fond gaze scanned the patches of aromatic plants, predominantly different hues of greens but broken by clumps of tall, pink foxgloves in their second flowering of the year. 'I've become quite adept at preparing healing potions over the years Eadwulf, the main reason Aslanga rarely uses her sharp tongue on me, I think, although I've also been useful in caring for the children. And I'm training young Freydis in medicinal skills. The jarl's daughter's a real aptitude for herblore. When I'm dead and gone, she can take over my work. Such skills are vital to a community.'

'Have you been a thrall for a long time?' he asked as they gathered their tools to return to the hall. It was almost time for the morning meal and he'd be needed to help with the serving.

'Too long, Eadwulf, she said with a sigh. 'It must be ... Well, it's nigh on eleven years since my husband died. Before that – about six or seven years I'd say – we gave up our freedom when we could barely afford to buy food. We were mere youngsters then, wed less than three years, with our whole lives ahead of us. Bjarni was a karl, owned his own farmstead, fifteen miles west of here. Our fields gave smaller yields each year until we had naught to sell, or eat. Much of our country makes poor farmland, you see; woodlands, heath and marshes cover a great deal of it inland. We gave ourselves to the jarl simply to survive,' she said, a faraway look in her eyes. 'That's probably hard for you to understand, Eadwulf, since you're not a thrall by choice, but there are many people in our land forced to do the same. Then there are others who forfeit their freedom because they committed some crime. Thraldom is their punishment; it can be for as little as a year or two or as long as the person lives, depending on the crime.

'Well, when Bjarni died after a fall from the roof of the hall while he was repairing the thatch,' Thora went on, gazing up at the high roof, 'I was left here alone. And Ragnar still had need of me. I thank the goddess, Freya, she didn't bless Bjarni and me with children, or they would have become thralls too. So,' she said, with a glance at Eadwulf as they left the vegetable gardens behind, 'many of our young men travel far away in the hope of finding new homes.' She paused, as though uncertain of how to continue. 'Others go raiding, to bring back coin or goods to trade to help their families survive the winter. Oh, I understand your indignation,' she said quickly as he scowled. 'But I tell you these things so you'll understand a little about our people and – rightly or wrongly – how the custom of summer raiding started. I'm not saying it's right, and I know you'll say that killing serves no purpose, but desperation leads people to act in ways they would not under normal circumstances. No man wants to see his family starve. Remember, our gods do not abhor killing as does your Christian god, but applaud men who give their own lives for their loved ones.

'But let's put such thoughts behind us. September is the

golden month and the sun still holds its warmth. Let's enjoy it before winter comes. Know how to use a flail, Eadwulf?' She smiled at his bemused expression. 'No? Well, tomorrow I do believe you'll find out. Tomorrow we begin threshing the grain.' Her face suddenly grew wistful. 'I pray that Thor will guide our men safely home. Summer's over and they should be here any day now. It's too long since we heard Bjorn's cheerful voice about the village.'

* * *

By the second week of September, Eadwulf felt he'd been relatively successful in avoiding any outright clashes with Ragnar's sons. Work in the fields with Cendred, ploughing after the harvest with a device called an ard, had kept him away from the hall during most days, and when the day's work was over, he would sit with Sigehelm, reading, or simply sharing thoughts, and Ivar and Halfdan could do no more than scowl at him in Ragnar's presence. But, returning from the fields late one afternoon, his stomach lurched. Ivar and Halfdan were sitting outside the hall with their younger sister, several other children around them, giggling as they bent over something in Ivar's hand. Ivar glared in Eadwulf's direction. 'Over here, Mercian. We need your assistance.'

'Go on, lad, I'm not going anywhere,' Cendred urged, nodding towards a pile of logs at the side of the hall. 'I've some wood needs cuttin' right here. I can't see 'em trying much with me choppin' right next to 'em.'

With a deep breath Eadwulf stepped toward the now silent

group and, as he'd anticipated, his presence was not requested in order to ply him with niceties. Ivar thrust a piece of parchment into his hand, a lengthy poem written on it.

'Read that to us, Mercian. We need to hear it again to fully appreciate it.'

'I can't,' Eadwulf lied, looking into Ivar's dark eyes. If he spoke the words of the vulgar poem he knew it would be reported to Aslanga. 'I can't yet read well enough.'

'So what *has* that sour-faced scribe been teaching you these past weeks? Could it be you're so dim-witted the words don't penetrate your thick head?'

The group of children tittered but Eadwulf was surprised to hear the boys' sister speak up. 'Let him be, Ivar,' Freydis said, frowning. 'He's probably telling the truth. Thralls aren't given the time for learning.'

But Halfdan seemed intent on prolonging their fun. 'How could anyone as thick as pig shit ever learn *anything,* other than how to grunt and wallow in the mud?'

A particularly loud thud as Cendred swung his axe into a log behind them made the children jump.

'Move away from here, you filthy Saxon,' Ivar yelled. 'No one in his right mind chops wood this close to the hall!'

'Another one thick as muck,' Halfdan joined in. 'Go back to your pig swill, Saxon!' The big man's fists balled and his eyes narrowed, but Halfdan was enjoying himself. 'See how the ugly hog snorts and stamps his trotters,' he sniggered. 'And have you ever seen such piggy little eyes? We really must pen him up with that fat old sow Burghild, and see if they produce some plump piglets for our pot.'

By now Cendred was seething, his every breath like that of a tormented boar, his eyes focused on Halfdan. He advanced on the shrieking children with a roar, his axe still in his hands – just as Ragnar stepped from the hall with a group of his men. With a hiss of drawn swords Cendred was surrounded and overpowered. The children scattered like mice with a cat in their midst, only Ivar remaining, unable to move away unaided. Eadwulf hardly dared move. Cendred was pinned to the ground, swords at his throat.

'I want him alive,' Ragnar seethed, before the over-zealous guards could finish Cendred off. 'Instant death is much too good for a thrall who dares to threaten a jarl's children. Throw him in the pit. I'll deal with him when he's had time to reflect on the folly of his actions.'

Ragnar stood statue-still, the enraged expression set into his stone-like features as Cendred was dragged away. 'By Odin, Scribe, I should never have listened to your words!' he threw at Sigehelm, hovering in the doorway. 'The Saxon dog had trouble written all over his face – and I knew it! Be very grateful I value your work as tutor to my sons. If I did not, then you'd now be in the same place as him.'

Sigehelm's face blanched and his eyes grew wide, but Ragnar said no more to him. His glacial stare fixed on his son, still hunched against the hall. 'Have your servants bring you inside, Ivar.' His tone was soft and ominous as he stepped through the doorway. 'You and your brother have a lot of explaining to do about what went on here.'

* * *

Over a week had passed and Eadwulf still didn't know what had transpired following Ivar and Halfdan's audience with their father, or how Cendred fared. Ragnar's men ensured that no one neared the pit and Cendred could have been dead for all anyone knew.

'What will they do to him?' he asked Sigehelm as they set out the trestles for the morning meal.

Sigehelm held Eadwulf in his steady gaze, releasing his breath as a weary sigh. 'I know you blame yourself for causing Cendred to behave as he did, child, but he's entirely responsible for his own actions. Ragnar is right to believe the man isn't safe to let loose. No sane person would advance upon children with an axe. But I did overhear the jarl issuing orders to have him moved into one of the huts by the end of the week. At least that will be somewhat better for him than remaining in that dreadful pit, open to all weathers – particularly if he is to be incarcerated for very much longer.' He shook his head sadly. 'I fear that whatever punishment Ragnar dictates for the Saxon, it will not be pleasant.'

* * *

Eadwulf rubbed his sleepy eyes and squatted on the river bank to fill his first pails for the day. The late September weather still held warm and dry and the sun had risen to greet an almost cloudless sky. Trees were turning golden, the grain was in and the threshing done. Preparations for winter would now begin in earnest and Eadwulf anticipated a hard day ahead.

Drawing the pail through the clear water he spotted a

kingfisher perched on a willow branch that trailed down to the silvery surface. He couldn't believe his luck. It was only the second one he'd seen at Aros and he was fascinated by the colouring of this tiny bird: the shiny, metallic blue-green of its back, wings and head, the little white parts around its neck and chin and the amazingly bright orangey-red breast. The dazzling mass of vibrant colour dived so fast Eadwulf wasn't sure he actually saw it move at all until the tiny thing flew back to its branch, a small, wriggling fish in its dark beak.

'Is this what you call work, thrall?' Halfdan's voice caused Eadwulf to lose hold of the pail and he struggled to retrieve it before the current could take it. 'Does Aslanga know of your fascination with our feathered friends and how long you spend staring at the damned things?'

Eadwulf did not respond to the taunts. What would be the point?

'Kingfishers are excellent divers, I'm told,' Halfdan said. 'They seem to know everything that goes on below the glassy surface that we see: all those fish and things. Wouldn't it be wonderful to be able to see what *they* see–?'

Halfdan's move was so fast that Eadwulf was sinking in the cold water before he realised anything had happened. The river deepened rapidly only inches from the bank but he surfaced quickly, gasping for breath.

'That's for getting us into trouble with Ragnar,' Halfdan sneered. 'Enjoy your swim. I'm sure Aslanga will be eagerly awaiting your return.'

Halfdan sped off and Eadwulf dragged himself onto the bank, dripping and shivering. The water was very cold and the early morning sun yielded little warmth. He cursed Halfdan. The wretched boy must have been watching, waiting to follow him.

Having no alternative, he trudged back to the hall in his sodden state. Aslanga would be waiting for the water.

* * *

Aslanga's fury seemed to flow from her in waves. Her dark eyes blazed, fixing resolutely on Eadwulf as he crept into the hall and placed the full pails by the door. Servants moved out of her way and two of Ragnar's men put their dicing game on hold. Sigehelm's quill hung motionless over his parchment and beside him, Ivar and Halfdan smirked.

Dripping wet and shivering, Eadwulf waited for the unwarranted tirade to begin. His mistress remained by the hearth, breathing fast, the floury whiteness of her face contrasting sharply with the black hair straying from beneath her head covering. Her choice of clothing was equally severe: a long-sleeved brown dress, fastened round her thin neck with a drawstring. Her plain white over-tunic was held at the shoulders by two simple round brooches, and from a chain around her neck hung a knife, scissors and keys: symbols of her complete control in the hall.

'Come here.'

A shudder of dread shot down Eadwulf's spine. Burghild's anxious gaze fixed on him as he stepped slowly forward. Without doubt, Halfdan had spun some highly incriminating yarn.

'What have you to say in your defence?'

'My defence of what, Mistress?'

Aslanga's sharp slap sent him reeling. 'Don't *dare* give me your insolence! I'll have you flogged for using that tone with me. Get up. Now.'

Not trusting himself to speak, Eadwulf obeyed. His face stung and he knew Aslanga would not believe anything he said.

'Let's start again. Explain, if you will, why you attempted to push my son into the river. Yes, you may well shake in your boots. Your actions will not go unpunished.'

'But I didn't–'

'Didn't what, exactly? Didn't expect to be seen? Didn't expect to fail? Perhaps you *did* expect to push Halfdan into the river and run off before he could see you?'

'Mistress, it was *I* who was pushed into the river.'

'You've certainly been *in* the river!' she snapped, eyeing Eadwulf's sodden clothing with contempt. 'And I know just how you came to be in there. Halfdan avoided your intended push by darting aside, after which you slipped on the wet bank and landed yourself in the water, precisely where you'd meant my son to go.' Aslanga shook with outrage and indignation. 'From the moment I set eyes on you, I could tell you'd not make an agreeable thrall.'

Eadwulf could barely contain his own indignation at the sheer injustice of this. He'd done nothing but obey Aslanga's orders. And he'd tried very hard to be amenable. That wretched boy, Halfdan!

'Nothing you say can lessen your guilt,' she ranted on, giving him no opportunity to defend himself. 'You stand there, feigning innocence, whilst the son of a jarl has suffered your disrespect and plots against his person. Did you believe it would be a great jest to see Halfdan soaked and bedraggled?'

Eadwulf shook his head, more by way of reaction to Aslanga's imbalanced condemnation than as answer to the question.

'Your disrespect is intolerable! I knew as soon as I saw the red hair that would be the case; the brash colouring comes with insolence ingrained at birth. It's a pity my husband failed to see that fact years ago.'

Eadwulf gaped, confused by this sudden line of thought.

'You are unfit to share our food, or our roof. For the next week you'll sleep outside and *if* we save you scraps from our table, you will also eat those outside.'

'Mistress, I swear I've done nothing.' Eadwulf could not believe such harsh punishment could be inflicted so unjustly. All evidence was based on malicious lies.

'Ulrik,' Aslanga shouted to one of Ragnar's men. 'Take the lying thrall outside. Use your belt and beat him soundly.'

* * *

Eadwulf spent seven nights banned from the hall. Oddly enough, he found it no great hardship. The nights had not yet turned bitter, nor had rainclouds released more than a fleeting shower, and after a long day's work he was able to sleep almost anywhere. Mindful to avoid the vicinity of Cendred's new prison, guarded by successions of Ragnar's ever-vigilant men, he'd found a nook between one of the storage sheds and a sturdy wicker fence, and piled fallen leaves under an old sackcloth to make a soft bed. Other rags afforded him some cover. For the first three days the pain of the thrashing made finding a suitable sleeping position difficult, but curled on his side was his preferred position anyway. Once asleep, he rarely roused before the cockerel heralded daybreak. Nor was he starved. The 'scraps' Aslanga sent out were not much worse than the usual leftovers given to the thralls. And on most days, Sigehelm sneaked him out a little extra.

Eadwulf was beginning to see a strength and selflessness in his quiet, god-fearing tutor that he'd overlooked before. Sigehelm had risked great punishment by these actions, but in Eadwulf's interest he'd simply ignored that possibility. Since arriving in this land, he couldn't remember a single time when Sigehelm had voiced concern for his own wellbeing: his concern was always for Eadwulf. It had just taken Eadwulf a long time to realise it.

Nine

Fallen leaves crunched beneath Eadwulf's feet as he collected twigs and branches for winter tinder in the small patch of woodland on the elevated ground behind the village. Accompanied by Toke, Aslanga's ageing Norse thrall whose dialect he found hard to understand, conversation was minimal. But away from Aslanga's sharp tongue, Eadwulf worked contentedly enough.

The October day had dawned fine and bright, but as the morning wore on the breeze picked up and heavy, grey clouds drifted in, threatening a wet and dreary afternoon. By now a commendable mound of firewood sat in the cart and just as Toke motioned they should be heading back, a shrill horn blast stopped Eadwulf in his tracks. He dropped the bundle of twigs he'd been about to toss into the cart, his heart racing. The horn must surely mean the village was under attack!

He grabbed Toke's arm and pointed across the ploughed fields at the people streaming toward the river.

The old man smiled reassuringly, his bony hand patting Eadwulf's arm. 'Bjorn,' he said simply, shoving Eadwulf into the cart before clambering up himself and rapping the rump of the ox with the reins. 'Bjorn has come home.'

* * *

Aros was in chaos. Eadwulf was jostled amongst the throng of elated villagers congregating in the communal compound, all too engrossed in their emotional reunions to consider the plight of the thralls proffering ale. He could barely squeeze between embracing families or those involved in amicable back-slapping. Returning fathers fussed over squealing offspring who'd made their appearance during their lengthy absence, others admired the swollen bellies of wives whose pregnancies had barely begun to blossom in the spring. Laughter and tears mingled freely; tears of joy for most, tears of sadness for an unfortunate few. Not all the men had come home; nor had all returned unscathed. Some scars were displayed with pride: a hideously scarred face or hacked-off earlobe was evidence of courage. But other injuries, such as loss of limbs or eyes, would ensure the bearers would never again go raiding.

The ale in Eadwulf's jug spilled copiously onto the grass and the men had insatiable thirsts, resulting in his frequent returns to the barrels in the hall. He'd caught Aslanga's glower the last time he'd sneaked in and knew he'd be sorely berated before long. Outside the doorway, Ragnar beamed as he congratulated the warriors delivering the plunder, including five human pieces of merchandise.

At Ragnar's side Ivar hunched on a stool, and beside him stood Halfdan. In their fine woollen tunics, their affected air of superiority contrasted sharply to the genial manner of their father. Pondering reasons for their surliness, Eadwulf didn't see the small dog wheedling between the shuffling feet. He tripped right over the yelping cur and fell flat on his face, half a jug of ale splattering down the right leg of a young warrior who seemed intent on squeezing the life out of a giggling woman.

The man was not pleased. With a throaty growl he yanked

Eadwulf up by the shoulders. Eadwulf squeezed his eyes shut, lifting his arm to protect his head, bracing himself for the blow. But nothing came, not even a clip round the ear. Tentatively, he opened his eyes ...and gaped at the face barely inches from his nose – with eyes as green as his own.

The young warrior pulled up to his full height and stood back, balled fists on his hips, continuing his scrutiny. A grin suddenly creased his face, setting his eyes twinkling. He tweaked his ragged beard and shook his head of wild red hair.

'By all the gods, what trick is being played on me?' he roared, his voice cracked with laughter. 'I leave my home, risking life and limb in the hope of bringing prosperity to our people and within so short a time my father finds a replacement for me! Now, lad, I know you're not my brother and by Frey's prick, you're too old to be my spawn. So where in Thor's name *did* you spring from?'

Eadwulf continued to gawk. It was like looking at a bigger and older version of himself. Eventually, he found his voice. 'I am called Eadwulf, and I'm a thrall. And I'm a Mercian,' he added, jutting out his chin.

'Well, Eadwulf, it's good to be proud of who you are. Why be otherwise? We cannot change what the gods have destined for us. How were you taken?'

'The r-raid on London...' Eadwulf stammered, hoping the man would not request the details.

'Your parents?'

'They're dead. Jarl Ragnar bought me with three others in Hedeby – for his wife.'

'So, you belong to Aslanga?'

Eadwulf nodded, feeling more miserable than ever to admit to that.

'And do you work hard for her, and escape punishment, Eadwulf? From your reaction to me, I'd guess you've had a few thrashings already.'

'She doesn't think a great deal of me, I fear, and yes, I've sometimes been punished – though I do work hard.' Eadwulf didn't elaborate on the beatings he'd had, or on the week he'd been banished from the hall, and wondered why he'd even admitted as much as he had.

'Her dislike of you isn't really surprising.' The warrior grinned. 'The lady simply detests red hair.'

'But lots of people have red hair,' Eadwulf huffed, gesturing to the man's bright thatch.

'Ah, there's a story and a half there, lad. Aslanga is...'

'*Bjorn!*' Ragnar's booming voice rang out. 'Get your arse over here and let the boy get on with his work!'

'Certainly, Father.' The warrior swung a low bow to his sire, bringing hoots of laughter from those around. 'We'll talk again, Eadwulf, when you're less busy.'

Eadwulf just nodded, dumbfounded.

'Don't forget tonight,' the woman yelled to the retreating back.

Without a backward glance Bjorn flicked out a wave and continued on to the hall. Beside the jovial Ragnar, Ivar and Halfdan glowered as their red-headed brother strutted towards them. Eadwulf followed to refill his jug, thankful they were so preoccupied in scowling at Bjorn they didn't even notice him pass by into the hall.

* * *

Preparations for the evening's feast were well underway. Women chopped and mixed with determination and a variety of foods covered the long tables. Aslanga had been watching her daughter as Eadwulf entered, her expression one of extreme exasperation. The pretty, flaxen-haired girl was kneading dough in a big trough, apparently with little success. Enveloped in clouds of floury dust with white streaks patterning her tunic, face and braids, Freydis muttered her intense dislike of the pastime. Eadwulf found it difficult not to laugh out loud.

'Careless, thoughtless boy,' Aslanga scolded as he headed for the ale barrels. 'Will you *ever* become steady handed enough to be of any use at all?'

Hearing her mother's acerbic tones Freydis glanced up and smiled at Eadwulf, her blue eyes full of sympathy – though whether for him or herself, he wasn't sure.

'Do you think we spend so many hours brewing ale just for you to slosh all over the ground?' Aslanga continued, glowering at Freydis until she bowed her head and resumed walloping the dough. 'How many other thralls do you see running in and out like you? That's right,' she answered herself with a flick of her hand, 'none. And if you return too soon again you'll forfeit your own meal tonight.'

Eadwulf sighed and strove to walk steadily with two full jugs to the door.

'Mayn't I go and welcome my brother home yet?' Freydis pleaded behind him.

'Bjorn's busy enough with your father without having you

clinging to his trouser leg,' Aslanga snapped.

'But it is *so* unfair!' the girl shrieked, with what sounded like an extra hard wallop of the dough. Her petulant outburst made Eadwulf jump, and ale slopped to the rushes. Silently cursing, he half turned to look, hoping Aslanga hadn't noticed.

'I want to see Bjorn!' Freydis demanded, stamping her foot. 'He's my favourite brother, and just because *you* don't like him, you think I should hate him too. But I don't! I love him to bits and–'

The resounding slap and ensuing whimper caused a wave of sympathy to wash over Eadwulf, but he walked through the doorway as though he'd heard nothing.

Ten

'Good people! Fellow Danes! Warriors of Thor!'

Ragnar's booming baritone caught the immediate attention of the occupants of the heaving hall. His ruddy face beamed and he raised his silver cup in salutation. 'Welcome home!'

The respondent cheers and hammering of fists on tables was almost deafening. Eadwulf froze, intrigued, the skewers of beef he'd been turning lying still across the hearth, in danger of being badly scorched. Euphoria swept the hall and he gawked at the sea of faces, all filled with admiration and pride.

The huge room was ablaze with light and colour. Torches flared and soapstone oil lamps and beeswax candles flickered, picking up the colours of the wall hangings and polished shields. The trestles had been set up and Eadwulf had laid out some of the mistress's cherished curved brass spoons and little knives with walrus ivory handles. Her fine, Rhineland pottery plates and bowls were stacked at the side, awaiting their freshly cooked contents. All had been such a rush. Aslanga had protested all evening at having to prepare a huge meal at such short notice.

In sudden panic, Eadwulf returned his attentions to the skewers. The meat didn't appear to be burnt, although one side was decidedly darker than the rest. Thankfully, Aslanga was still in the fireroom and could not have witnessed his inattention.

It seemed to Eadwulf that everyone had donned their finest attire for the occasion. Ragnar stood in his place at the centre of a table in an elevated position at the end of the room, where he could be seen by all. In his bright red tunic, with its glittering trims and heavy silver belt, he looked quite dazzling. Even the striped blue trousers and calf-length boots were in stark contrast to his usual drab attire. His flaxen locks were held by a black silk headband, colourfully decorated with a delicate tendril pattern, and his beard had been neatly plaited. Rings adorned his fingers and an armband of twisted gold lay testimony to his status in society.

To the jarl's right, Bjorn's red mane could hardly be missed, though the wild locks now hung tamed about their owner's collar. His red beard and moustache had been trimmed and Eadwulf could not help noticing how well he suited the emerald green tunic. Ivar and Halfdan sat at their father's left, after an unoccupied space which Eadwulf knew to be reserved for Aslanga. Both looked in jovial spirits, wearing splendid tunics of brightly dyed hues. Ivar's aides stood attentively behind him, though Eadwulf was surprised to note the absence of his snarling wolf-dog, since several dogs sprawled under tables by their masters' legs.

'An entire season has passed since we feasted together beneath this roof, my friends,' Ragnar resumed, all eyes following his gesture towards the high thatch. 'We celebrated Sigrblot at the onset of spring and gave offerings to the gods. Did not Frey accept our gift of the sacrificial boar? Was he not pleased that his statue was paraded around our village in the cart decked with fragrant blossoms? I say to you that Frey *was* pleased and *has* answered our prayers by giving us a plentiful harvest.'

A wicked grin lit up the jarl's face as his gaze swept the hall. 'And has not his sister, Freya, bestowed *her* most fruitful blessings on many of our women?'

Lewd comments and gestures erupted and men patted the swollen bellies of their scarlet-faced wives. 'Our harvest elsewhere has also been truly great,' he continued, his hand raised for silence. 'Tonight we celebrate not only our bountiful crops, but also the bountiful riches that will enable our village to prosper.' He motioned to the mounds of shining goods close to his table. Engraved bowls, plates and goblets, swords and daggers with hilts studded with precious gems, and golden chalices and candlesticks were heaped beside chests brimming with coins. 'Tonight we feast in honour of our warriors, whose plunder will fill our trading ships next spring.'

Ragnar flung out his arms to acknowledge the thunderous cheers, then again raised his hand. 'Tonight we eat and drink as much as our bellies can take. And you all know the standard of my lady wife's cooking!'

He offered an exaggerated bow to Aslanga, now standing with Thora and Toke by the fireroom door, dressed in her finest clothes. Over her yellow, pleated dress her azure tunic was edged with colourfully decorated appliqué and the shoulder straps fastened with jewelled brooches. And although her dark hair remained mostly covered beneath the matching yellow kerchief, Eadwulf was surprised to see a necklace of heavy amber beads around her neck. She acknowledged her husband's compliment with a gracious nod and her usually frosty features melted into a smile. More cheers reverberated round the hall.

'Tomorrow, when our men are recovered from the rigours of tonight's festivities,' the jarl chortled, pointing meaningfully at his mead cup, 'we have our first ceremony to the gods. To

Thor, the slayer of giants, god of thunder and storms, of travellers and warriors, we will offer thanks for guiding our men throughout their venture. As the sun leaves Midgard tomorrow, we will show Thor exactly how grateful we are and beg for his continued benevolence. Then tomorrow night, we feast in his honour. In three days' time we welcome the onset of winter.' Ragnar's tones became hushed, his face sombre. 'Before the morning sun casts its rays over the horizon, we make our yearly trek to the sacred grove to deliver our offerings to Odin. We entreat the All-Father for a mild winter and his blessings for a successful year...

'But these things are for later. Tonight we eat and get drunk, as only true Danes know how. Good health and the blessing of the gods to you all, my people!'

Aslanga took her place beside her husband and the feasting began.

The thralls kept up a hectic pace, serving food and running back and forth to the ale barrels and mead jars to refill rapidly emptied vessels. Toke and Thora served at the jarl's table, a relief to Eadwulf: he hadn't relished the thought of Aslanga and her sons finding fault with everything he served. The chicken and leek soup, always a favourite, brought many compliments. The aromatic liquid had been thickened with oatmeal and packed with chunky pieces of chicken, leeks and garlic, with additional carrots, onion and celery. Eadwulf's stomach whined pitifully as bowls of the steaming broth were carried to the tables. The skewers of meat followed. Greasy juices dripped down chins as jaws chomped on the succulent beef. A variety of freshly baked breads with honey or butter were offered to all.

Finally it was time for the dessert. Aslanga and Thora had mixed the batter for the berry pancakes earlier, leaving it in jugs in the fireroom, ready for cooking on the wide griddles. Mounds of forest fruits sweetened with honey had been stewed in pots over the hearth until they were mouth-wateringly syrupy, ready to be spooned inside the sizzling pancakes. Ragnar yelled for a barrel of his best wine to be opened and Eadwulf wondered how long it would be before arguments and brawls erupted. The door to the fireroom opened and trays heaped with golden pancakes were carried in, and his concerns were instantly curtailed as his stomach groaned anew.

'Freydis has barely touched a morsel,' Thora said, coming to stand next to him. 'I wonder what's upset her.' Eadwulf said nothing; it wasn't his place to relate what had occurred. 'Carry some pancakes over for the little ones, lad,' Thora continued, 'and try to persuade her to eat one. And tell Burghild from me they need to be in their beds as soon as they've finished. Most of the women will be retiring soon, leaving the men to their carousing. They do like to boast of their exploits.'

At the far end of the hall, close to the door, a table had been set up for the children of the village. Hollow-eyed and white-faced, Burghild sat with Ubbi on her lap, amidst several women from neighbouring families with their own charges. The matronly thrall had taken Cendred's punishment hard and, according to Thora, greatly feared for her own safety, should she unwittingly commit some minor offence. Her nerves seemed shattered in recent weeks. Even Eadwulf had noticed her constantly dropping things, her anxious gaze too often darting around the hall. He just hoped that Aslanga hadn't also noticed...

He swept his concerns for Burghild aside and focused on Freydis next to her. The jarl's daughter looked very pretty in an embroidered blue linen dress, with her shining blonde hair tumbling down her back. But by no means was she in festive mood. She refused to look at Eadwulf as he extolled what he imagined to be the delights of the pancakes, and pushed the proffered dish to join the others she'd rejected. Eadwulf had no time to dwell on Freydis's moods. No doubt she'd get over her pique. Passing Thora's message to Burghild he moved off about his work.

The women soon retired, Aslanga marching Ivar and Halfdan out with her, and the men shared riddles and tales of heroic deeds; bawdy songs drowned the flute player's melodies. And though still attentive to the demands for refills from the revellers, the thralls were now able to fill their own bellies.

Eventually, the jarl heaved himself onto unsteady legs.

'The food's been to your liking?' he yelled. Roaring cheers and hammering on tables with fists and spoons gave him his answer. 'The wines have titillated your discerning palates?' The same resounding reply. 'Have I not been a generous host tonight?' The men rose to their feet, those too drunk to do so buttressed between others who could barely stand themselves, and raised their cups to salute their jarl.

'Sit, if you will, good people. The day's been long and I fear your already buckled legs may buckle further before long.' He gestured amusedly to a few particularly drunken individuals. 'Once, I'd've been raiding at your sides. But now this old shoulder wound keeps me home, like an old, old man.' His tone was self-deprecating as he rubbed his injured shoulder. 'Tomorrow we share out the goods, though I'm told these few thralls already have owners. Pity,' he shrugged at Bjorn's grinning nod, 'Aslanga still hasn't forgiven me for not bringing back young women the last time I went to Hedeby!

'But before our beds beckon,' he said, quietening down the laughter, 'I'd like to hear from my rogue of a son what antics he's been up to for the *entire* summer. Enlightenment would be appreciated, Bjorn...'

To ringing cheers Ragnar's firstborn rose to his feet. He didn't appear particularly drunk, quite clear-eyed and steady, Eadwulf decided. He flashed a white grin and saluted the men with his own silver cup. 'We have, indeed, been away many months, Father,' he said, whilst heads nodded sagely. 'We've greatly missed the glorious summer as she blessed our homelands, causing the days to grow long and mellow and the corn to ripen...'

'Don't get sentimental on us, son,' Ragnar interrupted, bringing further hoots from the men. 'Much as I'm sure you feel glad to be home, don't tell me you didn't enjoy the thrill of the raids. You'd not be a son of mine otherwise!'

Laughter grew even louder when Bjorn said, 'Certainly, Father.'

'As I was saying,' Bjorn continued, 'Mighty Thor saw fit to render success in our quest and guided us home without disaster in stormy waters. I speak for us all when I say we feel honoured to have helped to ensure the wellbeing of our people for another year–'

Ragnar's loud cough stopped that line of thought and Bjorn

grinned roguishly. 'Our initial intention was to spend some weeks raiding along the coast of Frisia, but after a few minor raids we chose to sail on south to Iberia, which held promise of richer takings.'

'We'd thought you might sail up the Seine to pay your respects to Charles the Bald. I'm sure he's missed me these past six years. The Danegeld he so kindly gave us is in dire need of replenishment.'

'That option was considered, Father,' Bjorn admitted, nodding, 'but somehow the warmer climes held greater attraction.'

'I suppose it's understandable that you youngsters should want to make your own mark elsewhere.'

'Youngsters *some* of us may be, Father, but we certainly did make our presence known to the Frankish king! Our raids in Nantes from our camp on the island of Noirmutier proved very lucrative.' Bjorn motioned to the heap of plunder. 'Frankish swords are fine pieces of workmanship, as are their silver dishes and bowls – or goblets, like the one holding your own wine tonight. And as you see, their churches have kindly donated many Christian crosses and chalices to our safekeeping ...

'By mid-July we reached the north of Iberia, where the towns of Corunna and Santiago de Compostela offered us their warm hospitality and their church doors welcomed us with open arms! We gave daily thanks to the Christian god for his benevolence to poor travellers such as ourselves. It was in Corunna we found these five wandering the streets. Well, we found the two young ones wandering the streets,' he clarified, gesturing to the olive-skinned girl and boy. 'The other three beauties – although strictly speaking, we'd call them whores

– well, some of us merely happened to be inspecting the best brothel in Corunna, and since we couldn't bear to part company with three of their best er, *delicacies*, we made a quick getaway with them in tow.'

Laughter erupted and Ragnar had tears of mirth streaming down his face. Bjorn's tale was even holding Eadwulf rapt, though he noticed that Sigehelm's expression was grim.

'By the time we reached Lisbon it was August and very hot,' Bjorn went on, sweeping his arm theatrically across his brow. 'Lisbon is a well-fortified city and the Moors are formidable opponents. Their huge blades, called scimitars, are used with deadly precision, and after being twice repelled from the city walls, we thought it best to sail back north. But we do intend to go back, Father. Perhaps not next year, or even the next, but one year we'll return with better plans of attack. So, here we are, returned to you, my lord, with our offerings.'

The trestles stayed up for the night, more than a few men slumped across them, others recumbent on the rushen floor. Ragnar retired to his own sleeping room and Bjorn headed for the door, giving Eadwulf a mischievous wink as he passed.

At long last, Eadwulf fell to his bed, knowing that in only a few hours he'd have to be up again.

Eleven

'Eadwulf, it is past daybreak. We must stir before the mistress rises!'

Eadwulf vaguely heard the voice and felt someone shaking him, but he'd been deeply asleep and took some moments to rouse. 'The cockerel crowed some while ago,' the voice persisted, 'but I confess, even I was too weary to pay heed. We must not be lying abed when Aslanga appears!'

Eadwulf forced his heavy eyelids open and squinted at Sigehelm's worried face.

'Be quick now. Down to the river with your pails. I'll busy myself raking the ashes and stacking firewood. I hope to have a fire burning soon. A few others are already busy at their chores. 'There's much to be done after last night.'

Barely awake, Eadwulf did as he was told. Sigehelm was right, Aslanga would be unforgiving if she had to rouse the thralls herself. But the cold morning air helped, and as he plodded down to the river, a pail in each hand, he felt his senses reviving. The weak October sun had already emerged from its other world and the cockerel perched silently on the fence, his morning's work accomplished. Eadwulf didn't feel too guilty for being late; no one else was about either.

By the time he returned to the hall, Sigehelm was feeding sticks to the newly lit fire, the yellow flames greedily licking at the new wood. Surprisingly, Aslanga was still absent but most of the thralls were busily removing all evidence of night-time revelry, stepping carefully around a handful of men still snoring on the rushes. Dishes were piled ready for washing, trestles stacked away until later.

'We'll need as much water as you can bring,' Thora said, emptying the pails into a cauldron over the hearth and handing them back to Eadwulf. She wrinkled her nose at the heaps of food-smeared pots. 'A few journeys to the river, lad, quick as you can.'

Returning with his brimming buckets several journeys later, Eadwulf's attention was caught by a woman's giggle coming from inside the large, wood-planked barn. A man's throaty chuckle followed, and Eadwulf grinned. It wouldn't be the first time he'd heard couples engaged in noisy lovemaking, and in a variety of places, but he was curious as to which pair of lovers had risen for such an early-morning tryst after the late-night feast. But whoever they were, he decided, they definitely couldn't be thralls. Servants late to their chores risked a severe thrashing.

A hazy memory from last night suddenly crossed Eadwulf's mind and he wondered ...And since the door was already ajar, he supposed a quick peep inside could do no harm.

On first glance the barn appeared to be empty and he crept a little further in. Then a huge mound of barley straw in the far corner moved; a gentle kind of movement that rose up and down, slowly at first but gradually gaining momentum. The back of a woman's blonde head surfaced then disappeared, to be followed by a flash of bright red hair.

As he backed silently out again, Eadwulf smiled, pleased to have proven himself to be right.

* * *

By the time the morning meal had been served Aslanga had still not made an entrance and, having eaten his fill, the jarl summoned his men and headed off about his business. Nor had Bjorn yet returned to eat, which surprised Eadwulf. He'd have a long wait until the evening feast.

'It seems Aslanga has a gargantuan hangover,' Sigehelm said with an uncharacteristic smirk as they sat at a table to take their own meal. Our mistress rarely drinks wine but last night Ragnar refilled her goblet a few times too many.'

'On purpose, I imagine, so she'd retire and leave him to enjoy himself,' Eadwulf replied, returning the smirk as he tore off a chunk of bread to mop up his stew. His eyes flicked to where Ivar and Halfdan skulked in the corner of the hall. 'And those two are very quiet; didn't even join their father for the meal.'

'If you look closely, Eadwulf, you'll notice they're both somewhat pale and puffy-eyed this morning. Halfdan's been sitting there looking as though he would vomit and Ivar tried his usual tack of threatening to castrate me if I so much as speak to him again today.'

'I saw them downing mead last night. I hope they throw up all day.'

'Such uncharitable thoughts,' Sigehelm admonished with a shake of his head. But you know, Eadwulf, for once I wholeheartedly agree with you.'

'And exactly what do you two agree about, may I ask?'

The cheerful voice made them jump. Bjorn seemed to have materialised from nowhere, still wearing the tunic he'd worn for the feast, although it now looked rather the worse for wear. Spikes of straw bedecked his hair and Eadwulf was forced to mask his inappropriate laugh with a strangled cough.

'We were discussing the after effects of strong drink, as a matter of fact, Master,' Sigehelm said, flashing Eadwulf a questioning glance.

Bjorn grinned. 'What is there to agree upon other than such effects being utterly undesirable?'

'That hangovers are usually well merited,' Sigehelm supplied sagely.

'Well, I can see my two loving brothers look a little green this morning, and a little bird told me that Aslanga's also feeling under the weather. Shame,' Bjorn said, facetiously. 'But observe that I am not afflicted by such a malady. Sometimes there are better things to do than simply getting drunk. Fetch me a bowl of pottage, and a few chunks of that bread, would you, lad. I'm quite ravenous now.'

Thora ladled stew into a bowl for Eadwulf as Bjorn's genial tones carried across the hall. 'You wouldn't believe some of the things we've resorted to eating on our travels, Scribe. Ever tried octopus? No? Nor had I until we got to Iberia. It's not too bad – better than fish if you ask me...'

'I'll wish you a proper welcome home now, Master Bjorn,' Thora gushed, hurrying over as Eadwulf deposited his food. 'I had little opportunity to do so yesterday but my heart went out to you all the same. You made us all hoot with your tales last night.'

Bjorn rose and threw his arms around the Danish woman, lifting her off her feet and planting a smacking kiss on her cheek. Thora returned his embrace, sobbing tears of joy into his shoulder. Eadwulf and Sigehelm shared a bemused glance. It seemed these two shared a long-founded friendship.

'Let me drink in the sight of you,' Thora said, wriggling free of the vice-like grip and holding Bjorn at arm's length. 'You've been away so long, had us all fair worried for your safety. I've heard naught but your name from your sister's lips for weeks.'

'And where *is* Freydis?' Bjorn asked, glancing round. 'My little sister hasn't yet been to greet me. I noticed her in here last night, but she didn't run to me as usual. I confess, there were so many people to see yesterday, I quite overlooked her.'

Thora's brow creased. 'Freydis was in a strange mood last evening. I think she'd fallen on the wrong side of Aslanga, though over what, I can't say. She ate less than a sparrow at the feast and when you didn't arrive this morning she took Ubbi outside to amuse him until Aslanga rose.'

'Then I'll speak to the two of them as soon as–'

'I should think you've all had ample time to feed yourselves by now.'

The biting tones of Ragnar's shrew-faced little wife rang out as she strode into the hall, inspecting everything from the hearthfire to the mealtime food and last night's crockery. Nor did Bjorn's crumpled, straw-decked tunic escape her scrutiny. She was certainly hiding her hangover well, Eadwulf thought. Even her clothing looked crisp and fresh.

'I insist my sons have their usual tuition today, Scribe, whether they like it or not,' she said, shooting a look at Ivar and Halfdan that would brook no rejoinder. Her arm swept round the hall. 'The rest of you, the sooner we get this meal cleared, the sooner we start preparations for tonight's feast. Eadwulf, you will collect the nettles I need for the soup. There are still plenty growing by the river. Remember to pick the freshest leaves – they'll not sting too badly if you pick them carefully.

'Thank you for taking over this morning,' she added, addressing Thora and Toke. 'I must have overslept due to the late night.'

Bjorn let out an outright guffaw. 'Would you care for some pottage, Aslanga? You can always scoop the floating grease from the top.'

Aslanga cast her eldest son a look that could have turned a person to stone. 'The company has quite taken away my appetite,' she said caustically. 'I prefer to eat with those who do not look as though they've been rolling around in the straw with the pigs.'

Twelve

October was not the best month for nettles. The thick clumps that had sprouted profusely along the riverbank throughout the summer had now sadly died back. Eadwulf chuntered as he tried to find enough fresh growth to fill his bucket, his sleeves pulled down to protect his hands. He kicked the stubby plants, quite the opposite of the fresh, new leaves Aslanga had requested, wondering what she'd do if he returned with insufficient for her soup. Why did she want to make nettle soup anyway, when there were vegetables aplenty in the storage huts?

He followed the river seaward, plucking at the sorry specimens. The Kattegat Strait was less than a couple of miles away and the slate-grey water of the widening river flowed steadily towards its expansive freedom. Seabirds circled and the sharp, salty tang of the sea carried on the cold wind. There were fewer and fewer of the wretched nettles as he walked and he was on the verge of turning back when, on rounding a bend, he was brought up short.

Freydis and Ubbi were wandering about on the sandy flats at the river's edge, the jarl's daughter pointing out interesting-looking pebbles and stones. Ubbi's chubby face glowed in the bracing wind, but he seemed to be enjoying himself. Catching sight of Eadwulf staring down at them from the shrub-covered bank Freydis smiled and tugged Ubbi in his direction.

Eadwulf returned the smile, feeling envious of her thick coat of white fur. 'You shouldn't be here alone, mistress. It's a cold wind, although you are wrapped up well in your furs.'

Freydis's smile instantly dropped. 'I don't need a thrall to tell me what I can do! And – not that it's any of your business – the coat *is* very warm, thank you. It's made from the fur of an ice bear, and since they live near the edge of Midgard where it snows nearly all the time, I think it should keep me nicely snug ...

'Oh dear,' she giggled, 'don't I sound pompous.' Unsure of whether that was a question, Eadwulf said nothing. 'In truth, I wanted to be out of the hall before Aslanga could insist I knead dough again. And *someone* had to take care of Ubbi: everyone else was too busy.'

'I didn't mean to criticise,' Eadwulf assured, before the girl really took offence. 'I'm merely concerned for your safety, so close to the river with the little one.'

'I can look after us both very well,' she huffed, hoisting her little brother into her arms, where he proceeded to pull on her flaxen plaits. She jerked her head but Ubbi clung on with grim determination. 'I spend a lot of time playing with Ubbi, especially when Burghild's busy with other chores. Aslanga's not exactly the motherly type, in case it had escaped your notice.'

Eadwulf nodded, trying hard not to laugh at the child's antics and Freydis's growing irritation. 'I meant no disrespect, mistress, though perhaps some help in carrying him would be useful.'

'Oh, he walks well enough. He walked most of the way here, as a matter of fact.' She winced as Ubbi tugged a handful of hair and buried his face in her shoulder. 'And I am *not* carrying you all the way back!' she declared, pulling her braids from Ubbi's grasp and firmly lowering him to the ground. He thrust out his bottom lip and stretched up his arms, demanding to be picked up again.

'Perhaps he'd let me carry him,' Eadwulf offered, sizing up the sturdy child, 'although I'd need to ask you to carry the bucket, mistress.'

Freydis flashed a grateful smile. 'Let's see how far he can walk on his own first. He loves walking, as a rule. But what brings *you* so far from the hall? Are you collecting something?'

'I don't think Aslanga will be amused,' Eadwulf said, as they laughed at the shrivelled specimens in Eadwulf's pail. 'But I can't fetch something that isn't there!'

'Eadwulf!' Freydis suddenly shrieked. 'Where's Ubbi?'

Freydis was hard on Eadwulf's heels as they rounded a bush in time to see Ubbi paddling into the water, squealing with delight as it splashed round his legs. He waded further in until the water reached his chest, his squeals of glee soon turning to alarm as the current washed him off his feet, carrying him on downstream – and gradually further away from the bank, to where the water rapidly deepened. Unable to stay afloat, his dark head disappeared.

'Eadwulf! *Do* something!'

But Eadwulf was already diving towards where the child had gone down.

His first dive proved futile, the silt-laden water rendering visibility for more than a few feet impossible. Resurfacing quickly he caught sight of the boy, bobbing along a mere few yards away before disappearing again. He took several strong strokes and dived again, this time managing to clasp hold of Ubbi's shoulders and haul him up from the murky depths. But the panicked infant would not succumb to his rescue placidly. Gulping down great lungfuls of air he struggled and kicked so wildly that Eadwulf lost his grip. Ubbi sank a second time, to re-emerge several yards downstream.

Swimming for all he was worth, Eadwulf reached the gasping boy just in time to stop him from sinking yet again. In desperation he threw his arm across the child's shoulder and chest, his fingers clamping fast onto his left armpit. Then, with his strong legs kicking hard against the flow, Eadwulf, somehow, managed to propel them both to the bank.

He laid Ubbi face down on the pebbly beach and collapsed beside him, shaking with cold and exhaustion. Though not yet icy, the water had been cold enough to take his breath away as he'd made his first dive, and only his determination to prevent Ubbi from drowning had stopped him from abandoning his quest. And now the bitter wind was driving his sodden clothes against his skin. His panted breaths mingled with Fryedis's anguished sobs and the harsh screams of the gulls.

'He's not breathing!' Freydis suddenly shrieked, desperately rubbing the infant's back in an effort to revive him. 'And he's so cold ...Please, gentle Freya,' she prayed. 'Don't let my little brother die.'

Eadwulf knelt to take over her revival efforts and, after some moments, Ubbi suddenly coughed and spluttered, retching on mouthfuls of briny water. Eadwulf's relief was overwhelming, and as he helped Freydis to wrap the child in her thick coat, his streaming tears almost matched hers.

'I'm so sorry for all this, Eadwulf,' Freydis blubbed. 'I shouldn't have let Ubbi out of my sight. I brought him out here, just to get away from Aslanga's stupid chores! And it was my responsibility to take care of him.' Her tear-filled eyes looked straight into his. 'I don't know what I'd have done if you hadn't been here. I can't even swim… and Ubbi would have been swept out to sea and…' She stopped, unable to put the predictable ending into words.

Eadwulf didn't remind her that if he hadn't distracted her with those cursed nettles, she wouldn't have taken her eyes off Ubbi in the first place.

'I'll never forget what you did today,' Freydis assured him, with a wan smile, 'and I'll make sure everyone knows what a hero you are. I just wish I had a coat to wrap around you, too,' she said, suddenly seeming to notice his chattering teeth. 'But I have nothing else – although if you're not too weak to carry Ubbi, the coat is full enough to wrap around you both.'

Eadwulf was shivering too fiercely to refuse and, without a thought for the nettles, he lifted up the wailing child. Freydis placed her coat around his shoulders, fastening it with her brooch so that it enveloped them both before she sped off to the village to get help.

'Thank you, mistress,' he shouted at her retreating back.

Struggling with the squirming weight, Eadwulf forced his legs to move, sheer doggedness alone keeping him upright. He'd made little progress when a group of people came hurtling towards him, with Bjorn leading the way.

The jarl's firstborn unfastened Freydis's brooch and wrenched Ubbi from Eadwulf's grasp. 'Keep the coat tightly round the child,' he ordered, passing Ubbi into Toke's waiting arms. 'Ignore his protests. He's merely panicked, so get him before the fire as quick as you can and out of those clothes.' He motioned to two women. 'You two, go with them and help. Aslanga will undoubtedly instruct you further,' he added, dryly. 'I'll see to the lad here.'

Without the thick coat Eadwulf could not stop the violent shudders. 'Here,' Bjorn said, wrapping him in his own coat, then bending forward and tossing him over his shoulder like a sack of corn. 'Tell me if you're uncomfortable like that, lad,' he urged, setting off back to the village. 'It's just the easiest way for me to carry you, you see.' Eadwulf was too exhausted to even consider complaining. 'My sister said you'd pulled Ubbi from the river,' Bjorn went on. 'I don't yet know the details of this feat, of course, but no doubt I'll find out soon enough. Freydis was already singing your praises as we rushed from the hall.'

Eadwulf could do no more than grunt. It wasn't easy to speak hanging over the hard shoulder of his means of transport.

* * *

Bjorn carried Eadwulf into the hall to the rhythm of heartfelt applause, Freydis's vivid story having induced everyone to fervent admiration for his actions.'

'You've performed well for us today, boy,' Ragnar boomed as he made his way out. 'We'll talk later, once you've recovered, but right now I need to be in the stables.'

In dry clothes and seated by the hearth with a bowl of steaming broth, Eadwulf soon felt the cold numbness wane. His head slumped onto his cushioning arms and he dozed off, oblivious to the sounds and movements around him. On rousing he stood to resume his chores before Aslanga could scold him, but Bjorn would hear none of it.

Around the hall, women were busy with preparations for the feast and Freydis was hacking so wildly at carrots she spent more time retrieving chunks from the floor than chopping. As she worked she repeated her tale, with considerable embellishment of Eadwulf's bravery, her doe-eyed smiles making him squirm. Aslanga listened, so stony-faced at first he felt sure she'd demand the whereabouts of the requested nettles. But eventually her frosty expression melted.

'It's not every day we have call to praise the actions of a thrall, but today we cannot doubt that thanks are in order,' she admitted. 'Although I'm puzzled as to why two of my children were by the river in the first place,' she added, peering at Freydis in disapproval. 'Eadwulf was on an errand for me ...but you and Ubbi? I look forward to enlightenment regarding your actions, Freydis.'

She wiped her floury hands on her pinafore. 'Now, carry the prepared vegetables to the fireroom, Freydis. I was intending to make nettle soup, but vegetable it shall be.' With a half-smirk at Eadwulf, she swept herself out of the room.

* * *

The sun hung low in the near-cloudless sky, the late afternoon dry and cold with the promise of frost when darkness fell. Winter was nudging her icy nose into people's lives and they did not relish the prospect. They'd done all in their power to ensure the well-being of the village during the bleak months ahead and hoped their hard work would reap its dividend. All that was needful now was the blessing of the gods. In sombre mood, villagers waited for the ceremony to begin.

'Remember they are pagans, Eadwulf,' Sigehelm urged as they watched the sun touch the distant horizon, 'and we do not understand their ways.' He sniffed and pointed across the compound. 'See that flat-topped rock over there with the bowl and twig on top of it? That will likely be used as the altar, where the sacrifice will be made. The jarl and his entourage are already congregating about it and as soon as the sun disappears, the ceremony will start.'

Eadwulf nodded, staring at Ragnar in a flowing robe of brilliant white. His long hair was unbraided, held by a silver band around his brow; about his waist a belt held a long knife with a jewelled hilt in a leather sheath. At his sides, his three eldest sons and four men were all splendidly garbed.

'The jarl is acting in his role as high priest,' Sigehelm said. 'Today he'll lead the first of the rites to honour the gods, pleading their munificence during the winter months, when the land yields little sustenance. Blood sacrifices will be offered to demonstrate their sincerity.' Contempt soured Sigehelm's words and Eadwulf glanced about, fearing someone might overhear. Ahead of them Aslanga stood with her younger children and thralls, all too intent on their own conversations to have heard Sigehelm's words.

'The pagans believe the blood will strengthen the gods and urge them to look more favourably upon them,' Sigehelm continued. 'The sacrifice could be a pig, or more likely a horse, since Ragnar's spent so long in the stables today.'

Eadwulf baulked at the idea of sacrificing a horse: in Mercia, horses were prized animals. But he blanked out thoughts of home and concentrated on the present. In two days' time they would all attend the ceremony to Odin, the highest of the gods, but today it was to the red-headed, short-tempered god of thunder that people turned.

Thor was well loved in Danish communities. Warriors, farmers and those to be married, all prayed for his guidance and protection as he raced across the skies in his chariot pulled by goats, controlling lightning and the forces of nature. Many people were named in his honour, including Thora and Toke.

Ragnar stepped forward with raised arms and silence descended. Eyes followed Ulrik leading a proud old stallion towards the altar, its dappled markings identifying it as belonging to Ragnar. Recognising his master, the stallion whinnied and picked up his pace. Eadwulf sighed, envisioning the animal's sad end.

'It will be quickly over,' Sigehelm assured. 'Ragnar would not inflict unnecessary suffering on an animal that has been his favourite for many years.'

Ragnar caressed the stallion's neck, speaking in low, soothing tones, whilst behind them Bjorn slowly lifted the bowl and twig from the altar. The jarl's hand slid to the hilt of his dagger and he inched the long blade slowly from its sheath.

Death came fast, the wide slash across the horse's neck dealt with practised dexterity. Ragnar held on to the soft muzzle as the forelegs buckled and the animal dropped to his knees, then onto his side, shuddering in his death throes. Bjorn knelt to hold the bowl beneath the gash, collecting the life-blood as it gushed forth, and Ragnar sprinkled the bright red fluid across the altar and ground around it with the twig.

'Accept our offering, mighty Thor,' he intoned. 'Let the life-force of this noble beast be a token of our thanks and devotion, strengthening the ties between you and your humble servants. Look upon us benevolently throughout the coming year.'

'The jarl's priestly robes will be put aside for a day or two now. He'll attend the feast as chieftain tonight, and behave as loutishly as the rest of them!' Sigehelm ran his fingers through his hair. 'It is difficult for us to equate the two roles, is it not, Eadwulf? But, there's much in this land to be wondered at. And though Ragnar may truly mourn the loss of his favoured mount, he'll believe he chose wisely from his stables. The stallion had outlived his usefulness and would have died of old age before the year was out. According to their beliefs, great honour has been bestowed upon the animal by being selected for presentation to a god.

'The women will take over here now, preparing the meat for cooking,' he went on, gesturing towards the group huddled round the fallen stallion. 'I imagine it will be roasted on skewers as last night's beef, whereas on some occasions during my travels I've seen sacrificed beasts cooked in pits.

'Your bravery this morning seemed to impress our mistress,' he added as they turned to head back to the hall.

Eadwulf pulled a face. 'Perhaps, but Aslanga's opinions change by the moment.'

Sigehelm nodded at the truth of that. 'Nevertheless, I've never felt as proud of you as I did when Ragnar congratulated you. You are a true son of Mercia.'

* * *

For the celebratory feast in honour of Thor, Eadwulf was instructed to serve at the jarl's table and he concentrated hard to avoid splashing mead or dropping hot food on anyone's lap. He was also very aware of the wolf-dog, snarling at Ivar's feet. Aslanga's cooking triumphed again and the generous steaks of horse meat were savoured with gusto. He noticed that neither Ivar nor Halfdan was drinking mead tonight – but Bjorn was downing cup for cup with his father.

'I'm relieved to see Freydis happy again,' Thora said, passing Eadwulf on her way to the children's table with a jug of buttermilk. 'Whatever the cause of her dour mood last night, it now seems forgotten.' Eadwulf nodded, wishing the girl would just stop smiling at him.

Bjorn eventually heaved himself to his feet a little unsteadily and tapped the table with his scramseax to gain attention. 'It is now my duty to thank our illustrious jarl for this glorious feast,' he slurred, casting a silly grin at Ragnar, who looked anything but illustrious. 'You've done us very proud tonight, Father. You've given our sacrifice to Thor in the hope of his blessing this winter, and now we must ensure that mighty Odin is appeased. Isn't that so, Father?'

Ragnar nodded in inebriated acquiescence as Bjorn sank to his seat. A minstrel proceeded to sing a sad song of lost love, accompanying himself on his lyre. But few men listened, embarking instead on a session of riddle telling. Eadwulf tried to ignore Ivar and Halfdan's scornful looks as he moved along their table with his jug, but suddenly he found himself sprawled on the rushes, the jug's contents dripping from the jarl's boots – and the wolf-dog's slavering maw moving toward his face.

Ragnar sprang to his feet, arm poised to strike, but Bjorn yanked Eadwulf up before his father – or the dog – made contact with his target. 'And you two can stop that stupid noise!' he snapped at his hooting brothers. 'Eadwulf's not at fault here.'

'The fool gave me a dousing, there's no doubt of that!' Ragnar held out his leg to show a sodden boot. 'He was a clumsy imbecile, that's all there is to it.'

'It is *not* all, Father.'

'Well then, let's hear what you've to say and we'll call an end to the night. It's late and I've downed too much mead to think too hard.'

Bjorn nodded and glowered a little squint-eyed at Halfdan before facing the men. 'This boy,' he began, 'has performed a deed today that would do credit to the reputation of any warrior. He risked his life willingly, not on anyone's orders, to save that of another.' The murmurs of agreement were embarrassing and Eadwulf stared down at his feet. 'The boy has served at our table tonight, efficiently until now. Now it seems as though he clumsily fell over, so wasting a fine jug of mead.'

'Well then, are you saying he wasn't clumsy at all? Or that someone pushed him over?'

'Not pushed, Father, but tripped. I saw the offending foot being deliberately moved into Eadwulf's path as I waited for him to reach me with the jug. Honour dictates I don't squeal on another, but I'll be having strong words with someone tomorrow.'

'You don't know how close you came to licking the mead

off my boots, boy,' Ragnar growled, swaying ominously and sinking to his seat. 'But, Bjorn's right. 'You've shown courage today. And no doubt the boot will dry off.'

Ragnar dismissed the incident but Bjorn was of a different mind. 'I propose we show our appreciation to Eadwulf, who saved young Ubbi's life today. To our brave thrall: hearty thanks!' he yelled, raising his drinking horn.

The hall rang with Eadwulf's praises. His cheeks burned and, although he knew Bjorn meant well, he also knew that Halfdan and Ivar would not forget this. Before long they'd find something far more hurtful to do to him.

Thirteen

In the sombre, grey light before sunrise on October 14, the people of Aros filed from their longhouses and followed their priest in his flowing white robes. Guided by the fiery luminance of torches borne by a handful of thralls, the column moved in respectful silence along a narrow path that snaked between the cultivated fields and up the gentle slope behind the village. On the crest of the hill stood the sacred grove, a short way from the woodland where Eadwulf had recently collected kindling for winter fires. The ancient oaks loomed dark and ominous against the silvery-grey of the lightening sky, and Eadwulf shivered, overcome with sudden foreboding.

Fallen leaves felt wet and slippery beneath the mist enveloping his feet, and he stepped warily, trying to ignore the fearful flutterings in his stomach. Surely there was nothing to fear? He glanced sidelong at Toke, but the old thrall seemed lost to his own thoughts. He looked behind to the rear of the column where another four torches lighted the way for a wagon carrying Ivar, and hauling along a snorting pig. In front of him, Sigehelm walked beside Burghild and Thora, escorting Freydis and Ubbi, and ahead of them, Aslanga followed behind the jarl and his sons, Bjorn and Halfdan, accompanied by five of Ragnar's men.

The silent train streamed between the outer rings of trees to a clearing within. At its centre a solitary oak towered proudly over its attendants; a truly gigantic tree, the girth of its trunk of such immense proportions, Eadwulf thought it must be hundreds of years old. Its lower branches were thick and sturdy, reaching out and dividing into myriad, twisted routeways; its still abundant foliage evidence of the oak's jealous retention of its leaves long after most forest trees stood denuded and exposed.

Ragnar and his small group positioned themselves into the shape of an arrowhead, tapering away from the wide trunk, though one side of the blade exhibited a definite chink, a missing component. The single figure of the jarl comprised the arrowhead's tip, with Bjorn and Halfdan immediately behind and Ragnar's five men at the rear. And when the covered wagon rolled to a halt, Ivar was supported on his crutches to take his place at Bjorn's right, the chink in the arrowhead thus repaired.

Sigehelm's head was bowed, seemingly in respectful silence, as those around him. But Eadwulf knew better, and the fact that his tutor *needed* to pray at this time gave him little comfort. Aslanga held her head high, as befitted the wife of a jarl, and at her side, Freydis stared fixedly at her father, and clung to Thora's arm. Ubbi slept peacefully on Burghild's shoulder, wrapped in a blanket. Behind them, Eadwulf stood close to Toke, trembling.

Ragnar took two paces forward and turned to face the oak, his robes shimmering in the torchlight. Tilting back his head he reached out to the branches above.

'O ...di ...in,' he intoned, sinking to his knees. 'All-Father, lord of wisdom, war and death, mighty god of all gods...' Around the grove the people knelt, lifting their arms to the tree. 'We are humbled in the shadow of your sacred oak, knowing that you are close. I, Ragnar, priest of the gods, beseech you,

Father: hear the voice of your humble servant.'

'Odin, Odin...' The chanting began, rising to fever pitch before settling to a lilting hum; outstretched arms swayed like meadow grasses in the breeze. People were surely evoking the very presence of their god.

'The wheel of the seasons has turned and winter will soon be upon us,' Ragnar's baritone rang out. 'We bring our gifts of thanks and ask that you safeguard your people from the hardships of the frozen months. Let them live to serve you.'

A strong, unheralded gust swept the grove, whistling through the oak's branches. Torches listed wildly and the droning stopped. 'God of gods, lord of earth and sky, giver and taker of life,' Ragnar intoned, his hands reaching up to two black shapes, now perched on the thick branch above his head. 'We are unworthy to look upon your holy companions and avert our eyes in their presence.'

Eadwulf stayed on his knees, not understanding what was happening. He knew little about Odin's ravens other than what Thora had told him. Hugin and Munin – Thought and Memory – were the god's eyes and ears; awesome, black birds sent out each dawn to fly over Midgard, gathering information to report to Odin by the evening. He'd always dismissed such a story as pagan nonsense.

Ragnar rose and faced the kneeling crowd. 'To your feet, my people, and witness our offerings to the All-Father, who has given his sign of acceptance.'

The wasted body of Cendred was dragged from the wagon, his wrists bound behind him. Panic and anger surged through Eadwulf and he drew breath to cry out.

'Do not make a sound,' Toke hissed. 'Great insult to Odin if you do.' His eyes flicked up to the tree's thick branches. 'Could be you or me up there next.'

Cendred slumped, seeming resigned to his gruesome end after weeks of imprisonment. His filthy clothes hung limp on his half-starved body; his hair greasy and matted from his bowed head, concealing whatever expression was on his face. At his sides two of Ragnar's men stood grim-faced, and a few paces behind, Ulrik held a huge, heavy-headed axe. Close by, Bjorn carried a large coil of thick rope.

'Odin!' Ragnar shouted. 'May the lifeblood of our people's enemies please and strengthen you.'

Cendred was yanked to his feet and the heavy, flat handle of the axe-head crashed down on his skull. Eadwulf recoiled from the sickening crunch of shattering bones as Cendred's head caved in like a crushed eggshell under the force of Ulrik's strength. Had Ulrik used the sharp blade, far more than Cendred's head would have been split in two.

The lifeless body sprawled on the rotting leaves, his blood soaking into the earth. Bjorn severed the bonds holding Cendred's arms and rolled him over, rebinding his wrists above his head with one end of rope. The two warriors dragged the corpse beneath a thick branch close to the ravens and Bjorn hurled the loose end of the rope over it. Cendred's body was hauled up high, where Eadwulf guessed it would stay, dangling by the wrists to feed the crows.

A second man was dragged from the cart, whom Eadwulf recognised as a thrall of one of Ragnar's karls. He threw his body from side to side, frantically straining at his bindings, strangled, animal sounds gurgling from his throat. Eadwulf could think of no crime that could warrant such a death. But the Danes needed scant excuse to give a life to their gods and Ulrik's axe promptly despatched another offering to Odin.'

The third victim's frenzied attempts to beg for mercy gained him a blow to his head before the fall of the axe put an end to his miseries.

Finally the pig was hauled forward, squealing in terror at the smell of blood. Ragnar slashed the creature's throat and the carcass was hoisted up by its hind legs to hang next to the three men, its blood streaming to the forest floor. Eadwulf prayed to any god who would listen for this to be over soon.

Bright eyed and motionless, the ravens surveyed all.

Ragnar clutched the sacrificial knife above his head. 'Odin!' he yelled. 'Remember our gifts when winter comes. Let the season be kind, our huntsmen find success, and our people survive!'

The ravens lifted their wings to take flight and the strange, gusting wind raged a second time. The flapping of silken feathers hummed through the grove, then the black shapes soared into the distance to continue their daily tasks for the All-Father.

Filing down the winding path, people sang joyful songs of praise to Odin, while Eadwulf strove to erase the images of dangling corpses from his mind. His anger was slowly burning down, leaving the smouldering ashes of helplessness in its place.

* * *

The winter months passed uneventfully in Aros as people coped with the cold, dreary days and long, dark nights. With

Sigehelm's help, Eadwulf finally ceased to have nightmares over Cendred's death, though the memory would stay with him for a very long time. Sigehelm dismissed the timely appearance of Odin's ravens as pure coincidence. Ravens were not uncommon, he said, and the birds probably nested in the grove, since they disliked the dense forests. But Eadwulf was not totally convinced by his reassurances.

The daily routines of the season continued in much the same way as Eadwulf recalled of his life in Mercia: people busy with the necessary chores and retiring early to their beds. Yet food was plentiful: last year's harvest had been a bountiful one. People thanked the gods for their good fortune, many offering gifts at ceremonies in their own homes. At the Yule, when the old year was dead, a boar, a sheep and a horse were sacrificed and the gods entreated that the year to come should be a good one.

By the start of the last week of February it was still bitterly cold, the land white as far as the eye could see. It had snowed hard in the night and the wind snatched greedily at drifts that had amassed against the buildings, causing flurries of feathery flakes to spiral frantically around, making visibility unclear. Carrying a large basket of vegetables into the hall, Eadwulf battled with the heavy door, the biting northerly determined to fling it from his grasp. He triumphed in time to witness one of Haldan's usual tirades at Sigehelm. His throat constricted as he recalled the many times he'd griped like Halfdan – though he'd respected his tutor too much to be openly rude to him. But to Halfdan, Sigehelm was simply his father's property – and the boy treated him as such.

Sigehelm caught Eadwulf's eye and smiled, as though he'd read his thoughts. Ivar glanced up and witnessed the shared glance. The look in the boy's dark eyes filled Eadwulf with unfathomable foreboding.

* * *

Aalborg, Northern Danish Lands: February 852

Morwenna sat on the edge of her bed in the small chamber to the side of Rorik's hall, cradling the drowsy babe close to her heart and thanking God that the soft curls were not the fiery red of Beorhtwulf's, nor were his sleepy eyes green. The infant's gaze was as clear as the summer sky. Blue – like Morwenna's own. There had been no reason why Rorik should deny the child was his. By Morwenna's own calculations from the true date of his conception, his birth had been two weeks late. And it had been easy to feign a heavy fall once labour was already underway, making it appear that the fall caused the birth pains to start and the child to be born two weeks early.

The babe's round cheeks glowed pink in the lamplight as he drifted into a contented slumber, unaware of anything other than the security of a mother's love and warm milk to sate his appetite on demand. He would grow for many years believing himself to be the son of Jarl Rorik and his Mercian concubine.

Her heart filled with love for her new son, but the deep aching for the son who was lost to her would not abate. He was somewhere in this pagan land: some farmstead deep in the barren heath or perhaps on one of the many coastal settlements.

Please God that *someone* would bring news of a red-headed Mercian boy one day.

Certain the child was asleep she laid him in his cradle, hoping he'd sleep for some hours. It was late afternoon and soon she must help with the evening meal. Darkness was closing in and the icy cold would soon send people hurrying indoors. Another snowfall had been threatening all afternoon; as yet there had been only a few flurries, but she anticipated a thick covering by morning.

In truth, Morwenna's working life as Rorik's woman had caused her little discomfort, particularly during the weeks prior to the birthing, when her rotund form had made heavy manual work difficult. To their credit, the Danish women had respected her condition. Even Rorik's two wives accepted the new concubine into their midst: concubines were as much a part of Danish life as was polygamy, or summer raiding. In the early months, she'd worked with the women around the village, glad to be busy to keep her from utter despair. She'd been well fed and given cool tunics to wear during the summer, and warm, woollen ones as winter neared. But the long summer nights had been a different matter. Rorik would come to her, his breath stinking of ale, and callously use her exhausted body. Yet by the time her belly had swelled, he took pleasure in the belief that he had sown his seed within her and became almost tender. Morwenna could barely conceal her repugnance.

Though Rorik had sated his carnal lust elsewhere since the weeks prior to the birthing, today he'd declared his eagerness to resume his nocturnal activities with his Mercian concubine. The babe was now three weeks old and he would wait no longer.

An even greater dread now swamped Morwenna. Before long her womb could be swelled with a true child of Jarl Rorik.

Fourteen

April sunshine lifted Eadwulf's spirits and he worked contentedly enough in the fields at the foot of the hillside. Spring ploughing had been done soon after the thaws of early March, and now the corn was being sown. It had been a long day and by the time he reached his bed he could barely keep his eyes open. The hall was warm from the remains of the hearthfire and he soon fell into a deep slumber.

'Rouse yourself, Mercian.' The venomous whisper was so close to Eadwulf's ear that warm breath brushed his cheek. 'Far side of the byre. Now!'

Eadwulf's mouth went dry. He blinked into the darkness, but could make out no more than a shadowy form. Yet every fibre of his being told him it was Halfdan. Then the door creaked and he knew the boy had gone. For a moment he lay still, listening to the snores of the thralls and retainers along the benches, and wondered how long he'd slept. No light had squeezed through the doorway as Halfdan had left, not even the gloomy half-light of pre-dawn. Sunrise must still be some time off. He threw back his blanket, shivering, and shoved his feet into his shoes. Every instinct urged him to shout, alert the household to his predicament, tell them that Halfdan was going to ...to do what? The only certainty was that Halfdan intended him harm. And waking everyone was more likely to gain him a thrashing than offers of help. He grabbed his coat and crept from the hall.

Tiny pin-pricks of light dotted the ink-black sky and

moonbeams bathed the silhouette of the large byre ahead. Smaller buildings were strangely outlined, barns and food stores mostly, and the forge beyond Thora's vegetable plots. Frosty air chafed his face and pungent odours assaulted his nostrils as he neared the imposing byre. Cattle lowed softly in their stalls.

A rumbling growl stopped him in his tracks. So, Ivar was here with his snarling dog. His heart hammered as though it would burst through his chest, his immediate impulse to flee back to the hall. Too late ...

'You took your time,' Halfdan snarled, emerging from behind the byre. 'Get over here before we unleash the hound.'

Eadwulf stepped towards him, determined not to give him the satisfaction of sensing his fear. 'What do you want with me this time, Halfdan?'

A vicious punch to the stomach made Eadwulf double over and Halfdan knocked him to the ground. '*Master* to you, thrall! I told you before, a thrall *never* looks his master in the eye and isn't worthy of speaking his name!' Eadwulf struggled to catch his breath as the boy lowered himself to balance on one knee in front of him. 'Say it! Go on, or I'll–'

'*What* will you do – kill me? How would you explain that to your father?'

The Danish boy shrieked and booted him hard in his side. 'Say it, I said!'

Eadwulf gasped as hot pain shot through him. Halfdan grabbed his tunic and yanked him to his feet, shaking him as a hound would shake a captured hare. Overcome with dizziness, Eadwulf retched.

'You should see what you look like, Mercian – like the vomiting dog you are! Not so haughty now, are you? You'll be even less so when we've done with you.'

'What ...what do you mean? What are you going to do?'

'Perhaps you thought it acceptable to behave as though you were not our inferior!' Halfdan said, not answering the question. 'Our father is the greatest jarl in these lands, and you think you can look upon us as your equals! But you're no more than a piece of shit, dragged to our land on the shoes of our warriors.'

The wolf-dog's menacing growl struck terror into Eadwulf as Halfdan hauled him behind the byre, where a halo of candlelight illumined a group of figures. Wrapped in a thick cloak, Ivar lounged on a hefty log, his hunched back against the byre, his two aides at his sides. Eadwulf stood mesmerised by those deep, dark eyes, their reflected light forming fiery arrows that seemed to bore through to his very core.

Eventually, Ivar gestured to the ground, mere inches from the wolf-dog's slobbering muzzle. 'Sit down, Mercian. It's high time your brazen impudence was punished. That seems fair, don't you think?'

'If I knew how I've displayed impudence, I'd be able to answer,' Eadwulf replied, still standing.

Halfdan dealt another brutal kick, this time to Eadwulf's thigh, and swung his fist to down him before Ivar.

'You must know by now, Mercian, that my brother has a temper almost as quick as our father's – or our mother's, come to that,' Ivar snorted. 'Whereas I think before I act, and come up with solutions.' He propped his chin on steepled fingers, the wolf-dog's yellow eyes fixed on his face. 'And after much deliberation, I've made the decision to set you free.'

'That's impossible! Father would never allow it! Why should we–?'

'Hold your tongue, Halfdan! How typical of you to bluster before hearing a plan out. In a couple of hours it will be dawn,' Ivar mused, glancing up at the cloudless black sky. 'It will be a fine day I think, magnificently suited to the plan I've in mind.' He wagged a finger at Eadwulf. 'You will run; any direction you like. If you stay free, then so be it: you'll no longer be a thrall. If you succeed in remaining free until noon, which entails outwitting Viggi, you have my word that we'll never bother you again. Your word will also be required,' he shot at his scowling brother. '*Now*, if you will!'

'I give it,' Halfdan grudgingly returned.

'But if you're caught, thrall, there'll be little of you left after Viggi's finished with you. He already senses you're no friend of mine, for which he'll happily make you pay dear.'

Halfdan grinned, nodding approval of the plan. 'We'll tell Father we saw the thrall sneaking from the hall and disappearing behind the huts,' he enthused. 'We spent a long time searching, of course, before taking Viggi out to follow his scent. But alas, by the time we found him, he'd paid dearly for his insubordination.'

'A runaway thrall cannot expect mercy,' Ivar stated, continuing Halfdan's conjectures. 'Our father would probably have sent the dogs out himself, had we not already dispatched the best hunter of the lot...

'You will learn to show respect for your betters, *thrall*,' he suddenly snapped, tired of this dalliance. 'If you refuse to run, Reinn and Skorri here will drag you from the village and hold you until I release Viggi to follow your trail. Believe me, he'll reach you well before Ragnar is alerted to your disappearance.'

Eadwulf looked from Ivar's cold eyes to the feral, yellow ones of Viggi, finding no shred of mercy in either. The wolf-dog already strained at its leash to rip him apart.

'What shall we say to Mother when she asks where–?'

'Leave that to me Halfdan: I'll think of something. Now,' Ivar continued, 'you have our word, Mercian, that we'll wait until sunrise before following after you, so you need to put some ground between us or our hunt will be so much easier. Of course, I'll not be joining in the event; my brother and two companions will do the honours. But be very aware that Viggi's hunting skills are second to none!'

Eadwulf's stomach clamped tight. How could he agree to such a vindictive scheme? Yet how could he not?

Having no alternative, he ran.

* * *

Without a backward glance, Eadwulf sped between the food stores and huts towards the river, Ivar's words ringing in his ears:

Hunting skills second to none, second to none. Hunting skills second to none ...

He gave no thought to his direction, other than it being the nearest route out of the village, and he ran at almost breakneck speed, following the river upstream. He knew this stretch of land well and the moon was bright enough to cast some light. Panting wildly, his one panicked aim was to put distance between himself and the wolf-dog.

Hunting skills second to none, second to none ...

As the moon and stars faded against the lightening sky, the realisation that dawn was approaching struck him like a stab in the chest, and he was forced to slow his pace. He must think, take stock of his location and decide what to do next.

Now, several miles upstream, the river had narrowed, though it surged full and turbulent, carrying extra volumes of spring snowmelt. Distant hills were silhouetted in the moonlight, and Eadwulf suddenly realised that the forested slopes would afford him cover.

But first, he must cross the river. If he waded some distance along the water, the dog would lose his scent and there was a possibility that Halfdan wouldn't be able to fathom his route from then on. Once on the opposite bank he'd veer away from the river and take a direct route to the higher ground. Several miles of low-lying heath lay between himself and his goal, and he'd not be able to move quickly over such rough terrain. But the sky was paling fast and he had to reach the forest.

Again he broke into a run, heading further upstream until the gushing water appeared shallow enough to reach little higher than his knees. He wrapped his coat round his shoes to make them easier to carry, rolled up his trouser legs, and scrambled down the sloping bank into the river. Icy water pummelled his legs but he gritted his teeth and turned upstream. The riverbed was strewn with pebbles and rocks, most worn smooth by the flowing water but others sharp and jagged, making it difficult for him to find footholds; stringy weed entwined his toes. Each step was laboriously slow but he struggled on.

After less than a quarter of a mile he could no longer bear the river's icy embrace and scrambled up the slippery bank on legs so numb he could barely feel them. Cold air drove at his skin and he donned his coat and shoes between bouts of violent shivering. Somehow he'd managed to keep them relatively dry, though, as he'd expected, his trousers unrolled stiff and wet. But he'd no time to worry over trivialities and was too cold to stand still any longer.

A ribbon of pink lined the eastern horizon as Eadwulf careered on, the wooded banks and lush water meadows gradually changing into the desolate and uninhabited scenery of the heath. But he paid scant attention to the short, undeveloped vegetation sprouting its new season's green: the stubby shrubs and brackens; the purple flowering heather and yellow-blossomed gorse. He absently registered the occasional pine and spindly silver-barked birch standing conspicuous in its solitude. He ignored the scratches inflicted on his hands by the shrubs' sharp prickles as he tore past. His mind focused only on the low hills in the distance.

The arc of the rising sun signalled the start of the new day, engulfing Eadwulf in another wave of panic. The wolf-dog would now be after him! Where was there to flee to out here? Scanning the horizon he could see nothing but endless heath. The forest seemed further away the faster he ran. Why had he run into this open place where he was so exposed and vulnerable? 'Curses on you, Ivar! Curses on you, Halfdan!' he screamed. 'Why can't you just leave me alone!'

He could not have run any faster. His throat was raw from continuous panting and every inch of his skin was hot and clammy. On the verge of collapse he staggered on until the agonising stitch in his side allowed him to run no further. He threw himself forward, toppling onto a cushion of heather, where he stayed long enough to ease the stitch. He scrambled to his feet and ran again for the forest. As the land gradually rose the gorse and heather petered out, trees became more abundant and soon Eadwulf was into dense woodland. Then he heard that dreaded sound. Distant as yet, the barking struck utter terror in him. Which way should he run – deeper into the forest, or round the edges? Or should he find a tree to climb?

Panic gave little room for deliberation and he pushed deeper into the forest, dodging between the heavy oaks, the less grand birches, hazels, hollies and spindly saplings. Last year's rotting leaves still littered the floor and their odour filled his nostrils. But no birdsong rang in the treetops, no squirrels scampered along the boughs; only the sounds of the distant barking of the wolf-dog reached his ears. Perhaps his fear would allow them to register nothing else.

He stumbled on until brought up short. Ahead, huge oaks loomed and between them fallen branches blocked all pathways but the one along which he'd come. He searched frantically for a way through as the barking grew louder. But it was useless, and he knew he had no option but to face his tormentors. That vindictive boy, Halfdan, must have set off well before sunrise. How else could he have been so close behind...?

He picked up a stout branch and waited. The barking became a menacing growl and the great beast pushed from the undergrowth, dragging Halfdan after him on the short leash, with the two grinning Danish boys close on his heels.

'So, Mercian, time for Viggi's reward, I think,' Halfdan said slowly, straining to hold the snarling dog in check. 'Nice try at the river, by the way, but I knew you must have crossed *somewhere* once the water became shallower. Didn't take much to work that out! The broken branches and flattened grasses up the bank were a bit of a giveaway. And naturally, Viggi had no problem picking up your scent across the heath.' Halfdan picked gorse flowers and bits of foliage from his breeks with his free hand and smoothed down his tunic. 'Nothing to say, thrall? Then let's get this done with.'

Heart pounding, Eadwulf gripped the branch as Halfdan bent to unfasten the leather leash, the two boys peering from behind him, slavering in anticipation of gruesome entertainment.

'Release the dog, Halfdan, and it's dead.'

Halfdan spun round in alarm, treading on the hound's tail and falling against Skorri and Reinn, bringing them down with him. The dog let out a yelp and snapped at Halfdan's ankles, causing him to cry out in pain. The sight of his red-headed brother ready to loose the arrow from his bowstring caused Halfdan to emit such a startled cry that Eadwulf almost laughed.

'What are you doing here, Bjorn? How long have you been standing there?' Guilt coloured Halfdan's face and he seemed to shrink beneath Bjorn's scathing gaze.

'More importantly, what exactly are *you* are doing here? But before you attempt your feeble explanations, Halfdan, I'll answer your second question: I've been here long enough to see what you were about to do and apparently I'm only just in time to put a stop to it!'

Bjorn glowered at Halfdan, his arrow aimed unwaveringly at the dog. His gaudy evening tunic and baggy trousers were muddy and adorned with fragments of heath. 'I've been roused before daybreak with a tale of my brothers' wicked scheme and the request that I dash across miles of open land to deal with it. I'm now saturated to the skin and exhausted by moving faster than Sleipnir across the sky. Is it any wonder my temper's simmering close to boiling?' He released his breath with controlled calmness. 'What I demand, Halfdan, is an explanation: preferably one that sheds a more favourable light on these antics and possibly justifies your behaviour, which frankly I, for one, cannot condone.'

Halfdan hung his head, mustering up the courage to answer. 'We were apprehending an escaped thrall,' he lied, looking for support from his two minions. But they had shrunk into the shadows, fearful of the authority of Ragnar's firstborn. 'This thrall thought he could just run away – from the jarl!'

'And just why should he do that? Where do you think a boy, a foreigner at that, could run to in a strange land? And manage to survive, of course?'

'How should I know where he'd go? We just saw him running off.'

'And at what hour would that have been?'

Halfdan's brow puckered. 'Perhaps two or three hours before sunrise.'

'And you and Ivar are usually outside at that time?'

'No, but...' Halfdan faltered, clearly searching for a plausible lie. 'We were roused by noises outside.'

'So, you're saying that this would-be escapee made so much noise he could have roused the whole village?'

Halfdan stared at his half-brother, opening his mouth to reply, but the words seemed firmly lodged in his throat. At length he garbled, 'I saw the thrall running off when I went to the, um, latrine. I ran and told Ivar, who said that Viggi would soon find him. So we followed his trail to here...'

Bjorn's bowstring remained resolutely taut. 'Unfortunately for you, I have evidence to verify that events took place quite differently.' He shook his head, his expression more of sorrow than anger. 'And it's apparent that had I not arrived when I did, Eadwulf would now be little more than a bloody mound at your feet!'

Unable to find words of reply, Halfdan remained mute, returning Bjorn's calculating stare with cold-eyed defiance.

'Get back to the village, the three of you,' Bjorn said, flicking his bow. 'You've no idea how tempted I am to sink this arrow in that evil cur's skull anyway. Believe me, Halfdan, you'll not get away with this. I'm not the only one who knows the truth of your intentions for this day.'

Fifteen

Eadwulf's head swam with wild fears as he trudged back across the heath beside Bjorn. What yarns would Halfdan already have spun? Memories of events on the day he'd seen the kingfisher were never far away. Yet this time was different: this time the jarl's eldest son was on his side. At least, that's what he hoped. But so far, Bjorn had remained silent and grim-faced. The morning's events had clearly angered him, and unsure whether Bjorn held him partly responsible, Eadwulf dared not interrupt.

Bjorn suddenly stopped in his tracks. 'I've thought much about you over the past months, Eadwulf, and decided there's more to you than it would seem.'

Confused by the implications entwined in the sweeping statement, Eadwulf shuffled his feet. 'I know not how to answer, Master.'

Bjorn tugged at his beard, questioning green eyes boring into Eadwulf. 'Then I'll explain further. You're unlike any thrall we've ever acquired. You have that extra *something* that other thralls, even high born ones, do not. What is it that I just can't put my finger on?

'I realised months ago that Sigehelm was devoted to you,' he continued. 'He's a good man – despite his Christian ethics – and I believe he regards himself almost as what you Christians call your Guardian Angel?'

Eadwulf nodded slowly. He couldn't deny his tutor's selfless care for him. How often had Sigehelm kept alive the belief that Eadwulf would one day return to Mercia? *Remember who you are*! The words exploded inside his head and he squeezed his eyes shut as emotion welled.

'Then would I also be correct in believing you to be of noble blood?' Eadwulf's eyes shot open. He felt as though his skull had been pierced, his most intimate thoughts hooked out. 'Your entire demeanour would suggest that is so.'

Eadwulf did not want to lie to the man who had undoubtedly saved his life today, but he was not yet ready to divulge the entire truth. 'Sigehelm has cared for my welfare for as long as I can remember,' he supplied, evasively.

'You've not answered my last question,' Bjorn murmured, surveying the meadows across the river, the gentle rise and wooded slopes beyond. The village of his people sat at the foot of those slopes. 'We'd best get back,' he said, walking on and relieving Eadwulf of the need to reply.

They waded across the river and at the top of the bank Bjorn laid down his bow and replaced his leather boots. 'Who were your parents, Eadwulf?' he asked, adjusting the leather strap of his quiver across his shoulder.

Eadwulf shoved his feet into his own tired-looking boots, knowing that Bjorn would not be satisfied until he had an answer. 'My mother was Morwenna, the daughter of an Anglian ealdorman,' he said eventually. 'She was – *is* very pretty, so everyone said. I think she's still alive, Master, but Sigehelm says it's folly to cling to such hopes.'

'We'll talk about that later,' Bjorn said, laying a hand on his shoulder. 'But now, tell me who your father was.'

'My father's dead, so what difference does it make *who* he was?'

Bjorn momentarily considered the question. 'Nothing, I suppose, other than I'd hoped you may wish to confide in me.'

They walked along the riverbank in awkward silence. The deepening water no longer flowed in its menacing pre-dawn mood; sunlight danced on its surface and nettles sprouted profusely amidst the greening shrubs along the banks. Eadwulf mulled over Bjorn's question. Of all the people he knew, other than Sigehelm, he considered Bjorn to be the most deserving of his confidences. Yet Bjorn was a *Dane*, the jarl's son at that, so why did he want to know about Eadwulf's father?

Seeing no other option, he said, 'My father was Beorhtwulf, King of Mercia.'

A broad grin transformed Bjorn's sombre face. 'Then I was right: you're too proud to be aught but a king's son. I knew it the first time you spoke, after you'd doused me with ale. Such things can't be hidden. My brothers sense it too and–'

But whatever he'd been about to say remained unsaid. 'I'm sorry for your loss, lad, but I can't apologise for our raids. Raiding is necessary to our existence. But I do know several jarls who've raided in Saxon lands. Someone may know of an Anglian woman taken in London. Pity you don't know the name of your captor.'

'It was Jarl Rorik!' Eadwulf blurted. 'His nephew told me his name – the warrior who caught me as I tried to run from the manor. I think *his* name was Godfried. His men said Godfried's father was a king.'

Bjorn gave a humourless laugh. 'Rorik is my father's cousin, brother of Harald, who calls himself "King of the Danes". And Harald does have a son called Godfried. There's no love lost between Rorik and Harald. Rorik would happily eliminate his brother and take his place. Harald simply has more silver to buy the support needed to keep his position. But if you're certain of those names, Eadwulf, I may be able to discover whether Rorik still has your mother, or has sold her elsewhere. I can't promise anything, but we occasionally see Rorik at the autumn rites. Keep up your hopes, but don't harbour expectations of success.'

Aros gradually came into view, a cluster of dark shapes with columns of rising smoke that dissipated into the still morning air. Reminded of Aslanga, Eadwulf asked, 'Why is it your mother and brothers hate me, Master, yet you do not seem to do so?'

Bjorn squatted down on the grassy bank, motioning with his bow that Eadwulf should do the same. 'You've saved my life and helped me at other times,' Eadwulf ploughed on, finding only a thoughtful furrow on Bjorn's brow, 'whereas *they* do everything they can to hurt or humiliate me. I don't know why they do so, except that I'm a foreigner and a thrall. And they hate my red hair,' he admitted, his eyes flicking briefly over Bjorn's fiery mane.

The jarl's son hooted. 'Aslanga hates my hair as much as she does yours!'

'But she's your mother! Why should she hate your hair just because it's a different colour to her own?'

'Let me ask you, Eadwulf, what colour was your father's hair? No, let me guess. I'll wager it was red, like yours?' Eadwulf nodded, not seeing the significance of that. 'Well, Aslanga's hair is black as a raven's wing. What do you think that implies?'

Eadwulf shrugged. 'That she was born on a dark night?'

Bjorn snorted at his comical guess. 'What I'm getting at is *parentage*, Eadwulf. Offspring usually resemble *both* parents, in some ways at least, no matter how small those likenesses are. I am Ragnar's son,' he stated proudly, pulling back his broad shoulders. 'I'm told I have his muscular physique, his nose, the same square jaw, and his large hands. And one day I'll probably have a paunch to match!' He gestured to each feature in turn, grinning when it came to his well-muscled midriff. 'But,' he added, fingering a strand of red hair, 'not one thing about me bears similarity to Aslanga: not even my hair colour, or my eyes. Yet neither of those resembles Ragnar's either.'

Eadwulf's lower jaw dropped and Bjorn nodded. 'That's right, Aslanga is not my mother. Gudrun was my mother, Ragnar's first wife.' Eadwulf snatched at memories of Thora mentioning that name; it had meant nothing to him at the time. 'Gudrun died when I was a babe, so I don't remember her, though many in our village do,' Bjorn explained. 'I'm told she was a woman of great kindness and that Ragnar loved her so much he almost gave up the will to live during the months following her death, and he married Aslanga in an effort to lessen the grieving. Then Ivar and Halfdan were born – and lastly little Ubbi.

'I can't say whether Aslanga's made my father happy, but he did have a concubine for many years after Halfdan was born. Though as far as I know, he hasn't bedded her since Aslanga gave birth to Ubbi.'

Eadwulf caught the expectant flicker in Bjorn's eyes as he said all this, but could see nothing to comment upon. He neither approved nor disapproved of concubines.

'But Aslanga has never accepted me as a son. Nor has she ever attempted to raise me in any way at all. That task was given to Thora, whose love I have willingly returned.'

'So, your real mother had red hair and green eyes,' Eadwulf broached, trying to piece together the fragments of information. Bjorn nodded. 'And Aslanga and *her* sons hate you because you remind them of the wife Ragnar loved best.' Bjorn nodded again. 'So they all hate *me* because I remind them of you and your mother.'

'I believe that's how Aslanga sees it, certainly. But Ivar's hatred of me is most intense because I'm Ragnar's first-born, a status he desperately covets. Needless to say, his jealousy is constantly fanned by Aslanga. Ragnar's lands will be mine when I'm jarl and Aslanga's sons will need to seek their fortunes elsewhere. But Ivar's hatred of *you* is something else. It stems from some dream he had a few years ago.' Bjorn's gaze fixed into the distance. 'In this dream Ivar and Halfdan are grown men, leading an army against some king. Their army wins many battles until a red-headed warrior appears at the enemy king's side, bringing about my brothers' downfall. I don't know the details, so don't ask how all that comes about, but Ivar's come to believe that you will be that warrior one day – unless he can kill you first.'

'What foolishness to give credence to a dream!' Eadwulf gasped, springing to his feet. 'There are many red-headed warriors – and I know of no king who could need *my* help. Ivar will gain nothing by killing me.'

Bjorn patted the ground, gesturing to Eadwulf to sit down again. 'Yet you are a king's son, Eadwulf. Who knows what the gods have designed for your future? And, like me, my brothers sense *something* in you – perhaps a destiny to greatness. And they are fearful of it.'

For some moments he stared at his long legs stretched out before him, deep in thought. 'I've something to tell you,' he said, eventually, 'and it's not just some spur-of-the-moment idea. I've been considering this for some time, so here's the thing: from now on you'll belong to me. It may not be the freedom you so desire, but perhaps it's marginally better than belonging to Aslanga. At least my brothers won't have the opportunity to attempt another attack on you.'

Eadwulf said a quick prayer of thanks to whichever god was listening – until an ugly black cloud rained on his burgeoning joy. 'Master, I fear Aslanga would never allow it.'

'Aslanga will have no option but to agree when I threaten to tell Father the truth of her sons' actions today. She'll agree to anything to keep them in Ragnar's favour. I'll offer her Benita and Rico in exchange. So what do you say, Eadwulf?'

'I'll make you a good thrall and always do your bidding. I'll keep your tunics and boots clean, and polish your sword every day...'

'Then you can start by carrying my bow,' Bjorn said, chuckling at Eadwulf's exuberance. 'Remember, we'll still live under the same roof as my brothers, but as you'll be *my* thrall they wouldn't dare attempt to harm you.'

'What about when you go away on raids?' Eadwulf asked, jogging to keep up with him.

'I've thought about that, too. Next month I sail for the northern lands. Life aboard ship is truly exhilarating, Eadwulf, with the wind in your hair and the sun on your face.' He fixed Eadwulf with a steady gaze, before his features creased into a grin. 'But you'll soon see as much for yourself ...

'If your eyebrows rise any higher, they'll leave your face altogether! I know this is a great surprise, but you'll soon get used to the idea. And by Thor's bollocks, I guarantee you'll soon love the sea as much as the rest of us. You'll still be a thrall, but not unduly overworked. No crewman can sit idly on his buttocks for long.'

As they neared the village Eadwulf tried to make sense of his jumbled thoughts, relationships that had once seemed simple. 'Freydis does not hate you as do your brothers, does she, Master? Nor does Freydis seem to hate me,' he added, his cheeks burning on recollection of the doe-eyed glances.

'True on both counts,' Bjorn agreed.

'And Freydis doesn't seem very close to her mother, nor does Aslanga display any great affection for Freydis–'

'So what does that suggest to you?'

An idea was germinating in Eadwulf's head, which he strove to nurture. As they entered the hall, harvest time suddenly arrived. 'I think Freydis is not only your half-sister, but that Aslanga is not *her* mother either.'

Bjorn grinned and Eadwulf propped the bow against the wall. Sigehelm glanced up from his usual corner, concern draining from his face. Ragnar acknowledged his son's arrival with a mere nod as he ate, seemingly ignorant of the chase across the heath. Thora's face lit up at the sight of them and she dropped the ladle into the stew, hastening towards them with her arms wide. But Ragnar loomed before her, pulling her to him, squeezing her buttocks and whispering something that made her giggle.

'It seems Ragnar's grown tired of Aslanga's bony frame and razor-sharp tongue,' Bjorn murmured. 'It's been years since he bedded his concubine.'

Discovering that Thora was Ragnar's concubine was somehow not much of a surprise to Eadwulf: Thora had almost told him as much herself. But his next thought caught him totally unawares. 'You must think me quite simple for not realising that Thora is Freydis's mother.'

'Oh, I don't believe you to be simple, Eadwulf,' Bjorn smirked, sitting at a table. I knew you'd catch on eventually; the likeness between them is quite uncanny. And Freydis has Thora's knack with plants and herbs, and squirmy things that live in the soil!'

Eadwulf's mind was racing. 'Master, who was it told you about ...this morning?'

'It was Thora who roused me from my comfortable slumbers with Ingrid,' Bjorn replied, straight-faced. 'And you've Freydis to thank for alerting Thora. She saw Halfdan waking you and followed you out; saw and heard everything from behind the byre. It was a plucky thing to do,' he said, his smile revealing his fondness for his sister, 'considering the hound could have easily given her away. But I suppose the beast would have been focused on you at the time. Perhaps you should thank Freydis yourself.'

'How could I not? I owe her so much.'

'A bowl of that stew is needed for both of us, if you'd fetch it, Eadwulf. Thora's unlikely to disentangle herself for some time.'

Eadwulf ladled out the meaty stew, wondering what lies Aslanga's evil sons were presently telling her and his heartbeat quickened.

But he glanced at Bjorn and knew that everything would be all right.

Sixteen

Wessex: mid-March 853

A strong south-westerly picked up as the day progressed, pummelling the troop of thirty-strong Mercians and making the already arduous journey even more uncomfortable. Horses, too, were tiring; they'd been pushed hard today, and by mid-afternoon on the second day of travel, Burgred's patience was wearing thin.

'Damnable Welsh,' he muttered under his breath. If not for them he'd have had no cause to leave Shrewsbury and go grovelling to that old goat Aethelwulf again. But Mercian forces alone had little hope of defeating the cursed Welsh. He glowered at the churning black clouds that threatened to burst at any moment. But, rain or no rain, he'd not be stopping before he reached the Wessex Court.

'We'll be soaked before we even make sight of Chippenham, my lord.' The young thegn waited for Burgred's response, but when none ensued he ventured, 'There's a small village through those trees over there. Perhaps we could take shelter until the rain passes.'

'But it may not pass over today, Godric, and we haven't the time to waste. Do you think the Welsh will wait patiently for our return before they wreak further havoc in Mercia?'

Chastened, Godric held his tongue and drew back his horse.

Burgred loathed the wind. Rain he could cope with – but

wind seemed to penetrate to his very core, exposing the enormity of his sins. His own self-loathing constantly festered and only throwing himself into his duties as king could prevent the sickness from utterly destroying him. Vivid nightmares refused to sanction peaceful sleep. Morwenna's appalled expression on realising he'd betrayed them – *the people who loved him most* – hovered before him in his dream state, causing him to weep afresh. And the contempt in her eyes bored into the very depths of his being. But worst of all, the nightmares invariably ended with Beorhtwulf's damning proclamation: '*You'll burn in the fires of hell for all eternity*!'

He urged his sorrel into a canter. By his own reckoning they had another three hours in the saddle before they reached Aethelwulf's Court. But dead horses would be of little use and they'd soon need to slow to a trot and eventually, a slower walk.

He cursed again as the first cold raindrops spattered his face.

* * *

The arrival of the Mercians at Chippenham took the West Saxons by surprise. The blanket of low cloud had brought an early dusk and servants scuttled about the hall in the light of oil lamps, piqued that extra food would now need preparing. Aethelwulf received the message of Burgred's arrival with unaccustomed irritation as he sat with his wife in their bedchamber. Osburh had not risen today.

'Guests are the last thing we need whilst you're so unwell,' he said with a sigh, noting how cold she felt as he took her hand, and how bruised the skin beneath her eyes. His wife had been ill for so long, though his physicians declared there to be no real sickness to treat. Osburh was simply ageing and needed rest. Aethelwulf had no reason to doubt their wisdom: there were few signs of her once lustrous dark hair amidst the grey. In truth, Osburh had been weak since the birth of Alfred over three years since.

Osburh squeezed his hand, a sensation he'd always found comforting. 'I'll call Edith to help me dress,' she said. 'I cannot greet our guests in my night-gown. We must show them Saxon hospitality–'

'There's no need for you to put further strain on yourself,' Aethelwulf said, staying her hand as she made to push back the furs. 'I want you well again, and the only way you can regain your strength is by resting. I'll see that Edith attends you here and your meal will be brought to you when it's ready.' He embraced his wife, dismayed at the feel of her emaciated frame. 'And Edith will tell me if you don't eat it. And I mean *all* of it!'

'Yes, my lord,' Osburh replied with a feeble laugh. 'I shall eat every morsel.'

'And don't think to feed any to the dogs,' he ordered, grinning as he wagged a finger at her, responding to her light-hearted mood: he'd rarely heard his wife's laughter of late. 'As to our guests, Aethelswith can organise the meal tonight. She must prepare for the day she'll be running her own household. It's time she stopped pining over Cynric and moved on.'

Osburh nodded, though her eyes reflected deep concern. 'Be gentle with her, Aethelwulf. Our daughter felt Cynric's loss more deeply than you could know. But I believe she's finally accepted the need to wed another.'

'Then I'll keep my eyes open on that score. But now, I imagine our guests will be in dire need of refreshment. I can only assume Burgred's visit is of some importance for him to have continued on the road in this weather.

'And don't let young Alfred disturb you tonight,' he said, turning as he reached the door. 'You can't rest if he's jumping all over you. One of the young nurses can stay with him while Edith's here with you. Nelda perhaps? I know what you're thinking,' he added at his wife's sceptical grin. 'I, too, hope she can cope.'

* * *

Burgred and his retinue traipsed into the West Saxon hall, their long faces displaying their fatigue and discomfort in dripping wet clothes. Grooms had led their horses to be stabled and a servant hurried off to inform Aethelwulf of their arrival. Relieved of their sodden cloaks, they were invited to sit round the hearth and slake their thirsts with the welcoming ale.

Sitting so close to the roasting food was torment to Burgred's empty stomach and his nostrils flared unashamedly. But he basked in the blessed warmth and savoured the quenching ale as he watched the steam rise from his trouser legs. Wondering when Aethelwulf would show himself, he glanced about him. The long hall, with the rafters of its straw-thatched roof high above, was little different to most of Burgred's own in Mercia, its walls adorned with tapestries, shields and swords. The few shuttered windows were closed, the room lighted by the blazing fire and numerous oil lamps, and the rushes covering the floor were clean and sweet-smelling. Tables had already been erected and Burgred smiled, visualising himself seated at Aethelwulf's side. Desperately in need of Wessex aid, he'd swallow his pride and admit to Mercia's inability to deal with the Welsh alone, stress the need for unity between their kingdoms during these turbulent times.

Servants lifted hares and game birds from around the hearth, piling them onto the waiting platters. Though no spitted boar was offered – Burgred's arrival had been too late to forewarn the cooks – meat seemed plentiful. Trays of round loaves were carried in from the kitchens and, at the side of the hall, a table was being laden with cheeses and fruits; ale casks rolled into place beside it.

The woman ordering the servants had her back to Burgred, but he noted that her pale yellow overdress, finely embroidered with gold thread, was that of a noblewoman. Her hair hung down her back, as was customary for unmarried women, its hue almost matching that of her dress. As she turned, Burgred was transfixed by her beauty, and how her flawless skin, surrounded by its cascade of gold, glowed in the firelight. Aethelswith – yes, that was her name – Aethelwulf's only daughter. Burgred felt a rush of pleasure as he caught her eye and she smiled. Not the shy smile of two years ago but that of a self-assured young woman of perhaps fifteen or sixteen.

'My lord,' Aethelswith said, offering her hand as she came to greet him, flashing a smile so bright Burgred felt that sunrise had arrived many hours prematurely. 'I trust you've been made comfortable and provided with adequate refreshment? It is a wicked day for travel and the hour is late; you must be weary to the bone and quite ravenous. I can see from your persons you are saturated through.' She laughed, looking pointedly at Burgred's steaming legs before gesturing to the hooks around the walls. 'Your cloaks will dry overnight in here – but we must hope that none of you catch a chill.'

Burgred relished the touch of her smooth, slender hand and could hardly take his eyes from her face as he thanked her for her kind welcome. Rarely had he seen such natural beauty, which shone brighter than a thousand sparkling gems.

'Our meal will be served as soon as Father joins us,' Aethelswith assured him, her bright eyes suddenly clouding. 'He sits with Mother for hours these days. She has suffered ill health for so long, and is in our prayers constantly ... Forgive me, my lord,' she said, her cheeks flushing. 'I should not burden you with our worries. I simply intended to inform you that Mother will not be joining us in the hall; she takes many of her meals in her chamber.'

She flashed another dazzling smile. 'I shall oversee the serving of the meal tonight. But now, I must leave you to enjoy your ale. I hope Father can assist you in whatever the purpose of your visit may be.'

* * *

Aethelwulf savoured his meal amidst his guests, seated between the Mercian king and two of his sons. As the meal started, Aethelwulf had sensed guardedness in Aethelbald and Aethelberht, as in his thegns, so it was with some relief that he felt their mood lightening as the meal progressed. The Mercians, too, had cheered in the warmth of the hall and their wariness appeared to be abating. Such reserve was understandable: it was not so many years since Wessex and Mercia had been the most bitter of enemies.

The Mercian king ate heartily, as expected after such a gruelling journey. That his gaze constantly followed Aethelswith did not escape Aethelwulf's notice either: few men could ignore such beauty. But eventually, his belly full and mead warming his blood, Burgred raised the issues foremost on his mind.

'I come on no mere whim, my lord.' he began, passing the mead horn along and laying his hands on the table before him. 'I would not so abuse the alliance made between us before the death of my brother. But the Welsh grow stronger with the years. Rhodri Mawr inspires unity between their kingdoms, and in that unity they find strength. So far we've been able to hold them back, though their constant raids along our borders take heavy toll on the morale of my warriors and our people, and drain our resources. I come to you as a last resort, my lord, for I know that Wessex is sorely taxed by Danish raids along her shores.'

At Aethelwulf's slow nod, Burged continued, 'Yet I know that Wessex is strong and – as Mercia's true ally – you will consider our plea for aid, knowing the value of demonstrating our unity to all would-be marauders. I merely pray that the timing is right and Wessex can presently provide a strong force to add to our own. I believe the great increase in our numbers, and the knowledge that our alliance is strong, will make Rhodri Mawr think carefully about his designs on our lands.'

Aethelwulf tried to read the character of this man. Those

green eyes seemed sincere; certainly more so than on the previous occasion they'd met, when he'd found it difficult not to compare the man to his upright brother. But, kingship can make a man overcome selfish desires. Perhaps Burgred had grown in spirit as his ability to lead had developed. Aethelwulf firmly believed that the Danes could only be overcome by the unification of Saxon and Angle peoples. And now it seemed a joint offensive was needed to counter the Welsh ...

By the end of the meal, orders were issued to be dispatched to Aethelwulf's ealdormen. Without delay, armies would be mustered throughout Wessex. Burgred would return to Mercia to do likewise, and by the end of March all must be ready.

* * *

The fighting was fierce, often deep into Welsh territory, where the mountainous and heavily forested terrain favoured Welsh tactics of surprise attack and ambush. Their ingenuity impressed Aethelwulf, who had fought many battles in his time, most of them on open ground, with strategies well planned, armies well-ordered and positioned. Against the Welsh, strategies were meaningless. Aethelwulf's respect for Rhodri Mawr rose immeasurably. The Welsh were making full use of their own mountainous terrain. And why not? Aethelwulf would have done the same, had his kingdom been thus endowed.

No one could anticipate the next move of the Welsh. They were an almost invisible foe, the surveillance of unseen eyes a source of constant discomfort as they rode. Aethelwulf's men were ill at ease in unfamiliar territory, facing an enemy whose unorthodox tactics left them feeling much too vulnerable. No one knew where the bastards were until ungodly shrieks rang out from behind some rocky outcrop or forested slope. Many a night-time raid resulted in loss of Saxon lives, horses, and provisions.

But on open ground the Welsh were no match for the well-ordered forces of Saxons and Mercians, nor were the Welsh prepared for the vast array of men that faced them. By mid-April the Welsh had retreated into the mountains, though undoubtedly that was a temporary measure. But Aethelwulf felt the offensive had served its purpose: the Welsh had suffered immeasurable losses and would take some time to recover. And Rhodri Mawr was now aware of Saxon and Mercian unity.

Two weeks after Aethelwulf's return to Chippenham, Burgred arrived with his retinue. Although Aethelwulf had been aware of the intended visit – Burgred had previously asked permission to do so – he had not known its exact purpose, supposing it to be simply a sign of the growing unity between the two kingdoms. Yet he found he was not too greatly surprised by Burgred's proposal regarding how that unity could be even further fortified.

Seventeen

Chippenham: late May 853

The bells of Saint Cuthburga's church pealed their jubilation for all to hear, proclaiming the marriage of a beloved daughter of Wessex to a most eminent son of Mercia. Noble families from across the two kingdoms had come to bear witness to the union and celebrate with the royal couple at the sumptuous feast that would signify the start of their new life together.

Aethelswith listened to the bells, knowing she could not have looked more fetching. How could she not, after the hours of preparation she'd endured at the hands of Edith and her own closest friends, her maids of honour? Even her mother, though overly pale and weak, had fussed over her, and Edith had brushed her hair for so long she could feel her scalp tingling. Now she was ready to leave for the church, where her family and guests awaited her arrival.

And Burgred.

Aethelswith's four maids of honour, all unwed daughters of Wessex noblemen and of similar age to herself, perched on stools at the side of the bower, pretending not to watch her. Anxiety must be etched into her face. She gazed at the lovely flowers on the table, knowing that Edith had spent so long arranging them into such an exquisite bouquet. All she had to do now was lift them up ...

She bent to inhale their fragrance, the delicate scents causing a multitude of memories to surface. The spring had always filled her with such joy. The emergence of new life, and the blossoming flowers that painted the grey with magical colours, lifted her spirits and made her thank God she was alive. But today, thoughts of new beginnings filled her with dread; today she'd bid farewell to a life in which love and security were certainties, to begin a life with a man she hardly knew.

The wedding had been arranged so quickly, barely leaving her time to think about it. Burgred had paid the bride price, the terms of their marriage had been agreed and their betrothal announced a few weeks since. All that remained to complete the marriage was the Gift – the ceremony at which she would be given to the bridegroom. And by tomorrow morning the marriage would have been consummated – a thought that filled her with dread – and Burgred would have presented her with the morning gift. Not even the prospect of a generous gift of land and manors, or considerable coin, afforded her consolation. The thought of leaving her parents' home caused her stomach to lurch and she wrestled the urge to run to her father and beseech, *Please don't make me do this*! *Let me stay with you in Wessex*!

Edith, too, was watching her. Edith knew; Edith *always* knew how people felt. As the rotund nurse slipped a comforting arm around her waist, Aethelswith almost collapsed sobbing into her familiar embrace.

'Put on your bravest face today, Lady Aethelswith,' Edith whispered into her ear with a glance at the waiting maids. 'I know how you're feeling; you can't hide your unhappiness from your old nurse.'

Edith placed her capable hands on Aethelswith's shoulders

and turned her until their eyes met. 'Your parents believe you to be truly over Cynric. No, do not confirm or deny that, my lady,' she continued, raising a finger to Aethelswith's parting lips. 'What matters now is that you face your future with dignity and resignation to what must be. Though you do not love King Burgred, let your mind and body at least try to welcome him in. Love may grow, given time.' She shook her head sadly. 'Your marriage is doomed before it starts if you do not.'

Aethelswith took a steadying breath. She would never forget Cynric and would rather live her life as a maid than marry another. But, for a king's daughter to remain unwed was not to be. And Edith had spoken the truth: her future happiness was already jeopardized unless she showed some affection towards Burgred. 'You know I'll do my duty to Wessex, Edith,' she whispered, attempting a smile. 'That Father believes Burgred will provide me with a secure home cannot be questioned. But...' she paused, gnawing her bottom lip, 'I wonder whether he's allowed the opportunity of establishing this alliance to cloud his judgement.

'Oh Edith, I don't even know whether I like Burgred, let alone love him!' She stifled a half-formed sob, feeling ashamed of wallowing in self-pity. 'And Alfred – what is to be made of my little brother's behaviour?'

'He's but a small child, my lady, and does not take well to strangers. And no doubt he frets that Burgred will take you from him.'

Aethelswith shook her head. 'That he'll miss me may well be – and God alone knows how much I'll miss him – but it's more than that. You know full well that Alfred's never been shy of strangers; he sees enough of them, after all. Yet he took an instant dislike to Burgred, refusing to respond to any attempts at establishing friendship. And it's disconcerting the way he stares into Burged's eyes, as though he's boring into his very soul.' Aethelswith shuddered, but did not pursue the point. 'But your advice, as always, is sound, Edith. I'll not let you all down. Am I not a daughter of Wessex?'

'That you are, my lady, and I applaud your courage. I'd give you such a big hug if not for fear of crushing your lovely gown. Now, I believe you are ready.'

Aethelswith could delay no longer. She scooped up the beautiful flowers and her maids fell into pairs to lead her from the bower. And with a fine, military escort of six of Aethelwulf's finest warriors and the joyful tolling of bells, the bridal party walked sedately towards the church.

The sight of the pretty church always had a deeply calming effect on Aethelswith and she gazed lovingly at it as she approached, remembering the many times she'd joined her family at worship inside its solid walls. Built almost two hundred years ago during one of the few periods when Saxons and Mercians were not contesting ownership of the region, it had originally been a wooden structure, rebuilt years later in blocks of the creamy stone quarried not too far away. The western side comprised the sturdy, squat tower, and in the centre was the nave. The chancel harbouring the sanctuary and altar formed the eastern side, where Father Godwine would be now, praying for the welfare of the couple about to be wed.

The guests crowding around the porticus parted and Aethelswith envisaged the packed scene that would greet her inside.

This *should* be the happiest day of her life, but the words of that old rhyme refused to budge from inside her head:

Marry in the month of May and live to rue the day.

Gritting her teeth, she walked through the church door for the last time as an unmarried woman.

* * *

Surrounded by guests in their finest apparel, Aethelwulf waited in the high-ceilinged nave for the ceremony to begin. He gazed proudly at his beautiful daughter who had taken her place in the centre of the guests, her head modestly downcast, rendering it impossible for him to see her face, the emotions emanating from her clear, blue eyes. Circling her golden hair was a garland of intertwined green foliage interspersed with vibrant spring flowers. Her long-sleeved underdress of pale-blue linen adorned her slender figure down to her ankles, complemented by the darker cerulean of her calf-length overdress of heavier weave, the sleeves of which flared at the elbows to reveal a silken lining of still deeper blue. A multihued, tablet-woven trim decorated the scooped necklines and lower hems of both garments, matching the belt wrapped twice around her waist, knotted loosely at the front to leave the long ends hanging free. In her arms she held a glorious arrangement of colourful May blossoms. Aethelswith did not need bright jewels to look truly radiant.

Beside her Burgred stood erect, his richly ornamented attire indicative of his status. His dark green tunic was shaped by a black leather belt studded with rubies that matched the crimson wool of his cloak, the cloak itself lined with emerald green silk and held at his right shoulder by a brooch of elaborate gold strands. His golden crown displayed a solitary large ruby at that front. Aethelwulf felt the sudden need to adjust his own splendid crown. Although his attire was rich and well adorned, he felt quite drab compared to this bright Mercian peacock. But of more importance, for all his sparkle, Burgred did not outshine Aethelwulf's lovely daughter.

Burgred, the man to whom Aethelwulf would entrust the welfare and happiness of his beloved child, was still an enigma to him. He prayed daily that his doubts were unfounded; that Aethelswith would find happiness with this man, and her new status as Queen of Mercia. But, Aethelwulf had no doubt that forming a marriage alliance between Wessex and Mercia was an invaluable move.

At Aethelwulf's side, Osburh strove to appear well and hearty, but her gaunt frame could not be disguised. Her pale green overdress hung far too loosely from her shoulders, and beads of perspiration glistened on her forehead. The effort of standing for so long was taking its toll, but she masked her occasional lurch into his side with a squeeze of his arm and murmured praises of their daughter and her husband to be.

Behind them, all but the youngest of their sons displayed joviality on their sister's special day, at ease amongst the many notable guests. Aethelbald, the eldest since Aethelstan's death two years ago, acknowledged his father's attention with a smile, his dark beard and thick-set features lending him a handsome ruggedness. Aethelberht, too, grinned cheerfully, his gaudy apparel and ornamentation compensating for his wispy fair hair and sparse beard. Thirteen-year-old Aethelred's dark blond hair flicked about his face as his head turned this way and that to find some spectacle to provide amusement.

Only Alfred did not smile.

Tiny at Aethelbald's side and held firmly in his place by his tall brother's restraining hand, Alfred glared at the Mercian king. Aethelwulf frowned. Was the boy's behaviour simply a reaction to the thought of losing his sister, or something else? Could Alfred see something in Burgred that so eluded himself?

Guests murmured to each other as they waited for the priest to appear and indicate the need for silence. Eventually the clear tones of the choirboys drifted from the chancel, filling the nave with an air of beauty and solemnity. Father Godwine glided towards the bridal couple, his flowing robes sweeping the rushes of the earthen floor, his hands steepled, his head reverently bowed. Then, peering at the congregation until not a sound could be heard, he ushered the couple to the church doorway to make the customary vows.

Burgred took Aethelswith's left hand in his own and placed the gold wedding band on her fourth finger. Gazing into her eyes he made his vows, his voice clear and unfaltering: 'I, Burgred of Mercia, do take you, Aethelswith of Wessex as my wife. I will love you with my heart and protect you from harm. Never will you want for household comforts, nor feel the pangs of hunger. In the eyes of God, you will be my queen and mother of my children, and be recognized as such by our Mercian people.'

Aethelswith twisted the unfamiliar ring on her finger and glanced anxiously round the nave until her attention settled on Aethelwulf. The maelstrom of emotions raging in her eyes struck him like a surging tide: loss and desperation eddied with panic and fear; she was a sinking ship, abandoned by those she loved most. Aethelwulf was engulfed by an intense sense of guilt. If only he'd paid heed to his qualms, looked deeper into the character of the man he was giving his precious daughter to, allowed more time for the betrothal ...

Aethelswith's eyes momentarily closed and the calm waters of resignation returned. She turned and flashed a smile at Burgred, her eyes locked again with his and she made her vows, her dulcet tones carrying to the whole congregation: 'I, Aethelswith of Wessex, do promise to serve you, Burgred of Mercia. I shall be a loyal and caring wife, ensuring that your domestic comforts are met wherever the Mercian court may journey. Never shall I cause harm, or bring dishonour to your family. I will be a loving mother to our children, if we are so blessed.'

Aethelswith's cheeks burned red and Burgred embarrassed her still further by grinning in amusement. Father Godwine blessed the ring, his mellow tones reverberating around the nave, and as Burgred enfolded Aethelswith in his arms for the marriage kiss, the choir once again lifted its voice in song. The couple then walked into the warmth of the May sunshine as man and wife.

* * *

Alfred wove unnoticed through the forest of legs outside the church, heading towards his sleeping chamber where he could be alone for a while before hunger drove him to seek out Edith. He'd left the church with his father's permission and to Aethelbald's obvious relief, with instructions to go straight to either Edith or Nelda. His father had reluctantly agreed that Alfred would be better with his nurses than scowling throughout the wedding breakfast.

Alfred had not meant to scowl, had not wanted to spoil his sister's day. But his mind was in turmoil. The Mercian king was virtually a stranger to him, yet his thoughts were full of *bad things* about the man. That Burgred was taking his sister far away from him was enough to earn Alfred's dislike, but these upsetting thoughts caused him to detest the man.

Alfred found it all too perplexing. He entered his room, hoping that none of the servants would disturb him. He had much to contemplate.

Eighteen

Wilton, Wiltshire: late April 854

Aethelwulf rose with some difficulty, wincing as pains shot through his creaking knees, and rolled his shoulders, attempting to bring his muscles back to life. He was cold and stiff, but the calming effect of prayer had served its purpose: his mind had been freed to function with greater clarity, see solutions to problems which before had seemed insurmountable. He left the solemnity of the wood-planked church, now certain his decision was the right one.

Wishing to extend his solitude, he strode towards the river, watching the raindrops of an April shower dancing on its silvery surface. Along the banks, alders and willows were coming into leaf, their catkins still prominent on their branches. Nesting birds flew to and fro. He drank in the morning air, mulling over the issues to be presented at the Assembly. He jerked his cloak more closely round his shoulders, not wishing to address his nobles in a saturated tunic, and adjusted his simple crown, ensuring the small emerald was at the front.

'It is a most peaceful view, is it not, my lord?'

Deep in thought Aethelwulf had not heard anyone approaching. 'Indeed it is, Theomund,' he replied, noting that the quiet young Wiltshire reeve had taken special care with his attire for the coming meeting, his brown hair well groomed, moustache and beard neatly trimmed. 'The sound of running water has such a soothing effect, allowing the mind to concentrate on perplexing issues.'

A proud smile lit the reeve's face. 'It does, my lord, and the Wylye is also of great value to our manor. Trout and grayling are plentiful, salmon favour its waters for breeding, and we have eel traps a little downstream. If you stand here long enough, you'll likely see an otter or two, mayhap with their cubs at this time of year...' His cheeks suddenly flushed. 'I pray my boastfulness does not offend you, my lord.'

Aethelwulf patted his rapidly dampening hair and smiled at the anxious face. 'Not at all, Theomund; it's good to hear a man praising his own home. The Wylye is a delightful river and Wilton is one of my favourite manors. My wife is very fond of it, too. Your hospitality and generous table do you credit.'

'Well, speaking of food, my lord, the servants are ready to serve the morning meal. The guests are assembled and Lady Osburh has joined your sons at table.'

They strolled amicably back to the hall, the April shower already diminishing. 'It's a pleasure to see Lady Osburh looking so much improved,' Theomund remarked. 'She seems greatly relieved to see Alfred safely home, and happy to have celebrated Eastertide with most of her family.'

Aethelwulf nodded. 'The Easter services did Father Eldwyn proud, Theomund, considering the attendance of so many eminent members of the kingdom's clergy. Although the rebuilding of the church in stone is sorely needed,' he added with a raised eyebrow. 'Later this year, perhaps?'

'We anticipate the arrival of the stonemasons in June, my lord.'

'That is good news.'

They halted as Aethelwulf silently appraised the dilapidated condition of the old wooden church. 'We need to rebuild all our churches in stone,' he declared, punching his palm to stress his point. 'We've only to see how all those Roman structures have survived the ravages of time, some of them for well over five hundred years. Whereas our own ... No matter how sturdy the timber, wooden buildings are susceptible to rot, not to mention fire.

'And you're right about Lady Osburh,' Aethelwulf acknowledged Theomund's previous observation as they reached the hall. 'She's never happier than when amidst her brood. Alfred's absence has been a great trial for her, and Aethelstan's death three years ago did her health no favours. Now it's Aethelswith she frets about. Our daughter is seven months with child and Osburh constantly whittles over whether her new nurses are taking adequate care of her. If Edith were a few years younger, I do believe my wife would send her off to Burgred's Court!

'Now, let's enjoy our meal,' he said, as Theomund held open the hall's heavy oak door for him to enter. 'We'll not see daylight again until this meeting's over.'

* * *

From the centre of the raised dais Aethelwulf surveyed the gathering of some of the elite of Wessex, the hum of conversation filling the hall with expectancy and speculation. Most of the tables had been stacked away and nobles were seated along benches set in an open-ended rectangle around the firepit, all traces of April chill banished by the orange flames that crackled and spat as they devoured the hefty logs.

The reason for this gathering was ostensibly twofold, although Aethelwulf also intended to conduct further business, linked to a decision he'd made which would surprise some important people, perhaps anger others. The first reason – simply to attend the Easter services and honour the significance of Christ's Passion – had passed with the reverence the occasion merited. Now, two days later, it was time to attend to the second reason.

Alfred had recently arrived home.

Safe and well after almost a year of travelling across the continent to Rome, and conversing with the pontiff himself, Alfred, who had reached his fifth birthday on the journey home, was bursting with news. Unsettling tales had circulated of events that had supposedly occurred in Rome – and the magnates of Wessex required verification of those tales, and the implications they carried for Wessex.

At Aethelwulf's sides, his four sons remained silent. Suitably garbed in fine quality tunics, they were a sight to make their father proud. To his right, the two eldest nodded affably to anyone who caught their eye. At twenty and nineteen respectively, Aethelbald and Aethelberht were well aware of courtly procedure. Glancing to his left, Aethelwulf noted Alfred's calm appraisal of the gathering, unlike fourteen-year-old Aethelred, who'd already begun to shuffle. At Aethelred's far side, Osric whispered a friendly word of warning in his nephew's ear.

Aethelwulf nodded thanks to his brother-by-marriage. Though his hair was now liberally streaked with grey, Osric was still a handsome man. It had taken him a long time to get over the loss of his only son, though he'd held no one responsible for Cynric's death, accepting that a warrior's life was one of daily risks.

Also on the dais, Bishops Swithun and Ealhstan waited sedately next to Aethelberht, both attired in simpler garments than the elaborate vestments displayed during the Easter services. The frail Swithun, once Aethelwulf's mentor and spiritual advisor and now Bishop of Winchester, little resembled the robust man whose boundless energy had once inspired so many. He wore his usual white alb with a simple cross around his neck and a white cap covering what remained of his iron-grey hair. In sharp contrast, Bishop Ealhstan of Sherborne, Swithun's contemporary in years, had borne the passage of time with greater success, the slight salting of his dark hair only apparent at close quarters. His physique was still strong and well-muscled; Ealhstan had always been more warrior than cleric. He'd fought several battles against the Norsemen over the years and led Egbert's army alongside Aethelwulf to conquer Kent twenty-five years ago. In a crimson tunic, the only indication of Ealhstan's holy office was a ruby-studded cross around his neck and the faintest suggestion of a tonsure in his collar-length hair.

Content that all were ready to begin, Aethelwulf glanced at his scribe perched at a side table. Father Felix signalled his readiness to record the events of the meeting and Aethelwulf cleared his throat.

He welcomed the assembled, paying compliments to Theomund's hospitality and Father Eldwyn's Easter services before drawing attention to the sun-kissed boy at his side. 'I realise that some amongst you fail to see the sense in sending a young child on such a journey,' he admitted. 'But I tell you, my decision to do so was not made lightly. We live in perilous times. The Danes attack our shores with increasing frequency, only last year over-wintering again on Thanet. Moreover, last year our armies were called upon to assist Mercia against the Welsh. You will realise, therefore, why I was reluctant to lose my eldest sons at that time.

'You may ask why I should send anyone at all to Rome. Our learned clerics will doubtless understand my reasons,' he added, gesturing to the two bishops. 'I am convinced that the raids are God's punishment of us.' He noted many sceptical expressions, and several amused ones, as he'd expected: few men were as committed to their faith as he. 'Our halls have too often become places of degenerate conduct; excessive intake of mead can lead the best of warriors away from God. I fear the only person who can help us now is Pope Leo. Having received Alfred, I believe he will add his voice to our own in seeking God's forgiveness.'

One or two men cleared their throats as though to comment, but nothing ensued. 'I'm aware you are all eager to question my young son about his experiences,' Aethelwulf went on, 'but I urge you to remember that he is just that: young. However, I feel sure that Alfred will answer your questions with a dexterity that may seem unusual at such a tender age. If need be, I will assist with answers to any questions too complex for him to comprehend. But other than such instances, I shall leave Alfred to reply to your queries.'

Aethelwulf seated himself, patting Alfred's arm as he rose to his feet.

'Well, young man,' Swithun started, focusing kindly nut-brown eyes on Alfred. 'You are truly fortunate to have been able to undertake such a remarkable journey.' He held out his bony hands. 'Tell us what you found the most interesting about it.'

Alfred's amber eyes widened. 'I enjoyed every part of it, my lord, even the journeys there and back! And King Charles gave us a huge army to guard us through his land. The soldiers were very friendly, and told me riddles that made me laugh. We went through really dark forests, but I wasn't scared because our men kept a lookout for bears and wolves – and even robbers. And the Alps have snow on top of them, even in the summer.

'But what I liked best of all was the city of Rome.'

'Then pray tell us what was so intriguing about it.'

Alfred faced the scowling Bishop Ealhstan, his owl-bright eyes narrowing. 'I was just going to tell everyone about the wonderful things in Rome, my lord.'

Ealhstan shuffled, breaking eye contact, and Alfred's attentions shifted to those seated below the dais. 'The city is such a busy place,' he said, his high spirits returning. 'There are people everywhere ...and lots of stalls along the streets–'

'Can you remember, Alfred, whether the buildings are made of wood, like our own, or stone?' Swithun asked before Ealhstan regained sufficient composure to voice a question that seemed to be gnawing at him.

Alfred's small brow creased in thought. 'Most of the houses are made of stone, I think. Some are so old they're falling down! And some of their roads are made of cob ...cobblestones.' He glanced at Aethelwulf, who nodded to assure him he'd used the right word. 'I saw lots of big churches which are always full of people, and,' he added, his eyes opening wide, 'most of them have really interesting relics. Some are so old I couldn't tell what they were.'

Bishop Ealhstan coughed, patently intending to stop Alfred's ramblings. 'Tell us, Alfred, when you were confirmed by His Holiness, what exactly did he say to you?'

Aethelwulf examined his hands, knowing that the answer to that question would need to be phrased extremely tactfully. But he'd declared he would not interrupt unless so asked. And Alfred didn't ask; he simply answered the question in his usual direct and honest manner:

'Well, Pope Leo said I was his son, so I would now have *two* fathers! Then he said some strange words about wearing the vestments of the con ...consulate.' His nose wrinkled at that idea, and he gave a small shrug as he gazed round at the rapt faces.

'Then he put some funny-smelling oils on me and made me king.'

The communal intake of breath was followed by silence. That single snippet of information was what had kept Wessex nobility speculating for days. All eyes focused on Aethelwulf in anticipation of explanation, but Ealhstan voiced his questions first. 'Just what do you think His Eminence meant by that, Alfred? You are *not* king, are you?'

'No, I am not king now, my lord. But I know I shall be when I'm a man.'

'Then you'll probably need to live to be a hundred or more,' Ealhstan sneered. 'Look to your sides, Alfred. Your father is still king of Wessex, and after him, Aethelbald, Aethelberht and

Aethelred will each take the throne before you. And should King Aethelwulf, and then Aethelbald, live good, long lives, even Aethelberht may never become king. So why–'

'My Lord Bishop!' Aethelwulf barked, launching himself to his feet. I particularly requested that you show consideration of my son's age!'

Ealhstan bristled at the reprimand and opened his mouth to protest. But Aethelwulf cut him short. 'Is it not perceivable that a child of merely four years should feel overawed, and more than a little confused, amidst such pomp – and in the presence of so holy a man as the pope? Alfred has clearly confused the meaning of consulship with that of kingship.' He held out his hands and feigned amusement. 'How many here could say they fully understand the place of a consul in the society of bygone Rome?' Pleased to see many shaking heads he continued, "Then how much less would a young boy comprehend the meaning of being anointed to the consulship? The phrase refers to an outdated ceremony, intended only to show respect to the person on whom the honour is bestowed.'

Aethelwulf ignored Alfred's indignant scowl, knowing full well that the child had recalled the pope's words quite accurately. But to stress his point and quell subsequent unrest, he could not afford further contributions from his son.

'I have received written confirmation from His Holiness regarding Alfred's reception in Rome,' Aethelwulf stated. 'As a royal son of Wessex, Alfred enjoyed a generous welcome in the Eternal City, and I have no doubt that his education in both spiritual and secular matters has benefited from the experience. Regarding Alfred's confirmation, Pope Leo describes the ceremony as I have already done; it is customary to garb eminent visitors in the vestments of the consulate.'

Carefully, he unfolded a piece of vellum and held it up. 'This missive will be made available to anyone who wishes to read it. But I ask that it is treated with respect: it is precious not only to me, but to Wessex. It explains that Alfred was received by Pope Leo as a spiritual son, which means that, from henceforth, not only will the pontiff take particular interest in Alfred's welfare, but Wessex will be recognised as a Christian kingdom, devoted to the Holy See, as are our Frankish neighbours across the Northern Sea.'

There seemed little left to say regarding Alfred's visit to Rome and no questions were forthcoming. Even Ealhstan appeared satisfied that a child had not come home as king. Only Alfred seemed somewhat put out. But there were more important issues on Aethelwulf's agenda than a child's recollections of Rome. And flattery seemed to be the best way to introduce them.

'Around this hall, I see some of my loyal followers,' he started. 'Still others have been unable to attend this gathering. No matter; they have not been forgotten. My gratitude will extend to all who have served our kingdom well for many years.'

Wessex notables were used to gift-giving by their kings – grants of land being the usual way of rewarding faithful service – and faces told of hopes for generous acquisitions.

'It is my wish to honour some of you with gifts of bookland,' he explained. 'I intend to issue a general privilege of one tenth of royal demesne to the Church. From henceforth this tithe will be freed from all monetary obligations to the Crown: food rents, for example will cease. Naturally some responsibilities will remain the same, including military service, the amassing of the fyrd, bridge construction, and the building and repair of fortresses.

'I also intend the recipients of this privilege to include some members of the secular nobility,' Aethelwulf continued. 'Once the land is granted you may issue some portion of it to the Church, should you so wish – for example, as payment for masses to be said for your soul after your death. Whatever you decide, the land grants should benefit many of you financially, and perhaps spiritually. The charters, or "books", as we know them, will be drawn up by Father Felix, subject to the usual conditions,' he added as all eyes turned towards Aethelwulf's secretary.

Felix read out the long list of beneficiaries whilst Aethelwulf prepared to present the final issue on his agenda. His most loyal nobles had been rewarded, including his brother by marriage, Osric. He hoped the flattery would serve its purpose: their gratitude would render them amenable to his decision.

He mulled over his well-made plans. In a year's time he would journey to Rome: something he'd promised himself since the day he was crowned. Now he was ageing and had no time to delay. He must entreat the pope to offer God the repentance of Wessex for its sins. Opposition would undoubtedly focus on concern over who would rule the kingdom in his absence. He would propose the simplest of solutions: his two eldest sons would rule it between them. Aethelbald would take the greater part of Wessex, and Aethelberht the eastern shires, where, until two years ago, Aethelstan had presided as under-king.

Aethelwulf stepped forward, the movement silencing the hall. He glanced behind at his sons, for whose futures his every important decision had been made. As yet, Alfred was ignorant of Aethelwulf's plans for the following year, plans made long before the boy's return this Easter.

Alfred would make a second trip to the Holy City, to accompany his father.

Nineteen

Winchester: early January 855

On a cold and snow-brushed evening during the week following the twelve days of Christmas, Lady Osburh passed away peacefully in her bed. The lengthy illness had drained every modicum of her strength, rendering her so frail it seemed a puff of wind could blow her away. Aethelwulf had seldom left her bedside for days and the physician had been in constant attendance, although Osburh had rarely woken from her exhausted sleep. Bishop Swithun had shriven her and, surrounded by the family she loved so much, she had drawn her last breath.

Too choked to speak or even rise from where he'd slumped across Osburh's lifeless form, Aethelwulf gestured with a flick of his wrist that all should leave him alone with his wife.

Aethelswith's own overwhelming grief mingled with concern for her father and youngest brother. Alfred had not experienced death on such a personal level during the five years of his life and tears flooded down his face. So whilst others retired to the hall with Bishop Swithun, Aethelswith took Alfred's hand and led him to the sleeping chamber he shared with Aethelred beyond the hall. On the edge of the bed she sat him on her lap, stroking his head as he sobbed into her shoulder, his tears soaking the fine wool of her gown.

'Why did she have to die?' he wailed. 'Mother was always so good: God had no need to punish her.'

'No, He did not, Alfred,' Aethelswith agreed, struggling to

find words to explain the inevitability of death to so young a child. 'And you must never think He did. Death seldom comes as a punishment, sweet one.'

"Then why does Father believe that God has sent the Danes to kill our people as a punishment for not worshipping Him properly?'

Aethelswith tucked a wisp of hair beneath the head covering she now wore to signify her married status and nodded understanding of Alfred's question. 'But the death of people in their own homes is quite different,' she floundered, at a loss for a truly astute answer. 'We must all die eventually; no one lives forever. Some of us are fortunate enough to live good, long lives; others become ill or have accidents and die earlier than they would have hoped. Some very unfortunate people do not live past childhood. Mother was lucky enough to be granted quite a long life, well past her fortieth year. And, had illness not beset her these past few years, she may have enjoyed an even longer life, like Edith here.'

She threw a grateful smile at the old nurse who had entered with Alfred's meal: a chunk of bread with a slice of pork and a mug of goat's milk. Edith bent to lay the tray on a low bench and straightened up with a grimace. Her eyes were red and swollen with the tears she'd shed for her beloved mistress.

'We must remember that Mother had a happy life, Alfred, surrounded by people who loved her,' Aethelswith stressed, as much to comfort Edith as her young brother. 'Mother is at peace now, and would want us all to live our lives to make her proud. I'm sure we'll meet her again in Heaven, when she'll want to know about all the good things we've done.'

Alfred's sobbing breaths steadied and he seemed to mull over what she'd said. He yawned widely and Aethelswith realised just how deeply the grief had affected him.

'You must be hungry by now, young lord,' Edith said, offering him the mug of milk. 'You've eaten little all day.'

'I don't think I could manage any food,' Alfred replied, fixing apologetic eyes on Edith as he struggled to take a few sips of milk. 'My throat wouldn't open wide enough to let it through – and if it did, my stomach may throw it straight out again.'

"Then just drink the milk, Alfred,' Aethelswith said, knowing that further persuasion would be pointless. 'We'll get you settled and I'll stay with you until you nod off.

'I hope Aethelred's managed to eat something,' she said quietly to Edith. 'He was putting on a very brave face – though the face does not always reflect one's deepest feelings.'

Edith gave Aethelswith one of her most meaningful looks. 'I daresay I could name at least one other who's good at hiding their feelings, my lady. Believe me, it does no good to keep things bottled up. Problems often don't seem so bad when shared with someone you trust.'

Unshed tears glistened in Aethelswith's eyes and for some moments she stayed silent, fussing around Alfred's bed and plumping up his pillows. If she spoke, her voice would betray her and Alfred would see through her false bravado. It seemed that Edith had already done just that. She gazed at the rotund nurse perched on Alfred's bed, gently easing his nightgown over his head. Besides her parents and youngest brothers, Aethelswith loved Edith more than anyone else in the whole world.

Her throat tightened as she fought back the tears.

'Don't go back to Mercia, Aethelswith,' Alfred blurted as he settled into bed and reached his arms out to her. 'Stay at Father's court with us for ever. I know you'll be happier here.' Tears spilled down his face anew and Aethelswith sat on the edge of his bed and hugged him. If only Alfred knew how much she longed to do just that.

'*I* need you more than Burgred does,' Alfred sobbed. 'He's a man and can manage on his own: he has plenty of servants. You're my only sister and I want you here. And I don't like Burgred!'

'Oh, Alfred, if only it were possible for me to stay,' Aethelswith said, taking him by the shoulders as amber eyes searched her face. 'We can't always do what we want in life, which you will realise as you get older. But we must always honour the duties and responsibilities we are given, no matter how hard they may seem at times. And my duties lie in Mercia – with my husband.

'Try to sleep now, Alfred,' she soothed, stroking his cheek. 'I'll always love you dearly, you know that. My thoughts will rarely be away from you, and I'll try to visit more often, if I can – perhaps for a few days before you leave for Rome in the spring.'

Alfred nodded and lay down, though Aethelswith doubted her answer had greatly pacified him. Soon, his young body unwound, his features free of the agony of his loss. Aethelswith stood by his bed, listening to his rhythmic breathing for a while before turning to leave. In the solitude outside the doorway her own grief was unleashed, and her tears spilled. She swept them away and turned toward the hall. But, hearing Alfred's troubled mumblings, she slipped back into his chamber.

'I'll look after your lovely book, Mother,' Alfred murmured, his dream-voice muffled beneath the furs. 'And learn to read so well, you'll be proud of me...'

Aethelswith swallowed hard, the suffering in Alfred's voice triggering her own. A strange silence hung in the air and by the anguished expression on his face, Aethelswith was certain Alfred was still dreaming.

'Yes, I will try to be brave,' he whispered.

As will we all, Aethelswith thought, drying her eyes once again.

* * *

Later, certain that her younger brothers were asleep, Aethelswith returned to the hall to speak with Aethelbald and Aethelberht and satisfy the groanings of her own stomach. Her brothers sat by the hearth with Bishop Swithun, their cheerless murmurings affording the only sound. Servants hovered under a pall of downcast silence and Aethelwulf's thegns hunched at the tables, staring into their ale mugs. Aethelswith toyed with her food; like Alfred, she found she could barely swallow and resorted to a mug of goat's milk before sitting beside her brothers.

Arrangements for the funeral were broached, but in Aethelwulf's absence little could be achieved. Conversation lapsed into infrequent trivialities and eventually, Aethelswith retired to her own sleeping chamber. Her heart ached for Alfred, whose loss was even pervading his dreams. And Aethelswith would soon be so far away in Mercia, he wouldn't even have her to comfort him.

Mercia: her home now. The very thought caused all the unhappiness of the past two years to resurface. After her mother's funeral in four days' time, she'd have no excuse whatsoever to linger in her beloved Wessex. Burgred had returned to Tamworth at the start of the New Year and his men who'd remained to escort her home would be eager to be making a move. She must leave Alfred to deal with his grief alone and return to the husband who made her feel so inadequate. She slumped into a wicker chair, considering how astutely Alfred had assessed Burgred.

'Now, my lady, you need rest just as much as do your young brothers and should be in your bed,' Edith stated, interrupting Aethelswith's thoughts as she entered. 'Would you like anything fetching for the night – a mug of watered ale perhaps?'

'Nothing, thank you, Edith,' Aethelswith sighed. 'I am weary, but I think sleep may evade me for some time yet.'

Edith surveyed her with such understanding that Aethelswith's tears welled afresh. She had not felt such love emanating from a single soul since she'd left Wessex. Kneeling stiffly beside her, Edith's protective arms enfolded her.

'There now, my lady,' she soothed, 'no matter how bad things may seem today, there's always tomorrow. The loss of a mother is a terrible blow to a woman, but don't give up on life. There's always so much to live for, if only for the sheer joy of being alive ...

'Perhaps you'd like to unburden your problems on your old nurse. I know there's more than your mother's passing distressing you.'

Aethelswith nodded, wondering how much to say. But Edith deserved no less than the truth. 'I can't bear the thought of going back to Mercia,' she admitted as the tears flowed. 'My life's had no meaning since ...since the loss of my son.'

'I thought as much,' Edith said with a sigh. 'To have a babe stillborn is enough to break the strongest of women. But, my lady, there's always next time. Your poor, dead child is in Heaven, so do not grieve for him. But for you, life must go on, and you've shown yourself able to both conceive and carry a child. It was God's will that the babe did not breathe once he entered this world. And who are we to question the motives of Our Lord?'

'But you don't understand, Edith!' Aethelswith's fingertips ran down her wet cheeks. 'Burgred blames me for our son's death, thinks I willed it because I don't love him. God alone knows how I've tried to be a loving wife!'

'But the eyes rarely lie, my lady. Try as you may have done to be the wife Burgred wanted, your eyes would have told him he'd not captured your heart. And a man needs to know that his wife is his in mind and body.'

'But I just *can't* love Burgred,' Aethelswith whispered, taking a deep, steadying breath. 'He's not an easy man to love – not an easy man to *know*. Oh, Edith, I would have been better entering holy orders, where my soul could have sought comfort with God. But I wanted to do my duty for Wessex.'

Edith's face was soft with pity. 'Then you must assure your husband you want only to be a good wife. He must realise how much the child's death hurt you, too.'

Aethelswith hung her head, knowing the heartrending pain she felt would be reflected in her face. Then all the tortured emotions of so many months came pouring out: 'From the start Burgred has shut me out of his life, as though I don't exist,' she sobbed, 'always seeming somewhere far away, somewhere unreachable. I can't break through the stone wall he's set around himself. Sometimes he has such a haunted look on his face, seeming to be crying out for help to bear some inconsolable grief. Yet when I try to offer comfort he turns away and tells me not to be a nagging wife.'

She rose and moved to the shuttered window, uncomfortable about revealing the extent of her marital problems. But Edith would never disclose a confidence, and Aethelswith desperately needed to unburden her miseries.

'There's been no real opportunity for the two of us to speak privately since the babe's funeral,' she said quietly as she turned, lowering her gaze to focus on Edith, still kneeling by the chair. 'Burgred has blatantly shunned me and I feel shamed by it. He hasn't been to my bed once since that day. I so longed for a child to love, Edith,' she spluttered through trembling lips. 'I'm so very lonely in Mercia.'

'You *will* get through this awful time, my lady,' Edith said, rising awkwardly and proceeding to pull back the bed covers and lay out Aethelswith's nightgown. 'If only I could be with you to help you cope.' She sighed. 'But my duties are still with King Aethelwulf's family. Aethelred will be my major charge when Alfred's away in Rome. I won't have Osberht to think about then, either: he'll be with the king. I'll miss my husband – but I shan't tell *him* that,' she said, smiling at the thought of him. 'He's quite big-headed enough as it is! And I'll sorely miss that young rascal Alfred, even though I'll be able to reach my own bed earlier in his absence.'

Recalling Alfred's strange dreamlike words earlier, Aethelswith asked, 'Does my little brother often suffer from bad dreams, or talk in his sleep?'

'Well now,' the nurse replied, 'sleep has always been a problem for Alfred. Even as a babe he didn't nod off until late. And yes, he often speaks out loud. Most times the words he mutters don't make sense – they could be Greek for all I can tell! Sometimes he seems to be speaking with someone – like as not one of the family.'

'He had a conversation with Mother tonight, not long after he'd fallen asleep.'

'Understandable, after today,' Edith said, nodding sadly. 'Best not to wake him, my lady; his dreams don't seem to do him any harm. And Aethelred's such a sound sleeper it would take a whole army marching through his chamber to rouse *him*!'

Aethelswith smiled at the image as Edith glanced round the room. 'Now, your bed's all ready for you, my lady. Tomorrow will be another stressful day for everyone, with the funeral arrangements and all. Your father will need all the support we can muster. It was a godsend to have his close friend Bishop Swithun here when Lady Osburh passed away.' She cast a glance at the doorway. 'That Bishop Ealhstan would have been of no comfort to your father, whatsoever,' she whispered. 'He's not the type to offer solace to the bereaved, if you ask me, Lady Aethelswith.'

'I agree with you there,' Aethelswith replied, lowering her

voice to match Edith's. 'He's a cold natured man for a bishop. And Father told me Alfred didn't like him at all; he stared at Ealhstan and quite disconcerted him – just as he did with Burgred.'

'Try to put such thoughts from your mind, my lady. Let sleep refresh you ready for the morrow. I'll be here to see to your needs, as always.'

Alone in her bed Aethelswith listened to the wind whistling round the roof thatch, wondering whether it would bring in more snow. A heavy snowfall would mean conditions for the funeral would be difficult and uncomfortable. But it could also mean she may have to stay at Winchester for some time longer.

Twenty

Francia – Rome – Wessex: spring 855 – autumn 856

King Aethelwulf and his six-year-old son set out from Winchester on their long pilgrimage to Rome on an unseasonably cool and blustery morning in late May. Six days later, with their large entourage of bodyguards and servants appropriate for their safety and comfort, they crossed the narrow sea to the kingdom of the West Franks. Landing at Quentovic they rested overnight at the hostel of St Judoc before embarking on the journey of over a hundred and twenty miles to the Paris court of Charles the Bald. Half a dozen wagons carried many beautiful and costly gifts, mostly for Pope Leo and St Peter; others to impress the powerful Frankish king.

Aethelwulf found difficulty in containing Alfred's boundless exuberance. His son absorbed every sight, sound and smell along their lumbering route, inundating him with questions and observations until Aethelwulf silently screamed for respite. But, determined to ensure an interesting and memorable journey for Alfred, he put on a brave face, aided by a welcomed improvement in the weather.

'So we need to visit the Frankish king because you want him to help us if the Danes attack?'

Aethelwulf chortled at the bluntness of the question, glancing at Alfred as they rode at the head of the lengthy cavalcade. The verdant countryside of northern Francia was intoxicating, spring sunshine warm on his cheeks. Aethelwulf felt a rare sense of peace: this pilgrimage meant much to him – and to Wessex.

'That is true, I suppose,' he replied honestly, 'but I hope you'll keep it to yourself once we're at the Frankish court. Charles is a very important ruler – not only King of the West Franks but also a Holy Roman Emperor. It would be discourteous to pass through his kingdom without paying our respects, and the gifts will serve to convince him of our admiration and friendship.'

Alfred nodded, his face thoughtful. 'Has Charles always been bald, Father?'

Trying hard not to roar with laughter, Aethelwulf replied, 'I haven't yet met the Frankish king, Alfred, but I don't think he's at all bald. Indeed, several accounts say he's quite the opposite: rather hirsute. Which means *hairy*.'

'So why is he called 'Charles the *Bald*?'

Aethelwulf sighed, silently composing a brief and simple answer to that question. 'I'm told the title relates to a lack of *land* rather than hair,' he started. 'You see, when the emperor, Louis the Pious, died in 840, his three surviving sons were at loggerheads over who would rule Francia. Since Charles was the youngest son – as well as being the child of Louis' second wife – at first it was doubtful that he would have *any* land to rule over. But after three years of bitter civil war the empire was eventually divided between them, as Louis had wanted in the first place. The eldest son, Lothar, took the lands east of the River Rhine; Louis took the far eastern area of Bavaria, and Charles the lands west of the Rhine. Hence, Charles is the king of the *West* Franks.'

Alfred responded with a nod before resuming his scrutiny

of the landscape.

After five days of Frankish hospitality they left Paris behind, their numbers swelled by an additional body of mounted men provided by Charles to escort them to the border that separated his kingdom from that of his warring brother, Lothar. Alfred had thoroughly enjoyed the visit, having been permitted to spend the days being entertained by the emperor's eight-year-old son, who was also named Charles. Sometimes they played Frankish games that Alfred had never even heard of; at other times they explored the nearby woods and streams, under the watchful eye of a small troop of the emperor's soldiers. The two boys delighted in each other's company and, fortunately for Alfred, his new friend could converse in the Saxon tongue, albeit on a basic level.

Aethelwulf was well satisfied. The visit had been such a success that Charles had invited him to break the monotony of the journey home with another stay at his court.

As the days passed and spring ripened into summer they pressed on, south and east through Lothar's kingdom, the towering peaks of the Alps breathtaking in their splendour. At last they turned south towards Rome. On most nights they slept beneath the vast, clear skies; on others they managed to reach one of the many Christian hostels situated along the much travelled pilgrim route. But the long days in the saddle, or inside a bumpy wagon with Father Felix and the two priests, became a trial of endurance for Aethelwulf. The hot, dry air of the southern lands seemed to sear his lungs, sapping every modicum of his strength, the rutted roads causing horses to lame and playing havoc with wagon wheels. Dust from the dry tracks clogged nostrils and coated clothing, hair and sweaty skin with a layer of grime. And clouds of biting insects followed them relentlessly, determined for a taste of blood.

So it was with immense relief in late July that Aethelwulf saw the towering wall of the Leonine City. Named after the pope responsible for its construction, the wall enclosed a suburb of Rome on the right bank of the Tiber; the opposite side to the ancient city on the Seven Hills inside the old Aurelian Wall built nearly six hundred years ago. The Leonine City included the Basilica of St Peter's and the pope's residence, the Lateran Palace. Several churches, convents and pilgrim hostels for Saxons, Franks, Lombards and Greeks were also located inside the new walls.

'They've finished the wall!' Alfred yelled, dropping his reins and flinging his small arms wide, gesturing to the imposing new structures. 'Pope Leo had just started building the last time I was here.'

'I'm told the defences were designed to help safeguard the holy buildings from Saracen raids, Alfred. Many of our own towns, particularly coastal ones, would benefit greatly from similar fortifications,' he said, admiring the thick stone wall and sturdy towers. 'Such projects are unlikely to be undertaken in my lifetime,' Aethelwulf admitted, 'but perhaps during the reigns of my sons...'

He let the thought hang as they entered the Leonine City through the Saxon Gate and their long procession clattered through the cobbled streets, heading for the quarter known as the *Schola Saxonum* – the Saxon School. Situated next to the portico of the magnificent basilica of St Peter, the Saxon

School resembled most villages in Aethelwulf's homeland: a collection of wooden huts and stables around a communal hall and a simple wooden church. Run by Saxon monks, the Schola had been in existence for many years, its purpose simply to provide a place for all Saxon pilgrims to stay. Aethelwulf was pleased to note the buildings had been well restored following two fires that had reduced the hostel to little more than ashes in previous years. He'd sent a goodly sum towards its repair with Alfred two years ago and fully intended to donate further funds for its upkeep on this occasion. Elation filled him. After years of longing he was finally *here*, soon to meet the holiest man in Christendom ...

But, the news awaiting them on entering the *Schola* severely tempered his euphoria.

'You're sad because Pope Leo's dead, aren't you, Father?' Alfred said as they settled into the hut reserved for visiting nobility. Aethelwulf slumped on the low cot, in need of rest and a change of clothing. It was so long since he'd worn anything that wasn't caked in layers of dust. 'He was a very kind man,' Alfred continued at his father's nod. 'But the new pope will probably be kind as well.'

'He is called Benedict the Third, I'm told. And you're right; he's likely to be just as compassionate. It's just that–'

'You believe Pope Leo would have been more likely to help you because he'd already welcomed me,' Alfred supplied.

Aethelwulf nodded and pulled himself to his feet with a weary sigh. 'Now, before I throw off these stinking clothes I need a word with Osberht. The stabling here didn't look too generous and we've a lot of horses to house. Satan needs a wide berth or there'll be mayhem, and little of the stables still standing by morning. And don't think I'm joking either.'

It was almost a month later by the time Aethelwulf was received by Pope Benedict in the Lateran Palace. It was a brief encounter, after which he and Alfred, Father Felix and the two priests were politely ushered out as Benedict made his way to the council chamber for an urgent engagement with the notables of Rome. Though disappointed to have his long-awaited audience terminated so abruptly, Aethelwulf wasn't surprised. It was common knowledge that the city's appointment of the new pontiff was not proceeding smoothly.

Benedict was an austere man, unquestionably devout in his beliefs and the promotion of the Church but, unfortunately for Aethelwulf, Benedict was embroiled in conflict with Lothar and Louis, the brothers of Charles the Bald, who refused to approve him as pope. Consequently, Benedict had not yet been consecrated. But, refusing to give way to the two Holy Roman Emperors, Benedict spent much of his time with members of the Roman nobility, clergy and senate, determined to find a way to win this battle for the papacy.

The carefully planned ceremonies, during which Aethelwulf had intended to present the pope with his lavish gifts, were therefore postponed. On reflection, Aethelwulf considered that to be no bad thing. Benedict may not sit in the pontifical chair for much longer, and the costly gifts could be put to better use with the duly consecrated pontiff. So he resigned himself to viewing the sights of the Leonine City and the substantial remains across the Tiber of that bygone age of Empire, now interspersed with the shabby residential areas where most of Rome's population lived. His visits to the awe-inspiring churches and shrines strengthened his love of God, filling him with a profound sense of regret at his decision to leave the Church after his early education at Winchester. But regrets were futile and he rapidly dismissed them. As King of Wessex, Aethelwulf had been blessed with a wife he'd deeply loved, and sons who would continue to make the kingdom great.

Alfred was in a reverie of his own as the days passed in the wonderment of learning. At the tomb of the Apostle he said prayers for his mother, the simple act serving to ease the deep pain of bereavement that Aethelwulf knew he still felt.

The uncomfortable heat and humidity of summer with its swarms of buzzing insects gradually faded, giving way to the fresher air of autumn. By early October the uncertain occupancy of the pontifical chair seemed finally resolved. Though Aethelwulf had seen little of Pope Benedict, he knew from the gossiping Romans that Louis of Bavaria had sent a cardinal priest named Anastasius to be installed as pope. Anastasius's men had stormed the Lateran Palace and for a week Benedict had suffered the indignity of imprisonment. But the senate, nobles and clergy of Rome simply refused to consecrate the priest as pope. Anastasius's position was hopeless and Benedict was released to reclaim his position.

Following Pope Benedict's consecration on October 6, the people were in festive mood; the pontiff of their choice sat in his rightful seat, albeit without the approval of the Holy Roman Emperors.

Weeks stretched into months, the lingering warmth and blue skies of the Roman autumn gradually marred by the rains and cooler air of winter. The West Saxons unpacked thicker cloaks and dodged the heavy showers. Yet compared to the biting winds and freezing fog and ice of a Wessex winter, Rome seemed to embrace the perpetuity of a spring paradise. By the time spring did blossom again, Aethelwulf began making plans for the return journey. Since mid-October he'd been received in the Lateran Palace on several occasions. Exquisite gifts were carried in by his retainers and Father Felix stood by to record the joyous events. Golden chalices and gilded silver candlesticks, robes elaborately decorated with gold and silver thread, a beautiful ornamental sword and chests of gold and silver coin were amongst the offerings that delighted the new pontiff – and paved the way for amicable and constructive discussions between them. Aethelwulf would leave Rome with the knowledge that Pope Benedict would remember Wessex in his prayers.

At the end of May all was in readiness for their departure.

'When do we see His Holiness to say goodbye?' Alfred popped another grape into his mouth, looking expectantly at his father. They'd eaten a hearty meal of roasted pork, with pastries from the market and a variety of colourful fruits, and the hostel's hall buzzed with cheerful conversation. Beyond the open door, daylight was fading as the sun sank to the horizon across the stretch of sea the Greeks had called the Tyrrhenian. Alfred reached for an orange. 'Will you give it to him then?'

'In two days' time, and yes,' Aethelwulf answered the two questions, watching juice squirt into Alfred eye as he peeled the orange's thick skin with his small scramseax.

'So we meet with the pope in two days and you'll give him

the last of the gifts then,' Alfred said, trying to avoid cutting his fingers. 'I can't wait to see his face.'

* * *

Inside the huge Basilica of St Peter's on the first day of June, Pope Benedict held the magnificent crown of solid gold above his head. His lips moved in silent prayer as he lowered his arms to place the crown on the altar, beneath which lay the tomb of the Blessed Apostle. Aethelwulf felt truly humbled as the congregation of Romans and Saxons knelt together to be led in prayers by His Holiness the Pope. His gift had been well received; recognised as a true representation of his devotion to the Church and his deep love of God.

With Alfred and Felix at his sides and his retinue behind, Aethelwulf stepped from the solemnity of the basilica, feeling as though the hand of God had enveloped him. But silence ended as cheers erupted from the gathered crowds. Shielding his eyes from the afternoon sun he waved to the smiling faces below the wide steps and gestured to a dozen of his guards. The men disappeared into the basilica as Aethelwulf held up his hands to quieten the crowd.

'People of Rome,' he yelled in perfect Latin once he could make himself heard. 'You have heard that tomorrow we return to our own lands and wish to say farewell to you all. Thank you for allowing us to do so. The year we have spent amongst you has been one of the most enjoyable of my life and I thank you all for your generosity and hospitality to my companions. We will remember Rome's splendour, her wines, fruits and pastries for many years. But we'll remember Rome's people for ever!'

Resounding cheers filled the air and Aethelwulf raised his hands for their attention. 'It is now my turn to show my generosity to you.'

He signalled to the chosen men, each of whom now held a large sack. Positioning themselves across the breadth of the steps they began hurling out handfuls of silver coin. People jostled to catch them or retrieve them from the ground ...until the sacks were empty and Pope Benedict stepped out to stand beside Aethelwulf, as had been arranged.

'Return to your work now, my children,' Benedict said in a voice that projected itself forward without being greatly raised. 'Today you have been given a rare gift of thanks from one of the many thousands of pilgrims who visit our Holy City. But King Aethelwulf wants no other thanks than to see you return to your everyday pursuits and live the rest of your lives in peace and happiness.'

The people gradually melted away and Aethelwulf reluctantly took his leave of Pope Benedict. In the *Schola's* stables he chortled as Osberht told him of Satan's latest antics and they discussed preparations for horses and wagons to be ready for tomorrow's departure. Unlike Aethelwulf, Osberht could barely wait to get home.

'I just miss Edith, my lord,' the groom said with a morose shrug.

Aethewulf found himself laughing, though he knew the sentiment not to be funny at all. He had no wife in Wessex to miss, and the sadness of that thought added to the sorrow he already felt on leaving this glorious city.

Twenty One

Charles the Bald was delighted to welcome Aethelwulf and his entourage back to his court and keen to hear of their experiences in the Holy City. On the evening of their arrival they dined in the large stone hall, which was sumptuously furnished with thick, colourful wall hangings, and even thicker ones on the floor instead of rushes. Alfred recalled Charles explaining on their previous visit that these were called *carpets* and had been brought all the way from Persia.

As a notable guest, Aethelwulf was seated next to the emperor at the high table, with Alfred at his side. Content to enjoy the hospitality of the Frankish court and listen to the melodies of the harpist, Alfred glanced about, smiling as he caught the eye of his new friend, Charles, seated with three other boys at a separate table who, he decided, must be Charles's brothers. But at the high table, perched silently on the far side of the emperor, was a girl some years Alfred's senior. He glanced at her occasionally, presuming her to be Charles's daughter, Judith, although they'd not been introduced, nor had she dined with them last year.

Alfred thought that Judith looked a pleasant person. He liked the way her shiny dark hair flowed like waves down her back, and the colours of the swirling patterns on her embroidered gown. But Judith's pretty face was unsmiling and she constantly gnawed her bottom lip, taking frequent, anxious peeps at Aethelwulf. Alfred thought she was probably just shy in the company of strangers.

'It was unfortunate your stay coincided with the election of the new pope,' Charles was saying as a serving woman heaped his plate with roast venison. 'The selection and consecration to the papal seat is rarely a straightforward matter. I well remember the trouble over the previous pontiff, Leo the Fourth. The Romans are demanding the right to choose their own pontiff, independently of the Empire.'

'For some weeks the situation certainly seemed precarious for Benedict,' Aethelwulf confirmed, allowing the woman to place slabs of meat on his tastefully decorated dish. 'But everything was resolved by October and our stay was very enjoyable from then on.'

Charles washed down a mouthful of venison with a gulp from his wine goblet. 'You may also realise that my two brothers continue to threaten the peace of West Francia – though, having said that, Lothar passed away last November and his son, Louis, now rules in his stead. So I'm hoping we'll have some peace from that area whilst my nephew finds his feet.' He scowled, tapping the table with the handle of his scramseax in his agitation. 'It's my brother Louis causing problems right now. Bavaria's never been enough for him; he's greedy to get his hands on Aquitaine, despite the stipulations of the Treaty of Verdun. But I'll fight him to the bitter end to keep Aquitaine. I swear, Aethelwulf, it niggles them all that I got the lands west of the Rhine.'

Alfred's ears pricked when Aethelwulf murmured, 'Too often family members create the greatest problems for a ruler, no matter how extensive the kingdom.' Charles's bushy eyebrows rose in anticipation of elaboration, but Aethelwulf seemed not to notice and offered some compliment regarding the tenderness of the venison, and congenial conversation continued. But the remark troubled Alfred and he wondered whether his father was talking about his own family. Determined to ask him about it later, he put it from his mind by considering the Frankish emperor.

In appearance Charles was as dark as Alfred's father was fair, though like Aethelwulf, his thick hair and beard were well streaked with grey. He was a scrawny man with narrow shoulders and hollow cheeks, despite seeming to gulp down his food and wine with relish. His small, dark eyes and hooked nose made him look like a hawk about to swoop on its prey, but tonight, Charles played the genial host. However, Alfred wondered why he'd still not introduced his daughter, even though he occasionally spoke to her himself.

But, as servants cleared away the remnants of the meal, Charles turned and addressed Aethelwulf. 'My lord, may I present to you my daughter, Judith? She is a gentle and obedient girl and, as you see, comely in appearance and of childbearing age.'

Alfred silently sympathised as the girl flushed crimson. Too embarrassed to catch anyone's eye, Judith hung her head and chewed her bottom lip quite brutally.

'Come and greet King Aethelwulf properly, daughter.'

Looking utterly mortified Judith obeyed, stepping behind her father and curtsying as Aethelwulf rose to greet her. 'I am honoured to meet you, my lord,' she said in the Saxon tongue, with only the hint of a Frankish accent.

'And I'm delighted to meet the daughter of such an esteemed emperor,' Aethelwulf replied as she tentatively took his proffered hand. 'I'm sure you are a credit to your father. Your fluent use of the Saxon tongue is truly impressive.'

'I have an excellent tutor from your own lands, my lord – from Sussex.'

Aethelwulf smiled warmly at the girl. 'Then, with both intelligence and beauty, no doubt one day you will make some king a very happy man.' Judith shot a look of such panic at her father that Aethelwulf hurriedly added, 'Of course, the prospect of marriage may not yet have been discussed, in which case, please accept my apologies, Lady Judith.'

Judith gave Alfred's father a wan smile. 'My lord, I have been surrounded by discussions regarding possible husbands as long as I can remember. The daughter of an emperor must marry well,' she added, casting another glance at her father.

'Very true, my lady. I also have a daughter, and though I cannot aspire to the status of emperor, the daughters of all kings must marry for political reasons.'

Interest sparked in Judith's eyes. 'Your daughter married well, my lord?'

'Aethelswith is wedded to a neighbouring king. The match served to strengthen the unity between our two kingdoms.'

'And Aethelswith is happy in her marriage?'

'She is content enough.'

Alfred was taken aback by the outright lie: his father knew too well of Aethelswith's unhappiness. Perhaps he just didn't want to admit it to the Frankish emperor.

'Now, Judith,' Charles said, standing beside his daughter, 'would you like to take Alfred to see our collection of relics?'

Without waiting for her reply, Charles turned to Alfred. 'Your father tells me you have a passion for such things, and we have a goodly collection here. Many nobles making pilgrimage to Rome pay their respects at our court – as you, yourselves, have done,' he added, inclining his head to Aethelwulf. 'Many bring us gifts of unusual relics relating to the life of our Lord.'

Although surprised that he and Judith should be dismissed, Alfred couldn't hide his excitement at the prospect of seeing these relics. 'I would be pleased to see your collection, my lord,' he replied, considering how short Charles appeared beside Aethelwulf. Even Judith was as tall as her father.

'The relics are very interesting, Alfred,' Judith assured, holding out her hand with an encouraging smile. He placed his own small, chubby hand in Judith's slender one and allowed her to lead him towards the prized relics.

* * *

'Not all of the relics come from Rome,' Judith said as they sat together in a small chamber behind the main hall with box-loads of strange looking objects on the table before them. 'Some of these were brought to us from the holy city of Jerusalem. I can see that impresses you.' She smiled. 'Your eyes could not open much wider, young lord.'

Alfred thought Judith was one of the nicest people he'd ever met, and felt quite at ease in her company, though he still sensed she was upset about something. 'Are you are unhappy, Judith?' he broached. 'Is there anything I can do to help?'

'You are a strange one,' she said with an appraising look.

'You speak as someone much older than your six years.'

'I have been seven since before Eastertide!' Alfred retorted, causing Judith to giggle.

'Well, I am thirteen,' she said, suddenly sad again. 'Alfred, I want to tell you something, but you must promise not to tell anyone that I spoke to you of it.'

Confused, he nodded anyway. He was good at keeping secrets.

'At this moment my father will be speaking of a certain matter with King Aethelwulf.'

'Do you know what he'll be speaking about?'

Judith nodded and closed her eyes, twisting a long strand of hair round her finger. Her sudden outburst took him by surprise. 'It is all right for *you*, Alfred – you're a *boy*! I'm just a girl, no use for anything except presenting some lord with *sons*!' She covered her face with her hands and Alfred knew that tears were welling. He stayed silent, not knowing what to say or how to give comfort.

'I am sorry, Alfred,' she sniffed, taking a small, white kerchief from her sleeve to blow her nose. 'I have had many weeks to become used to this idea, but confronted with it directly I find I am a coward.'

'You are distressed because you are soon to be married?'

Judith stared at him for some moments before taking breath. 'Alfred, I am to marry your father.'

Alfred gasped, stunned by the revelation, and feeling certain that his father had known nothing about it before tonight. But Judith had known, and had been fretting about it for some time. No wonder she'd been behaving so strangely. He watched her staring down at her interlocked fingers, her lower lip quivering. 'It must be scary to face marrying someone so much older than yourself,' he said, laying a hand on her arm.

'It truly is, Alfred,' she whispered. 'I had hoped my father would choose a younger man for me, but politics must come first. I have always known that. My father believes the match will be good, politically, and is certain that King Aethelwulf will agree. Charles is a powerful emperor and – please do not take offence at this, Alfred – he believes that Aethelwulf will be more than pleased to ally Wessex to West Francia, nor would he wish to insult Charles by refusing him in this.

'I shall miss my home and family greatly,' Judith admitted, 'even though our kingdom is constantly under threat of invasion by my two uncles. And to make matters worse, we have the Danes raiding our lands again. We are told the Danes are becoming a problem in the Saxon lands too,' she continued, her eyes holding Alfred's. 'I know my father was impressed when he heard of King Aethelwulf's victory over them at Aclea. The Danes cause our people such hardship, pillaging and killing, and burning the crops. And they are almost unstoppable once they gain foothold in a land. Only two weeks ago a large band, led by a man called Weland, made their base at Jeufosse, from where they can strike at Paris and our palaces along the River Oise. I fear my father will soon have no option but to do battle, or else pay tribute to be rid of them.'

Unable to think of anything useful to say, Alfred just nodded.

'Tell me, Alfred, is your father a kind man?' Judith suddenly asked, tilting her head to one side. 'Perhaps I could overlook his age if he treats me kindly.'

They talked quietly about Alfred's father and siblings for a while before moving to retire for the night. 'Thank you for keeping me company tonight, Alfred,' Judith said, as they left the relics behind. 'I know we will be great friends when we are in Wessex and, although I shall be your stepmother, I will never try to take the place of the mother you loved so dearly. Sleep well, young lord.'

In bed in his chamber next to Aethelwulf's, Alfred wondered what his brothers would say when they heard about this coming marriage, particularly since they were all older than the girl soon to be their stepmother.

* * *

They arrived at Verberie three days before the wedding ceremony that would take place in the large stone church beside the palace on the first day of October. Alfred watched the scores of Frankish dignitaries and their retinues arriving to witness his father's marriage to Judith with interest. He'd faced crowds before, and could converse with his elders without embarrassment, but since he could not speak the Frankish tongue, Aethelwulf assigned Father Felix, a Frank himself, the role of Alfred's escort.

Verberie was one of several palaces along the Oise valley, and unlike anything Alfred could ever have imagined. Father Felix protested that such flagrant flaunting of wealth was offensive to God, but Alfred thought the palace to be absolutely splendid. The vast grounds were magnificent, with many lakes and canals surrounded by gardens bursting with trees, shrubs and plants, their autumn foliage vibrant in the sunlight. Statues lined the paths, some displaying people in minimal attire, which Felix hurried him past. The exterior of the palace itself was a sight to be seen, the walls of a smooth, pale stone, with round towers tapering to points at intervals. Inside, floors were covered with intricate mosaics, and frescoed walls told stories of ancient heroes. Servants scuttled about, making ready an enormous hall for the wedding breakfast.

Aethelwulf and Judith spent much of the three days rehearsing their vows and the order of the service with Archbishop Hincmar, who would conduct the ceremony. But today, as the sun rose to greet October, Judith was in her chamber being fussed over by her maids and female relatives and Alfred and his father donned their carefully selected attire. A little before mid-morning the ceremony would begin.

* * *

The imposing church was crammed with guests from all over West Francia, only Alfred representing Aethelwulf's family and Wessex subjects. He stood in his place of honour beside the emperor, whose sapphire-studded crown and cloak of gold silk bore testimony to his status in the Holy Roman Empire. And garbed in his finest green tunic and cross-gartered hose, Alfred, too, felt quite regal. Waiting for the ceremony to begin, he recalled Aethelswith's wedding day, the hatred he'd felt for the man taking her away from him. But he looked at Judith in her beautiful gown of rose-coloured silk and knew he could never dislike *her:* she was much too kind for that.

Nevertheless, Alfred dreaded arriving home to the scandal he knew the marriage would cause. And even worse, only yesterday Aethelwulf had revealed that affairs at home were in turmoil. The news had come in August, a week before they'd reached Charles's Court: Aethelbald had rebelled, refusing to surrender his kingship of the western shires on his father's return. Alfred frowned, recalling Aethelwulf's words to Charles about families and problems to kingship.

His father's familiar voice rang out, banishing such disturbing thoughts and filling Alfred with pride. Aethelwulf had spent so long with Father Felix, memorising the Frankish words of the marriage vows, determined to impress the gracious Charles. His splendid blue tunic and cloak, the jewelled crown that rivalled that of Charles, and the glittering brooches and belt buckle, all contributed to the impression of the wealth and power of Wessex.

Judith was facing Aethelwulf, and though Alfred could not see her face, he knew she would be trying hard to hide the fear she felt; fear of a journeying to a strange land, of leaving her home and becoming a wife. But she faced the ceremony bravely, speaking her own vows with clarity. Then, during the nuptial mass, Archbishop Hincmar placed a ring on her finger, anointed her and lowered a golden crown set with rubies onto her head. Judith was now Queen of Wessex. And although Alfred had known this would happen, he could not prevent a shudder: the wives of Wessex kings were *never* crowned as queen. Wessex nobles were unlikely to abandon a custom they'd clung to for the past seventy years, a custom stemming from a tale that Alfred knew well ...

Eadburh, daughter of the mighty Offa of Mercia, had married King Beorhtric of Wessex. Though beautiful, she was an evil woman who plotted the downfall of Wessex for her father. Relentlessly, she assured Beorhtric that his councillors were idlers, useless at running the kingdom, so he'd be rid of them. Beorhtric ignored her words, knowing them to be false, and in her fury Eadburh resorted to laying poison for the councillors. But the king accidentally drank the poison himself. Eadburh fled to Francia, taking much West Saxon treasure with her. Eventually she moved to Pavia, where she died a sad and lonely death...

The choir filled the church with such heavenly sounds that the fateful images were abandoned and Alfred followed the emperor as he led the guests through the high, arched doorway. He was hungry and the wedding breakfast an appealing prospect.

* * *

It was late in the year for crossing the Channel but the crisis in Wessex could not be ignored until spring. Fortunately, the weather held fine and the morning crossing was smooth. But by the afternoon conditions had changed, and they made a cheerless fourteen-mile journey from Dover to Canterbury in pouring rain, Judith not peeping out from inside her wagon throughout. Aethelwulf deemed this wet and dreary homecoming an inauspicious start to his young wife's new life in Wessex.

Weary and sodden, and heavy-hearted at the prospect of what he might hear, as evening approached he dismounted to greet his fair-headed son.

Aethelberht received them with cheerful cordiality and ushered them before the roaring fire in the impressive hall. Shadows danced on the tapestries that covered most of the high walls, masking the cold aura of the blocks of stone from which they were built – a reminder of the hall's Roman origins. Aethelwulf sighed. If not for these unforeseen events which would radically change the rest of his life, he'd be content to be entertained by his amiable son. He was thankful that Judith had cheered in the warmth of the hall and was enjoying the fresh bread and watered wine.

Content to relinquish his temporary kingship of the eastern shires, Aethelberht professed shock at his older brother's actions. 'I knew nothing of Aethelbald's intentions until he'd already turned his scheming into actions,' he proclaimed. 'I can only speculate that he's received unwise counsel in your absence, Father. Someone's put ideas into his head.'

Aethelwulf wearily massaged his temples. 'And we don't have to think too hard as to who that might be, do we?' he said, glancing at Alfred who was happily chatting to Judith. 'Bishop Ealhstan's been a constant companion to Aethelbald for some years, and that man's aspirations know no bounds. Nor do I have any illusions about Aethelbald's ambitions, or his impatience.'

'You're right, Father. Ealhstan's rarely left the West Saxon court since you departed for Rome. Nor has Ealdorman Eanwulf. And, of course, as king of the western shires, Aethelbald's had the financial resources to curry favour with some of our most powerful nobles.' Aethelberht played with his fingers, evidently uncomfortable at what he must reveal. But he took a resigned breath and said, 'I know how much this will dismay you, Father, but Aethelbald found little difficulty in persuading them all of your unsuitability to rule. With Danish attacks increasingly likely, he's used your age as his sharpest weapon. And I'm told he feels he should have assumed kingship of *all* the Wessex shires during your absence. So he's more than a little disgruntled with me as well as you.'

'Aethelbald's been disgruntled with someone or other for most of his life, Aethelberht, so don't take that to heart. I've no doubt it's me he's seething at.' Aethelwulf shook his head, contemplating this web of intrigue against him. 'You know, I can believe that Ealhstan and Eanwulf have played duplicitous roles in this,' he said. 'But the rest, those who've served me so well, and dare I say, loyally, throughout my reign? How could so many turn their backs on me now, after the generous grants of land?'

Aethelberht stared silently at the spitted meats being turned over the hearth, struggling to voice the reply that Aethelwulf knew to be on the tip of his tongue.

'Shall we discuss this now, son, or later?'

'Walk with me to the stables, Father,' Aethelberht said, glancing at Alfred and Judith. 'The rain has eased and I'd like your opinion of my new stallion.'

Horses shifted in their stalls as they entered the stables, Aethelberht's single oil lamp throwing a small circle of light into the dark building. Grooms had already gone to await the meal so they were alone, as Aethelberht had evidently wanted.

'You needn't fear to speak in front of Judith,' Aethelwulf said, caressing the neck of a handsome grey. 'She may be young but she's no fool, and she fully understands the situation in Wessex regarding the position of a king's wife. I've been honest with her in that. But try to understand, Aethelberht, the immensity of power held by her father, and his influence with the pope. The emperor would hear of no other status than queen for his daughter. This marriage was his idea in the first place. And no,' he said, lifting a hand to stay Aethelberht's half-formed comment, 'I could not have declined the offer. The match has much in its favour for our kingdom. Rarely a day goes by that I don't contemplate our resources should we face large-scale attack. Our alliance with West Francia should serve us well if we require aid.'

Aethelwulf heaved a weary sigh, knowing his long-winded explanation sounded no more than feeble excuse. 'I am old, son, may not last much longer in this world. But I had hoped to see out my life doing my utmost for Wessex. I anticipated a degree of outrage regarding my marriage and Judith's status as queen. I didn't marry in the hope of producing further heirs – though God forgive me, I believe her father expects that. Judith is young and, for the time being, will be accorded the privacy of her own bedchamber.' Aethelberht's brows rose at hearing such an admission, but he said nothing. 'But that I should lose my kingdom because of this marriage is proving a hard price to pay.'

Aethelberht averted his eyes and Aethelwulf sensed he was struggling to accept the idea of a Wessex queen. And, if a loyal son had condemned it, how much more so would the magnates of the kingdom?

Perhaps I should call a meeting of the Witan at Winchester?'

'You'll not be permitted back into the West, Father. Aethelbald has stationed men along all roads to prevent you. You'll need to relay your intentions to him via messengers.'

Aethelberht moved away and stood in the doorway, looking out at the puddled yard. Aethelwulf stared at his straight back; grieved beyond all telling at what he was hearing. At length Aethelberht turned to face him and said, 'I heard only yesterday that Aethelbald is prepared to face civil war in his bid to keep the western shires. He's been preparing his armies for weeks.'

* * *

Unwilling to subject his kingdom to the horrors of civil war, Aethelwulf agreed to Aethelbald's demands to meet with some of the most powerful nobles of Wessex. In the grim, formal atmosphere of the Winchester hall he fought desperately to present arguments in favour of retaining his own kingdom of seventeen years. But in the end it amounted to what he'd expected. Seating a queen beside him on the throne proved to be his greatest mistake: Wessex nobles had no intention of changing their practice of seventy years. In addition, Aethelbald's condemnations of his father's age and unsuitability to rule had done their work. Conversely, Aethelbald had impressed the magnates with his own skills of government; he was a proven leader of men who could raise an army swiftly – as he had recently proved.

Conscious of the looming possibility of battle, by the end of the harrowing day Aethelwulf was compelled to agree to a compromise. The kingdom would remain divided: Aethelbald would retain his *uncrowned* kingship of the western shires, whilst Aethelwulf and his new 'queen' would rule in the East. Aethelberht, Aethelred and Alfred would stay with them. On Aethelwulf's death, however, *all* of his sons would adhere to the terms of his will.

Aethelbald had seemed unable to meet his father's eyes during the meeting, whether through contempt or his own sense of guilt, Aethelwulf couldn't tell. Suddenly overwhelmed by unbearable sadness he thanked God that Osburh wasn't here to witness such betrayal by their son.

As he began the long trek back to Canterbury he wondered how Judith's father would react on learning that his daughter would be queen of only a minor portion of the kingdom. King Charles was astute enough to grasp the true implications of this 'compromise':

Aethelwulf had, effectively, been deposed as king of the West Saxons.

Twenty Two

Aros and West Francia: April – October 857

A little after sunrise on April 16, Eadwulf sat on his sea chest at his oar port aboard Bjorn's magnificent new ship, *Sea Eagle*, rowing hard through the Aros estuary towards the open waters of the Kattegat. The waving arms of villagers had long since disappeared, the cheering voices carried away by the strong wind.

It was a good day for sailing.

Eadwulf admired the striking design that Ragnar's shipwrights had created; this was a vessel well befitting the son of the powerful jarl. Along the length of the slender hull, twenty pairs of oars sliced through the water; shields hung over the uppermost strake, out of the way. Towards prow and stern the oaken strakes tapered, curving gracefully upwards, the prow ornamented by the carved eagle's head, its hooked beak wide, yellow eyes menacing. Bjorn's place would be at the prow for most of the journey, issuing orders that would demand immediate response.

Amidships stood the sturdy mast, the sail now collapsed until needed on the open sea. At the right of the stern sat the helmsman operating the steering oar. Already nearing his fiftieth year, Leif was one of Bjorn's most experienced crewmen. As their eyes met, Eadwulf returned his cheery salute, feeling good to be alive. It had been months since he'd rowed anywhere and his body complained at each stroke, but the sense of freedom under clear blue skies filled him with such elation he soon forgot his nagging muscles.

The *Eagle* glided into the wide bay beyond which the Kattegat stretched east to Skåne and south to the many islands and the Baltic Sea. Sunrise shimmered across the silver water, embracing the twenty dragonships anchored there: vessels from villages throughout Ragnar's domain, united under the leadership of their jarl's son. Eadwulf squinted at the impressive fleet, contemplating the large force it represented. The *Eagle* alone carried over forty men, and though most of the ships were shorter – a few thirty oars, others twenty or fewer – he calculated a total nearing four hundred men. And soon that number would be doubled.

The *Eagle* took her position at the head of the fleet and the stone anchors on the waiting ships were heaved up. The sails were raised, instantly catching the southerly wind, and the sleek ships pitched forward, like demons from the fiery land of Muspelheim sweeping over the sea. Rounding the headlands of the bay, they struck north into the Kattegat Strait. Bjorn paced the deck sharing cheerful banter with his crew, his well-fitting tunic accentuating his solidly broad frame, his red hair whipping across his face. Pride and exhilaration lit his face and Eadwulf considered how handsome he looked with his splendid beard and moustache, wishing the stubble on his own chin would hurry up and grow. This would be his seventeenth summer and he longed to have a beard to signify his manhood.

'Well, Eadwulf,' Bjorn said, squatting beside him and glancing up at the flag atop the mast, the white-tailed erne rearing from the water, a huge fish clutched in its talons. 'What do you think of her? Does she handle well?'

Eadwulf grinned, sharing his master's pride. 'She does that; she's light as a feather. I've never seen a finer ship.'

'Now I've seen ships in northern waters that would dwarf this one,' Bjorn said, nodding. 'Saw a Norwegian once, a fifty oar at least, with a huge sail. But size isn't everything, and I'm well pleased with this beauty. Her slim lines make for speed, a great advantage at times. Enjoy the break from rowing, lads,' he yelled, heading back to the prow. 'Once we turn from the Kattegat your backs will get little respite.'

In the mid-afternoon they veered west into the narrow channel that opened up into the wide Limfjord – a stretch of water that reached from the Kattegat to the Northern Sea, separating the two areas of Danish mainland. The fjord provided a much shorter route than sailing further north and through the unpredictable spring-time waters of the Skagerrak. Eadwulf knew it made sense to take this route – but the mere thought of it caused his emotions to run awry. Little over ten miles inland from the Kattegat, as the channel gradually became a wider sound, the settlement of Aalborg stood proudly on its southern bank.

Aalborg was Jarl Rorik's domain. And somewhere in that busy town could be Eadwulf's mother.

Eadwulf had known of Rorik's whereabouts for some years – Bjorn had not kept that secret from him – but they'd never had cause to sail this way before. Bjorn generally headed north to the Norwegian lands, or west to the coast of Skåne. But his master had promised that one day, they'd pay Rorik a visit.

Their first night was spent on one of the fjord's many

islands, and by late-morning the next day, they had reached the Northern Sea, following the Danish coastline south. They kept moving throughout most of that night, eventually casting anchor at the mouth of the River Ribea to await sunrise, and the arrival of the second fleet, under the command of Bjorn's cousin, Hastein.

Eadwulf had only vague recollections of sailing to the port of Ribe six years ago and he didn't dwell on that time. He drifted into a shallow sleep, to be wakened seemingly moments later by raised voices. His sleep-filled eyes were greeted by the glare of the rising sun, and the sight of Hastein's approaching fleet.

The *Jormungandr* swung alongside the *Sea Eagle.* Hastein's ship was an impressive vessel: eighteen pairs of oars compared to the *Eagle's* twenty, her slim lines just as alluring, the finely carved reptilian head at her prow equally ornate and fear-provoking. Unable to contain his joy at seeing his cousin again, Bjorn leapt from the side of the *Eagle* with the agility of a cat, to land sure-footedly on the *Jormungandr's* deck. The cousins embraced each other with much whooping and back-slapping. They made an interesting spectacle: the wild, red mane of Bjorn contrasting markedly with the neat gingery braid down Hastein's back and the short fringe across his brow. And, unlike Bjorn's hairy visage, Hastein's chin and upper lip were clean shaven. Both men were a little shorter than Eadwulf, though Hastein was less thickly built. But his biceps stood proud, and his strength could not be doubted.

Memories of Hedeby hit Eadwulf like a slap: of being trussed like a hog for sale, sick with physical weakness and humiliation – and a young man garbed in blue, eating a flatbread from one of the stalls, and tripping over a dog. That same young man had later come back, and his party had taken Aethelnoth. Eadwulf felt certain that the youth in blue was Bjorn's cousin. Dare he hope that Aethelnoth was still alive?

Swelled to over forty ships, the fleet struck south-west; the bright sails tacked into the bracing westerly and they made good time. By the end of the third day they were following the low-lying coastlands of Frisia. The wind dropped and they rowed through the night until daybreak, when the wind once more picked up. Under sail again they headed for Francia.

The weather was warming daily and Eadwulf's spirits were high when they sighted the Seine estuary late in the afternoon. As afternoon merged into evening and the western sky blazed crimson, they were sailing up the meandering, unpredictable river that would lead them to the heart of West Francia. But to navigate unknown waters in darkness would be foolhardy, and before long forty ships lined the banks of the Seine.

Eadwulf dumped down the sacks of supplies and made to return to the ship for more when he noticed Hastein squatting to sort through his belongings – and saw his chance to ask about Aethelnoth. Hastein's head jerked up at the unfamiliar voice and he cocked an eyebrow as their eyes met. Eadwulf waited for the verbal tirade to start: for a thrall to question a jarl's son could be construed as insolence. But Hastein grinned and rose to his feet.

'Your voice tells me you're not a Dane, and you could be the double of...' He tilted his head and grinned even wider. 'You could almost be his twin!'

'I am Bjorn's thrall,' Eadwulf said, taking in the cheerful Dane's appearance at close quarters. Hastein's skin was fair, pinking after the days of warm sunshine, with a sprinkling of freckles across his nose. A glint of humour played in his hazel eyes, the corners of his mouth seeming to be naturally turned up. 'Bjorn is a good master, and very considerate.'

Hastein hooted. 'Well, I've heard my cousin described as many things, some complimentary, some not quite so gracious. But *considerate?* That's a new idea. I wonder what his many women friends would think of it. Now, what was it you wanted? Oh yes, you wondered whether I remembered someone called Aethelnoth. Friend of yours was he?'

Eadwulf nodded, resigned to believing that Hastein wouldn't recall a slave from long ago. But Hastein not only remembered Aethelnoth, he couldn't sing his praises highly enough:

'Aethelnoth's a fair giant of a man, half a head taller than you – and *you're* bigger than most. Probably twice as broad as well! Legs like tree trunks, and a neck to match: a good, strong thrall to have about the village. And he's the best horseman I've ever seen; has a real way with the beasts. Once saved my father from what could have been a nasty fall from a huge, grey stallion he'd bought at Ribe – an evil-looking creature with madness in its eyes. Giermund's no horseman, but since he'd paid for the beast, he determined to be the first person to ride it!' Hastein chuckled at the memory. 'Well, it reared and bucked and my father hung on for dear life. Aethelnoth just walked calmly up, cooing to the angry beast. Unbelievably, it stood still, tossing its head a bit, but quiet enough for Aethelnoth to lead it back to the stables. My father was too stunned to request to be allowed to dismount!'

Dumbfounded at what he'd heard, Eadwulf waited as Hastein bent to untie his bedroll. 'The big man's been one of my father's bodyguards for some years now,' Hastein went on, peering up at him. 'Would've been with us now if Giermund could've spared him. So, my friend, I suppose the answer to your question could have been a simple yes: yes, I do remember Aethelnoth.'

The following morning they set sail upriver, Eadwulf's head still awash with thoughts of Aethelnoth. They made their first base thirty miles downstream of the town of Rouen, where they stayed for three weeks. Homesteads were sacked for food and plunder, and horses rounded up to be herded along the banks once they sailed on. Wanton slaughter and rape became the daily norm. And, unlike in previous years, Eadwulf raided beside his comrades.

But the main targets of their raids were the fine Christian churches, filled with such treasures that Eadwulf revelled in their taking. The Christ-God had no need of such exquisite objects when his scheming priests preached the shunning of worldly goods and the virtues of a life of poverty! The burning of each grandiose edifice elated him, his enthusiasm amusing Bjorn considerably. His master had expected him to baulk at the destruction of buildings devoted to his people's god, despite Eadwulf's assurances that he would not. But the mirthful glances were irritating, and he wondered when Bjorn would voice his thoughts.

Tomorrow they'd be sailing on, but today they were content

to enjoy the spring sunshine. Cheerful banter filled the camp, most of the men pitting their wits at the board game, *hnefatafl*, or the dicing game of *tabula*. Others were simply content with idle conversation. Bjorn and Hastein sat on their sea chests beside a splendid willow, and Eadwulf squatted next to them, cleaning Bjorn's boots.

Hastein shoved his unbraided hair back from his stubbly face, swatting at a persistent bank of midges hovering too close. 'Damned flies! I'll be covered in red lumps by tomorrow. The beasts seem to be acquiring a taste for my blood.'

'Can't expect to escape bugs this close to the river, Hastein, not in this weather. Perhaps you should just cover your arms.' Bjorn's features shaped into a puckish grin. 'At least that excuse for a beard you're cultivating should keep the tykes from devouring your chin.'

Hastein huffed, but ceased his complaining. For a while the cousins reminisced about childhood summers spent at Aros or Ribe, but soon their thoughts returned to the present. The ships were already laden with loot and they gloated over their achievements, their high spirits leading them to needle Eadwulf over the Christian doctrine of his people.

'This Christian god of yours seems only fit for women,' Hastein declared. 'What *real* god would ask his warriors to love his enemies? A man needs a powerful god like Odin or Thor; a god whose wrath is truly feared. How will a man defeat his enemies or cope with the hardships of winter should the gods not bless the raids?'

'And what will you tell your tutor of your exploits this summer?' Bjorn asked, poking him in his side with a stick.

'Will you describe how you enjoyed bringing about the fiery demise of all those churches?'

Eadwulf flinched at the sharp jab and scowled. 'I'll tell Sigehelm nothing!' he said, more tetchily than he'd intended. He opened his mouth to apologise but Bjorn waved it away, raising his eyebrows in anticipation of clarification.

'My life doesn't belong to Sigehelm, and I'm no Christian!' Eadwulf blurted, hoping the two irrepressible Danes would cease the taunts. 'Sigehelm knows how I feel. But I couldn't lie to him. If he asks, I'll answer truthfully.' He looked from one gleeful face to the other. 'Sigehelm wouldn't press me about my role in the raids, though he'll likely guess the truth.'

'Well, let's not dwell on the future right now,' Hastein said, before the mood became downcast. 'Tomorrow we move on. Let's see what further treasures we can wrest from this wealthy land.'

Twenty Three

In the afternoon of the following day they took up residence on what looked to be a conveniently placed island in the middle of the Seine, ten miles upstream of Rouen and inhabited only by a dozen tonsured monks in shapeless black robes. Wailing pleas to the Christ-god, the monks were hounded into the Seine where their heavy woollen habits ensured that most of them drowned, their bodies washed away downstream. Eadwulf felt no pity for such pretentiously pious men.

'By Thor's bollocks,' Hastein declared to anyone within earshot, 'this place will serve our purpose well.' He patted the sun-warmed wall of the tiny stone church against which he leant, watching his comrades piling provisions into the scattering of wooden buildings. 'We couldn't have asked for a place with better shelter and storage.'

Eadwulf followed his grinning master to join his cousin. 'And those vegetable plots could prove useful,' Bjorn added, pointing beyond the huts. 'Or perhaps not,' he grunted, as they strolled over to inspect the produce. He kicked at a row of holey cabbages crawling with oversized caterpillars. 'It seems the greedy little lodgers have already taken the lion's share.'

'But these could give us a few boilings to go with the livestock over there,' Eadwulf said, pulling up a couple of half-grown carrots and gesturing at the forming pods on spindly pea plants along the fence.

Bjorn scowled at the scraggy-looking cattle grazing on a small patch of enclosed grassland. Equally scraggy chickens strutted near the pens holding half a dozen lean pigs. But it was Hastein who remarked, 'If we can do no better than those scrawny beasts we may as well lie down and die right now! Of course, we can always throw out our fishing nets.'

'By Odin, cousin, you know how I hate fish!'

Bjorn's indignant face was so funny, both Eadwulf and Hastein creased with laughter.

Much of the following day was spent raising an earthen bank around long stretches of the island. The work was hard and sweaty, but fortifications were vital to their safety. The ships were carried inland, protected by the barricade from fire arrows that could deprive the men of their only means of transport home.

For over two weeks, Oissel Island provided an ideal base from which to move out and continue the raids. Using the few, small boats once owned by the monks, they rowed across in relays to their well-guarded mounts on the banks, and struck out, bringing chaos and destruction to the land. More churches and cathedrals were targeted and Eadwulf rode with Bjorn and three hundred men to sack Paris, returning with plunder that surpassed all expectations. The men found it hilarious that Charles the Bald despaired of ever ridding his kingdom of them. Nights were filled with merriment, aided by barrels of looted Frankish wine. Food was plentiful: bread was easily acquired from besieged villages and sheep and pigs were ferried across to supplement the island's meagre offerings. Eadwulf enjoyed these early weeks on the island, although his status as thrall was never completely overlooked, and he spent much of his time doing necessary chores. Bjorn eagerly anticipated their return to Aros, when he'd proudly report their successes to his illustrious father. He was also hoping the Frankish king would soon be prepared to pay a huge tribute to see the back of them.

But their good fortune was soon curtailed. The indomitable Charles saw the opportunity to lay his own siege: a possibility they had overlooked when taking over the island. By the start of the second week of June, Oissel Island was completely cut off from the outside world. Charles's soldiers lined the banks on either side of the Seine and arrows rained down on the Danes if they moved beyond their earthen barricade. Suddenly the island base did not seem such a good idea and Eadwulf commiserated with the two leaders, who shouldered all responsibility for the choice of site.

For three weeks they remained hopeful that the siege would not last, that Charles would soon withdraw his men for duty elsewhere in his beleaguered kingdom. Food supplies would last for some weeks yet. But as the siege dragged on throughout July and August, and Frankish soldiers remained an obdurate presence, stores were so low that starvation seemed an inevitable ending to the venture.

On a bright morning in early September, now twelve weeks into the siege, some of the men squatted against the wall of the church, despondent and lethargic from inadequate food. Eadwulf had never seen the two leaders look so low.

'Ragnar will never know how much plunder we took, how much we rattled that cunning bastard, Charles; never know why we didn't come back!' Bjorn raged. 'And it's my fault! The island was my choice! And look where it's got us: facing an ignoble death from starvation. Not a hope of reaching Valhalla.'

No one refuted his arguments, or offered consolation.

In the fading twilight at the end of the twelfth week one of their lookouts hurtled into camp from his post along the barricade, halting before the two leaders.

'The Franks, my lords – they've gone!'

Bjorn blinked a few times as though struggling to comprehend what he'd heard. But Hastein composed himself first. 'What, *all* of them? Are you sure?'

The lookout nodded emphatically. 'They just seemed to slink back and disappear, taking our horses with them. Our guards are probably dead ... The banks have been deserted since late afternoon, but we thought it best to wait a while before getting anyone's hopes up.'

Hastein eyebrows rose. 'Well, let's go and look, shall we?'

Hundreds of Danes lined the earthen wall around the island, all as flummoxed as their leaders. 'Who'd have believed it?' Leif muttered to Eadwulf. 'They seem to have well and truly vanished.'

Next to them, Bjorn shook his head. 'Don't be *too* sure of that, Leif. It could be one of that old buzzard's tricks: get us to lift out the ships, then attack. Fire arrows could finish us. And in our weakened state–'

'The very reason we can't afford to be so negative!' Hastein declared, dismissing his cousin's pessimism. 'We must make our move at dawn.'

'You're probably right,' Bjorn admitted, 'but it wouldn't surprise me to see the Franks reappear as soon as we do.'

In the grey light of approaching dawn Eadwulf accompanied Bjorn to the shore. After ordering the lookouts back to camp to prepare for sailing, his master headed for the water's edge to scan up and down the river. Eadwulf hung back, affording him solitude in his contemplations. Eventually, though clearly still perplexed, Bjorn turned away – and didn't see the archers rise from behind the makeshift barricade across the river. But Eadwulf did.

He yelled and charged full pelt, diving at Bjorn and knocking him down as arrows thudded into the earthen wall. But a single arrow hit home. Eadwulf's legs turned to water as searing pain shot through him and he crashed heavily against a huge boulder. He was vaguely aware of being dragged, followed by the sensation of floating.

Then darkness claimed him.

* * *

'Eadwulf! You must drink.'

Eadwulf heard the voice, somehow recognised it, but could put no name to it. Then water washed over his lips. That felt so good; his mouth was parched, his tongue thick and woolly. God of gods, what was happening to him? He hadn't even the strength to open his eyes.

'Open your mouth and swallow some water, Eadwulf. You can't go on like this!'

The pain! Someone was stabbing him in the shoulder. He cried out, tried to make his right arm beat his attacker away, but found it wouldn't respond. Why was someone making him drink if he was stabbing him? He couldn't even think straight, couldn't make sense of the pain, and sank back into that comfortable, dark place...

Something cool and damp was pressed onto his burning forehead and water trickled over his lips again. Suddenly he wanted to swallow it. He forced his lips apart and felt hands lifting his head up as water washed over his tongue. He swallowed and drew in more.

'Well done, lad. We'll soon have you on the mend. We should be ready to sail in two days, but don't worry, you won't be expected to row. After what you've done, you deserve to be ferried home in comfort.'

Eadwulf suddenly knew the voice belonged to Bjorn, but he was too drowsy to even try to understand what he was talking about. Perhaps if he returned to the darkness for a while he'd understand next time the voice spoke to him ...

'He's rousing again, Leif. Lift his head up and I'll try to get him to drink.'

He gulped greedily, too fast, and spluttered the last mouthful down his chin. The coughing hurt his shoulder and he felt again that agonising pain.

'Steady on, Eadwulf. Smaller sips just might go down your throat and not your chin.'

He forced his eyes to open and looked straight at Bjorn's grinning face.

'Welcome back, lad. I'm not sure where you've been for the last three days, but it wasn't here. No, don't try to move. You're not strong enough yet.'

'What ...what happened to me?'

'You don't remember anything?'

Eadwulf waded through the incomprehensible jumble inside his head. 'I remember a dark place, where the pain couldn't find me.'

'But you don't remember what caused the pain?'

He tried to move his left shoulder and flinched. 'I've been wounded?'

'You were wounded saving my life, for which I'll be forever in your debt. It was down on the shore ...at dawn ...three days since,' Bjorn prompted. 'To my shame, archers found me a sitting duck! My back must have seemed Odin-sent to them. Does that frown mean you're beginning to recall something?'

'Just fragments, like distant dreams, and archers aiming at us,' he murmured. 'And you, walking towards me. You haven't seen them!' He held his breath as the fleeting images flashed. 'The Franks haven't gone, have they?'

Bjorn was silent, as though unable to speak of the continuing siege, the inevitability of their deaths. But Eadwulf didn't need an answer. His master had been right: the withdrawal had been a trick. Though hadn't someone said they'd be sailing soon? Floundering in confusion he glanced about the little church. Sunlight poured through the tiny windows high in the walls and he knew it would still be warm outside, where the crew would be sitting around in their hopelessness. Bjorn was kneeling by his bedroll with Hastein at his side. Behind his head, Leif squatted.

'So it was you, Leif, who kept lifting my head so I could drink?'

'It was, lad,' the helmsman acknowledged. 'Getting real worried about you we were. You'd not swallowed a drop for days; been unconscious most of the time.'

Tentatively, Eadwulf touched his shoulder, frowning as his memory returned. 'I took an arrow, didn't I?'

Bjorn gently squeezed his right arm. 'What can I say, except that you took that arrow instead of me? I'd have been dead for sure had the arrow pierced my back and punctured a lung. The arrow went deep into your shoulder. It was a good thing you struck your head on that boulder as you hurtled me to the ground: that arrow took some digging out! It's Hastein we've to thank for the deft handiwork, by the way. He makes a fine surgeon: must be those long fingers.'

Eadwulf smiled at Hastein. 'My lord, I owe you sincere thanks.'

'You've more than proved your worth on this voyage, Eadwulf,' Hastein said, serious for once. 'And now you've saved Bjorn's life. It is I who should be thanking you. And without Thora's needles and silks, I could have done little – we would've had to seal the wound with a burning brand or heated iron. The barbs on the arrowhead meant we couldn't pull it out without tearing your shoulder to shreds,' he continued, grinning at Eadwulf's widening eyes. 'I had to make a very deep cut to release the wicked thing! So either stitching up the wound – or otherwise sealing it – was vital. Your unconscious state proved most convenient. But you seem to be truly back with us now. Do you remember Bjorn telling you we're soon to sail?'

Eadwulf nodded, perplexed. 'But I thought the Franks were still out there. Aren't they? They shot at us ...didn't they?' The three men shared a glance and he knew there was something they hadn't told him. 'Are we really sailing soon?'

'The Franks *have* gone; and yes, we sail in two days. But the siege is still on.'

Eadwulf gaped at his master. 'I don't understand.'

'The Franks have withdrawn, apparently to counter an attack on West Francia by Louis of Bavaria, one of Charles's brothers,' Bjorn explained. 'But Charles is a cunning bastard, as we know. He actually paid three thousand pounds of silver to some of our own countrymen to continue the siege in his stead! It was *Danes* who fired at us, Eadwulf. They'd moved in that morning at first light. And by Odin, if I ever come across that treacherous dog Weland again, I swear I'll tear him apart! He'll die the slowest of deaths possible. I'll–'

'I'm sure we all feel the same, cousin,' Hastein smirked. 'Weland would betray his own mother for a single piece of silver. But the point is, Eadwulf, it's because Weland is such a double-crossing cur that we will be leaving soon.'

'We've arranged an exchange, of a sort, with Weland,' Bjorn elaborated. 'We give him a share of our booty and he'll turn a blind eye to our departure.'

Eadwulf snorted.

'My sentiments exactly, lad: to betray your own country-men is beneath contempt; but to take our hard-won booty is doubly so!' The expression of insult on Bjorn's face made Eadwulf laugh. Red-hot needles shot through his shoulder and he gasped. Bjorn waited until he'd composed himself before speaking. 'Yesterday, Weland and a small party rowed across to the island under a white flag – which being principled Danes, we honoured. After much haggling, a price was agreed for which he was prepared to let us go. The amount has made a dent in our plunder, but considering how much we've actually got, it seems relatively little. Naturally, Weland is ignorant of how much we *have* taken, or he'd have undoubtedly pushed for more.'

'Can you trust him to let us do that, Master, let us go, I mean? Once he's got our loot, might he stop us sailing?'

'That's always a possibility, but two things make me believe he'll keep his word on this occasion.' Bjorn considered Eadwulf's expectant face and grinned. 'Firstly, whatever else Weland is, he's a Dane, and like all Danes, he enjoys duping non-Danes. And Charles the Bald with his Christian pomposity – not to mention his great wealth and power – has become not only the butt of jokes for all Danes, but also the main target of our raids. Charles's outrage when he finds he's been outwitted should be something to see, especially when he learns that Weland's no intention of leaving Francia yet, not when there's still rich pickings to be had.'

Eadwulf nodded. 'The second reason?'

'Ragnar, of course.'

Hastein and Leif grinned at Eadwulf's bemusement, and Bjorn laughed out loud. 'Weland's been a friend of my father's for years. Few kingdoms around the Northern and Baltic Seas haven't been besieged by those two. Weland was with Ragnar during the sack of Paris thirteen years ago. That would make Charles and Weland old acquaintances, I'd say. So I feel rather confident that Weland wouldn't wish to antagonise my father by starving to death his eldest son and beloved nephew.'

'It would be most unfriendly of him to do so,' Hastein agreed. 'He wouldn't be in a hurry to set foot back in our homelands either. But I still think the main reason for Weland's double-dealing is–'

'The booty,' Leif finished for him, scratching his head. 'You two seem to forget that I sailed with Weland and Ragnar for many a year. And a more devious bastard than Weland you're not likely to find. I can't see him being much afraid of Ragnar these days. He's got his own lands now, his own men; owes loyalty to no one. And you're right, Hastein; he'd sell his own mother for the merest glint of silver.'

'Then we'd best not turn our backs on the devil,' Bjorn conceded with a grimace.

* * *

At the end of the third week of September, Bjorn and Hastein's fleet eventually pulled away from Oissel Island. The lightening day saw a gradual easing of the downpour which had been heavy during the night, and the clear, sharp air smelt good. Relieved to be on the move the men concentrated on their rowing, reserving their thanks to Thor until they were well away from their island prison. Slumped on his sea chest beside Leif, Eadwulf felt wretched. His shoulder throbbed and he was much too weak to row. How could he justify his place on Bjorn's ship if he could do nothing but sit and watch others work? But he had no choice in the matter; hailed as Bjorn's hero he must endure the embarrassing praise and remain seated.

Leif's hairy visage was solemn, his darting eyes edgy as the ships glided past the riverbanks lined with Weland's men. Somewhere in their midst was his former comrade, undoubtedly revelling in his easily acquired wealth from both the Frankish king and his fellow Danes. As most of the men, Leif was not convinced that Weland would not renege on his word and attack. The booty had been exchanged for hostages in the diminishing drizzle at first light. Six warriors, each a chieftain in his own right, would be their only assurance of safe passage from the Seine. One of those six now squatted at the *Eagle's* stern, glowering. Other ships held his comrades: none to be freed until they reached the Danish lands.

Half-starved and brimming with anger after weeks of enforced confinement, the men rowed hard. They raided villages along the Seine without mercy, seizing food, burning homesteads and taking slaves. Five days after leaving the island they reached the open sea and veered north towards Frisia, sailing into creeks and estuaries to continue their raids.

Eadwulf stayed with the ships during these times as he'd done in past years. But he despised the feeling of helplessness, and though his shoulder only bothered him when suddenly jolted, he was still too weak to wield a weapon. He felt like a child again; the child who'd willed away the years to the day when he'd become a man, able to fight at Bjorn's side and make him proud.

Though his Mercian heritage still burned deep in his heart, Eadwulf had long since come to respect the Danish way of life: the elemental need to raid in order to survive. He thought of his father, a noble king who'd died a victim of one such raid, and his mother, snatched as a prize by the victor of that same incursion. And Eadwulf himself, thrust into a life of endless drudgery, his happy childhood gone forever. By rights he should deplore everything the Danes stood for. But he did not ...

Bjorn's kindness had saved him, taken him away from the relentless torment at the hands of Aslanga and her two spiteful sons. And for that, the jarl's eldest son had become his saviour, whom he would follow and obey without hesitation. Even during the raids in Francia, Eadwulf had participated without question. Bjorn expected it of him. Had he lived, Beorhtwulf would surely abhor what his only son become: a callous raider who dealt in death and destruction. And his mother, should she still be alive, must never know. Though, perhaps, having lived amongst the Danes herself, Morwenna would understand.

Now, even in his darkest moments, when his nostrils filled with the stench of burning and terrified screams resounded in his ears, Eadwulf thought of Bjorn and the men who had become his friends. And he smiled.

* * *

The amber glow of the setting sun danced across the waters of the pretty bay, highlighting a couple of the low-lying islands that formed part of the chain along the Frisian coast. The light offshore breeze now held a definite chill and the early October evening would soon rapidly darken. Campfires on the sandy beach already crackled and the men were setting whatever meats they'd obtained during the day's raids to roast. Eadwulf laid out breads, cheeses and apples with little concern as to how they'd been acquired. He'd have acted no differently to the other men, had his wretched shoulder permitted. He glanced at the thralls taken during the last week or so, hunched together with that terrified look Eadwulf recognised too well. He fought down the mixture of anger and sympathy he felt for their loss of freedom. To allow such emotions to dominate his thoughts would serve no purpose. He could not change the way of things.

The meal was devoured quickly; the Frisian wine downed too fast to be savoured. The men were still rebuilding their strength after the weeks of slow starvation, and the night-time meals were enjoyed more with a sense of relieved desperation than merriment. Thor must surely have smiled upon them to have saved them as he did. Though silver coin, elaborate swords and chalices, and other ornate goods were few in Frisia – the area had suffered many years of Norse raids – food was plentiful on most of the homesteads they'd raided. And since leaving Oissel Island, food was the one commodity the men still craved. Ample silver and gold from Francia was already in their possession; all they wanted now was to get home in good health. And tomorrow they'd be setting sail.

Just before they made a move towards their bedrolls, Bjorn rose to his feet, a big grin on his face, and addressed the fifty or so men seated around his campfire. At his master's left, Eadwulf paid little attention. Bjorn often ended the evening with jovial anecdotes and a summary of their recent achievements, goods accumulated. But after a few moments Bjorn raised his hands for silence, a serious expression on his face.

'In years to come we'll look back on this summer with mixed emotions,' he said, his eyes sweeping the faces, glowing in the flickering light. 'Our bulging sacks speak of our incredible success in Francia. Ragnar will be delighted that we laughed in the face of the pretentious Charles. But,' he added with a slow shake of his head, 'we've all felt the brush of death; all felt what it would be like to be barred from Valhalla. Sadly, but inevitably, we leave some of our comrades behind. Those men died as true warriors, doing their best to please the gods. Odin will smile upon them and open the doors into Asgard, where they can feast and drink in the great hall, Valhalla. But the rest of us...? Had we died on that cursed island, starved until our bodies could function no longer, we would not have been as fortunate as they. Valhalla would not have been our destination.'

He suddenly grinned and threw out his arms. 'But we are here. Alive! Perhaps a little thinner,' he jested, patting his midriff. 'Though in some cases – and note, I mention no names – perhaps that's not such a bad thing. Some of you will now be able to see your toes.'

The men hooted and Eadwulf noticed others gathering round Bjorn's group, drawn by the laughter. 'I, more than most, have reason to be grateful that I'm still alive,' Bjorn went on. 'And the one person responsible for my continuing good health is sitting right here beside me, still suffering considerable pain from an arrow, skilfully aimed to kill me. If not for Eadwulf's swift actions, I'd not be here enjoying this chat with you all now.'

Eadwulf shuffled as eyes fixed on him. He was not looking for admiration from the men and would prefer the incident simply to be forgotten. He'd merely acted instinctively to the sight of that cursed archer taking aim.

Hastein suddenly appeared between Eadwulf and Bjorn, a canvas bag in his hand, a great grin on his face. 'I imagine you're about ready for this, cousin,' he said, holding out the bag. 'If you continue to talk much longer, I fear Eadwulf may well slink away in embarrassment before you accomplish the intended purpose of this little gathering.'

'Couldn't have put it better myself,' Leif yelled round to the men from his seat at Bjorn's right. 'I swear our young master doesn't even shut up in his sleep!'

Bjorn threw up his hands with a feigned expression of astonished indignation before taking the bag from Hastein's grasp. 'Then I shall bore you all no longer with my inane chatter. No doubt I'll continue to talk to myself when I nod off. So now, at the risk of causing him still greater discomfiture, I ask that Eadwulf rises to stand beside me.'

Eadwulf silently groaned. Hadn't his master praised him enough already? Why couldn't he just let things lie?

He pulled himself up and shuffled between Bjorn and Hastein, trying not to look at the many grinning faces. Bjorn faced him and gripped his one good shoulder. 'I owe you my life, Eadwulf, for which I'll be eternally indebted to you. Never have I known a thrall with such courage as you. You could so easily have died in my stead...' Bjorn's voice was choked, and Eadwulf felt a lump in his own throat. 'You'll never know how much I prayed to the gods when you lay unconscious for so long, Eadwulf...when we all thought your life was ebbing away. Mighty Thor must have acknowledged your bravery, recognised your true, Danish spirit and the need for you to live. He knew that you are, without doubt, one of us.'

For some moments Bjorn gazed silently at Eadwulf, as though unable to put further thoughts into words. Then he opened the bag and withdrew something that glinted silver in the firelight. It took Eadwulf a moment to recognise what it was. An armband; a thick and heavy silver ring, embossed with spiralling stems and leaves, the open ends resembling the gaping maw of some sea creature. He stared at the object, unable to believe that Bjorn should bestow such a costly item upon him.

'Accept this gift, Eadwulf, as a token of my appreciation for the courage you've shown throughout our venture into Francia. I've already declared my heartfelt thanks for saving my life, and I know the men have valued your weaponry skills during the raids, and your comradeship. But, mere words can be forgotten, whereas this handsome token cannot.' The men cheered as Bjorn placed the silver band around Eadwulf's upper right arm then grasped him at the wrist to make the favoured greeting of warriors.

'Just don't lose it!' Hastein quipped, taking his turn to clasp Eadwulf's wrist.

The cheers and laughter eventually died down and Bjorn looked round the men, evidently about to speak again. Eadwulf fingered the unfamiliar band round his arm, his heart filled with pride, despite his embarrassment. He just hoped that Bjorn would now focus his attentions elsewhere. The night was already fully dark and a few men had started to yawn. It had been a long day.

'I've one last thing to say to our brave comrade before we retreat to our beds, my friends,' Bjorn began, turning back to face Eadwulf, who felt his face flush red again. 'After some in-depth consultation with Hastein and Leif, I've come to the decision that since you're now a Dane in all but heritage, you need a Danish name.'

Eadwulf blinked at this unexpected assertion. Changing his name had been the last thing he'd expected, and he wasn't at all convinced he liked the idea. He was Eadwulf, a Mercian, and always would be. Wouldn't he? His emotions reeled and he knew his confusion would show on his face.

Bjorn roared and the others joined him. 'Well, I can see that the idea has hit you like a slap with a wet fish.'

'It's not distaste at the idea, Master,' Eadwulf said quickly before Bjorn became offended. 'I'm just stunned. What name did you have in mind?' he asked, hoping he sounded pleased.

Laughter again rang out. 'Now, that's more like it.' Bjorn's voice trilled amusement. 'We believe that "Ulf" will suit you very well,' he said glancing sideways from Hastein to Leif, who were both nodding in agreement. 'After all, you do fight somewhat like a wolf. And Ulf is not too unlike your original name. But it's a popular name in our lands – and it will always signify your acceptance as one of us. A Dane.'

Ulf sat on his sea chest the following day as the ship ploughed north through the foaming brine, wondering how he'd explain all this to Sigehelm. Soon they'd leave Hastein's fleet behind at Ribe, and within the next two days they'd be back in Aros. Confusion made his head throb, to add to the pain of his shoulder. The armband would be hard enough to explain. But the name change...?

Sigehelm would see his acceptance of the name as a betrayal, a denial of who he was and his true heritage: everything he'd tried to keep alive in Eadwulf since the day the Danes destroyed his family, and his home. And made him the thrall he still was.

But now he was a Dane, and proud of it. He'd raided and killed like the rest of them. And Bjorn valued him so highly. Or did Bjorn still just see him as a useful thrall?

Confusion continued to rage. He sought desperately to find that comfortable, dark place; the place where he'd found such solace after he'd been wounded.

But oblivion eluded him.

Twenty Four

Aros: early October 857

'Well, Eadwulf, I'm truly glad to see you back. I confess I feared the worst. We all did.'

Sigehelm found it hard to keep his voice on an even keel. His relief at seeing his former pupil safe and well was marked, despite a whole day having elapsed since his return. He wanted to ask Eadwulf so many questions, but didn't know how to begin. He'd caught much of Bjorn's embellished account of events at last night's homecoming feast, but from Eadwulf he'd heard nothing.

Thora's uncharacteristically impatient tones interrupted his thoughts: 'The evening meal must be nearly ready when the jarl and his sons return from their rounds of the village,' she snapped at the thralls. 'The men won't want to resume their merrymaking surrounded by vegetable peelings and animal guts!'

Eadwulf would be a part of those celebrations, as Sigehelm had seen last night. Bjorn would insist.

It had been another hectic day. Family reunions continued and people pursued their work, hampered by the after-effects of last night's excesses. Sigehelm's own routine had changed little – he still had his tutorial and clerical duties to perform for the jarl – but the disruption around the village could not be ignored and he was pleased that the day would soon be drawing to a close.

'The autumn gales and treacherous waters of the Northern Sea could so easily have taken you,' he continued, shuddering at the thought. He would never lose his fears of those vast, grey depths.

'Ulf. My name is Ulf now.'

Sigehelm blinked at the terse rebuke, his quill poised over his parchment. He stared at Eadwulf, whose head was bent over the boot he was buffing, his body stiff, a pained expression on his face. 'Of course,' he acknowledged, 'I recall someone saying as much yesterday. But I can't remember the reason *why* you changed your name.' He glanced at eight year old Ubbi, practising his letters at the end of the table. But the women were making too much noise chopping vegetables for the boy to hear. 'Eadwulf is a fine old Mercian name; a name to be proud of.'

'I don't feel like a Mercian any more,' Ulf snapped, doggedly polishing without looking up. 'I'm not a Dane – and I'm still a thrall. I know that. But what's the point of harking on about my Mercian heritage? I'll never go back. And I've *earned* the privilege of being named Ulf, so please call me that in future.'

Ulf dropped the boot and polishing cloth to the floor, pushing back his hair as he raised his head. Sigehelm noted how the thick mane hung unkempt about his shoulders, in dire need of grooming. It had grown considerably since the spring. He held Ulf's gaze, desperately seeking the boy he once knew. But Eadwulf – Ulf – was now very much a man. The once boyish features had sharpened and red whiskers sprouted from his chin and upper lip. His physique was powerful and well-muscled, his every reflex that of a warrior. At seventeen he was a head taller than Sigehelm and looked so much like

... He swallowed hard. Ulf was a mirror image of how he remembered Beorhtwulf to be.

'Bjorn is my master,' Ulf said with a one-shouldered shrug. 'He re-named me Ulf and I must obey his orders. But it's more than that, Scribe! You've always had your God – your Christ. I could never understand your trust; your faith.'

Sigehelm struggled to grasp the connection between Eadwulf's change of name and his own faith. His former pupil was watching him, doubtless reading his confusion, and when he spoke his tone had softened.

'You've always taught me that Christ would be the salvation of his followers. But I could find no comfort in such a belief, Sigehelm, you know that. Bjorn has been my only salvation. If not for him, Ivar would have killed me years ago.'

'I do believe that when Bjorn took you under his wing it gave you relative freedom and the chance to get away from Aros and see some of the world. Heaven knows, you've not seen summer here for five years. You could undoubtedly sail one of those dragonships singlehanded!' Ulf's lips twitched at Sigehelm's quip but he said nothing. 'Bjorn certainly took you away from the intolerance of Aslanga,' Sigehelm continued, glancing about to ensure the mistress was still in the fireroom, 'and the constant taunts of Ivar and Halfdan. But whether Ivar would have killed you is doubtful indeed.'

'Believe it,' Ulf spat. 'You don't know the truth of it!'

Sigehelm gasped, the unexpected discourtesy astounding him. At a loss for words he looked away to collect his thoughts. He'd put down his quill in haste and unwittingly knocked over the ink pot. The black liquid streamed across his parchment, rendering his work utterly ruined. He felt the unaccustomed prickle in his eyes as memories of a day long ago resurfaced and he looked at Ulf.

Ulf glanced at the parchment and then at Sigehelm, his features impassive. He picked up Bjorn's boot and recommenced his polishing.

* * *

The hall was stifling, the heat from the hearthfire intense, and Ulf's face burned, his body uncomfortably clammy. Rowdy singing filled his head – or was it screams he heard? He needed time to think; time to contemplate the significance of recent events, unscramble his tangled emotions. His sense of self had become so deeply buried he didn't know who he was any more. Was he Eadwulf, or Ulf? Mercian or Dane? Whoever he was, he wasn't the same person who'd set sail for Francia in the spring. Did his deeds in Francia make him evil and depraved? If so, why had he done those things ...slaughtered and raped? They contradicted everything he'd once believed in; every principle his parents had instilled in him. But when all was said and done, he'd really had little choice over his actions: Bjorn had simply expected him to act in accordance with the rest of the men. When Ulf contemplated how he'd felt about that, he had to admit he'd had no objection to doing so. And once caught in the frenzy of the moment, there'd been no turning back, no time to consider the wantonness, the very wrongness of it all. And he'd so desperately wanted to please Bjorn and earn acceptance as a warrior. Being the lowliest member of his master's crew was no longer enough.

He slunk outside, the heaviness in his chest weighing him down. How could he have been so contemptible to Sigehelm, his one true friend; his one true link to his real self? Tomorrow he'd apologise, tell Sigehelm about Francia. He would not dwell on the raids. How could he explain to Sigehelm things he did not understand himself?

Drinking in the sweet, cool air, he basked in the peace away from the hall. The blue skies of the October day were now cloaked in the velvet shades of night, the waxing gibbous moon bathing the land in pale light. Millions of stars twinkled and beguiled, some swept in bands across the heavens like huge brushstrokes, others massed into clusters. Countless millions of others shone alone. His heavy eyelids closed, his tense muscles began to loosen, his mind to wander.

He'd seen so many night skies on his sea voyages over the past five years and never ceased to feel small and insignificant beneath such grandeur. He wondered whether Asgard lay somewhere beyond the stars, and whether Odin, Thor, Frey and other Danish gods were looking down on the antics of humans from their magnificent halls. Could the Christian god be there with them? It seemed to Ulf more likely that there were no gods at all, that Thor's storms and Odin's ravens were just part of the nature of things.

On clear nights at sea, when their sun compass was rendered useless and the routes of seabirds unseen, their navigators would use the stars to locate their position. Ulf had learned a little of that skill and could name several of the stars and constellations. The most important star was the North or Lode

Star, which was easy enough to find, since it sat between two great constellations with unmistakable formations. His eyes were drawn to a group of stars called Odin's Wagon, for Odin was ruler of the wagon road of the heavens. Ulf found this seven-star arrangement intriguing. Four of the stars formed the body of the wagon itself, the other three the pole, or handle. His gaze moved from the two pointer stars at the front of the wagon until it rested on the North Star. On the opposite side of the North Star from the Great Wagon, Cassiopeia sat in its great zigzag formation. He followed an imaginary line drawn from the open end of the first V of this zigzag and again located the North Star.

There were many old myths about these wonders of the heavens. Bjorn had once told him how the sun, the moon and the stars had been formed at the beginning of time. The story told of a hot, bright, glowing land guarded by the fire giant, Surt. This was the land of Muspelheim. It was said that the warm air of Muspelheim had drifted into the opposite cold, dark land of Niflheim, melting the ice and causing Aurgelmir, the father of the evil giants, to be formed. The gods themselves took the sparks and burning embers of Muspelheim and placed them in the midst of the vast space above and below the Earth. These became the sun, the moon and the millions of stars.

Ulf found the story little more than interesting. To him it was just that: a story.

At first Ulf had felt lost and alone at sea, surrounded by men more at home in their ships than on land. He'd been so young five years ago, so ignorant. But he was learning. Sailing with Bjorn, he'd seen places he hadn't known existed, places even Sigehelm hadn't heard of: trading towns and ports, peaceful villages, and mountains so breath-taking he'd felt totally humbled. Sometimes, they'd sailed into settlements to trade. At others they'd looted and killed.

He snapped his mind shut to the raids and thought of the Norwegian lands of the far north, close to where the world of humans abruptly ended and those strange and beautiful lights danced across the skies as the gods played. He'd quaked with fear the first time he'd sailed past the Lofoten islands to the fishing settlement of Tromsø. The crew had teased him relentlessly and he couldn't help smiling at the memory ...

'If we sail much further north,' Leif had told him, wide-eyed, 'we'll surely be thrust from the edge of Midgard into that wild ocean where the most hideous of all serpents, Jormungandr, lives. The monster will close his foul, gaping jaws around us and swallow us all in a single gulp!'

The men had kept up the pretence for days. Only much later had Ulf learned that ships often sailed even further than Tromsø. As a boy, Bjorn had sailed with Ragnar over the very top of the Norwegian lands, continuing east at the edge of a vast, cold ocean the Norwegians called the Whale's Road until they reached the land of the Finns. Bjorn had seen nothing of any monstrous serpent, just an abundance of whales and great floating lumps of ice.

A feeling of warmth swept through Ulf as he recalled those early voyages. The Danes had taken to him, a lad of thirteen, as one of their own, even though he cleaned and cooked and fetched for them. He had his allotted place in their company, and been respected for it.

Hearing footsteps he spun round to see a young woman coming toward him from the hall. Her unbraided hair shone like pale silk in the moonlight. She stopped and stood there, hands on her hips, glowering at him.

'I hope you're truly ashamed of yourself, Eadwulf. I feel ashamed *for* you!'

Ulf immediately bristled. 'You know your brother named me Ulf!'

Freydis advanced on him, fury shaping her features. 'Oh, I know all right. I also know *why* Bjorn gave you that name, and I commend your actions. But you seem to have let it go to your head! What gives you the right to treat Sigehelm with such disrespect?' she demanded. 'We've all benefited from his learning, and he's earned the respect of us all. And he cares for you more than anyone else in all of Midgard. He's a fine person with a noble heart, Christian or not. But you just–'

'And what gives *you* the right to try to put me in my place? I'm not *your* thrall!'

With a hiss of rage, Freydis leapt to stand barely an arm's length before him, tilting her head back to glare up at his face. Ulf glared defiantly back. 'I can put you in your place because you are a thrall!' she seethed, punctuating her reply with sharp jabs to his chest that sent jolts of agony through his shoulder.

His reaction was instinctive: he grabbed Freydis's wrist in a vicelike grip, fuming at the affront. Sudden pain contorted her face, a glimmer of fear momentarily flashing in her eyes. Then the anger took over. Her eyes fixed on Ulf's hand on her wrist before moving up to his face. 'I could have you flogged for this! Then my father would throw you into the pit and give you to Odin at next week's ceremony.'

'Then run and tell him, Freydis.' Ulf released her in a sudden gesture, his hand still raised, fingers splayed, clawlike. 'Run and tell Ragnar whatever you like. You're right; he wouldn't hesitate to have me strung up if he thought I'd laid so much as a finger on you. I'd be just another thrall to forfeit his life to appease your vengeful gods.'

Freydis stepped back, rubbing her wrist, her expression softening with uncertainty. Her eyes glistened in the moonlight, searching Ulf's face. He felt a wrench at his heart as he watched her gnawing her bottom lip. This was not how he'd expected to greet Freydis on his return. In the spring they'd parted as the friends they'd always been. And as long as that friendship remained within the bounds of mistress and thrall, it was acceptable in the eyes of the Danes. But Ulf's feelings for Freydis had developed into something so much deeper over the years.

'I don't understand you any more,' Freydis said, shaking her head. 'Where's the Eadwulf I knew, the Eadwulf who would not have hurt people's feelings? He seems to have been left behind in Francia, and a stranger returned in his stead.'

Ulf squeezed his eyes shut, stung by the accuracy of her observation.

'Can't you see that Sigehelm is very worried – no, he's *upset* about you?'

'I know!' Ulf snapped, turning his back on her. 'By Odin I feel badly enough without you rubbing it in. I'd already decided to talk to Sigehelm tomorrow.' He rubbed his aching brow, his shoulders slumping with weariness. 'And now I've made matters worse by offending you. And you have only ever shown me kindness.'

The sensation of her fingers on his back shot through him like a bolt. He caught his breath, its release coming as an involuntary shudder. Turning to face her he forced a smile. Freydis had such a troubled look on her face that he desperately wanted to hold her, assure her that he was still the same person deep inside. But a thrall could never take such a liberty with a jarl's daughter.

She smiled weakly in return. The front of her white pinafore was stained in patches, the colours indistinguishable in the moonlight: probably berry juice from the pancakes she'd made. Freydis had spent all afternoon in the fireroom, and a night of serving at the feast, and had every right to feel exhausted. Yet all her concern was for Sigehelm – and himself.

'I know my behaviour has been unacceptable,' he admitted, unconsciously brushing flour from her cheek. 'I just need a little time to adjust to new expectations of me.'

Freydis covered his hand with hers and turned her face into his palm. Her gentle kiss sent such a frisson of passion through him that he groaned. 'Freydis, we–'

'Hush,' she said, pressing her fingers to his lips. 'I know what you would say and I don't want to hear it. There is always hope. Don't give up on yourself, or on me ...But,' she went on, 'it appears I've been too hasty in my assumptions about you. I should know things aren't always what they seem. And I shall have strong words with my scoundrel of a brother. Ubbi knows he shouldn't eavesdrop on other people's conversations.'

'I did wonder how you knew about that.'

'I know a lot of things about you, Ulf. Did you think Bjorn and I wouldn't share our secrets? But don't worry; I never betray a trust – and Bjorn knows that.'

Freydis's smile was disconcerting and soothing all at once. 'I know that one day you must leave us to fulfil your destiny,' she murmured. 'You are the son of a king, and I know in my heart you have become a thrall for a purpose, as part of your learning about life, perhaps, or about people. I can see by your face you are sceptical. But, much as you've become a Dane in manner and appearance, underneath you're still the proud Mercian you were born to be. You will always despise our people for snatching you from your home and killing your father.'

She gazed up at the starlit sky and heaved a sigh. 'There is much about our world that we don't understand, Ulf. What is out there, amongst and beyond all those stars, for example? They are so far away that even the birds cannot reach them. And though our lives may be a continuous quest for knowledge, we can only ever scratch the surface of such mysteries. So we put our trust in our gods, who must surely know all things. And I believe that you *are* that red-headed warrior of Ivar's dream.' She laid her hand on Ulf's arm. It felt comforting and he savoured the sensation. 'It frightens me to think of it but what is fated to be, must be. You are destined to become a great warrior, and I a simple healer. We are surely opposites, you and I. But I know deep inside that you could never be evil. You are nothing like my two brothers.'

Ulf shrugged. He didn't believe himself to be truly evil; did not believe that killing in battle was evil. But, raiding the homelands of innocent people...?

'I've never shared my knowledge of your heritage with anyone except Bjorn: not even with Thora,' Freydis assured him with a small smile. 'And whatever Sigehelm knows about your parentage he would never divulge to anyone. His loyalty to you is steadfast, as is my own.' She reached up and took Ulf's face gently between her hands, standing on tiptoe to kiss his lips with a tenderness that felt no more than the brush of a butterfly's wing. She smiled again and turned to walk back to the hall, her silken hair white in the moonlight.

Ulf watched her enter the hall, the light from the opened doorway spilling across the bare earth. His legs suddenly went weak and he slumped down against the wall of the barn, his throat so taut he could barely swallow. The multiple emotions roused in him by Freydis had given him cause to hope for his own humanity. If Freydis could find some good in him, perhaps he wasn't the depraved creature he'd imagined.

* * *

Ulf looked down at his former tutor, taking in the silver streaks in his hair, the dark shadows beneath the soulful brown eyes. His long, grey tunic was worn and drab, like those of an ageing cleric.

'You should rest more, Sigehelm. No more sitting up all night studying those Latin texts.'

Sigehelm smiled at his former pupil, who'd just delivered a lengthy apology for his discourteous behaviour yesterday. 'Thank you, but I am well enough, just getting older.'

'But that's no reason for hastening the process along.'

Sigehelm's lips parted, a thought waiting to be spoken, his scrutiny of Ulf's own dark-circled eyes discomfiting. The early mist was slowly dissipating as the sun climbed in the pale sky, the assortment of barns and huts still blurred through the haze. Odours of wet earth and woodsmoke mingled with those of baking bread and pottage; thralls scurried between the buildings, their day's work underway. In the barns the laborious work of putting up the hay for winter fodder had already begun. Soon the slaughter of livestock and preservation of meat would begin, and animals required for breeding next spring herded into the barns. Ulf thought of the chores he must do before the jarl returned. Ragnar had ridden out at daybreak with Bjorn, intent on meeting with two of his karls, at loggerheads over some marriage settlement.

Sigehelm's face took on a familiar softness as he followed Ulf's gaze across the village and river beyond. 'How easy it is to ignore the things that cannot be taken from us, no matter how difficult we perceive our situations to be,' he said, turning to face Ulf. 'I'm glad you came to me this morning. I realise you must have swallowed your pride to apologise as you did. My lowly status demands neither apology nor explanation from you, but we've been through much together and I feel responsible for your welfare. Forgive me if you think I pry.'

Ulf raised his right arm and gave Sigehelm's shoulder a genial squeeze, an enquiring look appearing in his tutor's eyes at the sudden flash of silver. Ulf broke eye contact, not yet ready to explain how he'd earned the armband. 'It was entirely me at fault yesterday and I'm truly ashamed of myself,' he stated, ignoring the unspoken question. 'You've been my only lifeline all these years, Sigehelm, yet I chose to forget that in favour of my newfound status with Bjorn and his crew.'

'Then I should dearly love to hear an account of your summer ventures. Little has happened here during your absence; summer tasks have kept everyone busy as always. You probably already know that Ivar and Halfdan arrived back a few weeks ago?' Sigehelm gave an uncharacteristically low chuckle as Ulf nodded. 'Though they were reluctant to elaborate, I think they took little booty in the Low Countries.'

'And they are now on some errand for Ragnar?'

'They are, and we've been informed that the rest of the household will be joining them within the week.' Sigehelm ignored Ulf's half-started question as to exactly where they'd all be going, and added hastily,' I should be pleased to hear more of your adventures.'

They moved inside the hall to sit at the table where Sigehelm worked with Ubbi, away from household activities. The lively eight-year-old would soon be propelled in by Aslanga for his studies and Sigehelm arranged his parchments and scrolls into some sort of order as Ulf composed his thoughts.

'As you probably know, it was a joint venture,' he began, 'forty ships and close to eight hundred men of Ragnar and Giermund's lands. Giermund is the father of Hastein, Bjorn's cousin and our co-leader.'

Sigehelm nodded. 'This much I had heard, though neither Hastein nor his father is familiar to me.'

'No, but you did *see* Hastein once – on the same day that I first saw him.'

'I'm still none the wiser; you will simply have to explain.'

'Just one word may jog your memory.'

'And that word would be?'

'Hedeby.'

Sigehelm stiffened. 'A thousand images enter my head on hearing that word.' His dark eyebrows rose. 'A few more clues would be helpful.'

Ulf smirked, enjoying the game. 'A young Dane...'

'There were hundreds of those!'

'...in a blue cloak, and an encounter with a wandering canine.'

Sigehelm's eyes rounded in accordance with his mouth as recollection took hold.

'Aethelnoth...?'

'...is alive and well. At least he was when Hastein left Ribe in the spring.'

Sigehelm's shoulders slumped, the tension easing from his thin body. 'I've prayed for news of both your mother and Aethelnoth all these years and now at least some of my prayers have been answered. So, is there much to tell about the rest of your venture? Something happened to your left shoulder if I'm not mistaken. Your movements are unnaturally stiff, and I've seen you wince a few times.'

Ulf nodded, idly twisting the armband, not yet ready to explain.

'Bjorn has regaled us with tales of the booty taken and the number of Christian churches burned. All but four, he says. Is that so?'

Unable to look Sigehelm in the eye, Ulf responded with another nod, focusing on the thralls plucking chickens amidst chattering children.

But Sigehelm did not push him further. 'What I'd like to hear is how Bjorn came to bestow the name of Ulf upon you,' he said instead. 'Could he merely be wishing to make you a Dane, do you think?'

'Perhaps,' Ulf replied, 'though I think it unlikely. I'm still a thrall, aren't I? But as I told you, I did *earn* the name.'

'Then I'd like to hear how it came about.' Sigehelm tilted his head to one side in anticipation of the tale.

Ulf gazed at his fingers, intertwined on the table before him, knowing he'd have to relate the incident on that cursed island in order to answer Sigehelm's questions. He took a breath.

'Bjorn didn't exaggerate about the plunder we took, or the havoc we inflicted on the Franks. Charles the Bald despaired of ever ridding his lands of us. By the middle of May we'd made our base on an island in the Seine and for a few weeks it was ideal.' He lowered his voice and glanced round to ensure no one could overhear. 'I'll tell you the truth of events Sigehelm; I know you won't repeat it,' he added with certainty. 'It would cause embarrassment to Bjorn and Hastein if you did, especially when Bjorn's brothers return. Bjorn didn't actually lie – and the plunder taken speaks of the overall success of our venture – but he did omit part of the story. For twelve weeks we'd been within a hair's breadth of disaster; the reason we were so late returning to Aros. The wily old crow, Charles, imprisoned us on the island, attempting to either starve us to death or surrender to him. And after twelve weeks we'd barely any food left and things were desperate.'

'But evidently something happened to your advantage, or

you'd not be here to tell the tale,' Sigehelm said, ignoring Ulf's ignoble reference to the Christian king.

'No, we likely wouldn't,' Ulf agreed. And as succinctly as he could, he relayed the tale of the Franks' withdrawal and the unforeseen appearance of Weland's men in their place.

'Bjorn's own countrymen? But why?'

Ulf shrugged. 'They're raiders, interested only in increasing their booty. Weland was intent on relieving us of ours, after already receiving a huge sum from Charles to continue the siege in his place. So, in return for our loot, Weland agreed to let us go, duping the Franks still further by continuing his own raids in Francia.'

Sigehelm's opinion of such duplicity was evident, but he did not remark. 'You haven't yet told me how you were wounded. Or got your name,' he added, averting his eyes..

Ulf explained briefly how he'd taken the arrow in Bjorn's stead, and how Hastein had cut out the barbed head. 'Whilst camped in Frisia on the journey back, Bjorn rewarded me with this armband,' he said, his fingers inadvertently following the swirling patterns. 'And the new name was bestowed in front of all the men. How could I refuse and insult my master?'

'You could not, and your actions on that island would have made your parents proud.' Sigehelm smiled, holding Ulf's gaze. 'Nonetheless, when we depart from Aros in a few days' time, I suggest you keep the silver trinket out of sight. It might not be such a good time to draw attention to yourself, considering where we're destined.

Ubbi suddenly plonked himself next to Ulf, relieving Sigehelm of the need to answer Ulf's question, yet again.

Twenty Five

Canterbury, Kent: October-December 857

Alfred had watched his father growing increasingly morose as the weeks passed. At times Aethelwulf seemed to be drowning in his sorrows, unaware of the effects it was having on those around him. He often seemed lost in the past, his mumbled conversations with Lady Osburh heartrending to hear. He ate and drank little, despite Judith's valiant attempts to coax him otherwise, and his once robust body appeared to be wasting away, bit by bit. The ruling of the eastern shires was left to Aethelberht, who took it all in his stride, simply continuing as he had done for the past two years. He reported to Aethelwulf on matters raised at Council meetings and, at times, asked for advice as to the appropriate way forward. But Aethelwulf would fix him with his misty gaze, his reply always the same:

'You must do what's best for Wessex, son.'

Alfred often brooded over why things had come to this, frequently condemning his eldest brother for allowing his ambition to override his loyalty to his father. Weren't families supposed to stick together and support each other? How could Aethelbald betray the father who loved him so much? Alfred didn't understand; Aethelwulf meant the world to him.

The October afternoon was dark and cheerless. Alfred stomped from the stables, glaring at the heavy black clouds that threatened imminent release, piqued at the groom's assertion that only fools would ride out today. He'd so hoped to spend some time in the saddle, just to break the monotony of moping about indoors. On returning to the hall, he was greeted by the comforting glow of oil lamps and the chatter of servants as they worked at their chores. But then he spotted his father, huddled in his chair by the hearthfire, wrapped in a woollen blanket and staring into the flames. At his side, Judith patiently clasped the cup of buttermilk he was loath to drink. Seated opposite them, Aethelberht and Aethelred's faces were creased in concern. Their father looked particularly downcast today. Alfred joined them by the sputtering fire and Aethelwulf's sorrowful gaze shifted from one to the other.

"Where did I go so wrong?' he murmured. 'Aethelbald would've had the West anyway, after my death. Why couldn't he have just waited a few more years?'

'Don't torment yourself, Father,' Aethelberht said, reaching out to touch Aethelwulf's hand. 'We're all here with you, trying our best to get you feeling yourself again.'

The old king nodded at that, smiling wanly at Aethelberht's troubled face. He licked his parched lips and Judith again proffered the cup of milk. 'You must drink, my lord,' she urged, 'or you will become quite unwell. You have not taken more than a few sips all day, and I worry for you.'

'You are kind-hearted, Judith, and I couldn't wish for a more attentive nurse.' Alfred watched his father gaze at his young wife, her presence, as always, offering him comfort. 'I have failed you, too, my dear,' Aethelwulf whispered. 'You expected the life of a queen, yet you spend your days looking after an old man.'

'You have not failed me, husband. I am content just to be

here, with you and your lovely family. I have found love and friendship here that I could never have found in Francia. And that is all I ever wanted.' She held the cup close to his lips. 'But I would be happier still, my lord, if I thought my nursing was being of use.'

Alfred smiled at his stepmother, knowing that she spoke the truth. Judith didn't know how to lie. For the daughter of an emperor, she required little luxury in life.

'Then I shall drink, just for you,' Aethelwulf responded, pulling a face as the buttermilk slid down his throat. 'But that must suffice, for now. If you want me to eat later, my stomach must first rest.'

No one questioned the statement. Alfred knew his father found great difficulty in eating, the food often sitting too heavily in his stomach to stay down. A few nibbles were his limit.

As autumn turned into winter and the land was scoured by icy fingers of frost, Alfred spent most of his days reading poetry, or writing out the prayers he found so moving. Occasionally, he'd ride into the forest with Aethelberht and Aethelred and the royal huntsmen, in search of game, from smaller hares and birds to larger deer, and even ferocious wild boar. At almost seventeen, Aethelred was already adept in his hunting skills, but for nine-year-old Alfred, such talents presented another challenge. Yet he soon found himself enjoying the hunts and, although not permitted to attempt larger game, before long he was wielding his spear and bow with some finesse.

By the beginning of December, Aethelwulf appeared to have sufficiently risen above his miseries to potter about the hall, even finding time to discuss issues of government with

Aethelberht. But as the Advent progressed, ill-health struck, and physicians ordered the once powerful king to his bed. Too weak to refuse, Aethelwulf obeyed.

Christmastide was a dismal event in the Canterbury hall that year. Burgred had again refused to allow Aethelswith to visit her family. It was now almost three years since Alfred had seen his sister, although she continued to write, ever hopeful that her husband would soon give way. Alfred's dislike of the Mercian continued to grow. Judith spent most of her time at Aethelwulf's bedside, along with the chief physician and Father Felix, who sorrowfully informed them that the king was presently constructing his final will.

Aethelwulf was making preparations for his imminent death, and leaving his beloved Wessex to the mercy of his sons.

Twenty Six

Aalborg, Northern Denmark: mid October 857

In Jarl Rorik's hall on the shores of the Limfjord, the thralls were satisfying their own stomachs after attending to the morning meal. At one of the tables a young boy in dull woollen tunic and leggings dolefully scooped up a spoonful of pottage, watching his mother across the table feeding the lively, brown-eyed baby perched on her lap. His nose wrinkled in disgust as his blue gaze fixed on his little sister's bowl.

Morwenna smiled at him. 'Believe it or not, Jorund, you used to love your pottage mashed up when you were only ten months old like Yrsa.'

'But it looks all mushy, and I know I wouldn't like it now! Is there any meat in it? I like meat.'

'There is, but chopped into tiny pieces so she won't choke on it.'

Jorund seemed to think about that for a moment. 'You'd be upset if Yrsa choked, wouldn't you, Mama?'

Wondering where this conversation was heading, Morwenna nodded. Around them the remnants of the meal were being cleared away, and soon she must join the women at the looms.

'I wouldn't be sad,' he said at length, staring at the infant through half-closed eyes. 'If she choked and died you'd be able to love me more.'

Tears streamed down his cheeks and Morwenna reached

out to take his hand. 'Come round here, Jorund. Now, I want you to listen to me,' she said gently, shifting the babe to her opposite thigh, allowing him to nestle into her side. 'Yrsa's birth makes no difference at all to the love I feel for you.'

'But you're always fussing over *her* now; never have time to play with me or tell me stories.'

'Well, babies do take up a lot of time,' she agreed, wanting so much to ease his pain. 'But babies soon grow; soon walk and feed, and dress themselves. Why, it seems like only yesterday that you had to sit on my lap to be fed, and just look at you now ...almost six years old, and such a help to me.'

Jorund beamed at the praise and Morwenna cuddled him close, relieved that the hurt in his eyes had abated. 'You'll be a man one day, Jorund, strong enough to look after yourself in the world. But your sister will become a woman, and all women need their menfolk to take care of them. You are Yrsa's big brother and will have to make sure no one hurts her. Do you think you could do that?'

'If Yrsa becomes a weak woman and I a big man, then I will look after her,' he said, puffing out his chest. 'But won't Papa take care of her, too?'

'Yes, he'll do his best for Yrsa and make sure she chooses a suitable husband,' she started, knowing full well that Rorik would never take any interest in his daughter. 'But the jarl is away a great deal, especially during the summer.'

'I'm proud to be a jarl's son, Mama, though I see little of him,' Jorund responded with a frown. 'And Papa has so many children, he hardly notices me.'

Morwenna's stomach lurched. How different Jorund's life

would have been if he'd been born in Mercia with Beorhtwulf to love him and an older brother to spoil him. She had never abandoned the belief that Eadwulf was still alive, and one day she would tell Jorund about him. She glanced down at her drab tunic, thinking of her lowly status in Rorik's household – merely one of the many household thralls. Her position as the jarl's favourite concubine had, thankfully, ended: Rorik's lustful desires had long since turned elsewhere. Yet, even now, she rarely felt safe from his clutches. Rorik could seek out any of the women whenever he chose.

Memories of that day in early March last year sent shudders down Morwenna's spine. She'd been sorting through the remnants of winter vegetables in one of the huts, when Rorik had leapt at her from behind, his great weight plunging her to the floor. Taken so unawares she screamed like a banshee. Rorik roared with laughter, his vulgar mouth salivating on the back of her neck. 'By Thor's hammer, the sight of that arse takes me back a few years,' he taunted. 'I like a good scuffle with my mares and you always give me a good ride!'

He'd taken her then, flinging up her skirts and mauling her buttocks before thrusting into her. She'd fought for breath, her face pressed into the hut's filthy straw.

Morwenna had thought she would hate the child growing in her womb, that the babe would be a constant reminder of Rorik's depravity. But, although the brutal rape would stay with her for ever, just one look at the tiny face of her newly born daughter had been enough to change that. Morwenna knew she would always love the child, who was just as innocent of her father's cruelty as was her mother.

'Are you sad, Mama?'

Morwenna ruffled her son's blond head. 'No, I'm not sad; just thinking. How could I be sad when I have you? And I'm very glad to know that Yrsa will always have her big brother to take care of her. Now,' she said, wiping the infant's food-covered face, 'would you like to sit on the floor with your sister for a while? You could build a big tower and try to stop her knocking it over.'

'I'm good at building things,' Jorund enthused. 'And I'll watch she doesn't crawl near the firepit.'

Morwenna kissed his smiling face. 'I'm so lucky to have such a good son. And we'll all need to work really hard for the next week or two.'

'Because Papa will have more guests?'

'That's right,' she said, trying to mask her revulsion at the thought of the two young men who'd already been at Aalborg over a week. And in a few days' time, more of their household would arrive to enjoy Rorik's hospitality and attend the sacrificial rites to the gods. 'Rorik will have many guests, whom we must feed,' she explained, leading Jorund to a space in the hall where he could amuse his sister. 'Now, I'll be over there at the looms, so you can just call me when you've had enough and I'll put Yrsa in her pen. There are lots of nice wooden bricks here, see. Most of these were yours, when you were small.'

'I know,' Jorund replied. 'But I'm a big boy now. I'll soon be a man!'

* * *

The small convoy of wagons, carts and mounted men made its way up the low rise, nearing the final stage of its near sixty-mile journey north from Aros to Aalborg. After almost five days of trundling along dirt-tracks and making overnight camps, the travellers were bone-weary and not in the best of tempers. Despite having demanded to travel overland rather than sailing, Aslanga had constantly assailed Bjorn with complaints. But his countering platitudes served only to amuse Ulf and further incense the mistress.

Required to remain in Aros until yesterday, Ragnar had been obliged to take the faster sea route to Aalborg with his men. In his father's absence, Bjorn rode at the head of the column, and behind him a dozen men accompanied the two horse-drawn wagons carrying the jarl's family and female thralls. But Freydis had adamantly refused to be bumped along inside a covered wagon, claiming she'd be repeatedly sick, and took her place proudly beside Bjorn, proving to be as good a rider as any man. And not wanting to cause further offence by riding alongside them, Ulf accompanied Toke on one of the three carts.

Ulf avoided thinking of the impending sacrifices to Odin, but was plagued by visions of Rorik. In truth he remembered little of the man, other than the unkempt brown hair and hulking body, and he could not imagine how he'd react on seeing him again. Then there was always the chance that Ragnar's cousin was not the same Rorik.

Of the possibility of seeing his mother again, he dared not dwell.

At the top of the rise Bjorn dismounted and waved everyone forward. 'Have you ever seen such a sight?' he yelled as they gathered round, flinging his arms out wide to indicate the expanse of sparkling water before them. 'The Limfjord looks magnificent from up here. See that little island over there, Aslanga? We spent a comfortable night on one just like it not so long ago, didn't we, Ulf?' He swung his arm to indicate a sizeable settlement at the fjord's edge. 'As I'm sure you know, Aalborg is an important trading post. And Jarl Rorik is fortunate in being admirably located for sailing either east or west,' he added, pointing in both directions with further arm swinging. 'And at Lindholm Høje, over there on the opposite bank, is one of the biggest cemeteries in our lands.

'Just inhale that briny air, Aslanga,' he almost purred, breaking her glowering disapproval of Freydis's attire. 'Couldn't you just stand here all day, filling your lungs with the delicious odour?'

Aslanga's scowl was thunderous as she stalked back to her wagon.

Bjorn smirked and gestured at the sinking sun. 'I'd say we've less than a couple of hours before sunset, so we need to keep moving if we're to reach Aalborg before dark. We can probably assume that Ragnar is already there.'

* * *

Gleeful squeals drew Morwenna's attention to two brawny arms holding up a small, wriggling bundle. Panicked, she put down the ale jug and pushed through the chortling guests, trying to reach the man to whom the arms belonged. She got there just as Jorund did.

'Yours?' the grinning, red-headed man asked, handing over the giggling child. 'I think she liked being up there – better than tugging at my trouser leg at least.'

Grasping her little daughter, Morwenna opened her mouth to speak, but then closed it again and stared at the stranger's face. Those green eyes ...

'If the little one is your daughter, I assure you, I didn't hurt her. I merely held her up so her rightful owner would see her and–'

'Forgive me, my lord,' Morwenna mumbled. 'It's just that seeing you gave me rather a shock.'

'Well, I'm used to having an odd effect on women, but not usually one that causes them distress. You seem a little perturbed by my appearance.'

'In truth, my lord, you remind me of someone I knew in my homeland.'

'Ah. And where would this have been?'

'In Mercia, my lord: across the Northern Sea.

'I know of it, but have never been there.' The man's eyebrows rose. 'Of whom do I remind you?'

'My husband ...but he's been dead these past six years.'

Morwenna smiled down at Jorund, wondering whether she should say anything else about Beorhtwulf, but her son seemed to be engrossed in watching a dark-headed boy who was twisting energetically in an attempt to escape the grip of a sharp-featured woman of similar colouring. Jorund giggled as the boy pulled a funny face at him, pointing to the hand gripping his shoulder.

'You have my sincere thanks for retrieving my daughter,' she offered to the man, losing her train of thought and smiling at the boy's antics. 'I admit I laid a burden on my son in charging him with her care. But I fear I must do so again.

'Can you manage to play with Yrsa a while longer, do you think, Jorund?' At his nod she thanked the man again and took Jorund's hand to lead him back to the corner where he'd been building a tower of bricks for Yrsa, before she'd, somehow, escaped his supervision.

'I am Bjorn, eldest son of Jarl Ragnar, who is cousin to Jarl Rorik,' the red-headed man said as they turned to leave.

'I am called Morwenna,' she replied, facing him again.

'And who is father to your two fine children?'

'Rorik is their father, my lord, but–'

'I understand your meaning, my lady. Say no more. Now I must allow you to get back to serving ale. I hope the little one allows you to do so.'

Bjorn took his mug from the man at his side and walked away. Morwenna stared at his retreating back. 'He called me "my lady", she murmured. 'No one has called me that for years.'

Jorund wrapped his arms around his mother's legs as she wiped a tear from her cheek.

Twenty Seven

Whilst Bjorn's family enjoyed the hospitality of Rorik's hall, the thralls of Ragnar's household stabled the horses and unloaded wagons and carts. Indignant at being required to help, Sigehelm had suddenly felt the urge to thank God for their safe arrival at Aalborg and disappeared behind one of the huts. And since he was absent when a woman fetched them a jug of ale, no one saw reason to inform him.

'That'll teach him to shirk,' Ulf grouched, glancing at the now empty jug. He was as tired and hungry as the rest, but orders were orders. He hauled himself onto one of the carts and handed sacks of gifts for Rorik's family down to Rico. 'Just because he's a scribe doesn't mean he's above physical work now and then!'

'Our sleeping place,' Toke said, ignoring Ulf's bad mood and tilting his head towards a large storage shed. 'Girl who brought ale said hut used for vegetables. Space for ten, maybe more. No draughts perhaps: daub looks good.'

They carried straw from the barn into the hut, enough to cushion their bedrolls and mask the cold of the earthen floor. There was space to sleep a dozen men inside the windowless hut, but only the half-dozen Aros thralls would be using it. Pungent smells from sacks of onions mingled with the spicy aromas from storage jars on the shelves.

'It's not too unpleasant in there, provided no rats come seeking sustenance in the early hours,' Sigehelm remarked, standing outside as daylight finally faded into night. Toke and

Rico had already left for the hall to seek orders from Aslanga.

'It seems comfortable enough,' Ulf answered indifferently.

Sigehelm laid his hand on Ulf's arm, a bleak smile on his lips. 'I know the reason for your anxiety, Ulf, because I share it. But if Morwenna isn't here, I fear we must accept that she is lost to you forever.'

'I know that,' Ulf snapped, 'but I don't want to think about it. Curse Rorik for ever invading our home!'

Sigehelm drew breath to speak but released it again. Ulf knew he'd be thinking him to be the worst kind of hypocrite. 'I should go and find Bjorn,' he said, avoiding eye contact. 'He may need me for some chore by now.'

'And I must offer Burghild some respite from Ubbi. The boy wears her down with his boundless energy. Ubbi's no more high spirited than other boys of his age, but Burghild isn't a young woman. Do you know, Eadwulf, had I not feigned severity with you from an early age, I think you'd have led me quite a merry dance!'

Ulf didn't miss the slip, but didn't remark on it. In his heart he knew he'd never be anyone but Eadwulf.

* * *

They headed for the hall, passing groups of Aros men making for the barn to snatch some sleep before the meal. It was now fully dark, moon and stars hidden behind the thick banks of cloud that had blown over. One or two men carried lamps, curled fingers shielding the listing flames from the gusting wind. Loud jocularity professed their enjoyment of more than a few mugs of ale.

The hall door suddenly swung open, the flood of light from inside outlining a tall, bulky figure possessing an unmistakable air of authority. And not wishing to walk straight into the Aalborg jarl, Ulf and Sigehelm stepped aside. 'My lord,' they said, almost in unison, dipping their heads as they made to enter the hall.

Rorik threw them a disinterested glance and looked away. Then he turned back, holding out his arm to stay them. 'Frey's crotch, what trick is this? I could've sworn you to be Ragnar's son – but I've just left *him* inside my hall.' He scratched his own crotch and looked Ulf up and down, distaste replacing puzzlement on his face. 'But now I see you clearly, you've a different set to your jaw and your attire tells me you're just a mangy thrall.'

Ulf fought down the impulse to beat the ugly face to a pulp. 'You are right, my lord,' he said, despising the servility of his tone. 'The similarity must be no more than a trick of nature. Bjorn is my master.'

'They say we all have a double somewhere,' Rorik said, giving his crotch another determined scratch. 'I confess I've never seen such a likeness between two unrelated people before.' He turned to a big blond man at his side. 'What say you, Egil?'

Egil stared hard at Ulf, his eyes cold and calculating. 'You're right, my lord. It is strange.' He blinked several times and pulled at his plaited beard. 'But there's something about this thrall that stirs a memory in me somewhere. I'm just too befuddled with ale right now to figure it out. Perhaps I'll remember tomorrow.'

Rorik shot Egil an amused look and returned his attentions to Ulf, his amusement dropping. 'What's your name, thrall?'

'Ulf,' my lord,' he replied, returning the jarl's stare unflinchingly, silently thanking Bjorn for giving him the name. His old name may have been known to these two, even if his face were not.

Rorik's eyes narrowed. 'Well *Ulf*, Danish name you may own, but you weren't born on Danish soil with *that* accent.'

'So you've found your way here at last, you lazy churl,' Bjorn snarled as he stepped through the open doorway. 'You took your time with those horses. Serves you right you've missed the ale. You'll wait for your supper now – *after* you've finished the chores for me.' He jerked his thumb to the hall behind him. 'You, Scribe, the mistress is asking for you.'

Sigehelm disappeared into the hall and Bjorn turned to the grinning jarl. 'My apologies, my lord, but I can't abide idleness in my thralls.' He glared at Ulf. 'Why I ever took this one on, Odin knows.'

Rorik grinned and slapped Bjorn's shoulder. 'I like a man who allows no indolence in his thralls. I brook no nonsense from my own. Take a stiff belt to the women and a rod to the men. You'll have little trouble if you follow that advice.'

Bjorn's fists were clenched at his sides, knuckles white beneath the taut skin. But he feigned an obsequious smile. 'There can be no other way, of course.'

'You should keep this one clean shaven,' Rorik said, glowering at Ulf. 'And perhaps shave his head to prevent shocks like he just gave me. Should be a good meal tonight,' he added, turning to leave. 'And you'll have your pick of women. I only choose those whose tits and arses have plenty to squeeze.'

Ulf stood silently with his master as Rorik strode into the darkness. The hall door was closed now, the only light leaking through the cracks around it. Bjorn let out his breath as a long sigh. 'I'm beginning to think bringing you here was a mistake, Ulf. If Rorik thinks he's been duped in any way, Odin knows what he'll do. But there's something I have to tell you. I don't know how to do it, but you need to know, so we can decide what to do about it.'

'Can't you just tell me straight out?'

'No, I can't just tell you, Ulf. It's ...it's *difficult*.'

Ulf didn't press for more. 'I think Egil sees my likeness to my father and will soon make the connection. He and Rorik both know that Beorhtwulf had a son called Eadwulf.'

'Then they must not hear anyone call you that. Not easy, but I've arranged for our thralls to have their own table for tonight's meal. You'll not be serving ale, so no one's likely to shout out your name in front of Rorik.' Bjorn grasped Ulf's shoulder. 'Now, get some rest before we eat. But don't be surprised if someone comes looking for spices, or perhaps onions, in your sleeping chamber.'

* * *

Ulf lit the lamp and glanced round the hut. Sigehelm was right; it seemed warm and dry enough. He poked about, lifting the lids on spice jars, wrinkling his nose at their sharp pungency, and though he recognised the distinctive tang of some used by Aslanga, he could name hardly any. He tugged out some of the vegetable sacks, satisfied to find no sign of infestation by vermin.

Too fraught to sleep he left the lamp on a ledge beside the jars and wandered outside, squatting down to rest against the wall of the hut where it was sheltered from the sharp wind. He closed his eyes, picturing his mother's face, remembering how much she'd loved him – and how much he'd loved and depended on her. But a person can change over the years; time moves on and people adapt to new situations. And Morwenna – if she still lived – would have had a hard life as a thrall.

His heavy eyelids succumbed to the dark tranquillity and images of Morwenna and Freydis floated alternately across his mind. Rorik's snarling mouth was suddenly thrust before his face and all beauty vanished. He jerked his head back and stared at the hideous black teeth, rancid breath hot on his face. Morwenna's face was still there, bright in the glow from the lamp she held. Then Rorik's sour breath was assaulting his nostrils again. He shuddered and twisted his face sideways. So the ugly jarl was still in his dream – but not Freydis.

'Where's Freydis?' his own dream voice sounded in his ears.

'Come away, Burakki,' his mother ordered, tugging at the collar of a large, black dog.

'My lord Bjorn doesn't want your muzzle in his face! I'm sorry, my lord. Burakki would do no more than wash you from head to foot, though his breath would perhaps render you senseless. But to answer your question, your sister was playing a board game with your young brother but a moment ago. Were you not also in the hall just now ...?

'Are you unwell, my lord?' she asked, clearly puzzled. 'Shall

I send our healer with something to ease you?'

This was no dream: it really *was* Morwenna! Her face was just as he remembered, though her shabby, thrall's clothing was very different to the garb of the Mercian queen she'd once been. But she had evidently not recognised *him*. Had he changed so much? He touched his face, knowing his thick beard and moustache would disguise the features she would have remembered. And, of course, she'd assumed him to be Bjorn.

'I am not Bjorn.' He wanted to stand, but could not until the shaking stopped. 'My name is Ulf.'

'Then are you another of Bjorn's brothers, Ulf? You are so like him.'

'According to *Rorik* I should have my face and head shorn to avoid confusion!' he snapped, instantly regretting his words. 'I'm sorry. I seem to be having a bad day. But I'm not Bjorn's brother. Nor am I ill; just overtired.'

'Well, we all have bad days,' Morwenna said softly, 'some worse than others. And a good night's sleep will usually remedy the tiredness. I take it my lord Rorik didn't impress you with his suggestion – about your hair, I mean. But I also mistook you for Bjorn, for which I'm sorry. I came only to collect some extra pepper for Lady Freydis's soup.'

Ulf grinned, the scheming of Bjorn and Freydis becoming clear.

'We've all learnt to tread carefully and keep to our work,' Morwenna whispered, lowering her eyes. 'Of course, I speak for the thralls here. But if you are high born, you can stand your ground with Jarl Rorik without fear.'

'I *am* high born, my lady,' Ulf murmured, 'but Rorik

doesn't know that. He called me "a mangy thrall" – and in these lands, that's all I am.' He stood to retrieve the lamp from inside the hut and was now looking down on Morwenna's face. Like Freydis she was tall and willowy, reaching almost to his chin. 'But Bjorn allows me much freedom. He renamed me Ulf – for loyal service.'

With the extra lamp Morwenna would be able to see him clearly now, and her breathing had quickened. Ulf understood too well the inner battle she'd be fighting, the snatching at shreds of hope. He searched for the right words to relieve her pain, but could find none. Averting his eyes, he pulled at the neck of his woollen tunic.

'Who *are* you, Ulf, and why do you, like Bjorn, call me "my lady"? No-one in these lands has ever addressed me so.' She reached out to touch his sleeve, the corners of her mouth turning up in a smile. 'I had a son who swore that when he became a man, he'd *never* wear wool because it made him itch. It seems that wool has a similar effect on you,' she said looking steadily into his eyes. 'My son had green eyes too, the green of emeralds, like his father's...' Her words caught in her throat and she took a steadying breath. 'I dare not hope you are who I want you so much to be. I couldn't bear it should you tell me you are not.'

'Not Eadwulf, you mean?'

He opened his arms and she threw herself at him. 'Eadwulf ...is it really you? Pray God this is no dream from which I'll wake and find you gone.' She pulled back a little, drinking in the sight of him. 'You are a man, so tall and broad; so like your father. How could I have taken so long to see that?'

'The light...' was all Ulf could find to say.

'But I think you recognised me,' she said eventually, looking up at his face.

'I came to Aalborg in the hope that you'd be here,' he replied, smiling at her puzzled frown. 'Bjorn told me some years ago of Ragnar's cousin who'd led the raids in Kent and Mercia. And Rorik wasn't a name I was likely to forget.'

'But you could not have known that Rorik had taken me, surely?'

'I saw him push you into the cart on that day at Thrydwulf's manor. I recognised your gown, and your hair. But I didn't know where you'd been taken; you could have been sold to anyone. Bjorn promised to help me find out, one day.'

"And you, Eadwulf, were you taken straight to Aros?'

He shook his head. 'We were bought by Jarl Ragnar at the Hedeby market.'

'We...?'

'Several of us from the manor were taken: Aethelnoth, Alric, and some of the serving girls. Ragnar bought Sigehelm and me.'

'Sigehelm is still alive!'

'He is here, in the hall, though he would have avoided you until you'd seen me.'

Morwenna took Ulf's face in her hands, her eyes glistening. 'You've barely left my thoughts for a moment. I mourned your father for so long, but no one could tell me what had happened to you. And I could never lose hope.'

'My lady ...?' Bjorn's voice was hushed as he approached, carrying no lamp and peering warily into the shadows between the huts. 'I fear you may be missed if you stay here much longer. Dalla's already asked for you; it seems you're needed to deal with some of the children.' A flash of alarm crossed Morwenna's face. 'My sister is telling them a story, though stories do little to alleviate tiredness.'

'Yes, of course I must go.' Morwenna half turned away, then glanced uncertainly back at Ulf, drawing breath to speak.

'I suggest you go, Lady Morwenna,' Bjorn said, forestalling her. 'I'll explain the situation to your son – as far as I know it, of course. Take care not to make public your reunion with Sigehelm. There are some who can put two and two together too easily, and things could become more than difficult for all of you should they do so. I've told Sigehelm the same.'

'Every fibre of my being thanks you for caring for Eadwulf these many years, my lord,' Morwenna replied with a brave smile. 'I know you can make him understand about my life here. I simply had no choice.' To Eadwulf she said, 'I would have told you everything Eadwulf – later, in my own way.'

'Well, Master, what is this *situation* about which you're going to enlighten me?' Ulf smirked as Morwenna hurried away. 'Could it be that my mother believes my ears too sensitive to hear that she is Rorik's concubine?'

Bjorn pulled a face of feigned shock but seemed at a loss for words. He gave an extended shrug, releasing his breath as a somewhat elaborate whine.

'I've lived among Danes long enough to understand your ways,' Ulf said, still smirking. But Rorik's ugly face came to mind and his smirk vanished. 'I only hope he's treated her well. She's such a gentle soul.'

'I share your hopes on that, Ulf. But before we enter the hall there's something else your mother wished conveyed to you.'

'That I have brothers and sisters perhaps?' Ulf shook his head, his amusement returning. 'From what you so tactfully said about overtired children, even a complete imbecile could have guessed!'

Bjorn chuckled. 'Evidently, tact is not my strongest point. But surely the children I mentioned – only two of them, by the way – could have been anyone's?'

Ulf grunted. Such a remark did not deserve dignifying with an answer.

* * *

Ulf found it impossible to approach his mother the following morning. Sheltering from the high winds and threatening black clouds outside, people sat around the hall in convivial conversation, and any move in her direction would have been noted. He occupied himself by wiping down Bjorn's travel-stained cloak, glancing occasionally at Morwenna, who was shaping flatbreads with two of the women. And though she avoided eye contact, he knew she'd registered his presence.

Sitting beside Aslanga with Rorik's wives and a veritable gaggle of daughters, Freydis looked utterly bored. At another table, Ragnar and his four sons conversed with Rorik and three men so like him they could only be his sons. All seemed in good spirits, though like Freydis, Bjorn glanced often at Ulf. But hostile stares from Ivar and Halfdan were also directed at Ulf, and on one occasion, he caught Ivar staring at Morwenna

– before the dark stare slowly returned to fix on him. Like a startled hare caught in the torchlight, Ulf could not look away, until Ragnar made some jest and Ivar's scrutiny was broken.

Just before noon the jarls and their sons rode out to exercise their mounts and watch the fishermen raking in oysters and mussels along the fjord. The hall was peaceful once they'd gone, and since Ubbi was with them, Ulf sat with Sigehelm, hoping to catch Morwenna at some stage. Then Aslanga's shrill voice disturbed the silence.

'If you've naught better to do than sit around on your backside, thrall, you can get outside and chop some logs. Our good hostesses here,' she went on, smiling at Dalla and Helga, 'tell me the stack is low and the pile of timber is high.' Her outstretched finger swung from Ulf to Sigehelm. 'And you can do likewise. So get out and make a start.

'Now!' she shrieked, pointing to the door.

Not bothering to hide his furious scowl Ulf strode from the hall with Sigehelm on his heels.

The tree trunks were stacked under a lean-to shelter behind the pig pens, left to dry out after felling, with several long-handled axes propped next to them. Ulf noted the variety of timbers – from ash, beech, hazel, birch and pine to fruit-woods like apple, pear and cherry – and looked at Sigehelm in dismay. It would take many hours to make a dent in this lot. He seethed at this new attack on his favoured status with Bjorn. Aslanga had found a way of demeaning him before Rorik's women – and Ulf's mother, had she but known it. He vented his fury in powerful strokes that cut the trunks into lengths suitable for the hearth. Buffeted by the strong wind,

Sigehelm made slow progress at first, but by the time they'd built up a good sized stack, he'd become quite adept at his new-found calling as woodcutter.

Few of the men gave the two thralls more than a fleeting glance on their return from the shore and, deep in conversation with his father, Bjorn didn't notice them at all. But Ivar did, and his deep, calculating eyes fixed on Ulf. But he didn't linger and continued on to the hall with the rest of the party.

Sigehelm laid a consolatory hand on his arm and they, too, made to return to the hall – just as Morwenna appeared, heading towards them.

Perched on her hip was a babe; a little girl. A young boy bounced along beside them: Ulf's half-brother and sister, no doubt.

'I'm glad someone is pleased to see me,' Morwenna said, looking from Ulf's anxious face to Sigehelm's smiling one as she lowered the child to the ground. She reached out to take Sigehelm's hand. 'I'm so sorry to have been unable to speak to you sooner, Sigehelm. I can never repay the kindness you've shown to Eadwulf all these years. No, do not try to lessen or deny the extent of your care: both Bjorn and Freydis have commended it. You've always been the truest of friends to me. When I was a little girl, you were there for me. Even after I married, you found me again in Mercia.' She paused, her eyes probing into Sigehelm's, as though she'd just unearthed some buried truth. 'You loved me, didn't you? And I was just too blind, too self-centred, to see it. After all these years I suddenly understand why you left Anglia before my marriage. But you came back to me.'

'I could not stay away from you forever Morwenna, no matter how hard I tried.'

'And now you care for my beloved son. I do not deserve such a friend as you.'

His throat swollen with emotion, Ulf watched his mother take comfort in the gentle embrace of the man who'd so selflessly cared for her and her family for so long. At length she pulled herself away and moved towards him.

'We've already had our initial reunion, Eadwulf,' she said, enfolding him in her arms. 'Now we need time to become reacquainted and discuss the situation in which we find ourselves.' She stepped back a little, holding Ulf in a determined gaze. 'But, whatever happens now, should we never see each other again, I am content to know that you are alive and well.' She glanced at the two children, happily playing with pebbles. 'My life isn't likely to change, but in my heart I know that one day *you* will be free and return to Mercia.'

'I've been saying the very same these past six years, my lady.'

Morwenna flashed Sigehelm a grateful smile and bent to scoop up the small girl, then beckoned Jorund to join her. 'This is my son Jorund,' she said, patting the boy's shoulder. 'Jorund, meet ...er ...Ulf, a man from Jarl Ragnar's village. And this is Sigehelm, a very clever scribe who could teach even the dimmest of pupils his letters. You would love his wonderful stories, Jorund: all about heroes and great battles.'

Jorund beamed and peered up at Ulf. 'I shall be six in January, so I'll soon be as big as you. And I am learning my letters very well,' he added in a matter-of-fact tone, his blue gaze shifting to Sigehelm. 'And I really like listening to stories.'

Sigehelm grinned down at the boy. 'Then one day you'll be a tall, clever man, who'll be able to tell his own fantastic stories.'

'When I'm a man, I'll be a jarl, like my father,' Jorund responded. 'He's very brave and leads raids.'

'Jorund is very proud of being a jarl's son,' Morwenna supplied by way of apology at Sigehelm's grimace. 'Everyone has told him he should be so since he was tiny. And this is Yrsa,' she continued, 'who'll be a whole year old just before the Yule.'

Sigehelm smiled at the dimple-cheeked child. 'You have a very pretty name, Yrsa, and very pretty curls.'

Yrsa flung her chubby little arms around Morwenna's neck and just giggled.

Ulf surveyed the children, taking in their similarities and differences. In Jorund he could see Morwenna: the pert little nose and wide mouth, almond-shaped blue eyes and pale complexion, framed by a head of soft, flaxen hair. Yet there was a definite set to the boy's square jaw that was so like Ulf's own. In Yrsa, Ulf perceived features of both parents. Like Jorund, she had an attractively wide mouth, but although she had her mother's dainty, heart-shaped face and high cheek bones rather than Rorik's broad visage, Yrsa's longer nose resembled her father's. And like the jarl, the child was brown-haired and dark eyed. Long dark lashes swept her cheeks, her complexion of a naturally tanned hue.

'They are pretty children,' Ulf said, once Morwenna had set Yrsa into Jorund's care. 'I just hope Rorik treats them well.'

Morwenna smiled at the sight of Sigehelm, who'd wandered after the little ones, and now seemed intent on showing them how to play a simplified version of knucklebones with their pebbles. Ulf realised his tutor was simply affording a degree of privacy for his conversation with his mother, for which he was very grateful.

'He doesn't treat them ill,' she replied with a small shrug. 'But nor does he love them, or even acknowledge them as his own. He just seems to ignore them. Yrsa's too young to know but Jorund has become increasingly distressed by it of late.' She frowned, seeming to be considering her next words carefully, then took a breath to continue. 'There's something I must tell you, Eadwulf; but I'm finding it hard to get it out. I suppose the best way is to just say it...'

Ulf watched his mother's anxious face, fearing this 'something' would not be pleasant.

'When Thrydwulf's manor was raided, Rorik came to my bower and raped me.' Morwenna's words had poured out quickly, shame and embarrassment on her face.

'Don't dwell on it, Mother. I'd already guessed that Jorund was conceived at that time.'

'No, you don't understand, Eadwulf. That was not the case.'

Ulf stared at her, not understanding, and she took his hands in hers. 'Eadwulf, before I go on, I want to swear to you that what I'm about to tell you is the truth. You know I wouldn't lie to you, don't you?' He nodded. 'When Rorik raped me I was already a few weeks with child. The nausea and tiredness were already pronounced, as is the way in the earliest weeks. So, before you ask, no, I am not mistaken in this. Beorhtwulf was Jorund's father, as much as he was yours.'

Ulf gaped at her. 'Then, Jorund is my true brother, not my *half*-brother. Is that why Rorik ignores him?' He paused, trying to unravel the conflicting pieces of information. 'But that doesn't make sense,' he said at last. 'You said Jorund believes Rorik is his father, as does everyone else in the village. So what *does* Rorik believe?'

'To my everlasting shame I've let Rorik believe Jorund to be his child, though I doubt it would have made any difference had he known the truth.' Morwenna almost spat out the words. 'In my folly I thought Jorund would escape a life of drudgery if it was believed he was Rorik's son. But a concubine's son is little better than a thrall.

'I can never reveal any of this to anyone else, Eadwulf. Rorik would not hesitate to kill me if he learned the truth.'

Ulf hugged his mother, suddenly engulfed by an overpowering sense of foreboding.

Twenty Eight

By the time the evening meal had been served, most of the men in Rorik's hall were well on the way to being uproariously drunk. Ale had flowed since late afternoon and during the meal the mead horns were constantly passed round. Although the meal itself was a relatively simple affair, compared to that planned for tomorrow night after the sacrificial ceremony, the hall had a festive feel. Rorik seemed determined to impress his cousin with his hospitality. Torches flared along the walls and the tables were arranged in the usual U shape, with a few gaps between to facilitate the movements of the thralls bearing food and drink. Rorik sat at the centre of the high table, his guests at his sides, according to status.

The thralls eventually took their own meal at a table close to the ale barrels, from which they constantly refilled the cups of revellers. Ulf sat between Sigehelm and Toke, longing for his bed; the hour was late and before dawn they'd be heading for Odin's oak. He'd attended many sacrificial ceremonies over the years but had never become hardened to them. And he'd always felt extremely fearful in the presence of Odin's ravens. Even when the huge birds had not become manifest in the flesh, he'd felt that unnatural wind that heralded their arrival and the unnerving sensation of being watched.

The quartet of musicians was now setting up in the central area. Ulf recognised most of their instruments – hand drums, a stringed lyre, a bone whistle, a pair of rattles and some kind of long trumpet. But one unfamiliar piece looked just like a small section of wood with a tapering end and holes bored into its top edge.

'It is called a panflute, or panpipe,' Sigehelm told him, following Ulf's gaze. 'I've heard one played before; it can make a merry little tune or a sad one, depending on the mood the player wishes to create.'

The musicians bowed to the jarls and greeted their audience with outstretched arms. When the enthusiastic welcome abated they seated themselves on their stools facing Rorik's table. The lyre player performed first, accompanied by the man with the rattles. The tune was a lively one which had people clapping hands and tapping feet. Next, the panpiper and drummer played another lively tune, with an interesting little solo by the whistle player in the middle of it. Ulf was fascinated by the many different sounds and by the time they'd finished, everyone was in animated mood.

Everyone but Rorik, it seemed.

Beside the scowling jarl, Ragnar beamed his enjoyment of the evening and even Aslanga was enjoying the music. It seemed strange that Rorik should be in such a dour mood: he'd certainly had his fill of mead.

'Now, this instrument is a lur,' Sigehelm said, breaking Ulf's contemplations. 'See how it is shaped like a long, straight trumpet, just flaring a little at the end rather like a horn? Such instruments have often been used by shepherds and such like to call in their flocks and herds. It produces a rather doleful, haunting sound.'

Ulf nodded, watching the lur player preparing to play. In contrast to the previous presentations, his tune was a mournful one. Yet the audience seemed beguiled, and fuelled by the ale in their bellies, the desolate air brought a tear to the eyes of a few.

Rorik suddenly thumped the table hard with his fist and surged to his feet. 'Cease this dirge!' he roared, glowering at the lur player. 'Music should be for us to enjoy, not cause us to weep into our cups.' He moved slowly between the tables towards the terrified quartet. 'Soon your group will be required to play more cheerful tunes, but for now you will retire. And take these with you,' he said, kicking at one of the stools. 'I've business to attend to.

'I stand before you as your jarl,' he declared, addressing the hall after long moments of silence. 'Others are here as our guests; members of my own family and their retinue. All are welcome to share our hospitality. But tonight, something is preventing me from feeling even a little bit merry. And that dirge induced me to deal with it. Now!'

He drew a deep breath and exhaled slowly. 'As jarl I provide protection and leadership for my people, as is my duty. In return for which I ask – no, I *demand* – certain things.' He struck his left thumb with his right forefinger. 'One, I demand respect at all times. Two,' he continued, bending back the first finger, 'I expect loyalty to me and our community, and three, all must work hard for the benefit of the community.' He gave his third finger a few, slow taps, then struck his fourth finger hard. '*Instant* obedience! There can be no leadership without obedience from those being led. If I need to raise men to arms, I need to be certain they will rally instantly to my call. Are these not valid points, cousin?'

'You've covered the requirements well,' Ragnar agreed. 'All

members of a community must be prepared to follow their jarl in all things.'

Rorik nodded. 'Thank you, cousin,' but I have a fifth point to add. For a jarl to lead, he must know his people. And to know another person – on whom your life may depend at some stage – requires that person to be entirely honest with you.'

Ulf suddenly realised where this was leading. Across the room his mother stood rigid, clutching a stack of bowls, her eyes unwaveringly on Rorik. And the restraining hands of Sigehelm and Toke clamped firmly on Ulf's shoulders.

'If I am to trust a person – beside me in battle or simply preparing my food or reaping my crops – I need to be certain of that person's honesty!' Rorik yelled, striking hard at the little finger of his left hand.

'Morwenna! Out here before me, woman. Let's all have a look at you.'

Bowls smashed to the floor as Morwenna's legs gave way and she staggered against a table. Egil dragged her up and thrust her before the jarl, whose eyes bored into her like hot knives through butter. 'Have *you* been honest with me, woman?'

Trembling silence brought Morwenna a back-handed blow that sent her to the floor where she scrambled to her knees, blood streaming from a split lip. She stared up at Rorik for a moment before rising, steeling herself for further assault. Then a child's sobbing protests reached her and, recognising the sound, her head flicked round in desperation to locate the source. Ulf watched his mother's eyes follow Freydis as she took it upon herself to escort the distraught Jorund from the hall. Beside her, Thora carried little Yrsa. He choked back anguished tears but thanked the gods they'd given Freydis to this world.

But Rorik let pass the incident, too swamped in his own malice to be sidetracked. 'You are my *concubine*,' he snarled, making the word sound like something abhorrent. But Morwenna jutted out her chin and pulled back her shoulders. 'You are here as my property; my plaything,' Rorik continued, 'and as such *I* owe *you* nothing. I could have you slain any time I choose. But *you* owe *me* obedience, in bed and out of it. 'So, I'll ask again: have you been honest with me?

'Your precious Eadwulf can't help you,' he snarled, thrusting an arm toward Ulf. 'But I'm not asking you about *that* son of Beorhtwulf. He's of little concern to me.'

'The answer to your question is no, my lord. No, I have not been honest with you.'

'Then explain to these good, *honest* people, exactly how you've deceived me.'

'Jorund is not your son,' Morwenna said, a simple statement of fact.

The communal intake of breath was followed by intense silence. Morwenna frowned, seeming uncertain of what else to say, but Rorik was in no mood for patience and delivered a stinging blow to the side of her head. Ulf groaned, feeling her pain, and made to launch himself to his feet. But Toke and Sigehelm held him down.

Composing herself, Morwenna addressed the seated Danes as though the strike had not occurred: 'Your jarl raped me when I was already carrying my second child by my husband, King Beorhtwulf of Mercia.' All remained silent, waiting for her to continue. Ulf knew too well that accusations of rape meant nothing to Danes; even the women accepted that their men raped the female victims of raided settlements. 'But your *savages* killed Beorhtwulf!' she hissed at Rorik, 'and *you* took me as your prize. And until yesterday I didn't know whether my son was alive or dead. So why should I feel guilty about lying to you?'

Rorik raised his arm to deal another blow but seemed to change his mind. 'I remember well why I wanted you. And not just to stop that cur, Burgred, having you.' His words hit Ulf like a thunderclap: he hadn't known the full extent of Burgred's treachery. 'But now your looks are fading and I no longer desire you in my bed.'

'May I speak, my lord?'

Rorik scowled but gave a grudging nod, and all eyes followed Dalla as she came to stand before her husband. 'We are all now aware of how Morwenna has deceived you,' she said, her nervous gaze shifting between Morwenna and her husband, 'but I would speak in her favour.' Rorik nodded tersely, and Dalla pushed on: 'Morwenna has contributed much to the running of your hall these past years. She is adept in domestic chores, works without complaint, and is young enough to give us–'

'Weren't you *listening* just now, woman!' Rorik's chest heaved, his face grew scarlet and he stepped menacingly towards her. But Dalla held her ground. 'This thrall may seem obedient to you,' he conceded, 'but I say that none of us could ever trust her again!'

No argument to counter the vehement tirade, Dalla shuffled back to her women and Rorik focused again on Morwenna.

'Your brat of a son, Jorund, will remain a thrall for the rest of his life,' he spat. 'The girl is too young to be of interest to me.'

'She's your daughter!'

Another back-handed blow sent Morwenna sprawling. Rorik hovered over her, his lips curled back like a wolf over cornered prey. 'But she's also the daughter of a thrall – and too young to survive without a mother. And I wouldn't burden one of my *honest* women with her upbringing.'

'What ... what are you saying?'

'Simply that I've not yet decided whether the girl will live or die.'

Morwenna's agonised groan caused gasps of sympathy, instantly quelled by a flick of the jarl's hand. 'Either way, at dawn tomorrow you will be given to the All-Father.

'Take her,' he snapped, gesturing to Egil.

Ulf broke free of the restraining hands, aiming to leap over the table and choke the life out of Rorik. The last thing he saw before the blackness claimed him was the ugly face and a mouthful of blackened and broken teeth.

* * *

Ivar glared at his fair-headed brother slumped next to him with one elbow on the trestle, propping up his chin. Halfdan's usually well-groomed hair was dishevelled, sticky residues of food clung to his long moustache and his eyes were glazed: distinct signs of overindulgence in mead. Ivar sniffed, disgusted. He'd long since learnt that too much liquor blunts the mind. But his brother's mind had never been too sharp in the first place.

Perhaps that was why Ivar couldn't feel envious of his handsome sibling, who bore such a physical likeness to their father. In many ways he felt sorry that Halfdan couldn't see things as he did: the way of an intelligent, thinking being.

Ivar let his ideas flow. Halfdan had always been a weak strategist. He was one of those people who would act first and think later, although he was undeniably as unscrupulous as himself, and brave enough to face any physical threat. But Halfdan was better at following orders than issuing them. Still, Haldan had his uses.

Comfortable in a high-backed chair, Ivar ran his fingers through his wiry, dark hair. His own looks and colouring resembled Aslanga's, as did Ubbi's. But Ubbi was a strong, healthy boy who'd grow tall and straight like Halfdan, whilst Ivar's diseased body remained wizened and shrunken, his legs useless. From bitter experience he knew that no woman would ever come willingly to his bed. Even thralls, not at liberty to refuse him, shuddered as he used their bodies to sate his sexual needs.

He stopped the self-pity: such thoughts could become all-consuming and ultimately self-destructive. He'd lived with his deformities for long enough, after all. And no one dared poke fun at him. Ivar knew his own power over people, saw it in their eyes. They feared him, as though mystic powers compensated for his malformed body. He let them believe it.

Halfdan suddenly turned his head and squinted at him. 'A good night, eh?' he slurred. 'But right now I'm ready for my bed.'

'You did well, brother. We've waited a long time for such satisfaction.'

Yes, Ivar contemplated, things had worked out excellently. They'd finally wreaked vengeance on that red-headed Mercian in a most agreeable way. What better way than to force the scum to watch the humiliation and destruction of the mother with whom he'd just been reunited? But one small detail marred his near-perfect contentment.

Eadwulf was still alive.

Why couldn't his cursed half-brother have stayed in his seat and let the thrall leap over the table and attack Rorik? Ivar knew the answer: if Bjorn had not acted then Eadwulf – Bjorn's esteemed 'Ulf' – would have been joining his mother strung up in Odin's oak tomorrow. And Bjorn would not have liked that.

Ivar scowled, recalling how Bjorn had made his way round the back of the tables, so inconspicuously that even Ragnar hadn't noticed, and dealt a heavy blow across the back of the thrall's head with a clay jug, rendering him senseless. Bjorn had known that all eyes would be on Rorik and the Mercian harlot.

Halfdan was watching him, waiting for further comment: he'd learnt not to interrupt when Ivar was deep in thought.

'So, you managed to conceal yourself completely behind the pig-pens, Halfdan, and listen to their treacherous talk.' It was not a question. Ivar knew full well how earlier events had taken place. Halfdan nodded, grinning idiotically. 'Your stealth on this occasion has impressed me.'

Halfdan's brow furrowed and he took another slurp of mead. Ivar smirked. He could almost see his brother's small mind trying to work out whether the comment was praise or criticism. And Ivar would leave him wondering.

Halfdan suddenly leaned toward him and blinked several

times. 'And you were right about the woman. Being Mercian, I suppose she was likely to know the cursed thrall,' he burbled on, pulling a piece of hair from his mouth and shoving it behind his ear. 'But she's his *mother*! And then I found out about that boy!'

'You did indeed,' Ivar said, pushing him away. Halfdan's mead-soaked breath was enough to repulse an evil troll. 'We've learned much to our advantage.'

'Pity the thrall didn't get over that table.' Halfdan chuckled inanely at the thought. 'What do you think would have happened if–?'

He glanced at Ivar's glowering face and clamped his mouth tight shut.

Twenty Nine

Ulf was aboard the *Sea Eagle,* sailing north towards the beguiling Lofoten Islands. The heavy sail flapped and seabirds wheeled and screeched, guillemots, gulls and kittiwakes amongst them. Waves slapped the hull, sunlight glistened on the blue-grey water and the salty breeze ruffled his hair. Coastward, the green-swathed Norwegian mountains, intersected by steep-sided fjords, almost took his breath away. Colonies of black and white puffins with brightly coloured beaks perched on their nests along the cliffs and cormorants stretched, drying their wings in the sun. A sea-eagle swooped to inspect the ship to which it had given its name before plucking a fish from beneath the brine. Whilst seaward, foam-white sea-horses played on the water's surface and whiskered seals bobbed. The massive bulk of a silver whale shot great spouts of water high in the air, to cascade down again, rainbow colours of light dancing in their midst.

Somehow Ulf knew he was dreaming; yet he refused to wake up. His mind was cushioned by this sense of peace, taking him to where he wanted so much to be: this place out at sea with Bjorn and his crew, where he was valued, respected for what he was. He inhaled deeply, savouring the aroma of salty air. But the smell gradually lessened, evolving into the sharp tang of spices, mingled with the earthy smells of vegetables.

His eyes shot open. He was lying in a hut where sacks and jars were stored. Memory smacked into him like a raging torrent. His mother! Where was she now? Was it night or day?

Had the heinous ceremony already taken place? Pray the gods it hadn't and he could somehow save her. He tried to rise but his wrists and ankles were bound. He struggled until his skin was ragged beneath the bonds and blood seeped into his clothing.

'Help my mother,' he screamed. 'Save her from the cruel fate to which she's been condemned!'

But no one answered the pleas from his tormented soul.

Then the cockerel crowed.

Ulf's scream tore at his throat, his pain too terrible to bear. Morwenna's face shimmered across his thoughts, her words a balm to his searing misery: 'Let those who love you soothe your wounded soul.'

The pain eased and he drifted…

He seemed to be flying. He laughed as he glanced at his outstretched arms, a joyful sound that welled up from somewhere deep inside before rushing from his lips to be carried away on the wind. This must be what total freedom felt like. Beside him a flock of starlings swooped and spiralled in their exotic ritual, and he shared their sheer delight of the open skies. Then uncertainty hit, and he squinted into the blindingly blue expanse beyond the hazy, translucent clouds. Why was he flying? Was he now dead, not a solid body at all, but a spirit rising towards heaven? A woman's voice reached his ears, passing by in its ascent. 'Do not grieve for me, my son: I am free of the cares of this world now.'

Far to the west the sun was sliding behind the Welsh hills, splashing shades of vermilion and purple haphazardly across the blue. Above the landscape he soared, over fields of grazing cattle, corn ripening with the season's warmth, and winding blue streams. Soon he was hovering over the edges of a dense forest and instinctively he knew that it was Bruneswald. This beautiful, green land was Mercia: his home.

Then he realised it was not summer at all and he was not home. His mind grew angry and cast the scene away.

* * *

People were gathering. He could hear them milling around, excited; seeming to drift towards a common destination. When at last he forced his eyes to open, the darkness of night greeted him, relieved only by the oil lamp's dim glow. The cockerel had crowed long ago and his mother would be dead, killed in a way abhorrent to Christian souls. And Morwenna had always been a devout believer in Christ.

'Christ! Where *were* you?' he shrieked, pushing himself up on his elbows. 'How many more of your people will you abandon? I say you are no god!' His scathing laugh tore from his constricted throat and he sobbed like a child, wrapping his arms round his drawn up knees – and realised he was no longer bound! His chafed wrists had been bandaged and a sweet-smelling salve applied. Someone had been here while he was ...asleep? Tentatively he fingered the swelling on the back of his head, sticky with congealed blood, guessing he'd been unconscious for a time. He glanced at the closed door.

'The guards have instructions not to let you leave. You must remain in here, for your own good.'

Ulf twisted toward the familiar form emerging from the shadows. 'Sigehelm ...my mother?'

'...has gone to her Maker, Ulf.'

'Did she ...suffer much?' Ulf's own voice came as a laboured whisper and he waited, dreading the answer.

'She did not.' Sigehelm's voice was heavy with his own pain. 'Thora was permitted to attend her before the ceremony and the draught she persuaded Morwenna to drink numbed all senses, all thoughts. When your mother stood beneath the oak, I could swear she'd already left her body, and knew nothing of the falling axe.'

Ulf fell back to his bedroll, sobs of anger and unbearable grief racking his body.

'You'll not be permitted to see her,' Sigehelm said as his sobs lessened. 'Bjorn has ordered this, not Rorik. You'll stay in here until we leave in a few days' time. I'll bring your food and sit with you when I can. And there are others who wish to offer solace. But you'll see nothing more of Aalborg other than this hut. The door may be opened for light and air once you give your word not to try to leave.'

Despair threatened to destroy Ulf's very soul and he wept until succumbing to a deep and dreamless sleep.

* * *

Ulf had no idea how long he'd slept by the next time he roused but it was night again; a lamp still glowed from the shelf and no daylight seeped through the wattle walls. But he knew that Sigehelm would be somewhere, watching over him.

'You should go and rest, Sigehelm. As you said, I can't go anywhere.'

'Sigehelm's gone to eat, and fetch food for you.' Bjorn's voice was hushed as he moved to squat beside Ulf. 'You've eaten nothing for almost two days – but you've not exactly been with us for two days either. How's your head? I didn't mean to hit you so hard, but I had to stop you from striking Rorik.'

'You! Then you risked great disfavour from your father, not to mention Rorik.'

'They both understood my reasons.' Bjorn looked steadily at Ulf. 'But you need to understand how we – Danes I mean – see things. In our lands you're a thrall, Ulf, and as such, you belong to me. That is the way of things, whether you like the idea or not. In our law, a thrall has no rights, and a master is at liberty to treat him, or her, as he chooses.' He raised his hand to prevent Ulf's intended interruption. 'I tell you this to explain that no one had the right to interfere in Rorik's treatment of your mother. He had every right to mete out the punishment he did for what he saw as unpardonable behaviour in a thrall – as did my father all those years ago with that Saxon. But your behaviour is my responsibility. It's up to me to chastise you as I see fit.'

'Then why didn't you just kill me?'

'Perhaps you don't give a damn whether you live or die, but I do,' Bjorn snapped in Ulf's face. 'You're one of my crew and I'm greatly indebted to you for saving my life; you've also become a true friend. But if I'd allowed you to attack Rorik, I would have been compelled to see you meet the same end as Morwenna.'

Bjorn eyed Ulf's bandages with a frown. 'I ordered Rico to bind you in case you roused when everyone was at the ceremony. But it seems he doesn't know his own strength! You have Thora to thank for tending you, by the way.' He rose as Sigehelm entered with food and ale. 'I'll leave you in Sigehelm's hands now, but mull over what I've said. The good scribe would never forgive me if I let you come to harm. And Freydis would skin me alive.'

The next few days were the most harrowing that Ulf had ever endured, and he sank into a state of melancholy from which his succession of visitors could not retrieve him. At first he blamed himself for his mother's death: if he'd not come here she'd still be alive and little Yrsa's life would not be in danger of being discarded as of no consequence. But his self-recrimination soon turned to rage; a blistering fury that kept him pacing the floor of the small hut like some tormented beast. Rorik's face would hover before him and he knew that the callous jarl was responsible. It was he who'd ordered Morwenna's death, he who exhibited not a shred of compassion. Ulf could feel himself thrusting the knife into the jarl's cold heart.

And always, from the recesses of his mind, the treacherous face of Burgred would emerge. All blame lay at Burgred's feet.

Sigehelm came and went many times during these days, maintaining a respectful silence through Ulf's darkest times. Rico and Toke's visits were cut short, their fearful faces when he raged adding shame to the tangled emotions swirling in his head. Thora changed his bandages and applied fresh salves each morning, but it was not until the evening before they would return to Aros that Freydis appeared. Ulf had been dozing when the door quietly opened, but he sensed her presence; Freydis carried her own unmistakable fragrance, a mixture of the scented oils she bathed in and the aromatic herbs she handled daily. Her shadow fell across him before she knelt and reached out to touch his cheek.

'I'm so sorry for all your hurt,' she whispered. 'None of us foresaw such a disastrous turn of events. And, though it will give little comfort to you now, your mother was a good and kind woman, whom everyone admired, and–'

'I don't want your pity, Freydis, if that's all you've come to offer.' Ulf rolled away from her, knowing his words were unwarranted but unable to stop them. 'Save your pity for those two children in the hall – if that's where they still are!'

Freydis didn't move or become angry at his barbed response. 'I haven't come to shower you with sympathy, Ulf, though my heart truly aches for you. I just needed to speak with you before we leave Aalborg.' She paused, and his heartbeat quickened in dread of what she might say. 'Your brother and sister will be coming with us to Aros.'

He turned and stared at her, barely able to take in what she'd said. 'I've been unable to visit you in here,' Freydis continued, glancing round the hut, 'because I've been caring for them – Jorund and Yrsa, I mean. Jorund is distraught and cries almost constantly. And nightmares plague his sleep. Rorik would not allow *anyone* to miss the ceremony to Odin.'

An agonised groan racked Ulf's body. Freydis enfolded him in her arms, and when his body ceased to tremble, she brushed his tangled hair from his face and kissed his brow. 'It will take many months for your brother to forget that dreadful day, Ulf, if he ever does. But the pain *will* lessen in time. And Yrsa is too young to have known what was happening.'

Ulf nodded, fighting down the fury that threatened to erupt. Freydis didn't deserve to witness such a scene. 'I know Rorik wouldn't have suggested that we take the children, Freydis,' he said. 'So is it to you, or Bjorn, that I owe thanks?'

'Perhaps both,' she replied with a wan smile. 'The children have responded well to me. Yrsa frets a great deal, missing her mother, but I can cope with that and occupy her otherwise. And Jorund simply needs patience and kindness, which I haven't seen forthcoming from anyone in Rorik's hall. No one here is prepared to take responsibility for them. I spoke to Bjorn and he persuaded Dalla and Helga to sell the children to him. He told them that Jorund could provide him with a much needed thrall, and convinced them that gaining silver for Yrsa was better than merely disposing of her. Perhaps the suggestion was put to Rorik when he was drunk, but he agreed, and Bjorn has paid him.'

'But who will take care of them in Aros?'

'I will, with Thora's help of course. Their lives will be far better in Aros than anything they could expect in Aalborg. And they will grow up knowing their elder brother is close by.'

'And Ragnar will allow this?'

Freydis smiled. 'My father has never refused any request from Thora.'

* * *

In the afternoon of October 25, Bjorn's cavalcade arrived back in Aros. Life quickly took on a welcomed normality, although, as always during the winter months, Ulf spent his days willing spring to arrive. His own pain settled into a constant ache, deep in his chest, kept in abeyance by his daily responsibilities to his newfound siblings. But his murderous plans for Rorik rendered sleep a long time in coming each night, the opportunity of carrying them out a particular frustration to his raging thoughts. It could be years before he got the chance.

The children steadily became more comfortable in Ulf's company, though as yet, they did not realise he was their brother. The time for explanations would come later.

Yrsa responded well to the love and attention lavished upon her by Freydis and Thora, and was a cheerful little soul. With Jorund, progress was much slower. Although the nightmares gradually lessened he was prone to bouts of dark brooding, when he would withdraw inside himself, shutting out everything around him. His loss was magnified a hundredfold by the mental images that would not leave him. Thora was confident the boy would be mended within a year: the young are very resilient, she assured, and early memories fade. But Ulf was not so certain.

December came and with it the celebrations of the Yule. Ulf helped Rico to loop thick ropes round a huge oak log and drag it across the frozen earth into the hall, where the women and children decorated it with sprigs of fir and holly. Throughout the festivities it smouldered in the hearth, helping to bring light and cheer to the darkest time of year. A wild boar was sacrificed to Frey, the god of fertility, to ensure a good growing season in the coming year, with warm days and gentle rain. A goat was slaughtered, and people dressed in goatskins and sang in honour of Thor, who rode the skies in his chariot pulled by two goats. The roasted meats were eaten during the celebratory feasts, and unlimited supplies of ale and mead kept everyone in festive mood.

And Jorund smiled for the first time since October.

Thirty

Canterbury, Kent: early January 858

'Why did Mother have to die, Aethelswith?' Alfred sobbed into his pillow. 'What shall I do without her?'

A gentle hand touched his shoulder. 'Be at peace, young lord. Your mother has been with her Maker for three years now. And she would not wish her youngest son to be still grieving.'

Alfred woke from his dream, sweat-soaked and fraught with distress, and rolled to face the woman seated on the edge of his bed. Daylight writhed through the shutters and sounds coming from the hall told him it was morning. A cold, January morn, filled with sadness.

'Judith?' he mumbled, rubbing his eyes as he watched the blue-robed figure of his stepmother rise to open the shutters. He pushed himself up on his elbows, shivering as the cold air hit him. 'I think I was dreaming. I thought that mother–'

'I know, Alfred. Disturbing dreams can come at the worst of times. It is most likely that your father's illness has brought that harrowing time back into your mind.'

Judith picked up the heavy book lying on the fur cover of Alfred's bed and turned the gold-edged pages. 'A most exquisite thing,' she remarked. 'Given to you by your mother, I think you said?'

'Yes,' Alfred acknowledged, 'but only because I was the only one who could be bothered to read it all the way through. None of my brothers was interested enough, but I knew as soon as

I saw it that I wanted it. It's just so beautiful. I couldn't read at the time,' he admitted, frowning, 'so Father Felix helped me to learn it off by heart, and just recite it. So I suppose you would say I cheated.'

Judith lifted his chin between her thumb and forefinger, her blue gaze holding his. 'No, I would not call it cheating,' she said, her face thoughtful. 'It was very enterprising of you. I think that Lady Osburh would have known full well of your illiterate state, and valued your efforts all the more. So that is why she gave her precious book to you.'

Alfred smiled at her. He was very fond of Judith. Herself barely fifteen, she was always ready to talk and offer advice, especially since his father had been too ill to do so. And, unlike many others, Judith did not treat him like a young child.

'Then, reading your book and thinking of your mother before you slept explains your distressing dream,' Judith reasoned, twisting round her finger a strand of dark hair peeking out from under her head veil. 'During your slumbers such thoughts would have mingled with your fears for your father's failing health. Your dream-mind merely confused the details.'

Alfred blinked back the tears. 'Will God take Father from us soon?'

Judith was silent for some moments, seeming to battle her own emotions before replying. 'His passing will be soon, Alfred, so we must be very brave. I have kept vigil over him through the long night, and he is very weak. I have left the physician with him for now, though I dare not stay away too long.' Her shoulders slumped and in the brightening light, Alfred could see how tired she looked.

'Aethelbald should arrive in the next day or two, though I fear that Aethelswith and her husband may be too late,' she continued with a weary sigh. Tamworth is far away, and your fickle Saxon weather can so easily prevent travel at this time of year.'

Alfred scowled at the mention of his sister's husband. Although he'd not set eyes on Burgred for some years, his dislike of the man continued to fester, greatly fuelled by the fact that he had not yet permitted Aethelswith to visit her family in Kent.

Well aware of his feelings about Burgred, Judith did not comment on his reaction. 'Father Felix has ensured the terms of your father's will are clearly laid out,' she said. 'But Aethelwulf so hoped to see all his children, one last time...'

Alfred took her hand as her voice faltered and she gave him a sad smile. 'Aethelberht and Aethelred are about to attend the chapel,' she said softly. 'Perhaps you could accompany them, young lord.'

At that moment, Alfred could think of nothing more appropriate to do than pray.

* * *

Late the following afternoon Aethelbald arrived from Southampton with his large entourage. Notified of his arrival, Aethelwulf summoned his four sons to his bedside where, in the presence of Father Felix, his physician and his young wife, he struggled to explain the main issues of the document he'd recently had drawn up.

Alfred stared at the stone-grey hair, splayed lank against the pillows that propped his father up, and listened to the crackling whisper of the once forceful voice. Memories of his mother's final hours resurfaced and he strove to control his crushing grief. This was surely another such prelude.

In his will, Aethelwulf stipulated that the kingdom should remain divided. Aethelbald would continue his rule of the West Saxon shires, whilst Aethelberht would resume his earlier kingship of the East. Aethelred and Alfred were to be endowed with properties in the West, where, as king, Aethelbald would be custodian over them all.

Both Aethelbald and Aethelberht were compliant to these specifications – until Aethelwulf's final demand. 'I am adamant that my two youngest sons shall rule the West Saxon shires in their turn after Aethelbald,' the dying king rasped. 'I have worked to this end throughout my life, and will not abandon my most fervent desires now.' A wheezing breath rattled through his chest and he coughed violently, struggling to catch the breath to continue.

Aethelbald's dark good looks barely concealed his smouldering rage, though his voice remained calm and controlled. 'Father, this plan would be foolproof if I were not to produce heirs. But what if I were to tell you that I'm considering marriage within the next few months? Must any sons of mine have to stand down in deference to their uncles? Surely that is not how the laws of inheritance work.'

The red hue of Aethelbald's skin was deepening, a sheen of sweat glistening on his brow. Alfred cringed: his brother's temper was on the boil.

'The Danish threat escalates yearly,' Aethelwulf laboured

on, fixing his eldest son with a cold stare and ignoring the imminent outburst. 'Our kingdom needs strong and firm rulers: we cannot wait for babes to grow or allow lesser men to–'

Another fit of coughing ended whatever the king had been about to say and the physician ordered him to rest and regain his strength.

Aethelbald stormed from the bedchamber, leaving Aethelberht and Alfred staring after him, whilst Aethelred's amiable features crinkled into a wide grin. Then together they followed their eldest brother into the hall.

* * *

'It is simply not right that we should accept such terms,' Aethelbald fumed, his dark eyes moving from one brother to another in search of accord. Servants fussed round the table, clearing the last of the evening's meal, and Aethelwulf's sons had moved around the hearth to continue their discussion. Alfred watched, hoping that Aethelbald's rage would not be unleashed physically. 'Why should a dying man dictate to his heirs how the kingdom should be governed in future years? Surely the rules of inheritance stand for something!'

'But we've always known of our father's desires for the ruling of Wessex, brother,' Aethelberht reasoned, his pale eyes on his older sibling. 'And I believe he's shown wisdom in retaining this stipulation. Wessex can't afford to show a modicum of weakness, or the Danes would tear her apart. I'll certainly be vigilant where defence of the East is concerned and–'

'Oh, it's all right for you, Aethelberht. Any sons of yours

will rule in the East when you're gone! But as soon as I die, my sons will simply be ignored, unable to benefit from all the improvements I intend to make in fortifications and armed forces.'

Aethelberht bristled. 'It's unlikely our brothers will "ignore" their nephews, Aethelbald. They'd still hold a fair degree of sway in the West. But until such time, remember that *you* rule a far superior kingdom in both power and wealth than I do. 'And,' he stressed, 'Kent is far more likely to suffer Danish raids than your shires. Think of the times the pagans have overwintered on Thanet, or Sheppey, and how Canterbury suffered.' He picked up his mug and quaffed a mouthful of ale. 'So your griping won't wash with me, Aethelbald.'

His fists tightly clenched, his face thunderous, Aethelbald heaved himself to his feet. Alfred held his breath, waiting for a hefty blow to strike Aethelberht's head. But at that point Aethelred decided to add his grain of wisdom.

'You both seem to have overlooked the role of the Witan,' he stated, pausing to allow his words to take effect. 'If our Councillors deemed any of us – or any future "heirs" – to be unsuitable, we'd be tossed aside without a further blink. So where does that leave your laws of inheritance, Aethelbald?'

Just as Aethelbald began to give Aethelred a piece of his mind, Judith entered the hall. 'How can you think of your selfish quarrels at a time like this?' she admonished, her tired gaze moving between the solidly built Aethelbald towering over them all and the more slender Aethelberht. 'Surely you should show your respect in the home of a dying man – your own father!'

Tears coursed down Judith's cheeks. Alfred moved toward her to offer comfort, but Aethelbald beat him to it, putting his arm around her shoulders and gazing with surprising tenderness into her eyes. 'You are overwrought, Judith,' he said, 'and overtired. I know you didn't sleep at all last night. And we all owe you so much for the kindness you've shown us these past two years.'

'Thank you, Aethelbald.' Judith sniffed. 'I have much on my mind.'

Aethelberht put down his mug and stood to address his stepmother. 'You are naturally heartbroken at the thought of losing your husband, my lady. And thoughts of organising a funeral must be causing concern. But, we are all here to help, and no doubt Aethelswith will soon arrive. She will be of comfort to you.'

Judith sank to the bench beside Alfred. 'You are right about all of those things,' she admitted. 'I shall feel my lord's loss deeply, but I am also in great dread of returning to Francia. I shall be married off to some pompous lord and I may not have the same, er, *privileges* I have had here with your dear father.' She pulled a small handkerchief from her sleeve and blew her nose. 'I will miss you all so much.'

Alfred inanely patted her back for want of something more appropriate to do. He'd miss Judith but knew that, as a young widow, her future would be dictated by the will of her powerful father, Charles the Bald.

* * *

'Just what did you find so funny today?' Alfred asked his fair-headed brother as they headed for their bedchambers a little later. 'Don't you find Aethelbald's outbursts just a little alarming?'

'Of course I don't! He's just a big bag of wind. All puff and no punch.'

'How do you know that?'

Aethelred shrugged. 'He's always been the same: likes the sound of his own voice. But I've never seen him actually hit anyone.' Alfred looked thoughtfully at his brother. Nine years older than himself, Aethelred knew so much more about the other siblings than Alfred did. 'But, what I really found funny,' Aethelred went on, 'was the way Aethelbald kept eyeing up Judith!'

'I noticed that too. You don't think...'

'That he'll marry her after Father dies?' Aethelred's smile faded and he turned sorrowful grey eyes on Alfred. 'I can't imagine life without Father. Just speaking of his death turns my stomach to water.'

Alfred nodded, tears welling afresh. 'Father's always been there for us. Even after Mother died, we still had him.'

Aethelred wrapped his arms around Alfred's shoulders. 'Come with me to the chapel and we'll pray together.'

As they headed for the little church, Alfred repeated his earlier question, '*Do* you think Aethelbald will marry Judith?'

'I do,' Aethelred said, after a moment's thought. 'And I think it will cause quite a commotion in Wessex. But Aethelbald has powerful friends, as we well know from when you and Father returned from Rome. They'll back Aethelbald, no matter what unconventional things he wants. And we all heard Judith say she didn't want to return to Francia. I can't see her refusing Aethelbald if he offers her marriage. At least she *knows* him – and he's not bad looking, in a dark, hairy sort of way. At least he's not some fat old Frankish lord!'

'No, he's not,' Alfred agreed. 'And as we'll be living at the West Saxon court, at least we'd have Judith for company.'

* * *

A short while before noon the following day, Alfred was summoned to his father's bedchamber, watching with heightened anxiety as Aethelwulf insisted that even Father Felix and the physician should leave the room.

'Come close,' his father urged as the door clicked shut. 'I cannot raise my voice more than a whisper and I want you to hear clearly what I say. That's better,' he said, taking Alfred's hand as he came to stand by the big bed.

Alfred focused on the gaunt frame of his father, noting how the deathly pallor of his skin almost matched the leaden tones of his hair. He bit his bottom lip hard, still battling the welling tears.

'Do not weep for me, Alfred,' Aethelwulf said gently. 'I am ready to meet my Maker and will soon be reunited with your mother. But before I leave this world, I must speak to you about the future of our kingdom.'

Though puzzled as to why he'd been singled out for this talk, Alfred nodded anyway.

'I believe you were sent to your mother and me late in life

for a purpose, Alfred. 'Do you know what that purpose will be?'

'I know I shall be king of Wessex one day, Father. I believe what Pope Leo said. I think I shall be needed to defend the land.'

Aethelwulf smiled at that answer. 'I believe that too, so remember that you must prepare for that time. You and Aethelred must continue your courtly training when you reside with Aethelbald. Keep up your arms practice, and hone your riding and hunting skills. Become proficient in the use of spear and bow as well as sword, and enjoy your falcons. A king must prove superior in all these things. And continue to read and write the hymns you love so much. And one day you must marry and produce heirs.'

Aethelwulf slumped lower on his pillow, his eyelids drooping. 'I need to sleep now,' he whispered, his voice rasping from overuse. He reached out and took Alfred's hand. 'Be strong, Alfred. Never show your enemies your weaknesses, or they will leap on them and tear you to shreds. Promise me that, on my deathbed.'

Alfred leaned to kiss the sunken cheek. 'I promise, Father,'

'Then go with my blessing, my son. I know you will not let Wessex fall.'

* * *

Tamworth, Mercia: mid-January 858

Burgred slammed his fist hard on the table, causing his cup to brim over. 'Damn the woman,' he roared as a serving girl hurried to mop up the spilt ale. 'Can she give me no peace!'

Attendant warriors and the two visiting monks sped about their business but Burgred cared naught for their discomfort. His men were used to scenes of domestic disharmony in his hall. And those two mealy-mouthed clerics were only here to scrounge more funds for the Tamworth church, but as yet, they hadn't had the guts to come straight out and ask. Pah! He was surrounded by fools, sycophants and spongers.

His wife would be in the bedchamber now, weeping like the babe she seemed incapable of giving him. One still birth and two miscarried pregnancies were all Aethelswith had managed in almost five years. Oh, he was doing his part well enough, getting her with child, but she seemed incapable of growing a healthy babe in her womb. Again he was gripped by the terrifying thought that God was punishing him. He covered his face with his hands and let out a long groan.

'Are you ill, my lord...?'

'Just get out and give me some peace,' he yelled at the girl.

Peace? Would he ever feel at peace again? Even his wife detested him, all the more so in recent weeks. Aethelswith had not yet forgiven him for forbidding her to travel to Kent when the message of her father's impending death had arrived almost two weeks ago. And today, a second message had arrived, informing them that the old goat had died.

No, he would not travel all the way to Steyning in Sussex just for a funeral. Aethelswith could weep and rant all she liked. The weather may be snow-free now, but that could change overnight. Besides, Aethelswith was with child again and he couldn't put this pregnancy at risk. The child would not be born until May, but his wife must wait until after the birthing to see her family. Then, perhaps, if affairs of state permitted, they would visit Aethelbald at his Wessex court. At least Aethelswith's eldest brother was more tolerable than her God-fearing old saint of a father.

Resignedly, he headed for the bedchamber to make amends with his wife.

Thirty One

Aros – Birka: late March 858

As spring approached, Bjorn decided not to go raiding this summer.

'The truth of the matter is,' he said, facing Ulf and leaning back against the *Sea Eagle's* hull, 'the village is in dire need of goods that are best purchased from the Baltic lands.'

Bjorn silently mulled over his thoughts and Ulf watched the river frothing its agitation at the strong wind that seemed bent on preventing its entry into the Kattegat, the pallid sun doing little to warm the air. The snows had only recently cleared and trees showed little sign of greening, though downy catkins festooned the limbs of the willows trailing over the water.

'My loving brothers plan to try their luck raiding along the coasts of northern Britain,' Bjorn eventually continued, turning his back to the strong north-easterly, 'which leaves me to do the bartering and buying. We've bags of loot left from our raids in Francia for trading, so it makes sense that I be the one to do it. I'll not take the *Eagle* this time, since we'll not be raiding; just a couple of knarrs. We'll sail as far as Birka on the east coast of Sweden....

'That sour expression tells me you don't find the prospect appealing, Ulf – and I *know* you were hoping to see the Norwegian coast again. But I tell you, the Baltic lands hold their own unique charm. The island of Gotland, for example, is a veritable treasure chest for all kinds of manufactured goods, jewellery included. Gotlandic craftsmen create the most intricate brooches in bronze, gold and silver, as well as items from glass and amber. Many of our women would prove *very* generous to whomsoever should so provide,' he added, with such an exaggerated wink that Ulf burst out laughing.

'But alas, we need to purchase more useful items than jewellery,' Bjorn said, assuming an air of disappointment. 'The whetstones, fishing implements, tools and weapons on Gotland are exceptional. Of course we can also find some of those goods at Birka, as well as furs from the ice bear, brown bear, wolf, fox and squirrel, and soft down from the eider duck and Siberian goose to stuff our pillows–

'Ulf, are you listening to me?' Bjorn thrust his fingers into his hair and pulled his face in exasperation. 'I've the distinct feeling I've been talking to myself!'

'I'm sorry, Master. I have been listening but I was wondering how my absence will affect Jorund. He's only just started to feel at ease with me and my leaving for the summer may set things back.'

'I don't think your absence for a couple of months would be too much of a problem. Jorund has Freydis and Thora doting on him after all.' Bjorn paused, his brow creased in thought, then he said: 'But there just may be a way to solve the problem of your absence.'

'I don't ask, nor do I wish, to remain behind. I already long to be away–'

A flick of Bjorn's hand cut Ulf off. 'I hadn't contemplated the idea. I had something else in mind. Now, this is still only a possibility,' he murmured after further moments of silence, 'but what if we take Jorund with us?'

'But he's only six!'

'Are you saying you think the idea foolish?' Bjorn grinned and slapped Ulf's shoulder. 'I can tell you that I was only three the first time Ragnar took me into the Baltic, and I not only survived, I enjoyed myself immensely – so Ragnar told me. I remember little about it. I think I'll ask my father if we can take Ubbi as well,' he continued as Ulf gaped, too surprised to express his gratitude. 'I know Jorund has taken to my brother, and it will do Ubbi good, if only to get him away from Aslanga for a few weeks.'

Bjorn nodded curtly, dismissing the subject, and started back to the village. 'Tomorrow I'll inform the crew of my plans. Like you, they'll probably scowl – all hot-blooded Danes live for the spring when they can go raiding. But the smiles will return when I tell them about next year.'

'Next year…?'

'Next year,' Bjorn declared, thrusting out his chin, 'Hastein and I will lead a large fleet on the adventure of our lives.' He stopped in his tracks and faced Ulf, who grinned at the look of childlike excitement on his face. 'Next year, we sail south to the blue waters of the Middle Sea.' He took a deep breath and finished with a flourish, "Then we aim for that most celebrated of cities hailed as the centre of all Christendom.

'Next year we attack Rome!'

* * *

The two knarrs sliced through the slate-blue waters that sparkled in the late May sunshine, laden with goods for trading: wheat seed and oak logs for the most part, but also sacks of precious objects from last summer's raids.

'We are fortunate that across our own lands oak forest is abundant,' Bjorn had told Ulf as the ships were being loaded. 'We couldn't build our fine ships without it. Other timbers are not nearly as reliable. Of course, in some regions it is necessary to use a variety of timbers: ash, elm, birch and pine to name a few. People from the northern Norselands – whose lands are covered in pine forest, with perhaps a few birch in sheltered places, look forward to doing trade with us. Like ourselves, they are all people of the sea, who rely on their ships for everything from fishing to trading and raiding. And for sturdy hulls, solid oak is the shipwright's choice, every time.

'In Gotland, farming is important,' Bjorn continued, tweaking his short beard thoughtfully. 'The soils are fertile and the climate mild, and wheat grows well, so the people are always in need of high quality seed. And from Ragnar's lands alone we have ample to spare. I've seen wheat growing well in southern Norway and Skåne, but further north it's too cold and they rely on oats, barley and rye.'

Ulf was just beginning to feel alive again after the months of pain and anger that followed his mother's death. The familiar sensation of freedom on the open sea afforded salve to his injured spirit and he hoped it would have a similar effect on Jorund. Ubbi was overjoyed at being aboard the dragonship but with Jorund the joy crept upon him more slowly. At first, he'd cowered close to Ulf's oarport, lifting his white face occasionally to peep over the ship's side. But the combination of cajoling by Leif and Ulf and the beauty of the seascape gradually persuaded him to stand with Ubbi and marvel at the sights.

They wove between the islands that guarded the entrance into the Baltic from the Kattegat, the two largest, Sjaelland and Fyn, looming to east and west; Lolland and Falster lying further south. As evening neared they reached the southerly tip of Sjaelland and veered east, wheedling between many small islands as the slightly larger Mon appeared on the horizon. They camped on one of the tiny, uninhabited islands, sailing on at dawn through the narrow strait between Mon and Falster, heading for the open waters of the Baltic. In the middle of the hazy afternoon they reached Bornholm, a rocky island with steep coastal cliffs backed by dense forest: an ideal place for two boys to play and hide. But Bjorn had other ideas.

They traipsed along the pebbly beach behind the master's striding form, turning inland to climb beside a winding stream that spilled down to the sea. Ulf fell into step with Leif. 'Are we having a tour of the island?' he quipped.

Leif flashed a wide grin. 'We go to pay our respects to King Alfarin and secure his esteemed permission to stay on his island.'

Ulf contemplated the need for that. They'd never requested permission anywhere before.

'It's like this,' Leif explained at Ulf's puzzled frown. 'This may not look like much of a kingdom, but her king holds her jealously. Bornholm's warriors are a fierce lot, and few raiders dare approach the island, let alone attack it. But I'm glad to say that King Alfarin and Ragnar are old comrades. Alfarin's also acquainted with Bjorn, though they've not set eyes on each other since Bjorn was sixteen. So now we go so they can be reacquainted, for courtesy's sake. And because we don't want butchering as we sleep!' Ulf could not agree more and said so. Leif gave a throaty chuckle. 'You never know, we might even get a good meal out of this. Last time we were here we had a fair banquet.'

King Alfarin's fortress comprised a collection of wooden buildings surrounded by a thick stone wall that could repel most assailants, and which served as a refuge in times of attack for the occupants of the homesteads on the island. The large hall, with its carved doorway, internal support pillars and rich furnishing, suggested that Bornholm did not lack for wealth. Alfarin seemed pleased to entertain anyone who could break the quiet tedium of his everyday life, and did, indeed, insist they share his evening meal, proving to be the epitome of hospitality. Though his commanding personality left little doubt that he was the seat of authority on the island, his sallow complexion and yellow tinged eyes spoke of days with little to do other than drink mead and strong wine – which he wasn't averse to sharing with his guests. And his sturdy-looking wife, Svala, served them a hearty meal.

With heavy heads and queasy stomachs they set sail the next morning, Bjorn in a downcast mood at leaving the company of Alfarin's only daughter, a raven-haired beauty whose dark eyes never seemed to leave his face all night. The two boys stood at the stern, waving at the cornucopia of splendid vessels as the brisk south-westerly thrust the ships onward. They sailed through the night and by mid-afternoon the following day they pulled into a sheltered bay on the western side of the large Swedish island of Gotland, and moored at the crowded harbour of the small market town of Paviken.

Over the next two days trading was good. Though the market was small, the variety of goods was impressive, and by the end of the second afternoon, Bjorn had exchanged most of the seed and several Frankish cups and crosses for whetstones, Rhineland pottery, tools and farm implements.

'Bjorn's keen to be off to Birka first thing tomorrow,' Leif told Ulf as they watched the sun dipping to the watery horizon from their camp behind a sandy beach. Ubbi and Jorund skimmed pebbles across the water, lost to the pleasure of each other's company. 'He wants to spend some time there once we've done trading. He's a mind to look for a woman.'

Leif hooted at the look of astonishment on Ulf's face. 'It seems Ragnar's been pressing him to wed and produce a few offspring. And between you and me,' he added, tapping the side of his nose with his finger, 'Bjorn's been a bit disgruntled since Ingrid wed last year. So be prepared for him to be going a-wooing once our buying and trading's done.'

'A-wooing!' Ulf exclaimed. 'Now *that* should be fun to watch.'

'Hmm...' Leif gave his head a good scratch. 'But you know, lad, I wouldn't be surprised if we pull into Bornholm on the way home to see a certain somebody.'

They sat companionably watching seals bobbing in the water as the sun gradually disappeared, taking its light to another world. Ulf sighed. 'Bjorn's right: the Baltic does have its own majestic kind of beauty.'

'I know what you mean,' Leif said, getting to his feet. 'But we've work to do once we've finished admiring the views.'

* * *

By the following evening they were approaching the island of Björkö in Lake Mälaren, on which the market and trading centre of Birka was sited. The town presented a formidable appearance as they approached from the south in the fading light, presided over by a huge bare rock that seemed to loom from the depths of the sea, a stone fortress sitting menacingly at the top. Ubbi and Jorund simply gawked.

'This is the richest of all the trading centres in the Baltic,' Leif told them, 'so it stands to reason it'd be the target of raiders: hence the fortress, which is also a place of refuge in times of attack, like Alfarin's stronghold on Bornholm.' He flicked his chin upward. 'Just beyond the northern gate is the garrison that mans the place.

'Thor's bollocks!' he yelled as the ship rolled, too close to a large rock, barely visible above the water. 'I'd forgotten to look out for those cursed rocks. More defence strategies! Best do your own sight-seeing now, lads, whilst I do my job. And you'll be rowing soon, Ulf.'

They sailed through a defensive palisade that straddled the wide bay, the sails were furled and they rowed for the jetties of Birka's harbour. Tomorrow the trading and purchasing would begin in earnest.

* * *

As at Hedeby, Birka's market area was immediately behind the busy waterfront, where transactions were accompanied by the harmonies of mewling gulls, honking geese and shrieking children. Workyards and homes blended together just the same and the reek of rotting matter in the ditches along the walkways was equally gut-churning. People with skin colours and clothing as varied as meadow flowers in June vied for bargains, and the two boys were utterly enthralled.

After four days of hard bartering, Bjorn had acquired many of the items he'd set out to obtain; only the furs, necessary for the depths of winter, having eluded him.

'Come back this time next week,' a swarthy Swede in a leather jerkin told him in answer to his enquiry, straightening out the thin squirrel and fox furs on his stall. 'Varin'll be back by then. He's late this year, though I'm told he's on his way and to expect him within the week. They say his packhorses are well loaded, and his furs are top quality. Cost yer, mind – quality don't come cheap.' His tongue snaked out to moisten dry lips, his shrewd gaze ranging Bjorn from head to foot. Ulf turned his head to hide his smirk. His master did not flaunt his wealth like most high-born Danes, and many traders had displayed the same concern regarding his ability to pay.

'Varin promised me reindeer, as well as marten, wolf, bear and white fox. He may even fetch sable if the Lapps are trading, and ice bear furs if he got far enough north.' The stallholder drew his brows together. 'We don't get those beasts in our lands – the bears with fur the colour of snow, I mean. They come from the frozen lands of the north, close to the sea where the serpent Jormungandr swims. What man in his right mind wants to go up there, I ask.' He leaned forward, resting his hands on his stall, squinting at Bjorn. 'What were you hoping for, exactly?'

Bjorn held out his hands. 'I'll look at whatever you have, my friend. No promises though; it happens to be real quality I'm after. My father's a fussy man.'

'Aren't they all?' The trader grinned. 'Until next week then. Best be here early – furs go quickly, especially the good ones.'

Over the next few days their goods for trading rapidly disappeared and their newly acquired items gradually filled the holds in the knarrs.

'Three more days before this Varin's expected,' Bjorn said with a sigh as they lounged around their camp fire on the gentle rise behind Birka's palisade. To their left the walls of the fortress loomed, a constant reminder to any would-be miscreant. The long northern day was fading, the bustle along the waterfront slowing; the waters of Lake Mälaren lapped the island's shores and the breeze stirred the long grasses. Ulf swatted at a cloud of midges, smiling at memories of Hastein. It was almost a year since that day along the Seine.

The number of small circles of light dotting the town gradually increased and the two boys soon retired to their tent, drowsy after a long day. The laughter of night-time revellers carried to their ears and the men gazed longingly at the appealing scene. Ulf knew how they felt: they all needed a night of entertainment and pleasure.

'Let's just hope he's worth the wait,' Bjorn went on. 'Another few days here will be more than enough for all of us. But we need the furs so we've got to try our luck.'

'I thought you wanted to spend more time here, my lord – on *private* business.'

Bjorn momentarily glowered, then his lips twitched and he lurched to his feet. 'I've decided my "private business" can wait, Leif. Why waste time looking for a woman when there's a perfectly good brothel or two down there?

'Who's for a night of fun?' he yelled to his seated men.

The respondent cheer was enough to alert the entire town to their intentions.

* * *

By their twelfth day in Birka the novelty of wandering around the market had long since worn off for the two boys. Jorund gradually retreated into himself, his dark moods pervading the tent he shared with Ulf and Ubbi. Oddly, Ubbi found Jorund's sulks hilarious, and took delight in teasing the boy.

Bjorn had now traded the last of the loot from Francia and bought a variety of goods with silver coin: leather shoes, belts and jackets; items made from reindeer antler, like combs, spindle whorls, needles, gaming dice and even antler-handled knives, and walrus ivory for their craftsmen to carve into ornaments. Crates of iron from the northern lands would undoubtedly delight the smiths. And Bjorn had been well satisfied with Varin's pelts. Tomorrow they'd be leaving and Ulf hoped that sailing again might lift Jorund's spirits.

As they gathered their belongings early the next morning, Ubbi hurtled towards Ulf.

'I can't find Jorund anywhere,' he bleated, his eyes flicking to the dense woods behind them. 'Do you think he's just gone up there for a piss? He wouldn't have gone far on his own, would he, Ulf?'

Concern clouded Ubbi's dark eyes and Ulf wondered whether he felt guilty at having teased Jorund so much. He glanced down at the town, considering that his brother was more likely to have headed there. If he had, he'd be very difficult to find once the market was in full swing. 'Just give him a little longer,' he urged, squeezing Ubbi's shoulder. 'He knows we're sailing this morning. If he's not back soon, I'll see what can be arranged to find him.'

* * *

Too worried to wait for Ulf's help, Ubbi decided to search for Jorund himself. He darted between the scattered birches down the hillside and headed for one of the palisade gates, considering that his friend was unlikely to be roaming round the market. He squinted up at the fortress on that bleak rock, recalling Jorund's interest in it. Now *that* was a possibility ...

Once through the gate, he sped along the inside of the palisade as it swung to join the rampart that encircled the fortress, creeping past the garrison outside the northern gate, where voices through an open window conveyed the presence of off-duty guards. A confrontation was the last thing he needed and he moved warily on, knowing other guards could be patrolling. Keeping close to the rampart, only a few yards from the precipice that plummeted to the beach far below, he reached the tip of the headland.

And there was Jorund, statue-still, gazing down at the ships that bobbed like tiny toy boats on Lake Malaren's glassy water.

'Jorund! What on Misgard are you doing up here?' Ubbi blurted. 'You know we're sailing this morning!'

Jorund's sad eyes held his friend's. 'I just needed to be on my own for a bit – get rid of my bad mood before we sailed.' He retrieved a gold ring inset with a bright red stone from inside his tunic and held it out to Ubbi. 'Mama gave it to me, just before you all came to Aalborg and I was feeling jealous of Yrsa. She said it would always remind me of how much she loved me. Sometimes I can't get her dying out of my head, and looking at the ring makes me forget she's gone. I don't mean to be so miserable, Ubbi, especially when you've been so kind to me.'

Ubbi put his arm round Jorund's shoulder as the tears flowed. 'Well, I'm your friend, aren't I? I'll always be your friend, if you let me. And I owed your family a favour, anyway.'

Jorund stared at him and Ubbi laughed. 'I don't suppose your brother's told you how he dived into the river and saved me from drowning. I was only two, so I don't remember, but Freydis is always going on about it.'

'But I haven't got a brother! There's just me and Yrsa.'

'How can you forget someone that big? And Ulf's good at saving people; he saved Bjorn from an arrow in Francia.'

Jorund's little heart-shaped face creased in confusion. 'But I'd never met Ulf before he came to Aalborg, and Mother never mentioned him. Why didn't he live in my father's hall like all his other children?'

Ubbi frowned. Was Jorund really unaware of his relationship to Ulf, or had the loss of his mother blocked out all other memories? 'Rorik isn't Ulf's father, or yours,' he said, wishing he hadn't spoken about Ulf at all. 'I don't know who your father is – you'll have to ask Ulf about that. Only he knows, and perhaps Bjorn and Sigehelm. But no one ever talks about it. Certainly not to me.

'Come on,' he said, determined to cheer his little friend up. 'Let's get back before we both get a bollocking.'

Thirty Two

'Can't say I'm surprised to see you back,' King Alfarin said, mopping the last of the mutton stew from his bowl with a chunk of bread and popping it into his mouth. He took several gulps of ale and swept his sleeve across greasy lips. 'Svala's ears ache from hearing your name,' he added, grinning at Bjorn's expression of feigned ignorance.

Bjorn's crew had again been welcomed to Alfarin's hall and offered a bed for the night. Svala had provided another substantial meal, for which a goat had been slain to accompany the pottage, and was presently organising the servants for serving the dessert. Bowls of autumn fruits preserved in honey – juicy plums and sloes, bilberries, loganberries, blackberries, rosehips and rowan berries – would be served topped with dollops of skyr. Ulf licked his lips in anticipation of the smooth, creamy mixture made from buttermilk. Its touch of sourness complemented the sweetness of the honeyed fruits so well.

'Kata's normally quite a reserved girl, rarely speaks unless the subject's of importance: not one to waste time with frivolities or gossip, you might say.' Alfarin's fond smile told of his love for his only daughter. 'Sometimes I believe she thinks too deeply for a woman, worries about things of more concern to my warriors. And she'll speak her mind if she thinks an injustice has been done or an unwise decision made. Then there's no stopping her!'

From his seat with Leif and the two boys lower down the hall, Ulf followed the conversation with interest. At Alfarin's right, Bjorn was nodding vigorously, his elbows on the table, hands clasped together. 'Your daughter sounds just like my sister,' he said. 'Freydis doesn't like tittle-tattle either, but give her a subject she feels strongly about and she'll match any man's argument. And I confess, she's generally right in her opinions. But I feel she needs a woman of her own age to share her interests; someone with strong opinions, like Kata.'

Alfarin guffawed, banging down his ale cup and swivelling his bulk to face Bjorn. Even from some distance away, Ulf could see the mischievous glint in his eyes. 'It does sound as though your sister and my daughter would get along famously,' Alfarin said, still chuckling as he glanced round the hall.

'Just where *is* Kata?' he threw at his wife hovering with a bowl of skyr.

Svala scuttled off to find her daughter and Alfarin punched Bjorn's shoulder in playful jest. 'So you think my Kata would fit well into your family, do you? But what role did you have in mind for her, exactly? Remember, she's a king's daughter.'

Bjorn's face cracked into an enormous grin and he rose to his feet, all attention focusing upon him. 'My lord,' he started, bowing his head to Alfarin, 'and esteemed residents of this household.' He saluted each table in turn with his cup. 'You do us great honour by extending your hospitality to us for a second time. Be assured, my father will be made aware of every detail and hear our praises.'

'The honour is mine,' Alfarin assured. 'I couldn't have had a better comrade than your father. But I think you've a point to make somewhere here, a certain request to make?'

'I confess, I've counted the days to this meeting as we've

traded,' Bjorn admitted, feigned embarrassment on his face. 'You see, my lord, I've never made such a request before, and I've somewhat surprised myself in wanting to do so. But "wanting" is the only word that springs to mind to describe my feelings.'

'Would this, perhaps, be the object of your "wanting"?' Alfarin asked, rising to embrace his daughter who'd come to stand beside him.

Kata's dark eyes held Bjorn's as she tilted her head, a ready smile on her lips. She was a very pretty girl, Ulf thought, used to adoration, which, as the king's only daughter, she'd probably been freely given since birth.

Bjorn was entranced by this smiling beauty. His eyes fixed on her face with its ivory skin and pert little nose, framed by the shining black curls that cascaded like a bubbling waterfall down her back. Her shapely figure looked firm and lithe beneath her pleated, apple-green dress, the silver brooches fastening her white tunic glinting in the lamplight.

'You wish to take my little girl away from my hall and into your own? Would she please you as a wife?' Alfarin asked, his voice holding a teasing edge.

Kata showed no surprise at her father's directness, though her smile was replaced by a small frown as she waited for Bjorn's response.

Bjorn tore his attention from Kata to Alfarin. 'My lord, although we barely know each other, I feel that Kata and I were somehow meant to be. And I would be more than gratified to receive your permission to marry your enchanting daughter.'

A roar of approval filled the hall and Alfarin clapped Bjorn on the back whilst Svala hugged her daughter. Ulf knew the intended bride would not be consulted in the matter, though Kata's reaction left little doubt regarding her delight at Bjorn's reply.

'But…' Bjorn uttered the word quietly once he could make himself heard.

'You have a *but*?' Alfarin's beaming face transformed itself into a frown. 'Then pray tell us what this "but" would be.

'A simple request, my lord. I would ask permission for myself and my men to remain on Bornholm for perhaps another week or so in order for Kata and I to become better acquainted. After that time we would return to Aros to prepare my own family for our happy event. I would suggest a September wedding.'

Alfarin nodded. 'That seems a fair request. You're in no rush to be home?'

'It's early in the year; our trading's done and the goods will keep,' Bjorn replied, gazing adoringly into Kata's dark eyes. 'And I'd much prefer to spend the time with my bride-to-be. Properly chaperoned, naturally.'

Alfarin threw back his head and roared, his mirth rubbing off on everyone in the hall. '"Properly chaperoned" it shall be!' He slapped his meaty thigh, still chortling at the expression. 'My island's your home until such time as you return to Ragnar with your happy news.' He squeezed Bjorn's arm and turned to his daughter. 'Now that we've sorted out your future you can return to whatever kept you earlier, Kata. Tomorrow you may spend some time with Bjorn, but only in this hall, in the presence of your mother.'

Leif caught Ulf's attention and rolled his eyes. 'And just what does Bjorn think we're all going to do whilst he's off a-wooing his fair maid? Spend a week or so here, he says. A week my arse! Bjorn's no intention of reaching home before summer's done. He'd be bored to tears during the harvest. We'll likely be here at least three weeks – then probably take our time visiting Sjaelland or Fyn!'

'The ceremony will be here, I take it?'

Leif nodded. 'The bride's father holds the marriage feast in his own hall, and pays for it.' He suddenly smirked roguishly. 'Aslanga's face should be a picture when she's told she'll have to sail to Bornholm for Bjorn's wedding. Our master's not exactly the apple of the mistress's eye, is he?'

* * *

During the first week on Bornholm, Ubbi and Jorund played happily with the king's numerous grandchildren, released from many of their own duties whilst the visitors were here. But on occasion Ulf had caught Jorund staring at him, a puzzled look on his face. It was time to have a talk with the boy.

'You've found a good friend in Ubbi,' he said as they ate their morning meal together in the noisy hall. 'He told me you're his best friend now.'

Jorund glanced at Ubbi, chatting with Bjorn at Alfarin's table. 'I like Ubbi, too. And he looks after me, because he's older.'

'That's good to hear. Were you lonely in Aalborg, Jorund?'

'I wasn't lonely. Mother told me stories and taught me my

letters, and we played with my bricks and built towers and bridges. But when Yrsa was born Mother had no time for me. I was very unhappy, until she told me that all babies take up lots of time – and gave me this to remind me that she still loved me.'

Ulf stared at the ring inset with a large red garnet that sat in Jorund's small hand. A stabbing pain shot through his chest as he recalled the day Beorhtwulf had given it to Morwenna. She must somehow have managed to hold on to it for all these years.

'But I had no one else to play with,' Jorund said, tucking the ring back inside his tunic. 'None of Father's other children played with me. And Ubbi told me that Rorik isn't my father, so now I don't know who is!' Tears coursed down his face and Ulf held him close until he calmed. 'And I don't know why Rorik let Mother die. He just stood there and watched the man with the axe.'

Ulf knew that he would never forgive Rorik for what he'd done, but Jorund must be helped to live his childhood without hatred eating at his very being. He took a breath. 'I need to tell you something that will come as a great surprise–'

'If it's to tell me that you're my brother, I already know.'

'Ah,' Ulf replied, strangely unsurprised.

'I didn't believe Ubbi at first because Mother never told me about you. I just didn't understand.'

'You couldn't be expected to. I imagine it was a shock to hear it.'

Jorund stared dolefully into his buttermilk. 'It's definitely true, then? You're my brother, and Yrsa's? And our mother was your mother too?'

'I'm your *full* brother, Jorund,' Ulf explained, 'which means that we have the same mother and father. And we are Yrsa's *half*-brothers.' Jorund was silent, struggling with this new idea. 'Morwenna was mother to all three of us, you see, but Yrsa had a different father to you and me. Jarl Rorik is Yrsa's father. No, I'll not tell you our father's name because it's best not to talk about him in Aros. When you're older I'll tell you all about him.

'When our father died seven years ago, you and Mother went to live in Aalborg, where the jarl raised you as his son,' Ulf continued, choking on the necessary lie. 'And I've lived in Aros since then, which is why we'd never met. But after our mother died, you and Yrsa had to leave Aalborg because there was no one there to look after you. In Aros there are people happy to do so – and you can be near to me, so we can get to know each other. Can you accept what I've told you for the time being, Jorund? This has been a hard time for us both but now we must let our new friends help us.'

As though on cue, Ubbi charged towards them, thrusting his last piece of crust into his mouth and chewing rapidly. 'Coming to play, Jorund?' he asked, gesturing toward the children waiting in the doorway. 'Is that all right, Ulf?'

Ulf flicked his hand, dismissively. 'Go and enjoy your day!'

* * *

It turned out that Leif was only partially right about their stay on Bornholm. After two weeks, Bjorn informed his crew it was time to leave. It was mid-July.

'At the beginning of September I'll return here with my family for a mid-month wedding,' he said, his happiness evident. 'I can't wait to see my father's face when he learns whose daughter I'm to wed. We leave at daybreak,' he threw over his shoulder as he strode away, 'so go steady on the mead tonight.'

The men just glanced at each other and smirked.

Two days later, they arrived back in Aros where Bjorn's news caused the anticipated rumpus. Ragnar was overjoyed at his son's decision to marry – Alfarin's daughter at that! – and a beaming smile fixed on his face for days. For a week, evening meals became celebratory feasts, and a quiet place in the village became hard to find. And Aslanga flapped over the necessity of leaving Aros in Thora and Toke's hands.

'So you're all leaving again,' Freydis said, coming up behind Ulf as he plunged his head in and out of the horse trough by the hay barn in an attempt to cool himself. Westward the sun was sliding slowly down, spilling rays of liquid gold across the skies; the heat of the day reluctant to loosen its grip on the still evening air.

Ulf jerked upright, shaking his head like a shaggy-haired hound emerging from a dip in the river. Water droplets flew from his long hair and beard, showering Freydis, and she giggled at his embarrassed apologies.

'Don't apologise, Ulf. That cool water feels extremely good.' She pushed back dampened strands of hair and fanned her cheeks with her hand. 'I've been in the fireroom for so long I feel well griddled myself! I'd just stepped out to get some air and noticed you in the middle of your, er, ablutions. It's so good to have you all back.'

Freydis's blue gaze fixed on Ulf's face, a small frown replacing the smile. 'But you're sailing again in two days and you've only been back for a week. Life's so dull here when Bjorn goes away, and takes you with him.'

Not trusting his own voice Ulf watched the swallows circling and swooping overhead as they foraged for insect prey.

'Bjorn tells me you're going to Ribe.'

'He lowered his eyes to meet hers. 'He wants to take the wedding invitation to Hastein himself. I don't know how long we'll be there. We could be straight back, but I'm more inclined to think we'll stay for longer.'

'Those two have always been close,' Freydis said, smiling again. 'I remember Hastein's many summers here when I was a child. He's good for Bjorn: they're of a similar age and like the same things. And Hastein makes me laugh. It will be good to see him again.'

'It will,' Ulf agreed. 'And I hope to see an old friend of my own in Ribe.'

'Oh...?'

'Aethelnoth and I were childhood friends,' he said, unable to stop a grim laugh emerging from his throat, 'until we were both captured by Rorik's men.'

Freydis gently laid a hand on his arm, causing that involuntary frisson he'd felt before to surge through his body. He covered her hand with his and their eyes locked.

'Then I'm happy for you, she whispered, pulling her hand away, the moment broken. 'I hope you find him in good health and that your friendship can be easily renewed. People can change much over the years.'

'Hastein's told me all about Aethelnoth,' Ulf said, watching Ubbi and Jorund haring towards them. 'He's apparently a giant of a man, well regarded by Hastein's father.' A shadow of doubt crossed his mind as he contemplated Freydis's words. Aethelnoth may not want to renew a boyish friendship from seven years ago.

'Are you two *ever* coming in to eat?' Ubbi blurted as he and Jorund screeched to a halt beside the water trough and commenced to soak each other.

'Lady Aslanga's calling for you everywhere, Freydis,' Jorund added. 'She's ready to serve the soup.'

Their errand accomplished, the boys bolted back to the hall.

'I'm amazed at how close those two have become during your Baltic trip,' Freydis said as they followed behind. 'They're almost inseparable. But they'll be disappointed to learn they're not going to Ribe. Aslanga won't let Ubbi miss any more lessons.'

Ulf shrugged. 'They'll soon get over it; summer sunshine can work wonders.' Turning to face her, he said, 'I want to thank you for taking such good care of Yrsa, Freydis. She thinks the world of you, almost as though you were her mother.'

'Not really surprising when she spends most of her days with me and has her cot in my bed-chamber. No, I'm not complaining, Ulf, so don't frown. Your sister's a delight, and I do think of her as my own now. Of course we all know Yrsa is your sister, and I can never take your mother's place,' she added quickly, 'but you can't blame me for loving her.'

'I'm just grateful that you do care for her!' Ulf exclaimed, aghast that such a thought should cross her mind.

Freydis smiled in relief. 'Now, don't let Yrsa spoil your meal. If you allow her to climb onto your lap she'll be splashing soup all over your clothes.'

'You've been teaching her excellent manners, then?'

Her playful shove almost landed Ulf in the water trough.

Thirty Three

Ribe: late July 858

'My lord Hastein! Many men are coming!'

The red-faced youth slumped against the door frame of Jarl Giermund's hall to catch his breath, shoving greasy brown hair behind his ears. He stretched his skinny arms out wide. 'From a *huge* dragonship.'

His breathing steadied and he stepped towards a table where Hastein sat playing Tabula with one of his men. 'It came up the river, Master, and pulled ashore near our water meadows.' The spotty brow puckered as he pondered on the scene, his gaze flicking over Hastein's bemused features. 'It had a big bird on its flag – with a fish in its mouth! I was checking the cattle,' he added, lest Hastein should think he was shirking his duties, 'and I saw the men. Two of them with bright red hair.'

Hastein's frown was replaced by a grin as he turned to his mother and sister at their looms. 'It seems my cousin has chosen to visit us, he said.'

* * *

Bjorn's crew secured the *Sea Eagle* along the banks of the Ribea, a mile upstream of Ribe, and traipsed across the water meadows towards Jarl Giermund's village. Swatting at huge flies that swarmed around the lumbering beasts and avoiding cowpats, Ulf grinned. Bjorn bounced along like a child about to open a longed-for gift, impatient to see Hastein and his family again and relay his happy news.

But it seemed their arrival had been spotted. Hastein was waiting for them as they reached the village, conspicuous in a blue tunic against the greys and browns of his men. His welcome was a hearty one and Ulf stood aside with the rest of the men as the familiar slapping embrace ensued.

'Drink deeply, men. Refresh yourselves and rest.' Hastein beamed as they seated themselves in the hall. 'You won't believe how glad I am to see you here. We've not ventured far from the village this year and, by Frey's prick, am I bored!'

Bjorn's eyebrows rose. 'I'd have thought you'd be keen to set sail, cousin, even if only to trade. There can't be many years Giermund's stayed put. Where is my uncle, by the way?'

Hastein's reply was halted when a serving girl thrust an earthen jug beneath his nose. 'More ale, lord jarl?'

'Jarl!' Bjorn spluttered on his mouthful of ale. 'You're the *jarl* now?'

Hastein chuckled as Bjorn swept his sleeve across his wet beard. 'My father died a month ago, his long illness the reason we chose not to sail in the spring.' He glanced at his mother and lowered his voice. 'He'd been ill all winter; his racking cough almost tore him in two, and towards the end he'd been coughing up great clots of blood. By the time he died he'd been bed-ridden for some weeks, weak as a kitten and feverish. We rarely left his bedside, my mother, sister and me. Each breath rattled through his body. Then one morning the breaths just stopped.'

Bjorn squeezed Hastein's shoulder but it was Leif who said,

'Then it was for the best, my lord. No man wants his last days to be a burden on his family.'

'Truly spoken, Leif,' Bjorn said, finding his voice. 'And once the burial's over, the family can mourn him and get on with their lives. The funeral ceremony ...?'

'Giermund went to the next life in his ship, *Raven's Claw*,' Hastein replied. 'Not a sea burial; nor a burning at all. The funeral ship was buried on land, as is our custom here.' He smiled wistfully. 'My father had everything he could need for his future life – his sword and shield, knives and daggers, heaps of jewellery and silver. He even had spare clothes, fur rugs for his bed, enough food and ale to feed an army, with plates and bowls to eat it from. His two favourite horses, and Hopp, his shaggy hunting hound, were laid close beside him – and of course, a thrall to take care of his everyday needs. I just hope I do as well when I go. It was a joyous day for him, and will be long remembered by our people.' Hastein motioned in the direction of the open lands behind the village. 'His grave is in our cemetery.'

Conversation mellowed as serving women refilled their ale pots. Ulf downed the strong brew, its silky smoothness sliding down his throat, refreshing and enlivening him. Anxious for Aethelnoth to appear, he watched a skinny youth laying logs on the fire ready for cooking the meal. Aethelnoth was likely still about his work, but he'd undoubtedly appear to eat ...

Hastein's voice snapped Ulf from his thoughts. 'I rejoice in your happy news, Bjorn, and you have my heartiest congratulations, though you make me quite envious: it's time I took a wife myself. Alfarin's daughter, you say. I haven't set foot in

Bornholm for years. Kata must be quite something to snare you in her net.'

The new jarl glanced again at his mother. 'A wedding would be a welcome distraction for us all. This year's been hard for Bera, and Giermund's death has left a big void in her life. He threw back his head and chortled. 'And I can't think of a better diversion than the marriage of my cousin.'

Women were becoming eager to start the cooking and the men gradually moved back, allowing them space. Some headed outside and as Ulf rose to follow, Bjorn's voice stayed him. 'Ulf, I've news for you. Aethelnoth will be at the burial site about now. It seems he visits it every evening, out of loyalty to his master. But I believe there's also another reason,' Bjorn added with a glance at Hastein. 'Go find your friend, Ulf. You've time to do some catching up before we eat.'

* * *

The dark shape huddled next to the long, boat-shaped grave was motionless. If not for the straggling hair Ulf would have guessed it not to be human at all, just a pile of old clothes. The shape didn't flinch as Ulf approached, making his footfalls deliberately loud and kicking at stones. He stood for a few moments, waiting for some form of response, but to no avail. He reached out and laid a hand on the nearest shoulder and the straw-coloured head slowly lifted. Sorrowful brown eyes met Ulf's questioning stare, but no spark of recognition flashed.

'Aethelnoth...?' Ulf said, uncertainly. The face before him was not instantly recognisable as that of the boy he'd once known. Thick blond whiskers obscured parts of his lower face that the unkempt hair didn't cover, and other visible skin was deeply bronzed by the sun. Yet Ulf felt certain that this was Aethelnoth.

'What do you want?' the brooding shape murmured.

'Don't you know me, Aethelnoth?'

'Should I?'

Ulf crouched down beside his old friend. 'You would have done, once. But I've grown a bit in seven years – though not as much as you, it seems.'

The big man blinked and stared at Ulf. 'Seven years is a long time. I was only a lad back then. And I've been in Ribe for seven years. Before that...' He stared even harder. 'You can't be–'

'I'm a Mercian, Aethelnoth, the same as you. We knew each other as lads, before–'

Aethelnoth lurched to his feet, pulling Ulf up with him, his eyes narrowed, his stance threatening. He was as tall and thickset as Hastein had said. 'Tell me your name – and the name of your father!'

'I am Eadwulf, Aethelnoth. Surely you recognise my hair? My father was Beorhtwulf, my mother was called Morwenna and your father was Thrydw–'

Aethelnoth threw his thick arms around Ulf and hugged him until he gasped for breath. 'I hardly dare believe it,' he said, pushing Ulf to arm's length and looking him up and down. 'I'd given you up for dead years ago, yet there you stand, handsome and well fed. You found a good master at Hedeby then? How did you find me? Where in these lands do you live...?'

Ulf held up his hand to halt the onslaught of questions. 'I'll tell you all in due course, but right now I'm just overwhelmed at finding you again.' He glanced at the stone-edged grave. 'It seems your master was a good one.'

'He was that. Treated me well and gave me much freedom. I've sailed with him on many a raid, and I know he valued my strength and weapon skills. Yes, I'll miss Giermund – but I'll miss Hilde more.'

Aethelnoth stared down at the grave, a haunted look in his eyes, and Ulf suddenly realised who Hilde must have been.

'I'd loved her for years, Eadwulf, since she was captured on a raid in Frisia. We'd planned to be married, if we were permitted. And I think Giermund would have been agreeable. If only he hadn't died.'

Aethelnoth sank to his knees. 'She was buried alive in the ship with the master.' He squeezed his eyes shut and groaned. 'I can't get her screams out of my head. A month now and still I hear them.'

Ulf stared, appalled. He'd never witnessed such a ceremony, but knew the custom was prevalent in Norse lands. In some cases – if the slaves were fortunate – they were killed before burial. He knelt beside his distraught friend. 'We'll probably never understand some of their ways, Aethelnoth, but whilst we serve them there's naught we can do about it.'

Aethelnoth composed himself sufficiently to speak. 'I've a new master now.'

Ulf nodded. 'Hastein's a fair man, like his father.'

'You know him then?'

'He's the cousin of Bjorn, my own master. But even Bjorn didn't know about you until we met up with Hastein for the raids in Francia last year.'

'Well, I'll be damned. To think I'd've been on that voyage if Giermund hadn't needed me here. Hastein wanted me along, but we get scores of ships berthing at Ribe, it being a market town. Some of the foreigners like to take their chances on a few raids inland, so Giermund kept a contingent of warriors on the ready. The Norwegians are the worst: paying us back for our raids along their coasts, I suppose.'

Aethelnoth stared at the grave, his face fraught with grief. 'I know I can't bring Hilde back, but I feel close to her here. Never thought I'd love a woman that much.'

'We've both had our losses,' Ulf said gently. 'But I've one piece of news that may hearten you: Sigehelm is alive and well. He's been with me in Aros since Hedeby, and become invaluable to Jarl Ragnar and his family. He enthrals them all with his tales.'

'Your tutor could always charm the pants off people with his stories.'

Ulf grinned at that. 'Before we reach the hall, Aethelnoth, you need to know that my name is Ulf now.'

At Aethelnoth's enquiring look Ulf merely said, 'I'll tell you later.'

Thirty Four

Bornholm: September 858

'No more secret rendezvous with the generously accommodating Ingrid then, cousin. You'll be kept too busy producing a string of little Bjorns!'

Hastein hooted at the expression of pending doom on Bjorn's face. 'No going back now,' he added with impish merriment. 'Alfarin'd never let you off the island, and Svala would flay you alive, at very least. Not to mention that I would be most displeased to go all the way home deprived of a great feast.' He pulled an earlobe thoughtfully. 'On the other hand, if you should decide to abscond, I'd deem it my absolute duty to take your place beside the delectable Kata–'

Bjorn launched himself toward Hastein, fists clenched. 'I'll break both your legs if you so much as touch her!'

Ulf, Leif and Aethelnoth chuckled as they watched the antics across the large chamber provided by King Alfarin for the groom and his attendants. Bjorn's anxiety was manifesting itself in uncharacteristic outbursts of pique. Ulf felt a degree of sympathy for him. Tomorrow, Bjorn would take on the responsibilities of providing for a wife, making his vows before so many people. And once the mead-soaked days of feasting were over, Kata would sail back with him to Aros.

'Now, that's more like it.' Hastein laughed, holding up his hands to fend off the outraged Bjorn. 'Kata has eyes only for you. And you know it. Anyway,' he added with an air of mischievous mystery, 'I've cast my own eyes in another direction.'

Bjorn opened his mouth to speak, but shut it again, the unasked question swallowed, and squatted down to resume his rummaging through the wooden chest.

Numerous tunics already lay strewn across the rushen floor as Bjorn tried to select the most suitable attire for his wedding: Kata would look ravishing and he needed to match her standard. His everyday 'shabby' simply wouldn't do.

Ulf sighed. His master had umpteen appropriate tunics, all cut from high quality cloths and richly dyed, with intricate embroideries in costly threads. But only Bjorn could make the selection; he simply scoffed at anyone else's suggestions. He picked up some of the rejected garments and piled them on a chair and lifted a massive sword in a discoloured, leather-covered scabbard from the table top. 'I'll polish the sword now, Master,' he said, sliding the ancient weapon from the scabbard and holding it up. 'It's a beautiful thing. So old ...But it should shine like the sun when it's cleaned.'

'Good idea,' Bjorn responded from somewhere deep inside the chest. 'And Aethelnoth can polish my best boots. They're over there in the corner.' He flicked a wrist, gesturing in the general direction of the boots, and then suddenly raised his head to face his cousin. 'If Hastein doesn't mind, that is.'

'Not one bit,' Hastein replied. 'Fresh air will do these two good. And perhaps Leif could do with a breather. Then you and I, Bjorn, need to sort out this business of your marriage garb before Ragnar storms in to lecture you on the role of a good husband.'

Bjorn groaned and rubbed his brow. 'Tomorrow night I

intend to be so mead-sopped I can think of nothing but feasting on Kata's luscious curves.'

September on the island of Bornholm was very beautiful; a perfect time for a wedding. The forests were turning to golds and russets and the Baltic lapped the long beaches and craggy cliffs. Ulf and Aethelnoth sat together, enjoying the smell of briny air mingled with the woodsmoke of housefires. Women carried baskets of fruits and berries and in the storage huts vegetables were being put into crates and sacks. The mellowing sun shed golden light on the recently scoured fields beyond Alfarin's fortress: the harvest was in and there would be food aplenty for the wedding feast.

'Some sword that,' Aethelnoth said, watching Ulf still hard at work. Bjorn's boots stood cleaned and polished, and he leaned his head back against the hall, enjoying the afternoon sun. 'Your master should impress his lady love with that. Their first born son will inherit a beauty. Frankish, I'd say,' he mused, taking in the sword's impressive length and reaching out to touch the intricately decorated hilt. 'Look at the way it's inlaid with hundreds of pieces of silver wire. I don't care what anyone says, Frankish craftsmen can't be bested.'

'Stolen in some raid, no doubt,' Ulf agreed, smiling at his friend's relaxed mien. Thankfully, Aethelnoth seemed to be putting the horrors of Hilde's death behind him. 'It's a good few hundred years old, too. Well worth scrabbling about in that burial mound for.'

'A bit spooky, if you ask me. Couldn't Bjorn have made do with a sword already in his family's possession instead of digging up some reeking ancestor just to pinch his sword?'

Ulf shrugged. 'Meeting the ghost of an ancestor is believed to prove the link in a man's noble bloodline – as well as impressing everyone with his courage. Our own people once did the same.'

'Well, I'm glad we didn't see any ghost. We'd probably have shit ourselves if we had!'

They laughed as they recalled that moonless August night at the burial ground near Aros, a few days before they'd sailed for Bornholm. Just the four of them: Bjorn and Hastein; Ulf and Aethelnoth. They'd dug into the mound, the eerie silence broken by the regular slicing of their spades through the earthen barrow and the occasional screeching of an owl and calls of creatures of the night. Low humps of earth piled up steadily beside the burial mound, bizarre hillocks illuminated by the dim glow from a single oil lamp. Eventually the narrow entrance to the tomb was uncovered. But only Bjorn entered the musty chamber, locating the relic so quickly that, within moments, they were replacing the spadefuls of black earth.

'Well, tomorrow's the day,' Aethelnoth said with a smirk. 'You'll have a new mistress as well as a master, Ulf. Had you thought of that?'

'I try not to. But you needn't look so smug. From what Hastein said earlier, he may soon be wed himself.'

'I wonder which poor girl he's set his sights on. It'll have to be someone who can put up with his warped sense of humour.'

Ulf could only grin at his friend and shake his head.

* * *

On September 12 Bjorn married King Alfarin's daughter, Kata. It was Friday, Frigga's day, the day devoted to the goddess of the sky and wife of Odin. As the goddess of marriage Frigga protected the love of those married on her day, blessing housewives with fertility and successful management of their households. A bunch of keys was her symbol. As always, when confronted with the workings of the gods, Ulf retained an open mind – and a glance at Aethelnoth told him that his friend was decidedly disparaging.

Kata did, indeed, look ravishing. She had spent the morning sequestered with her attendants – including her mother and married sisters – to be stripped of all her old clothing and symbols of her unmarried status. She had been bathed before being dressed in a new green dress and white tunic adorned by jewelled brooches. On her head she wore the decorated silver bridal crown of her family with undisguised pride, her dark curls tumbling loose for the last time. At Bjorn's side by the stone altar in a forest clearing, she smiled radiantly, dappled sunlight playing on her crown and tunic brooches. And resting on the altar was a splendid sword, which she would give to Bjorn during the ceremony.

Bjorn had undergone a similar ritual, intended to remove all trace of his identity as an unmarried man, attended by his father and other men experienced in the state of wedlock. Ulf had stood well clear throughout the marital advice and bawdy jokes, grinning at his master's decidedly nauseous expression. Now Bjorn positively glowed, considerably more smartly garbed and groomed than Ulf had seen him for some time, and seemed unaware of anyone but Kata. His green tunic – quite coincidentally – matched the green of her dress, and from his belt hung the ancient sword, its stained scabbard scrubbed as well as Ulf was able.

The sun shone brightly on the joyful gathering. Accompanying the grinning Ragnar, Freydis and Ubbi's happy smiles contrasted markedly with the forced smile of Aslanga and the sullen faces of Ivar and Halfdan. Next to them, Hastein enjoyed the ceremony with his usual exuberance with his mother and sister, and Kata's many siblings, nephews and nieces beamed their delight with Alfarin and Svala. Other guests vied for a good view of the bride and groom. But as a menial, Ulf could only watch from afar.

Following the exchange of the dowry and bride price, sacrifices were made to the different gods. Thor demanded a goat, Freya a sow and Frey a boar. The blood from the slit throats was collected in bowls and sprinkled with fir twigs over the bridal couple and guests to sanctify the union. The exchange of swords and finger rings ensued, Bjorn offering his ring to Kata on the hilt of his new sword, and Kata presenting hers on Bjorn's ancestral one. Then, with the rings on their fingers the couple made their vows, pledging love and devotion, respect and loyalty to each other in the presence of so many witnesses.

At last Bjorn and Kata were married and it was time for the traditional run of the bride and groom back to the hall. Ulf thought this great fun, as the women ran on foot whilst the men charged ahead on ready saddled horses. So it was hardly surprising that Bjorn should arrive at the hall before his bride, ready to carry her over the threshold. It would be a bad omen for the marriage should Kata trip and fall in the doorway, which was a portal between worlds and a place where spirits gathered. Ulf huffed at that idea, but enjoyed the spectacle anyway. He laughed with the rest as Bjorn thrust his new sword into a supporting pillar of the hall, and watched intrigued as the elders of both families examined the scar. The Danes believed that the deeper the scar, the better the luck of the marriage. Bjorn's scar was very deep indeed.

* * *

The next four weeks passed in hazy revelry on Bornholm. Feasting became the everyday norm and the honeyed mead flowed. Ulf had never seen his master so happy. The guests remained to celebrate the annual sacrifices to Odin on October 14, for which Svala valiantly provided yet another great feast. To the Danes this further added to the joy of the season. To Ulf, it brought back sickening memories of last year's events in Aalborg, and it was in a state of brooding misery that he helped Ragnar's crewmen make ready the *Sleipnir* to sail.

Two days after the sacrificial feast they set sail from Alfarin's island, with an extra, tearful passenger aboard. But Kata's tears were short lived, her joy at being with Bjorn soon overriding her sorrow at leaving her family. She sat happily with Freydis in the stern, and Ulf smiled as he watched the new sisters sharing their laughter and thoughts so easily.

By October 19 the *Sleipnir* and *Jormungandr* were safely moored at Aros. Relieved to be home before the autumn gales whipped the sea into a frenzy, thanks were duly given to Aegir, the giant god of the sea, and his giantess wife Rán. Hastein, however, had still to sail back to Ribe. But Hastein could read the seas like the inscriptions on the runestones and Ulf knew he would not take unnecessary risks, especially with his mother and sister aboard. He'd sail only when the sky was clear, the Kattegat calm and the prospective outlook good.

After secluding himself with Ragnar for a lengthy period of talks, Hastein departed two days later, promising to return for the Yule should the weather permit overland travel. A sea journey in December was not to be contemplated. Ulf's parting from Aethelnoth was tempered by the prospect of seeing him again soon, then again in the spring, when they'd sail to the Middle Sea. But Ulf could only wonder about the subject of Hastein and Ragnar's talks, since not even Bjorn or Freydis could throw light on the matter.

'Possibly something to do with Hastein's new role as jarl,' Bjorn surmised as he wrestled with Ulf as part of his exercise routine. 'I think he's more concerned than he lets on about managing his extensive lands. Thank Odin I won't be burdened with such responsibilities for a few years yet. But if you succeed in breaking my head right off,' he growled as Ulf grasped him in a fierce headlock, 'I'll never get the chance!'

Bjorn and Kata settled contentedly into married life, Kata proving to be a willing worker and amenable companion to the other women. Ulf's life became a routine of chores. The usual work of Blotmonath and food preservation continued, though Ulf was more often engaged in repair work, which suited him better. Mending thatch, furniture and tools were tasks he enjoyed. Nor did he object to helping the ironsmith at his forge.

And on most days, he had his rendezvous with Freydis to look forward to.

As the weeks passed, Ulf realised that Sigehelm knew of his dangerous relationship with Ragnar's daughter. The worried gaze that followed him as he slipped from the hall each night left little doubt of that. But, as dangerous as he knew the meetings to be, Ulf could no more put an end to them than stop his heart from beating. He'd never felt as *alive* as he did in her arms, never smelt such sweet fragrance as that suffusing her silken hair. The softness of Freydis's skin and the suppleness of her body filled him with such ecstasy he could scarce draw breath. Wrapped in her arms, all sense of danger simply melted away.

Then the Yule was looming and Ulf eagerly awaited Hastein and Aethelnoth's arrival. And to everyone's surprise but Ragnar's, when the party from Ribe did arrive three days before the festivities, Hastein's mother and sister were amongst the guests.

'It's good to see you again, cousin,' Bjorn said, hugging the frozen Hastein then embracing Bera and Astrid as they came into the hall. Hastein had travelled on horseback with half a dozen of his men, Aethelnoth amongst them, and all looked stiff as boards. Outside, the air was bitter enough to seep through the thickest furs, the scant layer of winter's first snowfall beginning to freeze on the ground as the afternoon progressed. 'Prise off your coats and come to the fire. Warmed ale and hot griddle cakes will soon thaw you out.'

The hall door opened again and Ragnar appeared, snowflakes speckling his greying hair and beard. It had just started snowing again. 'Frey's great phallus!' he yelled as an icy gust tore the door from his grasp and flung it back with a crash. 'A thousand curses on this weather!' He pushed the heavy door shut and swept the snow from his cloak before tossing it aside and coming to greet his guests. 'Not a good time for travel, Hastein,' he said, yanking his nephew to his feet and engulfing him in his meaty embrace, 'especially with ladies along.' He gave Bera and Astrid a dutiful kiss and seated himself, pulling Hastein down next to him. 'In Odin's name, sit down, Bjorn! I'm not fond of people looming over me.

'Good to see you've made it in one piece, though,' Ragnar went on, his attention again on his guests. 'It's not the easiest of routes you've travelled. The heaths and marshes between here and Ribe can be treacherous if you stray off the paths. And it's easy to do just that when all's beneath the snow. You're fortunate the snows have only just started as your journey ends. But you're here now, and we're all glad about that. Let's hope there's no more snow before your trek home. Now sup up and get warm; the meal shouldn't be too long. And your sleeping quarters are ready, should you wish to rest before you eat,' he assured Bera. 'Now, I need to check all's well in the stables, so I'll leave you to make yourselves at home. Bjorn can keep you company, as can Ivar and Halfdan. Hear that, you two?' he bawled across the hall. 'You can play Knucklebones later. Come and be sociable for once!'

Ragnar hauled himself to his feet, ready to leave. 'We'll resume our talks tomorrow, Hastein. We've several details still to clarify'.

* * *

'Do you polish that damned sword every day?'

Aethelnoth grinned and sat beside Ulf as he burnished Bjorn's wedding gift from Kata. The rest of Hastein's party huddled round the fire, enjoying the warmth, and Aethelnoth had taken the opportunity to spend some time with his friend.

'Mmm,' Ulf murmured. 'This, and the one from the burial chamber.'

'Rather you than me,' Aethelnoth said, waving at Sigehelm across the hall. 'I hate cleaning and polishing. At least I can spend most of my days at Ribe in the stables.' His chest puffed out in pride. 'I'm head groom now, as well as chief bodyguard.'

'Then I'm happy for you; you were always good with horses.' Ulf's glance strayed briefly to the preoccupied guests. 'What do you make of these talks between Hastein and Ragnar?'

Aethelnoth frowned thoughtfully. 'I think they're the real reason we've traipsed all this way in the middle of winter.'

'I'd gathered that much myself,' Ulf retorted. 'But what are the talks about? I just hope Ragnar isn't putting the downers on this Middle Sea voyage. I think he's peeved he can't go himself,' he added, lowering his voice. 'And his two sons over there make things worse, griping that Hastein should be dealing with his new responsibilities instead of gallivanting around the Iberian coast – and that Bjorn should have more care for his new wife.'

Aethelnoth hooted. 'Since when did having a wife cause the Danes to hold back? There'd never be any raids if they paid heed to that load of bullshit. Anyway, why are these talks of so much importance to you?'

'I don't know,' Ulf replied. 'I just have a feeling they involve something I won't like.'

Thirty Five

The twelve days of Yule passed with much jollity. The usual boar was sacrificed to Frey to ensure a prosperous growing season and some folk garbed themselves as goats in honour of Thor. People got drunk and ate too much and the Yule log smouldered in the hearth. But the time for Hastein to return to Ribe soon neared, and by the first week of January the weather was bright and though bitterly cold, was dry enough for travel. Hastein would be departing in the morning.

Freydis was so tired. The celebrations seemed to have gone on for ever and she was beginning to feel she'd never see anywhere but the fireroom for the rest of her days. She sighed wearily. Perhaps she should tell Ulf she couldn't meet him tonight. But the thought of seeing the disappointment in his eyes caused her resolve to vanish rapidly.

Aslanga suddenly laid a hand on her arm. 'Let us eat now, Freydis. You've worked hard these last days and you look bone tired. I've already told Kata the same and she's gone to the hall.' She tilted her head toward the olive-skinned girl loading the trays. 'Benita can help Thora finish off in here. Come,' she insisted, ushering Freydis to the door.

Though surprised at this unaccustomed concern, Freydis needed no second prompting to leave the serving to others.

At the end of the meal Bjorn rose to his feet and held up a hand for silence. Freydis smiled, wondering what tales he'd amuse them with tonight. She noted the starry-eyed way that Kata gazed at her handsome husband, and feeling more than a little envious of the couple's happiness, she glanced at Ulf as he poured mead for the guests.

'I'll make this brief,' Bjorn said, sweeping his audience with his cheerful gaze, 'because I know my esteemed father wishes to address you all when I'm done.' He turned to grin at Ragnar and Hastein next to him. As always, Ivar and Halfdan's faces remained sullen. 'But for what I've got to say, I'd like my beautiful wife beside me ...

'Well,' he resumed, as Kata reached his side and he grasped her hand in his own. 'We've been wed for almost three months now. And I can say that those months have whizzed by so fast that I could scarce distinguish night from day.'

'That's because you've scarce been out of the bed-chamber!' Hastein yelled, to the hooted delight of everyone.

Bjorn flashed a grin at his cousin. 'True, I suppose. But just look at what I've had to occupy me *in* the bed chamber!' He engulfed his wife in his arms as the hall erupted into a cacophony of whistles and lewd remarks. 'I said I'd make this quick, so here's the thing: by July I shall be a father!'

The roars of approval ricocheted round the hall until the beaming jarl rose to his feet with raised hands. 'To my mind you've been perhaps a little precipitate in sharing your excellent news, son. Three months is a relatively short period of time. But your secret's out now and can't be taken back.' Freydis could almost feel her father's delight at this news: a babe would be a welcomed first grandchild. But Aslanga's frosty expression revealed that she was not at all pleased. 'Perhaps a few more weeks would have allowed you to be certain,' Ragnar was saying. 'But I'm sure Kata knows her own body – almost as well as you do, son!'

Kata blushed scarlet at the bawdy comments and Bjorn tactfully steered her in the direction of her seat amongst the women. 'Thank you for your wise observations, Father,' he said with a bow. 'We'll be sure to inform you if our news was too, er, *precipitate*.'

Ragnar stood and faced the hall. 'Bjorn's news was no surprise to anyone,' he started, grinning again. 'Earlier than expected, I'll grant, but still expected sometime soon! But what I have to say will come as a surprise to all of you, with the exception of my wife and one or two others. And now, arrangements have been finalised.' He smiled down at Hastein, smartly attired in a tastefully embroidered brown tunic, his gingery-blond fringe neatly trimmed, his face clean shaven, as was his preference. Freydis would miss him when he left for Ribe.

'And now it falls to me to inform you all to what I refer,' Ragnar continued. 'Freydis, my daughter, come forward.'

Puzzled, Freydis tried to ignore the questioning eyes boring into her as she rose. Aslanga had abandoned all trace of her earlier concern and now displayed nothing but disdain. Her father was smiling – but Freydis knew well that his smiling pleasantries were often a prelude to reprimands, or orders that were not to be questioned.

'You have always been a dutiful daughter,' Ragnar said as she crept to his side, her heart thudding wildly as he took her trembling hands. 'You've been of marriageable age for some years now, during which time I've met no man good enough to assume care of you. And I'm a patient man when my daughter's happiness is at stake.' He smiled, slowly nodding. 'But now the perfect man for you has approached me, requesting you as his wife.'

The words bounced about inside Freydis's head until she could hardly think.

Sweet Freya, my father's going to make me marry. No! It's Ulf I love, Ulf I've given myself to. I could never love another!

'No need to panic, Freydis,' Ragnar said, gently lifting her chin. 'You'll find this man more than meets my exacting standards as a husband for you. He has status and lands, is not lacking in fine looks and, er, other manly attributes.'

Though the jest raised a few titters, most ears were pinned, waiting for the name. Freydis wanted to scream, *'Who are you talking about?'*

Her father shifted position, fixing an unsmiling gaze on Aslanga, who returned his stare with frigid calm. But, though his eyes addressed his wife, his words did not. 'You will be the wife of a jarl, Freydis; the only fitting position for the daughter of a jarl.'

Silence descended; Aslanga visibly recoiled at the barb and Thora's hand rose to her breast. To hail a concubine's daughter as the true daughter of a jarl was against all protocol.

'Perhaps at this point, I might address these good folk?'

Unable to wrench himself from the silent battle with his wife, Ragnar absently nodded, and Hastein rose to his feet. 'It must be apparent that the man to whom Jarl Ragnar refers as "the perfect man" for his daughter is somewhere in this room,' Hastein stated, sweeping them all with his hazel gaze. 'Might I introduce myself to you now as that very person?'

Freydis almost keeled over. She'd known Hastein all her

life, but as nothing more than Bjorn's cousin and friend. Never had she considered him as a potential husband!

'I realise how much of a surprise this must be to you, Freydis,' Hastein said, concern in his eyes, 'but I assure you, I'll make you a good husband. You'll be happy at Ribe, and your father and I have decided that Jorund and Yrsa may come with you, if you wish. I'm sure Ulf would agree you care for them so well.'

Ulf acknowledged Hastein's enquiring look with an expressionless nod and Freydis's heart reached out to him. A thrall could not disagree with requests from his betters. She forced a smile, her mind awhirl with screaming words of refusal. But she could not contest her father's decision: she was duty bound to obey.

'I am honoured to be chosen by you, my lord,' she said, choking on the lie. 'You will not find me lacking as a wife.' The hall erupted with cheers and Freydis stood beside her father, too distressed to move; her dreams crushed like grains of wheat into flour.

Thirty Six

Wilton, Wessex: Christmastide 858

Christmastide at Wilton was a joyful affair, the snow-free weather allowing many of the kingdom's ealdormen and clergy to contribute to the festivities and spiritual devotions over the twelve days. The hall was decorated with the customary sprigs of evergreens from surrounding woodlands and a Yule log glowed merrily in the firepit, reminders of the Saxons' own pagan heritage. For the sons of King Aethelwulf, it was also a time to remember events of the previous Christmastide, and the imminent death of their father. As always, time had played a great healer and, although neither of their parents would ever be forgotten, the immediate grief of loss had long since subsided.

Much to Alfred and Aethelred's relief, as well as that of the elite of Wessex, Aethelbald had soon become reconciled to reigning only in the western shires, and appeared to hold no grudge against Aethelberht's rule of the East. The two brothers communicated often, and news of events and developments in the two parts of the kingdom were shared between them. Since Aethelwulf's death, little had actually changed in the government of either region. Aethelbald continued to be guided by the ealdormen and bishops appointed by his father, and Aethelberht was supported by the powerful nobles of the East who had saved Aethelwulf from dishonourable exile.

Aethelberht had managed to find time to join his brothers

for three days during the Advent, but Alfred's beloved sister was, yet again, conspicuous in her absence throughout the period. However, Alfred refused to be too saddened by that. The birth of Aethelswith's daughter in May had already given them cause to celebrate. To Aethelswith's delight, and Burgred's evident discomfiture, in early June they'd all travelled to the Mercian hall at Worcester to welcome little Mildrede into their family. And besides, Alfred told himself, any long journey at this time of year was a risk, particularly with a young babe.

During the first and most holy of the Christmas days, once the long church services were over until the evening, the royal household and its many guests gathered round the tables to partake of the festive fare. Alfred had soon seen enough of food, and keen to be reading his poetry, he found a quiet corner away from the noise in order to enjoy it. He'd read little more than a few lines when he saw his stepmother approaching.

'You have eaten your fill already, young lord?' Judith asked, smiling as she sat next to him on the bench. Alfred greeted her and smiled back. 'Like me, you seem to become easily bored with the art of overfilling your belly.'

Alfred laughed at her peculiar expression. 'I just find it a waste of time, my lady. There are more useful things to do than making oneself feel ill. Besides, the table will be laden all day. The servants will see to that.'

They chatted for some time, simply enjoying each other's company. Alfred had always felt at ease with Judith, and no one he knew could match her kindness and generosity. Occasionally, however, he'd caught the hint of sadness in her eyes, especially when she gazed at her new husband. But, ignorant of its cause, he felt helpless to offer her comfort.

As she glanced across to the high table, Alfred noticed that same sadness flash again. It was the opportunity he'd been waiting for.

'I know you think me rather strange at times, Judith,' he started, shooting her an apologetic look,' but I was wondering what it is that sometimes make you look so sad. Aren't you happy being married to Aethelbald?'

Judith contemplated the question for a few moments. 'Do you remember how I felt at the prospect of marrying your father?' she asked, once she'd gathered her thoughts. Alfred nodded. 'I was truly terrified of leaving my home in Francia, and marrying a man so much my senior. But in King Aethelwulf, I found a gentle soul, a soul in need of affection and comfort. He was not in love with me, nor I with him.' She gave a small, reflective smile. 'Your father could never love anyone as he loved your mother. But he treated me with such kindness and respect that I came to love him in a different way; as a daughter loves a father, perhaps. My own father had rarely shown any interest in me, other than as a valuable asset with which to secure a propitious marriage alliance.'

She paused, and Alfred waited patiently for her to continue, hoping she'd actually answer his question this time.

'King Aethelwulf never recovered from Aethelbald's betrayal,' Judith said at last. 'He never stopped loving his son, but I believe that during those two years in Kent, your father gave up the will to live. He just wanted to be with Lady Osburh.' Alfred's throat suddenly seemed so swollen, he could barely swallow. 'And now I've been married to King Aethelbald for ten months, and I cannot say I've been unhappy for most of that time. I am still here, in Wessex with you all; I am still a queen, and am always treated like one. Aethelbald is very kind, and shows me great fondness and respect.' She sighed and looked intently at Alfred. 'If I had stayed in Francia, I could have been married to a cruel and uncaring man.'

Alfred nodded, sensing that the answer to his question was on the tip of her tongue. Judith's attention strayed again to Aethelbald at the high table and, for a few moments, she seemed lost to her thoughts.

'Although our marriage was against canon law and Christian custom,' she continued eventually, still relaying facts that Alfred already knew, 'our union has served us both well. It took little time for our ealdormen and thegns to become accustomed to the situation, and now, to our great relief, even the holy bishops seem to have accepted our marriage.'

Alfred wondered whether Judith had forgotten all about his question as she gazed round the festively decorated hall with a small smile on her lips. She straightened the folds of her purple gown and adjusted her head veil, her lips seeming to have sealed. But Alfred had broached the query once, and felt bold enough to repeat it.

'No one could ever fool you, young lord,' Judith said in reply, an observation she had often voiced before. 'Your eyes and ears miss nothing. Yet since you are so persistent, I shall tell you why I sometimes feel a little sad. But,' she added, waving a forefinger at him, 'you must promise not to repeat what I say.' Alfred nodded and Judith drew breath to continue.

'Over the last few months I have come to love Aethelbald

dearly. He is everything I could want in a husband, as I have just explained to you. But he does not love me, and I don't know how to make him do so.' Judith suddenly looked so forlorn that Alfred put his arm around her shoulder. 'I know he wanted me because of my status,' she said, raising a delicate white hand to touch Alfred's comforting arm. 'I was still the crowned queen of Wessex, after all. And I am also the daughter of a powerful emperor, which made me doubly desirable. But I live in hope that Aethelbald will, one day, grow to love me for just being myself.'

Aethelred came to join them, relieving Alfred of the need of a suitable response. He had none to offer. Aethelred held his belly in his hands, a pained expression on his face. 'I swear I never want to eat again. But the venison is simply mouth-wateringly irresistible. Right now I think we should flog the cooks. My discomfort is entirely their fault.'

Alfred and Judith laughed, but Judith's brow suddenly creased. 'Did my lord Aethelbald seem quite well when you left the table, Aethelred?'

Aethelred looked at her troubled face, evidently deciding that this was not the time to be flippant. 'Come to think of it, I don't believe my brother ate a great deal, Judith. I was sitting next to him and I can't say I noticed him actually eating for some time. He was quiet, too, despite the frivolity around him, which I must confess to being party to. Oh, and I do believe his wine cup hadn't needed filling since we sat down. But whether or not Aethelbald felt unwell, I couldn't say. He showed no signs of being in pain.'

Judith nodded, as though she'd expected that reply. 'Aethelbald has barely eaten for days. He has been feeling unwell for some weeks now, but has tried hard to hide it. He does not want physicians fussing over him.' She glanced again at her husband, now speaking with Bishop Ealhstan. 'But he has promised to allow a physician to examine him after the Christmastide. Illness can come upon us so suddenly,' she said, worry creasing her pretty face, 'yet it can take so long to leave.'

Alfred thought of his eldest brother, Aethelstan, who had died when Alfred was but a child of two. He knew that Aethelstan's illness had lasted for some years before eventually resulting in his death. Learned physicians had been unable to find a cure, since they'd never understood the cause.

He sincerely hoped that whatever Aethelbald's ailment might be, it was something quite different to that of Athelstan's.

Thirty Seven

Aros: late January 859

The stillness and uncanny silence were unnerving and Ulf tensed, fearful his footfalls on the frozen earth would be detected by someone. But at well past midnight on this icy night, Ragnar's village slept.

He kept to the shadows of huts and store-sheds, moving only when the bright gibbous moon claimed refuge behind the scattering of dark clouds. Inside the barn he leant against the wood-planked wall as his eyes adjusted to the gloom, the silence intense. He recalled an October morning, many years ago, when he'd peeked into this very barn, inadvertently witnessing another young couple enjoying a tryst in the straw.

Filled with sudden foreboding he thrust his hands through his hair. What perilous game was he playing? What *right* had he to put Freydis at risk of being disgraced in the eyes of her family; cast aside by Hastein? What right had he to betray Hastein's trust – or Bjorn's?

He had no right at all. And tonight he'd tell Freydis that their meetings must end, though the mere thought of it tore his heart to shreds.

Footsteps were nearing: two people at least. His heart pounding, he dived behind a mound of straw. If Ragnar's men had come to find him, he was dead for certain. The barn door creaked open.

'I'm so sorry, Ulf ...so sorry.'

The distress in Freydis's voice was palpable, but he dared not move. He could hear her moving into the barn, searching for him in the shadows. She was barely feet away now. 'I was so sure I hadn't been seen.'

Her words were engulfed in heartbroken sobs. Moments passed and Ulf prayed that it was only Sigehelm with her, come to warn of the dangers they faced. Unable to bear the suspense any longer, he raised his head, just enough to see over the straw...

Large hands grasped his tunic and yanked him to his feet. Freydis shrieked as an iron fist slammed into Ulf's stomach and he doubled over, gasping for breath. Then the fist cracked against his jaw, sending him tumbling back. His head reeled, but the pitiless hands hauled him up, every vigorous shake accompanied by enraged words: 'What in Thor's name are you playing at? What kind of fool do you think I am?'

Ulf sought out the face of his fuming master but could see only the vague outline in the darkness. He opened his mouth to speak, but could not find the words. And though he was bigger and stronger than Bjorn, and would doubtless prove the victor in an outright fight, he offered no resistance to the assault. He couldn't deny that Bjorn's rage was justified.

'Give me one good reason why I shouldn't kill you right now!' Bjorn fumed, shaking an almost hysterical Freydis from his arm. 'By rights I am honour bound to do just that – or else throw you into the pit.' He turned to his sister, sobbing on the straw. 'But if I did, then your dishonour would be no secret. If anyone hears of this you'll be brandished a whore. Did you think of that, sister?

'How could you betray every trust I had in you?' he hurled at Ulf, his released breath a loud, exasperated groan. 'It's my own fault, I suppose, for giving you too much freedom. But I thought you were different to other thralls, that you valued integrity and trust. And I can't deny you've shown great courage.'

'I beg you, brother, let us both go and you'll never need to see either of us again.'

'Just how far do you think you'd get, before the dogs picked up your scent? And if they didn't rip you both to shreds, Father probably would! No, Freydis,' Bjorn said firmly, 'you'll marry Hastein. He doesn't deserve to be treated this way, nor would my own honour allow it. He's a good man, and I could want no better husband for a sister I happen to love dearly.'

Freydis rose and Bjorn held her gently as she sobbed into his shoulder. Ulf turned away, overcome with shame at the misery he'd inflicted on people who meant so much to him. But he heard Freydis's whispered voice.

'What do you intend to do with Ulf?'

'Ulf must leave.'

'Won't you take our word that we'll not see each other again?'

'I can't risk the possibility of you breaking that promise. Love can cause people to lose all sense of right and wrong.'

Tense moments passed as Bjorn said nothing, his every breath imparting his anger. Nauseous and dizzy, Ulf recalled the night he'd fled from Ivar's wolf dog. Bjorn had been his saviour, then.

'What are we to do?' Freydis could bear the silence no longer. 'Please, Bjorn, help us!'

'You will simply carry on as though nothing has happened. As I said, you *will* marry Hastein – and if you want Ulf to stay alive, you'll spend your days going cheerfully about your work. As for you, Ulf,' he said with a sigh that hovered in the darkness, 'the only certainty is that you must go; when and how I've still to decide...

'And don't think I'm unduly concerned for your hide, thrall. If anyone learns of my part in your deceit, I'd be deemed unfit to be called a Dane, let alone the son of a jarl!'

Ulf drew breath to beg forgiveness but Bjorn was too angry to listen. 'Don't say anything,' he hissed. 'I don't want to hear your voice again tonight.' He turned to his sister. 'Get back to the hall, Freydis.'

Freydis lingered uncertainly in the doorway, silver tears striping her white face in the moonlight. Then she obeyed, her footfalls gradually fading into the distance. Bjorn's breaths were slow and loud as he strove to control his turbulent emotions. 'I need my bed,' he said at last, his hands circling the sides of his head. 'I'll think more clearly tomorrow.' On reaching the door he threw over his shoulder, 'My orders to you, Ulf, are the same as those I gave Freydis: complete your chores as usual and say nothing to anyone, not even Sigehelm. When I've decided what to do, you'll be the first to know.'

* * *

By the first week of March, Ulf still had no idea of Bjorn's intentions for his future. Whether he'd be forced to flee from Aros, pursued by men intent on stringing him up to mollify the gods, or sold elsewhere, he didn't know. Bjorn had become an indifferent master, who spoke to him only to give orders or curt thanks. Gone were the cheerful conversations and shared trust: Ulf had destroyed all that by allowing his love for Freydis to override his better judgement. The lengthening days and prospects of a summer at sea held no allure for him now. Engulfed in misery he shied from contact with anyone, especially Sigehelm, and focused on the tasks assigned to him.

Then Hastein arrived for his spring wedding, and Ulf felt as though his life had abruptly ended. Relieved to have arrived safely at Aros the Ribean guests chatted with unrestrained cheerfulness. Too early in the year to risk sailing, their overland journey had been beset by its own perils. Melting snows had rendered large tracts of land waterlogged, impassable in places. Re-routing had added miles to the already lengthy journey and wolves prowled too close to their camp, drawn by the scent of fresh horsemeat. But today all thoughts of travel were left behind; it would be several weeks before they returned to Ribe.

Aethelnoth grinned across the hall, but much as Ulf was pleased to see his friend, it took considerable effort to return the grin. He focused on repairing a broken stool, resolving to speak with Aethelnoth later.

It was when Ulf was serving ale that evening that Hastein beckoned him over. At the young jarl's side, Bjorn held out his cup for a refill, then abruptly turned his head. Hastein seemed not to notice the friction between them, his own joy in life overriding all else. 'So, Ulf, you'll attend with Bjorn and Aethelnoth to prepare me for my wedding?' he asked.

'I'd be honoured,' Ulf replied, ignoring the pain that seared his chest.

'You know what's required: strip me of my old identity and all that. And since I no longer have a father to advise me in the finer arts of matrimony, with all its joys – and intrinsic responsibilities of course – my mother's brother will stand in his place. A more debauched character than Uncle Arne I've yet to meet!' Hastein grinned, nodding toward a corpulent figure slumped on the bench a few feet away, more than a little drunk already. 'It should prove interesting to hear his advice on taking care of a wife!'

'I can give you all the advice you need there, cousin. Kata believes the sun shines out of my arse – and I've no mind to disillusion her just yet.'

'Then I'll look forward to your wise advice, Bjorn, though I'm sure you won't mind if I ignore most of it. Until tomorrow then, Ulf, and remember, it's Aethelnoth's job to clean my ancestral sword, not yours, so don't let the scoundrel shirk on that score! The sword's in good condition anyway, been handed down in my family for a few generations, so we didn't need to dig about in a burial mound to get it. Not nearly as old as Bjorn's, of course, but the craftsmanship is very fine and I think Freydis will approve.'

It was past midnight when Ulf eventually climbed into bed, having spoken with Aethelnoth for some time – though he'd kept his friend ignorant of his feelings for Freydis. Aethelnoth did not deserve to be burdened with such knowledge.

* * *

Ulf could recall little of Hastein and Freydis's wedding other than it had seemed like a repeat of Bjorn and Kata's. He'd witnessed the rites and traditions of the marriage ceremony as through a dense wall of fog. The long days of the honeymoon had been agony as family and guests celebrated in wild abandon. With each day's close Hastein steered Freydis away to their bed, leaving Ulf fighting back tears of misery, regret and jealousy. He found little solace in knowing that Freydis had had no choice in her marriage and must learn to make the most of her new role in life.

Too soon it was time for Hastein and his bride to leave. And though the day was cold for the second week of April, it seemed the entire population of Aros had gathered to bid farewell to the jarl's lovely daughter. Emotions ran high; Ragnar's embrace of his only daughter fierce and long. Freydis composed herself throughout, until she turned to Bjorn and Ubbi, when fortitude deserted her and her tears flowed. And when she eventually tore herself away it was only to sink into Thora's waiting arms, the pain of their parting viewed by most through misty eyes.

For Ulf, the pain of losing Jorund and Yrsa added to that of losing Freydis. But with his young brother and sister his emotions need not be curbed and he hugged them unreservedly.

'You're doing well,' Sigehelm whispered at Ulf's side. 'I'm proud of you.'

Ulf was well aware that Sigehelm had been watching him, most noticeably when Freydis had come so close to wish them happiness. The brief flash of desperation in her eyes had almost caused him to cry out, only Sigehelm's touch on his arm preventing him.

Freydis eventually moved to stand by her smiling husband, ready to climb into the wagon with Jorund and Yrsa. Unaware of the great changes about to occur in her life, Yrsa giggled excitedly. But Jorund was on the verge of tears, unable to bear the thought of being separated from Ubbi.

Ubbi suddenly hurtled from Ragnar's side to clasp his friend by the shoulders. 'When I'm a man I shall journey to Ribe and beg Hastein to allow you to become my thrall, Jorund. Just like Bjorn asked for Ulf,' he proclaimed. 'I shall pay handsomely, of course.'

'Then I'm sure we can come to some amicable arrangement,' Hastein replied, giving Ubbi a hug before moving to take his pony's reins from Aethelnoth. 'But until that time, we'll take good care of your friend and his little sister. Freydis would cut off my ...er ...well, she'd certainly attack my person in some way if these two youngsters suffered any harm.'

'Thank you, Hastein,' Ubbi replied, grinning at everyone. 'So, that will not be many years, Jorund. And Father says I can spend this summer in Ribe, so we'll not be parted for long.'

Hastein shouted final thanks to his hosts and mounted his waiting pony, and soon the wagons and carts rolled steadily away. From the back of her wagon, Freydis momentarily caught Ulf's eye before turning her attentions to Ragnar. 'You *will* keep your promise and bring Ubbi to Ribe in the summer, won't you, Father? And I'd like you to see how good I am at managing the lands whilst my ...my husband is away. I'll make you proud of me, you'll see.'

Ulf headed back to the hall to hide his misery.

Thirty Eight

Aros: mid-April 858

Losing Freydis served to galvanise in Ulf all the hurt, all the insult, resentment and rage that had accumulated over the years. Faces of his tormentors loomed in his head as he worked, opting for the most physical of tasks on which to vent the anger boiling in his guts. His chest heaved as he shovelled the stinking manure out of the stables, remembered words ringing in his ears:

I know that, one day, you will be free and return to Mercia ...

You are destined to become a great warrior...

Remember who you are ...

But Ulf needed no reminder of who he was. He was Eadwulf, atheling of Mercia: the proud son of King Beorhtwulf. And it was time to take his destiny into his own hands; put an end to his miseries on the whims of others. No longer would he let the injustices done to his family go unavenged. He was not a child any more; he was a man, strong and skilled in the use of seax, sword and battleaxe ...

He was no man's thrall!

The decision surged into Ulf's mind as though it had always been waiting, just hovering on the periphery of his consciousness. Tonight, when Aros lay silent in sleep, he would flee. That would give him several hours start before the chase began – the baying hounds, and men intent on stringing him up to pacify the gods. He had no fears for the welfare of his young brother and sister; Freydis and Hastein would take good care of them. And one day, he'd return to Ribe and take them home to Mercia.

But the crushing misery that engulfed him at the thought of betraying Bjorn almost destroyed every shred of his resolve. He'd already betrayed his master once, simply by loving Freydis, and was still uncertain as to whether he'd ever really be forgiven. A second betrayal was tantamount to openly obliterating all ties of friendship and respect between them. Bjorn might initially be distressed that Ulf could do this to him, but that distress could soon turn to rage. Above all else, Ragnar's son was a Dane, whose injured pride would demand its own retribution. He'd probably lead the hunt.

And yet, to find his real self, and avenge the deaths of his parents, and the damage done to those two young children, Ulf realised he must steel himself from conflicting emotions and forget his life of the past seven years.

Now the decision was firmly lodged in his head and there was no evicting it. After years of obeying orders, Ulf would seek out his own path to follow.

And his first stop along the way would be Aalborg.

* * *

Little under an hour had passed since the occupants of the hall had retired for the night, but Aros had already descended into silence. Ulf stepped warily towards the stables, the pale light of the quarter moon enough to betray the movements of an escaping thrall. He prayed to all the gods that if anyone had witnessed his leaving the hall, they'd think he was simply going to relieve himself.

A night bird suddenly screamed, the sound splitting the air like a lightning bolt, swift and terrifying; a portent of doom. Ulf shook the thought away and focused on getting to the stables.

An old sack slung across his back contained chunks of food wrapped in a cloth, and a waterskin tied about his waist would be fastened to the pony's saddle, once away. It was all the sustenance he had for the sixty-mile journey, until he could steal more from somewhere. He'd face that problem when it arose. Of more immediate concern was the lack of a weapon: those he used at sea were forbidden to him, a thrall, once back home. The journey to Aalborg alone could be fraught with dangers. And for killing Rorik ...? He'd just have to rely on finding some discarded implement on reaching the town. Or else use his bare hands.

He pulled open one of the two rickety stable doors, cringing at the creaks and groans it made as it shifted in irregular jerks. Unsettled by the sounds, ponies shuffled, the odd whinny causing Ulf's heart to race. Tugging the door shut behind him, he murmured softly and they soon calmed. His voice was one they'd heard regularly over the past weeks, after all.

Shut away from the moonlight, the darkness was intense, and Ulf stared into the large, wattle-walled building until his eyes grew accustomed to the gloom. He inched his way towards the pony he'd previously selected, fumbling along the wall behind him until he located a lightweight saddle and bridle. Lifting them down he moved across to the stall, ready to back the pony out.

The creak of the door stopped him in his tracks. He peered over the side of the stall, his eyes fixing on a dark shape outlined in the doorway. It appeared to be a single man, motionless, and likely staring into the sudden darkness. Silently, Ulf laid down the saddle and crept to crouch down at the end of the stall. He peered out, his ears strained to detect movement.

The sudden thwack of a foot striking a wooden pail pinpointed the man's position: the bucket always sat in that particular place against the wall. Ulf dived out, colliding with a solid figure and landing on top of him on the earthen floor. His victim yelped, too stunned to retaliate, as Ulf rained blows to his head and stomach.

'Enough, you damned fool! Are you so intent on leaving that you must kill me to do so?'

Ulf recoiled at the sound of the familiar voice, pulling himself up and staring down at the object of his fury. But his shock was rapidly replaced by rage at being called 'a damned fool'. 'I'm doing exactly what you want me to do, Bjorn,' he snarled. 'You made it quite clear I had to leave. I just decided it would be at my own instigation.'

Ulf's use of the name was deliberate. Never again would he call anyone 'master'.

Wincing at the effort, Bjorn dragged himself up to face him, so close that Ulf could have reached out to touch him. He could just make out Bjorn's features now, and the slight tilt of his head as they stared at each other.

'Though I didn't know it was you sneaking up on me,' Ulf admitted, breaking the awkward silence. 'I imagined you'd be curled up in bed with Kata ...But don't expect me to give up my plans. I *will* leave, even if I have to knock you out or truss you up to do it. If I stayed, you'd never be able to trust me again. You'd always be thinking I was plotting to flee. And you'd be right. It could only end with me dangling from Odin's oak.'

For some moments Bjorn did not move or speak, but at last he leaned wearily against the wall. 'We need to talk about what you're intending to do,' he said quietly, all trace of outrage gone from his voice as he slid to the floor. Warily, Ulf sat beside him. 'I'll overlook your attack on me if you can see reason,' Bjorn went on. 'There are things I need to say before you embark on this foolhardy venture – which, as you said yourself, could only end up one way. No matter whether you knock me out, or even kill me.'

Ulf felt the attention full on his face, glad he couldn't see the look in Bjorn's eyes. The hurt would be too much to bear. 'I know you've been tormenting yourself with the belief you could have saved your mother, Ulf, but you could never have done so. Morwenna's fate was sealed as soon as Rorik discovered her secret. And we won't go into the possibilities of how that could have happened, right now. But, if I know anything about you at all, the need to wreak revenge on Rorik has been gnawing at your guts ever since. Oh, you put up a brave enough show on our Baltic trip, and I'd hoped you were coming to terms with the events at Aalborg. But now I realise the warrior in you would never let that happen. You won't rest until Rorik lies dead at your feet. Or you at his.'

Bjorn ignored Ulf's grunt. 'I know you don't want to hear this again, Ulf, but your relationship with Freydis was also doomed from the start. I'd seen the two of you becoming very close over the years, as, no doubt, had Sigehelm. But discovering that your feelings for each other had developed into such passion hit me like one of Aegir's spiteful waves. If I hadn't noticed Sigehelm staring at the door as you left the hall each night, I might never have known what was going on. The look on the scribe's face said it all. I'll say no more about that night. I'm not proud of the way I lost my temper. But Hastein is my cousin, and honour dictated–'

'Is this leading anywhere, or is that it?' Ulf's anger was rising again, roaring through him to match the frustration he felt at the disruption to his plans; this wasted time. 'As far as I see it, there's only one way I'm getting out of here. And that's right through you. I'll probably have to kill you – whether I want to or not.'

Ulf heard the sudden intake of breath, imagined the pained look on Bjorn's face and felt the familiar pulls of loyalty, admiration and gratitude.

'You'd do that, would you?' Bjorn's voice was a mere whisper but the hurt rang loud. 'You'd actually kill me?'

'It would never come to that, and you know it. Your men would be here long before I got the chance.'

'Answer the question, Ulf. *Would* you kill me if I tried to stop you leaving?'

'I don't know, Bjorn. Settling my score with Rorik means more than anything else to me right now.' He sighed, his anger tempered by a sensation of deep sorrow. 'I'd never willingly harm you, you must know that. But–'

'Your desire for revenge overrides all else. I understand that, and I'll admit, you've suffered a great deal. I, for one, wouldn't be sorry to hear of the demise of that obnoxious swine, Rorik.' Bjorn paused, seeming to consider what he would say next. 'And I know that losing Freydis almost broke you. Believe me, I've been expecting you to do something like this for weeks. In fact, I've watched you slipping food into bags for the past few days. That's why I followed you out here now; you seemed particularly on edge tonight.

'And you're right, Ulf. I still believe that your leaving Aros is vital. But not like this. You've already spelled out the inevitable consequences of that.'

Ulf waited as more precious moments passed, angry with himself for even listening to all this. Bjorn was just playing for time; coaxing him to stay.

'In two weeks' time we set sail for Ribe,' Bjorn reminded him, 'then on to the Middle Sea. You know how long we've planned for this, and how much the venture means to me and Hastein. Well, I believe your leaving might well be achieved once we get to Ribe. And that way, no one in Aros would know you'd even gone until my return.'

'But how...?'

'Don't ask me that, Ulf, because I can't yet give you a full enough answer. But I've been toying with the idea for some time and things are just starting to come together. And I think you could find your way from Ribe to Aalborg easily enough.'

Ulf grunted. 'How do I know you won't have me thrown in the pit once we leave these stables?'

'I suppose you'll just have to trust me, won't you?'

Thirty Nine

Aros –Ribe: late April 859

Thirty colourful sails snapped taut, gripped in the vicelike jaws of a howling wind that drove the dragonships north through the Kattegat. Like a swarm of grotesquely-headed beasts the ships soared over the foaming brine, gaping maws blood-red, salivating with the expectation of fresh kill. Nearing the Limfjord, Bjorn turned his back to the *Sea Eagle's* prow and faced his men, his hair and cloak streaming out behind, eyes glistening with the sting of wind and sea spray. 'To fortunes greater than we have ever known!' he yelled, punching the air above him. 'And the charms of olive-skinned women with hair as black as night! What red-blooded Dane could ask for more?'

The crew cheered and whistled but Ulf silently concentrated on his rowing, mentally preparing himself for the days ahead. As they sailed past Aalborg, he smiled grimly to himself, imagining his return to the town, very soon. How that would be achieved, or how he'd even get away from Ribe, he had no idea. He'd put his trust in Bjorn, and so far, Bjorn had kept his word. He'd not ordered Ulf thrown into the pit, nor even referred to the incident in the stables again.

The following afternoon they sailed into the estuary of the Ribea, and while the rest of the fleet berthed at Ribe, where the men could enjoy the port's many attractions, the *Eagle* continued upstream to Hastein's village.

Freydis was too busy catering that night to offer more than

general greetings. Ulf felt relieved at that; just seeing her was enough to tear his emotions to shreds. But he did manage to catch Jorund alone.

'Are you and Yrsa happy here?' he asked, taking in the boy's decent tunic and sturdy shoes compared to the shabby clothing Aslanga provided for her thralls. 'You certainly look well cared for.'

'We are,' Jorund replied, his eyes briefly finding Ulf's as he made ready his bed. 'Freydis and Lord Hastein are very kind to us. And Yrsa and I have plenty to eat and nice clothes. But...'

'Come on, out with it,' Ulf prompted, ruffling his brother's hair.

Jorund's face crumpled. 'It's just that I've no friends here. The other boys keep telling me I'm just a measly thrall and won't let me play with them. They aren't nasty when Freydis is around; *then* they pretend to like me! And I miss Ubbi.'

Ulf hugged his brother, knowing too well what it felt like to be an outcast amongst other children. 'I'll speak to Hastein, or Freydis, if you like. But if the children think you've gone crying to the master or mistress, it could make matters worse.'

'I know. I've just got to find a way to make them like me on my own.'

* * *

The following morning, Hastein and his crew were down at the river, loading their ships for sailing, leaving the hall strangely quiet. Ulf wandered outside, noticing that even the *Eagle's* crewmen were nowhere to be seen. Thralls were busy at their chores, and small children chased about, shrieking excitedly. Ulf watched them, envious of their joy in life; it had been a long time since he felt that carefree. He wondered when Bjorn would inform him of his plans. The joint fleets would be sailing with the morning tide and any move Ulf made would have to be soon...

The sudden arrival of the master he was about to desert startled him from his thoughts.

'Let's go inside so we can talk away from all this mayhem,' Bjorn said, gesturing to a group of lads about to embark on a punch-up, before heading for the hall door. 'I've sent our men with Hastein so we'd be left in peace,' he began, his voice suitably lowered once they were seated indoors. A handful of women were now busy sorting through skeins of wool by the looms along the far wall, chatting to each other as they worked. Ulf tugged at the neck of his tunic. Anxiety was making him nervous. 'I don't want anyone overhearing what I've got to say, even though I still can't give you any last minute details until later.'

Ulf just nodded, willing Bjorn to divulge his plans quickly. He wasn't in the mood for a long preamble.

'Agonising over the best way for you to get away unseen has caused me many a sleepless night,' Bjorn confessed. 'And I've had no one to talk it through with, other than Leif.'

Ulf stared at him. 'Leif knows I'm about to run...? I thought you said no one else would be involved in this. Does he also know about my relationship with Freydis?'

'Leif's a trusted friend, Ulf, who happens to think highly of you. I told him about you and Freydis weeks ago, and he's been as concerned as I have over what could be done. We've pondered on it many times. He doesn't know about events in the stable, though. I won't tell anyone about that. But he does know that you'll not be sailing with us.

'I'll tell my sister exactly what I'm about to tell you. Though her heart may bleed for want of you, she'll continue to care for Hastein, for whom she feels great affection, if not the deep love she has for you.'

'Then I'd be grateful if you'd tell me quickly what you've decided,' Ulf croaked.

Bjorn held Ulf's gaze. 'You've been far more than a thrall to me, Ulf, saving both my life and Ubbi's after all. But we both know that you and Freydis need to move on. And if things in Aalborg go as you intend, news of Rorik's regrettable death will reach Aros before too long. Of course you and I will be far away in the Middle Sea at the time,' he added with a wink, 'so no one's likely to suspect you.' He suddenly grinned impishly. 'I wonder if you'll ever think of us when you're back in Mercia.'

Ulf gaped, but subsequent explanation was forestalled by the arrival of Freydis, laden with bread for the morning meal. Close behind her toddled little Yrsa, toting a flatbread wider than herself.

'We'll talk later, Ulf, as soon as Leif returns. Then I'll speak to Freydis.'

* * *

By early afternoon Leif was back, and once the helmsman had downed a second mug of ale, Bjorn led them to the cemetery where Giermund was buried so they could speak openly. Cross-legged at the edge of the graveyard amidst a profusion of spring flowers, they were silent for some time before Bjorn said, 'Of course you realise that Hastein won't initially be told of your leaving. If he notices your absence during our boarding and moving out, I'll be very surprised. But if he does, I'll simply say you've fled and nothing can be done about it. Hastein's fleet will be waiting at the mouth of the Ribea by sunrise, so our sailing can't be delayed.'

He plucked a couple of shiny yellow celandines, examining them as though that were his sole purpose in life. 'What I'll tell him later on I don't know yet. I just hope some feasible explanation grabs me.' He paused, inadvertently crushing the small flowers he'd held so tenderly just moments before. 'Hastein will be dismayed by the thought that you've run, Ulf, I know that much, and will want explanations regarding your motives. But one thing is certain: Hastein must never know that any involvement has ever existed between you and Freydis. I won't see my cousin so hurt.

'Do you both understand?' he said, his green gaze flicking from Ulf to Leif. 'Forgive me for laying this demand at your feet too, my friend. I know you always speak and act with prudence – but my fondness for my cousin...'

Leif gave a dismissive wave. 'I understand, Bjorn. You have my word that Hastein will hear naught from my lips.'

'Nor from mine,' Ulf affirmed as Bjorn squinted at him in the sunlight.

Bjorn nodded. 'The only time this can be done is today: late this afternoon, or early evening, while there's still light.

Tomorrow we sail, and you must be gone before then.' He gestured to Leif, who took his cue:

'This morning, when most folk were busy with preparations for sailing, I sort of borrowed one of Hastein's ponies and rode into Ribe. I'd a job avoiding our own men, and some weren't entirely convinced I'd been sent on my own to purchase extra provisions. Can't say I'm surprised, mind you. Not a very likely story, is it? I bought a couple of coils of rope to carry round with me, look more convincing, like. Anyway, my real motive for going was to find an old acquaintance of Ragnar's and mine – someone we've met up with many a time over the years: Kaupang, Hedeby, Birka ...We've even enjoyed a few mugs together here in Ribe. He's a Norwegian, an old seaman who spends more time aboard ship than we do. I found him exactly where I'd expected – down at the quay with his ships. Like us, he sails tomorrow.'

Leif shifted his bony backside into a more comfortable position on its hard seat. 'Olaf hasn't changed a bit since you and I last saw him ten years ago, Bjorn – though you were little more than a lad yourself then. He sends his regards and hopes we can all meet up again soon, Ragnar included. Next year perhaps?'

Bjorn shrugged. 'Perhaps, although I can't answer for my father. I recall Olaf as an irascible old rogue, but deep down, he's a good sort. Talked a lot about his family – probably because he so rarely sees them.'

'How did you know he was in Ribe?'

Leif shot Ulf a glance and picked up a sharp stone that appeared to be the major cause of his discomfort. He lobbed it across the grass, prompting the screeching alarm call of a startled blackbird. 'Hastein mentioned it last night,' he said, selecting another stone to hurl. 'Few ships berth at Ribe without him knowing about it. Seems Olaf's been in Ribe this past week and – here's the best bit – he's short of crew for his voyage. A few of them decided they'd rather not go home right now and disappeared a few days ago. Beats me why they'd do that, but do it they did. Olaf's mad as can be, but has no way of finding them.'

'So you asked him to take me on. But isn't he just sailing to the Norwegian lands?'

'The first bit of that's true enough, but not the second,' Leif said, glancing at Bjorn, who nodded for him to continue.

'Well, lad, on leaving Ribe, Olaf'll first be making a detour up the Limfjord to Aalborg for a day or two – says he's got some cargo bound for the place and he's hoping to recruit a few more crewmen there. It's an interesting town, Aalborg,' he added, staring at Ulf and nodding slowly, 'and we think you'll find plenty to occupy you whilst you're moored up.'

Ulf's looked from Leif to Bjorn as the implications of the steersman's words hit. But neither man spoke, leaving him time to digest this new development. Olaf would be taking him straight to Rorik's door.

'Does Olaf know what I intend to do in Aalborg?'

Bjorn shook his head. 'Though he might guess, especially if the hue and cry's raised before you set sail again.'

'Anyway,' Leif continued, breaking the awkward pause, 'after dropping off the goods for his own people, Olaf'll be on the move again. You'll not like what I'm about to say, Ulf, but say it I must. He plans to raid along the coast of Northumbria, then work his way south along the Mercian and Anglian coasts. There's some very convenient rivers along the way too.'

Seeing the way to Mercia open up before him, Ulf disregarded thoughts of raids in his homeland. 'And he agreed to me leaving him once we're over there?'

'He did. And I've paid the old scoundrel enough to hire several more men in your stead.' Bjorn suddenly shot a worried look at Leif. 'You *did* remember to give him the purse?'

'I did that. And very pleased he was to accept it.'

'Then it's all set.' Bjorn heaved himself to his feet and started back to the hall. 'You need to get to Ribe before nightfall, Ulf. No goodbyes to anyone, not even Jorund and Yrsa, and Freydis will keep them out of the way when we leave tomorrow. As to your absence from the meal tonight, should anyone notice, I'll say you're doing some job for me.'

'And the crew?'

'I'll tell them what I tell Hastein: that you've fled – unless you've any better ideas. And don't worry about having no coin. I've another purse put aside, for you. You'll need most of it once you're back in Mercia, so keep it out of sight until then. As long as you sail with Olaf, you'll be well fed, but after that...' Bjorn flashed a roguish grin. 'I don't want you to waste away due to starvation – especially after I've gone to all this trouble to send you home.'

* * *

With the hood of his coat pulled up to hide his conspicuous

red hair, Ulf pushed through the crowds still thronging Ribe's waterfront, the early evening air thick with the smell of fish and brackish water. He tugged the sack slung across his back ground to his chest: it contained all his worldly possessions, including the heavy purse and silver armband from Bjorn, and he couldn't risk the chance of a thief snatching it. Drawing comfort from the feel of the dagger Leif had given him pushed through his tunic belt he moved on, keeping his head bowed. Scores of vessels were moored along the quayside, many loaded for sailing with the morning tide. Crewmen sat aboard or on the quay, drinking companionably, their voices mingling with the screams of seabirds seeking last minute scraps. He didn't glance at the men guarding Bjorn's fleet. Most had known him for years and would recognise him too easily.

He located the Norwegian dragonship, *Fenrir*, exactly where Leif had told him, along the most southerly of the jetties. She was a fearsomely beautiful-looking craft, as long as Bjorn's *Sea Eagle*, her prow supporting the head of the great wolf after which she was named.

Ulf's scrutiny of the ship was cut short by the appearance of someone peering at him over the vessel's side. The greying hue of his long, lank hair matched the trailing moustaches and plaited beard: a man easily old enough to have once caroused with Leif and Ragnar.

'Step aboard,' Olaf shouted down in answer to Ulf's query. 'We're a fair way from your lot here, but best keep your hood up till daylight's gone.'

Ulf boarded the longship, nodding at the group of hardened-looking men talking quietly over their ale. They eyed him with ill-disguised suspicion before returning his nod and resuming their muted conversation.

'They'll treat you fairly – Ulf, is it?' – Olaf said, 'as long as you pull your weight. Can't expect them to be too friendly till they know what you look like, can we?'

'I suppose not,' Ulf agreed, his lips twitching.

'Well then, seat yerself and we'll eat some bread and good, strong cheese and down a few mugs. The rest of the crew'll stay in the town till we sail.' Olaf flicked his chin to indicate the length of the ship. 'We're all loaded for off, so I've a few more men aboard with me tonight. Don't want no buggers trying to relieve us of our stuff, do we?'

Ulf eventually closed his eyes to Ribe's flickering lights. In a few hours he'd be sailing away from the life he'd known for the past eight years. What lay ahead, only time would tell. All he could see was the bloodied knife in his hand.

And Rorik, dead at his feet.

Forty

Aalborg: late April 859

The *Fenrir* spent a day and night at sea, following the Danish coast north before veering east into the Limfjord. Ulf slept little during his allotted rest periods, his thoughts preoccupied with possible ways of killing Rorik. And then, having achieved that, he'd have the problem of disposing of the body. At the very least, it must not be found until the *Fenrir* was well clear of the Limfjord...

By the time they reached Aalborg, Ulf still had no answers to his problems.

Sunrise shimmered over the shallow waters as the *Fenrir* glided alongside the Aalborg wharf. Olaf's crew secured the great ship as the port roused from its brief sleep. A few men were already sauntering about or shifting goods, but Ulf's attention was fixed on the dozen dragonships berthed further up the quayside.

'Looks like the Aalborg jarl's about to set sail on his raiding,' Olaf said, as though reading Ulf's mind. 'That's Rorik's ship, the *Nidhogg,* in the middle over there,' he added, pointing to a huge vessel with the head of a ferocious dragon atop its lofty prow. Ulf nodded, thinking how well the feared dragon of Niflheim suited Rorik's nature. 'So, until they pull out, there'll likely be a lot of coming and going around here; all the more reason why we need to be extra vigilant with this beauty.' Olaf's gaze swept his beloved ship. 'I've never left her unattended yet, and don't intend to start now.

'I've put you on the first watch, Ulf, along with Sven and Koll and their mates. You'll stay aboard till noon, and make sure you're seen from the quay – put any thieving buggers off. If you feel like a nap, check with yer mates. No more than two of you sleep at a time, the other six stay wide awake – not so much as a yawn. And no one leaves this ship, so if you need a piss, it's still over the side. Am I making myself clear?'

Ulf nodded and Olaf grinned. 'Right then. I've arranged four different watches to take us to sunrise tomorrow, then we'll start over. Two days is all we'll have here, just long enough for me to deliver those crates of goods over there and recruit a few more men. Most of the alehouses'll be heaving with this lot in town,' he said, nodding at Rorik's fleet, 'but there are enough alehouses here to accommodate a vast army. Anyways, at least you'll get two full nights off, lad. You've looked fair down in the dumps during our journey here, and a few mugs and buxom women should cheer you up before we sail.'

Ulf gave a grim smile. 'You're right, Olaf. A night on the town is just what I need.'

* * *

The arrival of the second watch came as a relief to Ulf. By noon he was more than ready to stretch his legs, and itching to get out to the jarl's hall, a short way from the southern edge of the town. He'd planned to spend the first day here just watching, and figuring out some way of getting at Rorik. Then tomorrow night, just before they sailed, he'd strike.

But Ulf hadn't anticipated the solidarity of Olaf's crew. The seven men with whom he'd shared the morning watch seemed to have claimed him as one of their own, taken for granted that he'd spend his time ashore in their company. In actual fact, Ulf had enjoyed his hours on watch, playing board games with the jovial bunch of men. He'd even managed a much-needed nap. But once ashore, Ulf had a task to do that was utterly at variance with socialising.

He spent the afternoon wandering about Aalborg's small market with his new shipmates, sharing food and ale, and tales of places seen and memorable raids. But, as dusk closed in, Ulf racked his brains to find a means for going off on his own. Oddly enough, it was the brawny, dark-headed Sven who provided one for him.

'We'll be back on watch at sunrise,' Sven reminded his comrades, his voice already a little slurred,' so it stands to reason we can't spend all night on the ale.' He took another slurp and tweaked his beard thoughtfully. 'Olaf'd flay us alive if we didn't turn up for our watch on time. So here's what I suggest...'

A wicked grin spread across Sven's face. 'There's a certain establishment I know that stays open all night.' The men nudged each other, knowing full well what was coming. 'Now this place is the lodging house of some very lonely women, just longing for some wholesome – and generous – male company. So, as long as we've silver in our pockets, I say we go and keep those lovely ladies company.'

The brothel was a large, wood-planked structure, close to the centre of the town. Oil lamps glowed on benches along the outside walls, illuminating the handful of women strutting there, eyeing up potential clients and vying for trade. The whores' bawdy comments induced further merriment in the men, and Koll swept a gaudily dressed woman up in his arms and disappeared into the building.

'We'll not see him again till daybreak,' Sven said, eyeing up the remaining women.

'Best make your choice quick,' a brash redhead informed them, hitching her skirts up to her thighs and nodding in the direction of an approaching group of prospective clients. 'If you're too picky, you'll end up all on your own, out on the town.'

Sven threw an arm around the woman's waist and pulled her to him, before heading indoors. The rest of the men soon followed suit, leaving Ulf to be jostled inside in the midst of the recent arrivals. The large room was heaving with eager clients, further aroused by the distinctive smells of sex that the reek of stale ale failed to mask. Whores paraded round the tables, the expanse of naked flesh increasing as they competed for masculine attention. Lewd banter and raucous laughter added to the grunts and groans coming from inside the booths edging the walls. Pairings were made quickly as men pulled women onto their laps, lust-filled gropes triggering further giggles and squeals. Several pairs headed outside, too impatient to wait for a vacant booth.

Ulf inched towards the door, certain that no one would notice his leaving. And with so many couples copulating in sheltered nooks outside, who was likely to question his whereabouts? He could easily have been occupied in one of those cosy niches himself.

He slunk away and out into the night, hardly able to believe his luck.

* * *

Dusk was giving way to darkness as Ulf neared the Aalborg hall. From the shadows of one of the huts he stared at the light streaming through the partly-opened door, his ears attuned to the hum of voices and the occasional burst of laughter. Savoury aromas of cooked meats drifted on the night air and his stomach rumbled. He'd eaten nothing since mid-afternoon, but that wasn't likely to be remedied for some time yet. His thoughts returned to the events of his last visit to this place: his confrontation with Rorik on the night of their arrival, and his own unbearable urge to beat the ugly face to a pulp; of the hope that shone in his mother's eyes when they'd met outside the storage hut, and how boldly she'd faced up to Rorik's accusations. Then the cold barbarity of her death ...

Ulf's grief surged anew, gripping him pitilessly for some moments before being swamped by the smouldering rage he'd lived with for the past eighteen months. He leaned against the hut to steady himself, willing the trembling fury to abate. He'd achieve little if he allowed his emotions to control his deeds. For what he was planning, he needed a clear head and rational thought – and a steady hand.

Yet again, Ulf reached for the comforting feel of Leif's dagger through his belt.

A few thralls traipsed back and forth from the hall, and Ulf moved further into the shadows. Remnants of the evening meal were carried into a largish hut, which he knew served as the kitchens, and a cask of ale taken back to the hall. Evidently, the meal was over and the usual drinking would continue.

After what seemed like hours of uneventful waiting, Ulf was suddenly alerted to movement. The hall door swung open and a group of Rorik's men made their exit.

'Another couple of days and we're off,' one of them said as they headed for the barn. 'By tomorrow, Godfried should be here with his ships. King Harald just had to send his son along to make sure Rorik doesn't pocket his share of the plunder, didn't he? But I suppose Friesland's as much Harald's domain as Rorik's – although the fool never seems to get there too often.'

'The sooner he drops dead the better it'll be for all of us,' another voice declared. 'Call himself a king ...! Rorik'd make a far better one, is what I say.'

'But if Harald meets an untimely end, his son'll expect to step right into his shoes,' the first speaker returned. 'Mind you, Godfried's young and strong, and not one to stay home in Viborg like his miserable father, waiting for booty to come to him. He'd not be a bad leader to follow – but don't tell Rorik I said that.'

The chuckles diminished as the men made their way into their sleeping quarters and Ulf settled down for a long watch, reminded of his own encounter with Godfried all those years ago. But now was not the time for such recollections and he focused on the grim task ahead.

He knew that the jarl's sleeping chamber was inside the hall, so getting to him during the night would not be an option, especially if he was sharing his bed with one of his wives or concubines. But at some stage, Rorik would likely need to piss out all the ale he'd drunk. And then Ulf would need every ounce of his willpower to stop himself from unsheathing Leif's dagger. Rorik must not disappear before the *Fenrir* was ready to sail.

More time passed and, lulled by the dark silence, Ulf battled the overwhelming urge to close his eyes. He stood to rouse himself and crept closer to the hall. Shadowy figures had begun to emerge, disappearing round the side of the hall to relieve themselves before heading back to their beds – and Ulf needed to know whether Rorik was one of them. But, as night moved closer towards its inevitable clash with the dawn, he'd seen no sign of the jarl. Surely the man's bladder must be bursting by now! And before long, Ulf would be obliged to return to the ship, still ignorant as to how he'd accomplish Rorik's death.

Tomorrow night he'd try again, and tomorrow night, failure was not an option.

Just as he rose to make his retreat, the door opened again. And this time there was no mistaking the hulking figure of the Aalborg jarl.

Ulf held his breath, his body suddenly rigid. Bloodlust swept through him like a raging torrent, powerful and all-consuming, until he could see nothing but his chance – perhaps his only chance – of killing Rorik. His resolution to wait until tomorrow vanished with the thrill of that single thought as he watched his prey disappear behind the hall. Silently, he stepped out of the shadows, Leif's dagger already gripped in his hand.

The hall door swung open again and Ulf dived for cover as someone else emerged to follow after the jarl. He caught the muffled voices as the two acknowledged each another in passing, then Rorik was in full view again, reaching for the door and entering the hall.

Ulf stood there, staring after him, cursing himself for missing such a perfect opportunity. He turned and crept away, knowing only too well that tomorrow night was his last chance.

Everything hinged on the timing of Rorik's need to piss.

* * *

The second day followed much the same pattern as the first, and another visit to the brothel was a foregone conclusion. Ulf did his best to hide his escalating anxiety, feigning cheerfulness as the men laughed and jested, and joining in as they shared descriptions of the women's charms by extolling the attributes of the non-existent 'Inga', with whom he'd supposedly spent the night.

As he'd expected, the brothel was busy again – with so many ships in port it was unlikely to be otherwise. Most of his crewmates were soon blissfully engaged, either grunting in one of the booths or cavorting around somewhere outside. The April nights had lost the bite of winter, and sexual romps beneath open skies exerted the usual pull on men of the sea.

Ulf sat around for a while, waiting and watching for the best time to take his leave. But the sudden arrival of a curvaceous young woman on his lap delayed any possibility of him going anywhere. At first, he was quite disgruntled, seeing her as a further hindrance to his plans, and refused to respond to her persuasive advances. So it wasn't surprising that before long she lost her patience.

'I've a queue waiting for my favours,' she announced tartly, jumping off his knee. 'So if you can't be bothered to do what you came here for, get yourself off to an alehouse.'

Not wishing his crewmates to witness his reluctance to ravish the girl's voluptuous body, and thereby question his virility, Ulf declared his preference for a romp outside, and led her to the door.

He selected an empty space between the brothel and an adjacent hut, and the girl set to work. Her skills in her chosen profession were considerable, and for some time Ulf succumbed to her ministrations. She spoke little – not even enquiring after his name, which suited him well – simply doing her utmost to make his experience satisfying and memorable. The interlude served to ease some of the crippling anxiety that had built up during the day and he paid her well, having delved into the purse from Bjorn for a handful of coin. She walked off without so much as a smile, undoubtedly in search of her next client.

Ulf was now free to head to Rorik's hall. He'd thought about doing little else all day as he'd battled to control the fits of panic, when his heart thundered and he sweated like a hog. But the sexual release had induced in him calm and lucid thought, and as he approached the hall, his mind was focused solely on the ugly jarl's end.

* * *

Ulf guessed that midnight could not be far away when he arrived to watch the play of events around the hall. The post-meal drinking was lasting longer tonight, and seemed to be taking its usual toll. Angry voices carried through the part-opened door, suddenly broken by what sounded like a table being hurled over. Someone yelped, followed by a deathly hush. Then mayhem erupted ...

A tangle of bodies fell through the doorway, arms and legs flailing, and Ulf stepped swiftly back between the storage huts. Suddenly, Rorik was there. His outraged roar rang out and the tangle instantly unravelled.

'By Odin, I'm tempted to put an end to the miserable existence of you six imbeciles! If we weren't short on crew for the sailing, I'd do just that.' He turned to the beefy man at his side. 'Take some of your men, Egil, and lock these fools in one of the huts. They can reflect on their stupidity for the rest of the night. And it'll be a long one at that,' he added. 'After all the mead I've downed, anyone who wakes me before mid-morning can expect a flogging.'

Ulf cringed behind some empty food crates as Egil and a handful of men followed Rorik's orders. Fortunately, the chosen hut was not in his direction and he resumed his watch.

'Pity you had to witness that, Godfried,' Rorik was saying, addressing a younger man who'd come to stand next to him. 'The men are fired up, impatient to be away raiding, and tempers can fly at such times.'

'I take no offence at the antics of your men, Uncle. Believe me, I've seen far worse.' Godfried gave a throaty chuckle. 'But I fully concur with your sentiments regarding rising too early tomorrow. Since we're sailing at first light the following day, this could be our last chance to sleep a little later for some time. Now, I've a full cup of mead waiting for my attentions, and I see no reason to waste it.'

Rorik threw an arm round his nephew's shoulders and they returned to the hall. The door closed behind them and darkness returned. From inside, voices were now little more than a muted buzz, the threat of spending the night locked in a hut evidently hitting home with the men. Ulf crept back to his former position, squatting down for the interminable wait and contemplating his plans.

He'd already registered the arrival of the half-dozen longships during his morning watch aboard ship, so wasn't surprised to see that Godfried was here, especially since hearing Rorik's men discussing his anticipated arrival last night. But, Ulf reasoned, Godfried's presence shouldn't make any difference to his plans. His major problem still lay in finding a way of getting Rorik alone, with or without Godfried's presence in the hall.

The more he racked his brains, the more he was convinced that his only chance lay in Rorik's need to relieve himself during the night. And even then, the timing had to be right. Too soon after he'd retired there were still likely to be thralls about, and too close to sunrise would be too late for Ulf. The *Fenrir* sailed at dawn. Ulf felt no qualms, no trembling fear at what he must do; he just hated the idea of everything hanging on chance. But the possibilities arising from Rorik's threat to anyone who roused him too early, added to the fact that he slept in a private chamber, could prove useful when Ulf came to making his getaway.

It was well past midnight before the men made a move, many of them heading for the huge barn. And once all seemed settled for the night, Ulf crept closer to the hall to continue his long vigil.

The sky was showing the first signs of paling when Rorik staggered through the door. He moved slowly towards the side of the building, one hand trailing along the wall to support himself. The night's excesses were, evidently, exerting their ugly after-effects, and Ulf smiled grimly: Rorik's reflexes would be considerably dulled. He pulled up his hood, drew Leif's dagger from his belt, and stepped out to follow.

Not bothering to enter the roofless hut that served as household latrine, Rorik stopped to release his waters against its outside wall, the hiss of the steady stream breaking the silence. He swayed a little as he refastened his belt, and leaned his brow against the wall to steady himself. Ulf pulled down his hood and waited for him to turn...

He struck fast, gripping Rorik in a fierce, one-armed hold and pressing him back against the hut whilst bringing the dagger up and thrusting it deep into the soft flesh beneath his breastbone, angled towards his heart. Rorik stared down in confusion at the hand clasping the hilt of the knife lodged in his chest. Then his eyes moved up to fix on Ulf's face, growing wide as recognition hit.

'That's for my father, King Beorhtwulf,' Ulf whispered, feeling the thrill of victorious vengeance course through him. 'And this,' he added, twisting the knife,' is for my mother, Morwenna. Neither of them deserved to die. Unlike you...'

Already dead, Rorik's eyes were still wide as he slumped against Ulf.

For some moments, Ulf stood there, locked in the deathly

embrace with a man he'd dreamed of killing for so long. Now the job was done and, as long as nothing went wrong, he'd be aboard the *Fenrir* and sailing out of the Limfjord before anyone even realised the jarl was missing.

The lightening sky signalled the rapidly approaching dawn, and there was still the possibility of someone coming to piss. Ulf needed to get rid of the body, and quick. He glanced at the dense thicket barely twenty yards away. That had always been a possibility. Then he looked at the hut and wondered...

Inside the old hut, the latrine consisted of a deep pit bridged by a wooden plank with a hole in it for use as a 'seat'. Ulf had made use of it himself when he'd been here on that ill-fated visit with Bjorn. Next to the pit sat a shovel and a mound of soil, with which users were expected to cover their own excrement. Many didn't, and the place usually reeked.

The ideal burial place for the brutal jarl.

Ulf released his hold on the dagger and eased the heavy body to the ground. Then, gagging at the stench as he opened the door, he dragged the corpse inside the hut, and kicked the wooden plank away. Carefully, he pulled his precious dagger from Rorik's chest, wiping it in the soil before returning it to the sheath at his belt. Blood gushed from the wound now that the dagger had been removed, and Ulf shoved the body quickly to the edge of the pit ...

Rorik dropped, and landed with a muted slap in his stinking grave.

Ulf shovelled in the soil until certain that the body was no longer visible, and replaced the wooden plank. Guardedly, he opened the door. All was clear, so he used the edge of the shovel to remove any trace of something being dragged inside. Then, checking that the coast was still clear, he made his retreat to the ship, exulting in his triumph.

* * *

Ulf watched the islands of the Limfjord slip by, and by mid-morning the *Fenrir* veered north, heading for the Norwegian lands. He'd already said his goodbyes to those he loved, and those he knew he'd never forget, and now he was heading home to Mercia. Exactly when he'd get there, however, he'd no idea: Olaf was already considering a trading trip to Gotland after taking the supplies up to his people in the Lofotens, with a stop at Kaupang on the way back. So by the time they'd done all that, it would probably be too late in the year to sail again. Ulf would be stuck in Olaf's village for the winter.

But Olaf swore he'd be crossing the Northern Seas the following spring. The old seaman had heard that trading was good in some Northumbrian city. And of course, there was always the possibility of a bountiful raid or two...

Ulf knew nothing about Northumbria, except that it lay to the north of Mercia and, like the Mercians, the people were descended from the Angles. But once he was on Anglo-Saxon soil, he'd find his way to Mercia, no matter how long it took. He was in no particular hurry, now. The first object of his revenge had been dealt with, and he'd ride on the elation of that success for some time yet.

And firmly lodged in his head was the absolute certainty that, one day, he'd deal with his loving uncle, Burgred.

Printed in Great Britain
by Amazon

51486171R00249